FOR THE LOVE OF
MAUDE

DENISE LIEBIG

FOR THE LOVE OF MAUDE
Copyright © 2013 Denise Liebig

Cover Design & Print Format by The Book Khaleesi
www.thebookkhaleesi.com

ISBN-13: 978-1544939636
ISBN-10: 1544939639

Print Edition Published 2017
Printed in the United States of America
Library of Congress Control Number: 2017907643 CreateSpace Independent Publishing Platform, North Charleston, SC

www.deniseliebig.com

OTHER BOOKS BY DENISE LIEBIG

Dear Maude

Forever Maude

Subscribe to Denise Liebig's website
and download the Free Novelette,
Remembering Skye

www.deniseliebig.com

This book is dedicated to the memory of my parents, whose stories of the past were the sparks that ignited my imagination to pen this work. Without the wonderful experiences they shared and those they created for me in my childhood, the following pages may have never been written.

~ * ~

PROLOGUE

The blank paper begged to be covered in words, but the more I stared at its nakedness, the more it teased me, reminding me of my lack of focus. I wanted to crumple it and remove the challenge of filling its space. A paper shredder came to mind, a pair of scissors, a match; but I was alone in a white room, filled with only a metal desk, gray office chair on wheels, and *the paper*.

I opened the solitary drawer, extending across the front of the desk, and found among its contents a pen and pencil, a gum eraser, an ink well, a fountain pen, and a blotter—modern and antique side by side, just like my life.

I scooped out the contents of the drawer and deposited them in a pile on the desk.

In need of inspiration, I separated the pencil from the other objects and placed it on the paper. It was orange, sharpened to a fine point and lacking the teeth marks my collection of pencils was known for in college. Unsanitary, but it guaranteed that no one would want to borrow one and forget to return it. I graduated with all my pencils intact—a small victory for a girl who lost everything else.

I ran my fingers across the paper, wishing the words

would just appear, the ones that would tell my story from the beginning. Unfortunately, I'd forgotten where that was. I was lost somewhere in the middle, flailing around while everyone else went on with their lives.

I moved on to the tortoise-shell green fountain pen with a slight chip on the tip. "It needs a new nib." I closed my eyes and shook my head. "I shouldn't even know what that means—no one born in 1990 should." With a quick swipe, I relocated the pencil and fountain pen, along with the ink bottle, blotter, and gum eraser into the drawer and slammed it closed.

A blue ballpoint pen remained next to the paper, on the right, as if it knew which hand would reach for it. I did its bidding, grabbing the thing and giving the end a quick *click* to reveal the tip.

I hadn't written a word since I buried the journal. Addressed to my grandmother's deceased aunt, Maude, whose friendship, wisdom, and understanding I sought even after she died, the journal had become my lifeline to the world I left behind. Now I was alone among strangers—no Maude journal, no family, no husband, just scientists who treated me as more of a specimen than a human being.

It was the first opportunity I had in months to be without an audience and think—to do something, anything, with a blank piece of paper. So, after a deep breath, I finally touched the pen to paper and began to write:

Dear Maude,

I miss you every day. I'm sorry I haven't written in a while. I can't—not because I lack writing supplies, but because putting my words on paper makes the last two years real. Then I'd have to admit that I'm a time traveler.

I also ask myself every day why I accepted that stupid scholarship from Evergreen Research Corporation in New York, and their job after graduation that threw me into this position. I'm still waiting for an answer. I should be the envy of my college classmates, who are probably stuck in cubicles, knowing a window office is the best they'll ever achieve. After all, not everyone can say they graduated in 2012, worked in 1910, and then lived in so many other years that they lost track. Even if I could say these things—and so much more—I wouldn't. Some secrets are best left hidden—or written in journals like the one I hope you found by now, buried beneath the oak tree you often described as your favorite childhood treasure-hunting spot. Besides, the world isn't ready to discover just how manipulated history could be if Evergreen has its way.

Of course, even after I joined Evergreen, I could have smiled and nodded and gathered information for four years, then gone home to Oregon like it never happened, just as Evergreen wanted. But no. I had to meet Dell with Holtz & Sons (H&S)—the good guys, the ones who have been doing it longer, the ones who allow history to simply happen.

Worse, I did what I always promised myself I wouldn't do—I gave up my future to be with a guy, just as Mom did and Nana Rosie before her. Unlike them, though, I didn't get pregnant. How could I? Dell and I never consummated. This is ironic, considering our son and his descendants are the "S" in H&S.

I'm so confused! With time travel, nothing is linear, especially time itself. Not only that, but Holtz & Sons' brilliant plan to fake my death and Dell's, then hide in history backfired...

The pen fell from my hand before I even realized I dropped it. Unable to write another word, I pushed the paper away and rested my folded arms in its place, then scooted the chair backward with my feet until my forehead met my wrist. I closed my eyes and shook my head.

"You're sure in a pickle this time, Toots!" Maude's wise sayings had a funny way of finding their way into my head and making sense of stressful situations.

My own reply bounced up to my ears from the surface of the desk. "Yeah, a big barrel of them."

I took a deep breath and left the comfort of my arms to once again stare at the paper. I pulled it to me, then brought the pen to join it:

If Evergreen hadn't wanted to keep me single by killing Dell, we wouldn't have had to fake our deaths in the first place! Then Dell wouldn't have gotten so hurt that he needed the technology of 2125 to recover.

I can't get that image out of my head, Maude. He was wrapped up in more bandages than a mummy, and what wasn't covered was bruised or bloody or both.

FOR THE LOVE OF MAUDE

I looked at the pen, wishing the words that came from it would somehow create a better picture of Dell in my mind. Sadly, it just balanced between my fingers, blue and unmoving until I started to write again:

> *I didn't think he'd be gone this long — maybe a week or so, but months? I should have demanded to go with him! He said I wasn't ready for the future, but I'm not ready for this either. We should be hiding in history together, honeymooning in various eras, while remaining dead in the eyes of Evergreen. Avoiding their discovery and whatever wrath they might impose upon me — their once most important asset — should be my only concern. Yet, here I am alone, stuck in the past under Holtz & Sons' protection, constantly shuffled between safe houses in time frames that run together like spumoni on a summer day. What little they tell me, seems to be a bunch of lies. They keep promising a reunion with Dell, only to disappoint me each time.*
>
> *I'm in the basement laboratory of one of their safe houses now, and it's almost time to leave for my next one. I'd better stop. I'll write more later.*
>
> *Love,*
>
> *Emily*

I placed the pen on the desk, stretched my arms high above my head, then rose and walked to the door. I turned the knob and pulled it toward me.

Before I could even step a foot across the threshold, I was

greeted by a middle-aged woman, dressed in a standard white lab coat that covered her black slacks. Most of the basement employees were from the future, but their uniforms gave nothing away. Her graying brown hair was short and grazed the bottom of her ear lobes, offering her otherwise bland appearance its only trace of personality. "Yes, miss?" she asked.

"Hello, I was just wondering, *when* am I?" That was my favorite question, a little time travel humor.

The woman just stared.

"I'm sorry," I said. "I didn't catch your name." I knew I wouldn't either.

With Evergreen's technology improving by the day, H&S security was high, and my name and location changed like the wind. The personal side of things—names, smiles, and small talk—were often lost in the shuffle. Only high-level H&S employees were privy to my real name, and as an extra security measure, I often didn't learn theirs.

I smiled at her silence and asked my real question: "I don't suppose we'll be leaving any time soon?"

"Yes. As a matter of fact, I was asked to fetch you in five minutes."

Fetch? What am I, a stick? I smiled and kept my comments to myself. "Isn't that great news? I'll be right out."

I closed the door and stood against it, staring at the desk and the letter it held. *What was I thinking? I buried my journal and its secrets for a reason, to keep it safe. I don't need to defeat that purpose. Besides, if Maude found the journal as a child, she'd have lived the rest of her life knowing most of this already.*

I walked to the letter, folded it up tight, and placed it into my jeans pocket. When I left the room, I found the same employee standing just outside. "I need to use the restroom before we depart," I said.

She walked with me to the ladies' room and waited outside as I promptly tore the letter into small pieces and flushed them down the toilet.

CHAPTER ONE

There I stood, teetering on the precipice of where I'd been and where I needed to go. Dell, my mom, and my life were somewhere down the tunnel on my right. I squinted into its long darkness, eventually losing sight of the taillights from the car I'd just exited. I continued to strain my senses until the echoing engine noise left only silence. Then I took a deep breath before slowly turning to my left and the approaching welcoming committee.

I was in one of the H&S basement laboratories, subterranean portals to the past and future, equipped with more security than Fort Knox. Located beneath structures they called "safe houses," their labs were connected to elaborate systems of high-speed tunnels that allowed time travel via specially modified vintage automobiles. I could still smell the exhaust from the light blue 1957 Corvette, whose driver had just delivered me.

I looked around the giant warehouse space in search of my husband; as usual, I was left disappointed. I tried to remain hopeful each time I traveled, but I was growing tired of playing the H&S waiting game.

Crash!

FOR THE LOVE OF MAUDE

In his hurry to greet me, a man leading a gaggle of white-coated lab workers dropped a metal clipboard on the shiny, gray epoxy floor. The sound echoed off the cavernous walls that surrounded me, a loud reminder that I was, in fact, living a nightmare.

"Mrs. Holtz!"

Like geese, the group arrived in a V-formation with the man in front extending his hand in my direction.

I gave his soggy hand a shake and counted my blessings when he quickly released his grip. "Please call me 'Emily'!" Since he'd used my married name, I knew I could safely offer my first, but my new last name still didn't feel right. I hadn't used my maiden name, Stanton, in years, and without Dell, Holtz was just another name, one I hadn't earned.

"Yes, thank you, Miss Emily...and hello. So glad to see you. I'm...blah-blah...and these are my colleagues...blah, blah, and blah."

He lost me at "Hello."

His use of names should have signaled something in my brain about his position with the company, but all I could do was stare at the green piece of yuck stuck between his front teeth. *Spinach?* I squinted to get a better look. *No. Definitely lettuce.* A victim of lumpy beds and constant travel, I hadn't slept well in weeks, maybe months; I'd lost track. Watching the man's lips move was the only way I could focus on his words that seemed to drift in and out like waves on the ocean.

"We're just so delighted to..."

Wow, is that a cold sore? I shifted my focus to the crusty mass at the corner of his mouth.

"But I'm sure all this talk of technology and break-throughs can wait for Mr. Holtz."

His words finally drew my full attention as his flapping lips met in an arrogant grin.

I cannot believe you just said that! Science wasn't my strongest subject in school, but I always pulled A's in it, as well as every other course I studied. *Just because I'm tired doesn't mean I'm stupid!* I fought through a number of scenarios in my head, most of which required more effort than he was worth. Regardless, I didn't have the energy, but my mouth did. Thus, against my better upbringing and my position as the boss's wife, I decided to allow my now cranky disposition to wipe the smile from his face. I ignored his last comment and offered "Nice to meet you all!" to the rest of the group.

Two other men and one women, all in lab coats with nondescript black slacks beneath, took turns shaking my hand.

Then I smiled at Mr. Lettuce Teeth. "I take it you're in charge?" It was obvious, but I needed to know for sure.

"Yes, I am!"

With his mouth no longer the center of my attention, I noticed the perfectly combed brown hair and amber eyes that looked at me as if I were a field mouse or, rather, a lab rat. The man was in his late twenties and his clammy handshake reminded me of Mr. Wilson's, the Evergreen employee who helped train me to live in the past. Since I wasn't paying attention when the introductions were made, I decided to rename Mr. Lettuce Teeth "Willy."

When he eagerly remained before me, smiling confidently, I pelted Willy with a barrage of questions, which I flung out in such rapid succession that he staggered backward, as if he had actually been struck by them. The stunned look on his face was priceless. I referred to that method as the "Tommy Gun Approach," named after the gangsters' weapon of choice in the 1920s. Similar to them, I felt justified; in fact, I had nothing to lose. Therefore, I led with, "When and where am I?" I noted the reaction carefully, trying not to blink as I did so.

"Well, uh…"

I smiled. "Oh, that's all right. I know you probably can't tell me. And where is Dell?

"Uh, I'm not—"

"—at liberty to say?" I finished for him, then added, "Of course."

At that point, my smile grew, while the one in charge stopped smiling entirely and began to shuffle uncomfortably. I had him. Answering my questions was far above his pay grade. Most valued their jobs enough to avoid unnecessary conversation with me, but that was not the case with Willy. His colleagues masked their smiles from behind tightly stretched lips, staring at the ground in the process. I felt like their hero as I kept guiding the bullets.

"Shane, then?" I asked, referring to Dell's younger self, whom he had plucked from his past to provide assistance in his absence.

"Uh…" Willy drew his clipboard toward his downturned face.

"Right!" My smile only grew broader. "And how long shall I be here?"

"Well, we really don't—"

"—know?" I smiled, pretending to be helpful.

The clipboard was now in full use as Willy feverishly flipped through the pages, most likely in search of his lost importance.

I was unrelenting. "I'm quite tired." I worked up a yawn

and patted my open lips.

"You're—"

"Yes. The journey."

"Oh. Well, uh…"

Then, a brave one stepped out of the group and walked toward me. He reached for Maude's suitcase, a vintage, rigid-sided reminder of home that I refused to travel without. "May I?" he asked.

"Of course!" I ignored the now distraught Willy, who had been reduced to a babbling idiot in front of the co-workers whom, judging by their reactions, he had belittled for years. I couldn't resist the urge to shoot one more bullet his way. "Finally! So kind of *someone* to offer!"

As I brushed past, I cast a backward glance at Willy, who was staring in pale disbelief while his co-worker and I, as well as his career, faded away.

We walked down a long, white hallway dotted with picture windows, behind which were housed banks of instruments and more employees in lab coats. Neither the lab worker nor I spoke as he escorted me to a large metal security door. I just wanted sleep, without all the fanfare, and I appreciated the silence; I knew I'd probably said too much already.

After punching numbers into a keypad beside the door, he bent down so his retina could be scanned by a small screen above the keypad. The vault-like door made a clicking sound, and the guard standing next to it turned the wheel on its face and opened it just enough for us to pass through. Such security measures were common to other labs, and I wasn't surprised to find many similar doors down a long series of cavernous hallways. The final entrance placed us before a stainless elevator door, next to which the lab worker pressed the up button.

"It was nice meeting you, Miss Emily," he said.

"You too, uh…" I searched the front of his coat for a nametag I knew wouldn't be there. *I guess I should have been paying attention earlier.*

His forgiving smile drew me into his handsome features and held me there. "Barnaby. Samuel Barnaby," he said.

I could only stare. The man was just under six feet tall, with light brown hair and bright eyes that now danced at my reaction. *How did I miss those big, hazel eyes? And his face is nearly perfect. Look at that mouth, those lips, those teeth! Am I that dead?*

The open elevator door saved me from further embarrassment as the heat from a familiar, hot blush crept up my neck, and reassured me that I was very much alive. I rushed inside and turned to see Barnaby pushing the first floor button.

"Have a pleasant stay," he said. Then he handed me the suitcase and stepped out of the elevator.

The door closed before I could reply, and stood in front of me like a giant mirror, reflecting the crimson blush on my cheeks. I looked away but caught my reflection on the other stainless walls that surrounded me. Unnerved by my unwanted embarrassment, I just stared at the white tile floor beneath my feet. *Nice, Em. One minute, you're taking Willy out at the knees, and in the next, you're making a fool of yourself over his co-worker. After losing so much of who you are, I can't believe blushing at the sight of a good-looking man is one of the few things that remain.* I fanned myself with my hand and tried to regain my composure. *And what about Dell?*

When the elevator door opened, a sight as welcome as a ray of sunshine in midwinter gave me a second wind and temporarily cast my thoughts to the back of my mind.

I found myself in the safest of all the so-called safe houses, the one in which I spent the majority of my time. Located on a secluded island somewhere in the Atlantic off Great Britain, it was where I was first sent shortly after Dell's accident. I grew to regard it as a home of sorts—or at least a place where I knew what to expect.

I eagerly stepped out of the elevator and dropped the suitcase onto the runner-covered wooden floor that led me down a hallway and out to a great lawn. A blanket of fog and sea mist slowly enveloped me while I filled my lungs with cool air and held it there, savoring its freshness. As I gradually exhaled, I was drawn to the cliff's edge, where an invisible ocean roared its greeting.

The fog, mixed with a cool breeze, felt like fingers running through my loosely held hair. I longed for it to be Dell's touch, to smell his musky scent overwhelming me as he cradled my face in his strong hands and drew my lips to his. I imagined my fingers melting into his soft, light brown curls as his hands traced their way to the small of my back, his muscles straining the fabric that tried to contain them.

The sting of tears, mixed with the misty air, sent streams down my cheeks to drip unhindered from my chin. *I didn't agree to this, Dell. We're supposed to be hiding in history together. Why did you leave me here alone?*

A crashing wave brought my attention back to the cliff's edge and the fact that it lacked a guard rail to keep me from plummeting to the jagged rocks hidden below. I wiped my chin and retraced my steps to the house, watching it fade in and out of focus behind the shifting fog. Its stone façade stretched the length of at least a football field somewhere in the white vapor, which also masked several Victorian spires, resembling broken pencils beneath the fog that hid their tips. Windows sprinkled along the multistory walls blended into the stone, reflecting only the morning haze. The craggy rocks and heather that surrounded the remainder of the house were nowhere to be seen in the ever-thickening fog.

I usually visited the house prior to or during 1908, and since it came without a name of its own, I referred to it as "The 1908 House." It may not have required a name, but I did, and the aboveground staff addressed me as "Lady Milton." I didn't mind; it had a nice ring to it.

What wasn't so nice, though, was the garment that met me at the door when I reentered the house. Although my location was secluded, I was still required to wear the proper clothing of the day, just in case. Among the garb was my nemesis, the ever-ill-fitting corset. Even though the house was staffed with H&S employees, precautions were always enforced to ensure time-period continuity, and that extended to my wardrobe. I mistakenly hoped the fog would hide the jeans and white T-shirt I was wearing, but I was wrong.

My lady's maid stood just inside the door, holding my new wardrobe and the Maude suitcase, and giving me the time-to-take-your-medicine look.

"Hello, Goodwin," I said. It had been several months since my last visit, and I was genuinely happy to see her, despite the corset.

Like all the staff, Goodwin was always dressed and pressed in black, her skirts just clearing the floor, and she wore a loose bun that held her brown hair in place near the crown of her head. Her quick smile softened her otherwise overly proper appearance that came complete with a British accent. "Milady, shall we?" She gestured toward the hallway and my doom.

We climbed the stairs to the familiar bedroom with its overstuffed canopy bed. The only somewhat-modern convenience was the attached bathroom that came complete with indoor plumbing. The French doors that led to the balcony and its usual view of the lawn and ocean beyond, now served as a barrier from the fog.

A coal-burning fire kept the chill from the air as Goodwin helped me don my outfit. Within minutes, I was wearing white stockings and a union suit that looked like a tank top attached to knee-length drawers, with ruffles at the shoulders and hems. Then I stood, and tried not to pass out, as Goodwin worked behind me, lacing my white cotton, boned corset. She attached the stockings to garters on the front of the corset and buttoned a pair of black Oxfords on my feet. The next layer was a fitted top, sleeveless and trimmed in lace, which covered the corset, and an attached petticoat that went to the floor. Then, she covered it all with a floor-length skirt and separate top made of white silk, lace, and enough buttons to render its removal impossible without assistance.

"Last one," she said.

"Good."

Goodwin let out a brief giggle. "Now that wasn't so bad, was it, milady?"

"No, it wasn't. Thank you, Goodwin."

But it really was. It had been almost two years since I first traveled to a time other than my own, yet I still found it difficult to adjust to all the fuss. The costume changes, hair styles, manners, and especially the staff were more than I could process at times. Before the ink on my college diploma had dried,

FOR THE LOVE OF MAUDE

I went from plugging quarters in dorm basement washing machines in 2012 to having a personal maid to dress me more than a century earlier. It was a bit much.

I reached for the hairbrush on my dressing table, but Goodwin beat me to it.

"Why don't I do that for you, milady?"

Granted, she was far better at doing my hair than I was, but at the rate I was going, I had no hope for improvement. From making my bed to making dessert, I was scolded at every turn.

"No, milady, allow me."

It was a staff conspiracy that extended to all the safe houses. I couldn't lift, lend, or offer a hand to save my life; that was ironic, because in my family, not working was an evil punishable by the humiliating and ever-frustrating, "Sit on your hands!"

"Sit on your hands, and watch how it's done," my maternal grandfather, Papa Bob, would say when I messed up. Nana Rosie's favorite line, if I complained about working, was always, "Poor thing! Sit on your hands, so you don't hurt yourself." Then there was Mom's dreaded, "Sit on your hands and think about it!" The only one who didn't make it a punishment was Maude, Nana's aunt, who liked to say with a wink, "Sit on your hands and listen to a story." Maude always had my back.

In the end, I was an overachiever with a vivid imagination, sitting on my hands so much they were losing circulation.

My lack of purpose, as well as the island's isolation, was driving me crazy. I wanted out. Since the majority of the house was surrounded by unpassable rocks and dense heather, I spent hours surveying the cliff from the lawn and upper floor windows, trying to find a path to the water and my escape. The only route was a slippery stone staircase that ended at a gated dock, where boats dropped off monthly supplies. The delivery process, although often unnecessary, lent authenticity to our seclusion. The dock was guarded by James Hogg, a burly man whose swollen nose told the world of his love for whiskey.

Hogg was the only one who stood between me and freedom.

I baited him for weeks with bottles of whiskey from the house stores, which the staff supposedly used for cooking. At first, I smuggled him a new bottle twice a week.

"Cheap, but it'll do the trick." James smiled, bearing a set of brown, rotting teeth as he uncorked the first bottle and took a drink. "Doesn't hurt to sample the merchandise."

After that first sip, he never questioned my motives.

"Much obliged, Lady Milton. It becomes lonesome on these waters in the spring, and I sures can use the company!" He looked longingly at the bottle as if I had just set him up on a blind date with a super model.

"Glad I could help!" I said with a smile.

After a few weeks of that, I was certain the staff would start to notice the sudden reduction in their whiskey supply. Therefore, when I wasn't outside, I was combing the dank basement for any sign of a wine cellar or some other cache of alcohol. Original to the house, the basement had an exterior entrance through a weathered wooden door, hidden within the stone foundation. Behind the door, an iron railing guided me down a series of flagstone steps into the darkness, where a maze of musty, unlit hallways crisscrossed beneath the house. Within a few days, my search was rewarded with the discovery of a small oak door with rusty iron hinges that creaked loudly as I pulled it toward me.

I waved the candle I was carrying at the stone floor, hoping to scare off any rodent friends living in the room. None emerged. "We're so far from civilization the rats haven't even found us." I surveyed the floor a second time. "Good thing. I'd just freak out and scare us both away."

With my free hand, I drew the long coat I was wearing around me, then stepped into the room. An initial survey by candlelight was all I needed. The space was filled, floor to six-foot ceiling, with shelves of alcohol, some still in crates. "Perfect!" I said, despite the musty stench that greeted me.

I wiped off a few of the bottles and saw dates as early as 1757. "Amazing! This would sell for a fortune on the internet." I scanned the rows of shelves for signs of whiskey.

Within a few steps of the entry, I found what I was looking for—a crate labeled "25 Year Old Pure Pot Still Whiskey."

I pulled out one of the filthy bottles and tried to blow off the dirt. Unfortunately, I was holding the candle too close and succeeded in blowing it out instead.

"Brilliant, Emily." I stood in the pitch-black room, completely disgusted with myself. Electricity wouldn't be installed in the house for decades, and I was fresh out of matches.

Fortunately, during my childhood, I was known as the "Queen of Hide-n-Seek in the Dark." None of my friends could ever find me, and I always made it to home base without being caught. I even had a crown.

With my title to back me, I licked my fingers and squeezed the remaining heat from the wick, then stuffed the candle and the bottle into my coat pockets. I felt along the shelves for the small door and found my way to the exit without much effort. The trip down the hall wasn't so uneventful, however, when I nearly knocked myself out on a low-hanging unlit lantern that swung dangerously from an overhead beam.

"Stupid thing!" I screamed in the dark. Rubbing my head only seemed to make it worse as I felt the charcoal from the candle wick transfer from my fingers to my forehead.

To avoid any further trauma, I held my left arm above my head to protect it and used the right one to feel the walls as I shuffled my way down the corridor to the staircase. When the blood began to drain from my left hand, I bent my arm at the elbow and rested my head on my forearm.

"Just call me Rudy." I tried to amuse myself with the thought of Rudolph Valentino and the cape he wore in his sheik movies. I grew up with Maude's vast library of old VHS tapes, recordings of films from the silent era that she played until the machine ate most of them. *I love silent movies! If I wasn't stuck on this stupid rock, I might be watching a few right now.* My mood soured even more as I worked my way to a small light that was coming from the staircase in front of me.

I emerged from the basement filthy, covered in dust, cobwebs, and candle soot, and blinded by the midday light. I felt less like Valentino and more like a vampire or a rodent. *I'm the only rat this place every produced.*

I squinted back the light and half-ran inside and to my room, quickly closing the door behind me. "Phew!"

Since I was the only guest occupying its halls, the house was staffed with fewer than ten people, who mostly kept to their quarters except at dressing and meal time. Luckily, it was not one of those times.

Without the aid of yet-to-be-popular makeup, I attempted to explain the nasty bump on my forehead as a mishap with a falling branch. The poor gardener could only scratch his head as he wandered the grounds in search of the offending tree and its wayward offspring.

My next trip to the cellar was made with several candles, deposited like bread crumbs along my pathway. I even lit a few of the lanterns I passed, with the exception of the one with which I had previously collided. It was easy to find; it was the only one that had come unattached from the beam that held it, precariously hanging upside down by a single nail. "Jerk," I said every time I passed it.

I spent several days sharing bottles of watered-down whiskey before finally letting my friend, Mr. Hogg, enjoy a nice bottle of the twenty-five-year-old Irish whiskey, which I delivered right after lunch.

"Anything, anytime, anyhow, Lady Milton. Just let me know what you need, and it's yours!" He wiped the liquid from his chin as he eagerly gulped another swig from the bottle.

He was mine.

I had a perfect view of his shack from the cliff above. The bottle was empty by the time the kitchen staff had cleaned the lunch plates and were preparing for dinner.

They won't miss me for hours! I hoped, anyway.

I carefully descended the cliff stairs one at a time, holding the cold iron railing in one hand and another dusty bottle of the basement's finest in the other.

When I finally reached the bottom, I stared at the water with only one regret: "I wish I hadn't caught a cold and dropped out of swimming lessons when I was five."

Although I couldn't swim a stroke, I could row—or at least I hoped I could as I looked at Hogg's emergency boat rocking gently against the dock to which it was tied.

I adjusted my dress and walked, bottle in hand, to the guard shack and the snoring man who inhabited it. Empty bottles greeted me as I stepped inside and placed the one I was carrying on a table near the door. "He won't even notice the missing boat when he wakes up to this," I whispered, turning the "1865 Irish Whiskey" label toward him and dusting it off with my fingers.

I watched him sleep while I carefully reached across him to free two oars from their posts along the wall. I held my breath as I succeeded in grabbing the first one, but just before I had my hand on the second, a wave hit the dock and caused one of the empty bottles to roll across the floor of the shack and collide with another bottle.

I froze.

When the wave subsided, so did the clanking bottles on the floor. Mr. Hogg didn't even flinch. Relieved, I quickly grabbed the second oar and left the shack for the small boat.

The first few yards of rowing were the most difficult as I tried to gain enough distance from the dock that the boat wouldn't be sent crashing back into the rocky cliff. My arms felt like wet noodles by the time I made it beyond the breakers.

When originally formulating my plan, I noticed that there was no clear view of my destination from either the dock or the house above. Anxious to get off the island, I decided it was worth the risk, so I kept rowing, pushing the boat in the direction from which the people delivering food would arrive in two weeks. My back was to the uncharted course as I fought the current and my corset to widen the gap between myself and the island. I rounded the cliff to one side and soon lost sight of the house, which gave me a chance to look behind me at the route I would have to take.

Far in the distance, I saw a sliver of land with a blinking light at one end. I could only stare in disbelief.

"Great," I finally muttered. The disappointment was overwhelming as I calculated the gulf that separated my little boat from the distant shore. "It must be at least twenty miles away! It will take me days to get there if the current doesn't send me somewhere else first."

I scanned the horizon for a different, closer sign of land, but I couldn't find one.

I sat rocking in the little boat for several minutes, trying to think of a workable Plan B before I finally admitted there was none. Defeated, I pulled in the oars and held them as I lay back in the boat, staring up at the slightly overcast, bird-filled sky. "God, I'm so stupid!"

The seagulls overhead seemed to reply, *No argument here. Duh-duh-duh.*

I tried to ignore them but couldn't contain my frustration. "Now what?"

The gulls failed to respond; rather, they appeared to lose interest and simply flew away.

"Whatever!" I offered at their departure, lying in an ever-growing puddle of sweat and self-pity.

"No wonder the deliveries come in bigger boats…with motors on them. Maybe I can fashion a sail with this stupid corset I'm wearing! I think it's made out of whale bone or something."

At that point, the sound of the rocking boat seemed to mock my poor decision as well, offering *lap-lap-lap* against the wooden sides.

"God!" I screamed at the universe. I knew my only option was to turn the small boat around and try to make it back to the dock alive.

Once I was close, I drifted just outside the breakers for several minutes, trying to determine what kind of wave would safely deliver me to the dock without destroying my boat and me in the process.

It took several minutes of concentration before I realized that the roaring crash of foaming waves, a constant reminder of my mortality, periodically took a break. The pause was only long enough to allow a rolling wave or two to take the place of the brutal ones, but it was just the opportunity I needed. After several minutes spent watching for the least foamy set, I finally rowed as hard as I could toward the dock.

Somehow, it worked.

Unfortunately, by the time I tied up the boat, I was completely exhausted. I set both oars on the dock and crawled out of the boat, barely finding the strength to roll myself onto the wooden planks and close my eyes. I lay there for several minutes, grateful for the sliver-filled dock below me.

"Think of that one on your own?" asked a male voice that was all too familiar.

I squeezed my eyes closed tighter as if that would block out all sound.

The planks creaked beneath the approaching footsteps. They stopped within a few inches of my feet, and a shadow covered my face as I continued to hide behind my eyelids.

He took a seat on the dock next to me, laughing hysterically.

I slowly opened my eyes just in time to see him blowing his nose into a white handkerchief. The top of his light brown head was unmistakable; it was an unfortunate shade lighter than Dell's. "Hello, Shane," I mumbled.

"Oh, Em, you never disappoint!"

I stared at the younger, less appealing version of my husband and exhaled in disgust. "Speaking of disappointing, why are *you* here instead of Dell?"

"Nice try, Lady Milton, but in this house, *I'm* the lord of the manor."

"Excuse me?" I sat up, quickly forgetting about my tired body.

"Yes, my dear, I'm Lord Milton."

"No, you're not. Dell is!"

He grinned and shrugged. "Tomayto, tomahto."

"What?! You have to be kidding me!"

"Would I kid my lovely bride?" He wiped his eyes and returned his handkerchief to his pocket.

Then, an especially loud snore drifted out of the guard shack.

"Hmm. I hear your partner in crime." Shane stood and walked over to the source of the noise and emerged, holding the bottle of whiskey. "And, I see you've found my stash."

I just stared at him.

He walked toward me with the bottle, grabbed the oars from the dock, and hung them in their rightful resting spots. Then he returned to my side, extending his free hand down to me. "Milady…"

I was too tired to argue, so I let him help me up.

He held my hand until we reached the stone staircase,

and he walked close behind me to keep me from falling backward while I slowly dragged my exhausted body to the top. It was humiliating.

So much for my escape.

CHAPTER TWO

Whenever I saw Shane, I had to fight an overwhelming urge to punch him in the nose—or, at the very least, slap him. Although he was Dell's younger self and shared his handsome features, muscular physique, and a similar hair color, his personality overrode any further resemblance. He seemed to have a gift for finding and pressing all my buttons, winding me up until I could hardly breathe. Then, he would just sit back and smile as I fought to compose myself.

After my incident with the rowboat, Shane led me into the library and helped me to lie down on one of the couches. He pulled a chair up next to me and ran his fingers along my arm as he spoke: "So, darlin', what made you think those dainty little thin's were meant for rowin' twenty-five miles in shark-infested wata?" He tried to mimic the Southern accent Dell used when I first met him; he only succeeded in sounding ridiculous.

I immediately sat up and swatted his fingers from my skin as if they were insects. "I didn't know we were so far away!"

"Well, that makes me feel better." He shot a crooked grin

in my direction. "Still, what were you thinking?"

I loudly exhaled through a pair of flapping lips. "I'm bored." *Not really…just with you.*

He looked around the room, scanning the overstuffed shelves that occupied three of the four walls. "Do you need more books?"

"No, Shane. That's clearly not the answer."

"Well, I think I could manage a puppy. Would you enjoy that?"

"Are you kidding me?"

"Of course not, darlin'. You can have whatever breed you wish."

"Shane!"

"What, darlin'?"

"I'm *not* your darlin'!"

"Okay. Then what name do you prefer?" His blue eyes danced as he licked his lips.

I shivered in disgust. "Stop it!"

"Why? I'm only trying to please my bride."

"I'm not your bride either."

"Well, in this house you are."

"Then I want a divorce," I demanded.

"Did you forget where you are, my buttercup?"

"Then move me to the mainland and find me a lawyer."

He shook his head. "Sorry, sweetness, but that's not possible."

"And why not?"

"Because this is the safest place for you right now."

I was quickly losing patience and found it more and more difficult to stifle my urge to pummel him with more than my words and attitude. "I don't care about being safe, Shane. I just want to be with Dell!"

"But you are, dear."

"No, I'm not! I'm with you."

"Well, technically, we're the same person," he said.

His arrogant grin caused the steam to boil up inside me, until it finally exploded. "You might be Dell at twenty-five, but you need every bit of the ten years that separate you two to become even remotely close to the man I married!"

That did it. He finally stopped talking and stared down at his lap. Then he slowly rose from his chair and walked over to the window.

After a few minutes of silence, in which I somehow managed to regain my composure, I felt my conscience start to take over. *Way to go, Em! You weren't raised to be cruel and insulting, to argue like that, even if some people—like Shane—bring it out in you.*

I dragged my sore body off the couch and joined Shane at the window. "I'm sorry."

He didn't respond.

"I didn't mean to hurt your feelings. It's just…I miss Dell so much!" My voice started to crack, so I inhaled and exhaled deeply to regain control. "I'm tired of traveling to different times and safe houses with the promise of seeing Dell…only to be disappointed. Plus…you make me crazy."

He spoke without turning from the window. "I take that as a compliment."

I bit my tongue, feeling my conscience and self-control fade in the wake of a new round of venomous comments, lying just below the surface. Before I could spew them in his direction, however, Shane reached down, gently grabbed my hand, and turned me toward him.

"There's something I need to tell you, Emily."

The sadness in his eyes immediately brought tears to mine.

"Dell?" I fought to breathe as the image of Dell, broken and bruised from head to toe, flashed before my eyes. I stared at Shane's Adam's apple as it moved in response to the lump of courage he must have swallowed.

"His injuries were…life threatening."

Dell had prepared me for that grim possibility on our last visit, but Shane's words made my fears real. Tears instantly streamed down my face. "Is he…?"

Shane held my other hand in his. "No, but he suffered extensive internal and external injuries and was placed in a recovery chamber to heal."

"A what?" I asked, feeling lightheaded.

"Let's sit." Shane guided me back to the couch and sat next to me, handing me a clean handkerchief. "He's in a medically induced coma within a hyperbaric chamber that will allow him the time and environment he needs to heal."

"Will he recover?"

"Em, I can't answer that question."

"What do you mean? You can travel in time to the past *and* the future, and you can't even tell me if Dell's going to be okay?"

Shane drew several deep breaths before continuing. "He asked me not to do that."

I had to grip the handkerchief with both hands to keep them from flying in the air. "He what? When was this? Does he talk in his sleep?"

"Em, please calm down!"

"Really, Shane? You're telling me that I might never see

Dell again, yet you want me to be calm?"

He ignored my outburst and continued without making eye contact. "After his surgeries and before he went into the chamber, he asked an associate to retrieve me from my time so he could speak with me. Dell asked me to take care of you until he recovers." Finally, Shane looked into my eyes as I wiped away the tears, making a soggy mess of his handkerchief. "Emily, he wants his recovery to be in real time. In other words, if it takes him six months to recover in the future, then we won't see him for six months in the time we're occupying either."

His words left me speechless.

"He also made me promise not to go into the future to check on his recovery."

I quickly found my voice. "Why? That doesn't make any sense."

Shane looked at me, then at his lap. "I don't know how to say this."

"Just spit it out!"

His eyes slowly met mine again. "Dell wants us to...become acquainted with each other before we learn his fate."

"Why?"

"If he doesn't live, Em, then I'm meant to take his place."

"You're what?!" I felt certain that insanity was a family secret he had just accidently revealed, but I needed clarification. "Are you both nuts? Does Dell think I can just substitute you for him?"

He didn't reply.

"You're at a different place in your life, Shane. I'm in love with the you who is ten years older. It's not as easy as simply replacing one of you with the other!"

Shane nodded. "He warned me that you'd react this way."

"Oh, he did, did he? Well, good for him! If he knows me so well, he should also have known better than to leave me behind with his younger self, knowing that I'd rather row twenty-five miles with my scrawny arms than be with you!"

With that, I stormed from the room and straight outside, determined to row myself to death before I set foot in that house again. My focus was so undeterred that I failed to feel the giant rain drops descending from the sky in an ever increasing stream. Every step became more labored as my skirts wicked water from their long hemlines to the waist like a roll of superabsorbent paper towels. By the time I reached the top of the stairs leading to the boat dock, I felt as if I had gained fifty pounds, and I was soaked through to my corset. Unfortunately, my very thin leather shoes were also no match for the puddles I slogged through to get there, and I could already feel the bottoms of my feet wrinkling up like prunes.

I stopped briefly to scan the black sky above and on the angry horizon, as well as the white-capped waves that were crashing into the cliffs, slamming the small boat into the dock below. I didn't care—the weather was no match for the storm brewing within me.

Shane reached my side and grabbed the back of my hand just as I extended it toward the railing that would have guided me down to the dock. I tried to pull away but found his grip was unbreakable.

"You'll die out there!" Shane yelled. He was standing behind me, but the newly formed wind gusts took his words and threw them in the opposite direction.

"Funny, I thought I was already dead!" I screamed in reply.

He drew me closer to him so that he could speak in my ear. "Do you think I want this? I didn't choose you either! Dell chose for me!"

I stopped struggling—he was right, and I knew it. I had only been looking at things from my own perspective.

Shane loosened his grip, allowing me to face him. "I just miss him, Shane!"

"I know," he replied, defeated.

He led me back to the house where Goodwin was waiting to assist me to my room and a hot bath. Although she must have witnessed more of my foiled escapes than I would have preferred, she acted as if that sort of thing happened all the time. I imagined the remaining staff knew as well.

Later, in the dining room, our dinner was a quiet one. Surrounded by mahogany paneled walls, broken on one side by tall curtains that were almost seamlessly drawn together, Shane and I sat at opposite ends of a long, rectangular table covered in a delicately woven linen tablecloth and set for two with crystal, china, and silver. With the exception of the occasional "Please" and "Thank you," we ate in silence.

Once the plates were cleared, Shane rose and looked in my direction. "Shall we?"

I nodded and stood as one of the footmen pulled my chair out for me.

Shane reached my side and offered me his arm to escort me to the library. "We need to talk," he said in a raspy voice.

Great. Dell might die, and now I've given Shane pneumonia!

Inside the library, a roaring fire filled the room with its warmth, casting a comforting glow on the spines of the books lining the many shelves. Shane placed two wingback chairs in front of the fireplace and offered one to me.

"Thank you." I sat with my feet pointing toward the flames, still feeling as if I had lost a toe or two in the rain.

Shane leaned forward and placed his elbows on his knees. "Can we call a truce?" he asked.

"Yes," I said, not hesitating.

"Good, because I don't see how I can keep my promises to Dell without us being friends."

"You must think I'm horrible."

"No. You're just in love. I realize that my company isn't what you want to keep right now, but I'm here for you regardless. Also, please don't think ill of Dell for asking for my help. He loves you and only wants to keep you safe while he recovers."

I shook my head. "But when Dell first introduced us, he was so jealous of you."

"I suppose he thinks you might want to be with someone younger."

I thought back to the last conversation I had with Dell, when I had jokingly suggested that Shane step in for him on our real honeymoon. The memory left me speechless.

After pausing several seconds, Shane said, "I didn't come right away, you know."

"I had no idea."

"He asked me months ago, but I simply went back to my time and proceeded with my life."

"Simply?" I asked. Dell might have been recovering in the future, but he was from the past—sometime in the 1800s—and so was Shane. "I doubt it was simple for you to return to your time as if nothing happened. Then, once you finally readjusted, you returned to the future just to babysit me. It sounds more complicated than anything. What changed your mind?"

"It was a who—Johann."

"You mean the older version of you and Dell?" I asked.

"Exactly."

Despite the use of different names, the whole relationship between Johann Holtz and his younger selves, Dell and Shane, was confusing at best. The mere mention of parallel lives sent smoke pouring from my ears. It took me a few seconds before I could return to the conversation with Shane and ask, "How did he convince you to come here?"

"He showed me a hologram of my future—of you, me, and our son. I couldn't refuse after that."

My throat went dry. "Was it you or Dell in the hologram?"

"Johann knew, but he wouldn't tell me. He didn't want to influence my behavior in any way."

"Wow. You people sure don't appreciate interference!"

"No, we don't. If it isn't organic, we don't participate."

I could feel the confusion mounting. "Then why did he ask you to leave your time to be with me?"

"To protect the mother of my son," he said flatly.

The future of H&S hinged upon the birth of the son I was meant to have with Dell, but that, just like my honeymoon, wasn't quite going as planned. I married Dell because I loved *him*, not his company's plan. I fought the urge to laugh like a lunatic while simultaneously patting my head and rubbing my belly. It took several deep, cleansing breaths to put the whole ridiculous situation back into perspective. "I guess I'm just a glorified incubator." I smiled over at him. "You sure know how to make a girl feel special."

A grin crept across his face for the first time since we had entered the library. "Yeah, well, you're not so bad yourself!"

"Touché." I laughed, then asked, "What now?"

"We simply wait it out," Shane said, staring into the fire.

"Lovely. Why here?"

"It's not called a safe house for nothing," he replied.

"What about the other safe houses?"

"But this one suits you so well." He turned from the fire to admire the neckline and corset-enhanced bodice of my dress.

Perv! I glared at him until we finally made eye contact. "Let me rephrase that. Why can't we go to a different safe house, one I've never been to before?"

"Because you're not trained."

I scooted to the edge of my seat. "Then train me! I want to learn. Besides, I have nothing else to do." I actually missed school and didn't mind admitting it.

"We don't work that way, Em. Evergreen taught you to live in 1910 society with no regard for how your presence would impact life there. Changing the past to their client's advantage is the Evergreen way, but that doesn't fit too well with H&S's well-established organic approach to history. Our methods require extensive preparation at our headquarters in the future."

"Then teach me all about it. Send me to the training, Shane," I pleaded.

"You know I can't. The future isn't for you, Emily."

"I still don't understand why."

"Because your being there might influence your decisions that may, in turn, change the future. We can predict outcomes, Em, and your traveling into the future doesn't come with favorable results."

"But, Shane, we could be here for years!"

"Then so be it."

I suddenly wondered how many bottles of whiskey it would take for Mr. Hogg to turn the other way as I sneaked onto one of the delivery boats.

Shane saw my far-off look and must have misinterpreted. "Have you changed your mind about the puppy offer?" His perfectly straight, white teeth glistened almost demonically in the fire light.

"You're impossible! I'm going to bed."

Instead, I found a pair of shears and an empty flour sack in the staff kitchen and borrowed them without being noticed while the staff was busy cleaning up after dinner. I'd appropriated a similar pair once before, when the lack of Evergreen staff assistance led me to cut myself out of my Coming Out gown and corset. I gently ran the blade along my thumb pad, hoping the sharpness of the newly acquired pair would serve me as well. After I absconded with the scissors, I hid them above the wardrobe in my room until after Goodwin helped me out of my dress and torturous corset.

I waited almost half an hour after the maid left me alone before walking with the items, as well as the corset, into the bathroom. I propped the dreaded undergarment up behind the sink faucets for inspiration. Then I took the sack, rolled the top portion open numerous times, and placed it in the sink. I stared at my reflection for several minutes, searching for the nerve I possessed in abundance earlier. "This had better work!"

I grabbed a fistful of my blonde hair with my left hand and pulled it away from my head. Then, with my right hand,

I proceeded to cut the hair just below my ears. Afterward, I just stared at the handful of long locks I was holding. My hair had never been cut; an occasional trim, but never an official haircut. I wanted to cry as I stuffed those lifelong pieces of myself into the sack.

"There's no going back now," I told myself. "Besides, long hair wasn't as popular in the 1920s." I grew up hearing Maude's stories of her flapper days. Her eyes always took on a special far-off light whenever she spoke of her wild ways. "Now, maybe I can see firsthand what Maude was talking about."

When I found the nerve again, I proceeded to repeat Steps One, Two, and Three, until my hair overburdened the flour sack. I spent the next half hour trying to even out my pathetic attempt at a bob before giving up entirely. "You look ridiculous!" I screamed at my reflection.

I grabbed the fat sack of hair and my corset and flung them both into the fireplace. It took several seconds for the coal embers to ignite the new items, but once they did, the smell was nauseating, forcing me to open the balcony doors to air out the room. I sat beneath a blanket, shivering in front of the fire, as my corset and hair bag were reduced to ashes and indistinguishable bits and pieces. Once the nasty stench dissipated, I closed the balcony doors and climbed into bed. My bare neck felt cold as I tried to find sleep, knowing that the morning would only bring drama.

CHAPTER THREE

Apparently, as a younger man, Dell possessed quite a temper, because I thought Shane was going to rupture something vital in his neck or head when he saw my haircut. Of course, my method of revelation probably didn't help matters.

I chose breakfast to make my new appearance known by walking into the dining room as if nothing was different. The sound of a tray crashing to the ground behind him made Shane look up from his morning paper. He first cast a glance at the broken dishes on the floor, then the ashen-faced butler, who just stared at me while I walked past. It all seemed to happen in slow motion when Shane turned from the butler to me as I seated myself and nonchalantly spread my napkin across my lap.

"Clear the room!" Shane screamed.

The staff nearly ran from their posts, and I stood to go as well.

"Sit!" Shane's words echoed throughout the room.

I sat.

He placed both hands, palms down, on the table and just stared at his plate while his face grew a deeper shade of red by the second. After a dozen or more deep breaths, Shane finally spoke to the table: "Dell always painted an amazing picture of you to me, and your beauty and intelligence topped the list. When I first met you and looked into those blue eyes, I saw those things as well. Imagining you shaking that blonde hair of yours from the pile it occupied atop your head...Well, let's just say that kept me up at night. And your wit! I've never met anyone who could rival you." His eyes met mine. "But I don't see those things anymore. Instead, I see a spoiled little girl who now resembles a child and makes poor decisions like one too. You want the 1920s? Well, you'll have them just as you want them, without any training. Meet me in the lab in twenty minutes!" With that, he wiped his mouth with the napkin and left the room.

I felt horrible. I just stared at my plate for a few seconds, then left the dining room and slowly walked to the bedroom. Goodwin was there to meet me and wouldn't make eye contact. Before breakfast, I had dressed myself in a simple frock that hid the fact that I wasn't wearing a corset and left the room before Goodwin arrived. She now helped me remove the outfit and handed me a 1920s-era dress to replace it, accompanied by a modern-style bra, then exited the room without a word. The dress was an off-white cotton, and with the exception of the drop waist, it bore no distinguishable pattern or design. It was hideous.

Fifteen minutes later, the lump in my throat felt like a cramp of shame as I carried my Maude suitcase to the elevator, hidden behind a closet door, and pressed the button that would lead to the lower basements. When the elevator arrived, a sturdy brick of a man stepped out and held the door for me to enter. I stared at the floor as we rode in silence to our destination.

Once the doors opened, the man stayed behind me and quickly ushered me from the elevator, down the hallways, and through the security doors. The lab technicians we passed refrained from making any contact as we walked to the end of the last hallway, which opened into the garage area of the basement laboratory. Near the far end sat a shiny, black 1920 Silver Ghost limousine, which had transported me to different times on many occasions. Its giant headlights seemed to be the friendliest eyes in the room. Shane was already seated in the front, with the chauffeur, clad in a gray hat, wool jacket, and leather gloves, positioned to drive on his right. Meanwhile, the man from the elevator led me into the back.

I was barely seated before the car started to move at a far greater speed than I expected. The black cloth seats did little to keep me from sliding back as I struggled to find something to hold onto in the ever-accelerating vehicle. I closed my eyes to keep the nausea at bay and to avoid seeing the usual strange, iridescent colors of the tunnel-like void through which we were being transported.

The trip ended within minutes, but the lump in my throat remained a constant reminder of my stupidity. *Perfect, Em. Shane is angry, as you expected, but you've also alienated yourself from your only ally in this crazy place!*

The chauffeur remained seated as his male passengers exited. No one offered me their assistance, so I opened the door and stepped out on my own, then joined the other two at the far end of yet another garage-like space. Chivalry was a perk of the job that I grew accustomed to experiencing, and the blatant lack of it felt like a slap in my already humiliated face.

Without looking at me, Shane introduced the man from

the elevator. "This is Louie. He's your shadow. Don't bother talking to him. He only speaks Italian."

Aside from being extremely muscular, Louie was also quite good looking. His dark brown hair was greased into a wave at the back of his head, and his chocolate brown eyes were surrounded by equally dark eyelashes that framed their almond-shape as if he were wearing eyeliner. The tiny laugh lines at the corners of his eyes made it appear as though he would smile at any moment. His remaining features all worked together to give his face a symmetrical balance that made not staring at his striking appearance almost impossible.

I tried not to blush as I offered Louie my hand, but Shane grabbed it instead and led me to one of the window-lined rooms just steps away. Its cold whiteness was further accentuated by rows of fluorescent lighting that covered almost every inch of the free space on the ceiling.

"Sit." He released my hand and pointed to a blue, plastic chair that looked like a garage sale reject, the only seat in the room.

Shane and Louie stood just outside the door as a group of women in white coats descended upon me like vultures on fresh roadkill. Without introductions, they closed the door, pulled the blinds, and unceremoniously removed my dress and gave me a smock to wear in its place. Then they cut my hair—again. When they were through, they brushed the loose hair from my neck and shoulders, then made me stand as they removed the smock and chair. One of them swept the hair from the floor, while another entered the room, carrying a different outfit.

Had I been able to feel anything other than self-pity, I

might have noticed that the dress she was holding was beautiful and didn't require a corset. It was an apricot-colored taffeta with off-white beads that ran the length of the dress. It fit perfectly and was accented with two long strands of pearls that extended to my thighs. I was given a pair of silk stockings that I put on just before I was handed shoes that matched the dress perfectly, right down to the beadwork. I barely stepped into the shoes before one of the ladies knelt on the floor next to me and rolled my stockings down below my knees. Another walked into the room carrying the plastic chair and a new smock, which she placed over my dress, then motioned for me to sit in the chair. A second chair was brought in that soon housed a stubby, mustached woman who proceeded to apply makeup to my face. The products smelled like the rendering plant from which I was certain they escaped, and the noxious odor began to turn my stomach.

I finally found my elusive inner voice. *I don't even like makeup! I can't imagine this ending well.* The woman's well-established facial hair and bad breath also competed for my interest as she worked her magic, applying liberal amounts of matter to my reluctant face. I could almost hear my *au naturel* pores crying in protest and slamming shut with every brush stroke.

Once she was finished layering me with her caustic paint, the woman removed the smock and both chairs, and I was left standing alone in the empty room. The whole transformation took only minutes and was performed without any form of conversation.

When it was complete, Shane stepped inside and met my eyes. He held them for several seconds without looking away. For the first time, I saw Dell in his eyes, and I longed to run to him; instead, I just stared.

Shane finally broke the silence. "At least you don't resemble a little boy anymore." Then, he turned and walked out of the room.

I was crushed.

Louie walked with me to the limousine and watched me open my own door and enter the back seat. The chauffeur and Shane were already seated in the front. I was glad no one required me to speak, because the lump was growing by the second and would have prevented me from doing anything except cry.

The Ghost was parked on a platform that ascended from the basement floor. A similar lift was used at Dunston House, where Dell and I went after our wedding. The memory of that day, coupled with my recent experiences, was suddenly more than I could bear. The tears descended in streams before I could stop them.

Louie elbowed me and handed me a handkerchief.

Wow. There's a gentleman in there after all. I tried to smile my thank you, but he had already turned away.

Once the elevator stopped, the driver proceeded toward a set of double-doors that stood across the warehouse space we now occupied. Two men opened the doors from the inside, and we drove onto a busy street, lined with single-story warehouses. Each had open bay doors that were accepting and producing deliveries from various trucks and wagons, as well as pedestrians pushing carts or carrying parcels of different sizes and shapes. The aroma of rotting produce and leaded exhaust filtered through the loosely sealed car windows along with the goose-like honking of rubber car horns.

I had visited the 1920s only once before, back when I buried the Maude journal at night. Seeing my surroundings during the daylight fascinated me.

Fortunately, in my attempt to discern our location, I had a perfect view of the street from my spot in the back seat. That was where my luck ran out, however, because when I turned to look back at the doors we had just exited, Louie reached behind me and grabbed my shoulder, forcefully pulling me sideways toward him onto the open bench and placing a rag on my nose and mouth. Struggling was useless as my world quickly went black.

* * *

I came to in the dark, the only occupant of the parked limo's back seat. When I sat up, I noticed that the chauffeur was still sitting behind the wheel. He must have heard me moving on the bench, because he turned to hand me a train case that matched the Maude suitcase, which was lying on the floor at my feet.

I reached for the case and pulled it toward me. "Thank you."

"You're welcome, miss."

Great. I've been formally reduced to "miss" again. I guess I burned "milady" with my hair.

I set the case on my lap and opened it. Although it was dark outside, the sky was clear, and the full moon shined into the back seat, serving as the dome light the vehicle lacked. Inside the train case, I found the makeup the mustached lady used on me, as well as a few extras, such as facial cream and real bar soap. "I've missed you—or at least most of you," I whispered into the case. I singled out the blush and eye-

45

shadow and gave each a scowl.

I was so excited about my new treasure chest that I failed to look in the mirror attached beneath the lid. The reflection of the moon in the glass, however, soon left me horrified. "Now I know why makeup isn't my thing in any time period!"

My previous tears had created streaks of color from my eyes, cheeks, and lips that blended into dark smudges, running the length of my face.

Wonderful.

I used the moonlight in the mirror, Louie's handkerchief from earlier, and a fair amount of saliva and face cream to remove the trails and streaks. Then, giving it my best effort, I applied fresh makeup, trying to recall the colors and placement the mustached lady had used. *It would have been nice if someone had offered me a mirror in the lab. I have no idea how I looked when the makeup was fresh.* I studied my face some more. *It couldn't have been too bad, though. At least it held Shane's attention for a while.*

I ignored the slight tremble in my bottom lip as I replaced the covers on all the cosmetics and closed the lid to the train case. "Is this mine?" I asked the driver.

"Yes. Mr., uh…Well, it was a gift."

I just smiled. *Poor guy doesn't know Shane's name in our new time. Neither do I, for that matter.*

It was the nature of the H&S time-travel beast that the changes in my wardrobe, name, and identity were already handled for me, almost exclusively without my knowledge, prior to my arrival in a new period. Unlike Evergreen's brief orientation, followed by their on-the-job training approach to time travel, H&S implemented intensive training for all their employees, everyone except for me. I wasn't an employee; I was the boss's wife, meant to simply hide in safe houses and await Dell's potential return. And now, I'd blown it with Shane, my only source of information.

Sitting in the dark, without the security of arriving in a safe house, made Shane's words, "… without any training" dance around my head. *I guess their solution was to knock me out rather than explain anything to me, then throw me to the wolves. Some solution.*

"What am I meant to do now?" I asked the back of the brown-haired chauffeur's head, which was still covered by the gray hat.

"This is your home, miss."

"I thought we were in a parking lot," I said, peering out the window. The number of cars that surrounded us was almost impossible to count from my seat. From Cadillacs, Packards, and Studebakers to Hudsons, Bugattis, and the occasional Duesenberg, the cars were all in mint condition, similar to ones at the vintage car shows Mom's boyfriend, Tom, and I used to attend eighty years in the future.

Without a reply, the driver stepped out and opened my door for me. I was pleasantly surprised and took the hand he offered as I stepped out of the Ghost and looked around. An enormous white house illuminated the night in the distance beyond the sea of parked cars. Its modern façade looked like the missing front tooth from a celestial smile that beckoned to me in the darkness. Devoid of windows, the flat, stucco front jutted from the ground beneath it and was broken only by garage-sized double front doors. These stood atop a wide set of about a dozen white, marble stairs that led into the house beyond.

I turned back to the dark limo and the train case I had placed on the seat, as well as the Maude suitcase on the floor below, then met the brown eyes of the chauffeur.

"I'll see to those, miss." He offered a smile.

"Thank you," I said, my voice wobbly.

I didn't know how to take his kindness. Fortunately, he had no expectations and simply left me with a nod. I was still groggy and slightly confused from being unconscious, but I finally snapped out of it and slowly zigzagged through the stream of cars toward the front stairs of the house. My pace quickened, however, once I realized that the majority of the vehicles were occupied and doubled as bordellos behind their fogged up windows. "Eew!" My disgusted protests were hardly audible above the sounds coming from the surrounding cars.

When I finally negotiated the front stairs and opened the massive right door, I hoped to find refuge in the house; however, I was greatly mistaken. The entire scene before me was a drunken example of bad behavior.

I looked around, almost unable to keep my mouth from dropping. *Wow, and I thought frat parties were crazy!*

The crowd noise was deafening, with cackles of laughter rolling in and out in spurts. Although a full jazz band was playing in a corner, I could barely hear them.

People and clothing hung from every free surface. Ladies' undergarments descended defiantly from the chandeliers in the entryway, as well as from the other light fixtures visible from the doorway. As I walked farther into the house, I noticed that everyone was either smoking cigarettes or extinguishing them in empty drink glasses or the potted plants unfortunate enough to exist in the area. *I wonder how long we have before the whole place catches fire.* I shook my head.

Stronger than the smell of smoke was the stench of alcohol that also left a sticky mess all over the Italian marble that covered the first floor. I almost lost a shoe in an effort to simply walk forward. To make matters worse, I had a busting headache.

"Where's the kitchen?" I asked everyone I passed.

They all gave me different answers.

I finally worked my way through the drunken masses to a swinging kitchen door, where an angry, white-clad caterer turned me around and shoved me back into the crowd. "Water!" I screamed at the top of my lungs, only to be drowned out by the cackle of a half-clothed female whose wrinkles told me she should have known better.

I needed air, so I walked toward an open set of French doors and out onto a deck that led to an Olympic-sized swimming pool. Although the fresh air was welcoming, the sight before me was not. The pool and surrounding area were filled with more nakedness than I'd seen since I visited Papa Bob and Nana Rosie's summer camp in the woods of Oregon. The thought of my crazy, hippie grandparents brought a smile to my face that retreated in an instant, when an extremely hairy, overweight man streaked past me.

I'd had enough. I turned around and tried to head back into the throng but was stopped by an unmistakable voice coming from behind me: "Hiya, sis!"

I turned around to see Shane in all his naked glory, with half-clothed women hanging from him like ornaments on a Christmas tree. If I would have had anything in my stomach, it would have escaped at that moment.

I was speechless. Whatever inkling of Dell I saw in his

eyes earlier had been replaced by mindless blue orbs swimming in a pool of bootlegged alcohol.

"I'd hug ya, but, well, uh…" he slurred.

His entourage giggled like school girls at his debauchery.

I was furious. "Nice party!"

"Gosh, sis," he said. "Don't be that way. I'm just having a little fun. You see, I was bored." In an obvious effort to mock my words spoken in The 1908 House library, he tried to make his lips move as he exhaled but only succeeded in spitting in the face of the woman next to him.

She giggled in delight. "Oh, Oscar, you're such a silly boy!"

"And you, my little chickadee, are such…a…silly…girl!" He leaned down to kiss her.

I couldn't watch. "Stop!"

He stood straight, almost unable to catch his balance, relying instead on a pair or two of the female legs that seemed to be attached to him.

"Well, she's sure mouthy for fifteen!" one of the women said in my direction.

I just looked at Shane, who threw one of his crooked smiles at me.

"That's right, ladies…fifteen going on twenty-four!"

They all gave a little giggle, despite their ignorance of the true meaning behind his words.

I shook my head. *This clearly isn't one of those occasions when looking young for my age is paying off.*

"You see, little sister, anything goes here. I bet even *you* can succeed at that!"

I hated him at that moment, and I had to turn away to keep him from seeing the tears forming in my eyes.

Louie was now standing at my side. I tried to remember the Italian I had picked-up from the many subtitled movies Mom had insisted I watch. "They give you culture," she always said. At first, they only gave me a headache while I tried unsuccessfully to read the subtitles and catch the action on the screen at the same time. But the straight-A student in me soon learned to skim the words and travel the world with my crazy, eclectic mother—all from the comfort of our living room couch.

"Uh, Louie, *mi camera*?" My feeble attempt to locate my bedroom was barely audible above the noise the house was belching in our direction.

He just stared at me.

"*Italiano*?" I asked.

He nodded.

Feeling my linguistic inabilities mounting by the second, I tilted my head to the side and rested my cheek on the back of my hand, held in a sleeping gesture. Then, I proceeded to make snoring noises.

His eyes traveled from me to Shane. I shot Shane the nastiest look I could, effectively wiping the smile off his face and simultaneously off the faces of the women around him. He nodded at Louie, who then led me to a room upstairs that overlooked the pool.

"*Grazie*," I offered.

He nodded, then left the room.

The noise was beyond belief, and I had no interest in watching or hearing my husband's younger self gain his poolside revenge on me, so I proceeded to the attached bathroom, where I piled blankets and pillows into the bathtub and closed the door.

I slipped off my dress and climbed into the tub, wearing my slip, then drew the pillow around my ears. Nevertheless, I couldn't drown out the voice of reason screaming in my head: *Well, Em, you asked for it, and you got it, the 1920s.* But it wasn't what I expected at all. I shook my head inside the folded pillow and felt it brush against my bare shoulders.

"From the frying pan into the fire, aren't you, Toots?" Maude's wise words, once again, found their way into my thoughts at just the right moment.

You're right, Maude. I guess I've just substituted a skillet for a bathtub, which makes sense, considering I'm drowning.

The mere mention of water drew a well of pent-up tears to the surface and sent them streaming down my cheeks.

I miss you so much! You're my best friend, Maude, and when I buried your journal, I felt like I buried you all over again. Cutting my hair was stupid and juvenile and all those things Shane accused me of being, but that's not me. I'm not bored. I'm just…lonely. I have no point of reference, no anchor, no purpose. As crazy as this might sound, I did what I did for the love of you, Maude. I've always wanted to be just like you. I sure don't want to be myself right now. I wouldn't wish this on anyone. There was only one you, and right now, I'm stuck being me.

Sleep eventually found me but not before I cried myself in its direction.

CHAPTER FOUR

The stench of the night before, coupled with a fair amount of vomit, greeted me the next morning as I opened the bedroom door and descended the stairs to the first floor. It was almost more than I could handle. A cleaning crew was making the best of the mess, wearing full-sized handkerchiefs over their noses.

Wow! I'm sure they're being paid a fortune. I looked around at the carnage. *They couldn't pay me enough, though.*

In an effort to find some breakfast, I stepped over the garbage and corpse-like guests sprinkled liberally across the floor and walked into the only clean room on the first floor, the kitchen.

"Leave!" The same caterer who had greeted me the night before now stood within inches of my face. He was a dark-haired man with beady eyes and no sense of humor.

"Excuse me? I live here!" I was starving, and I was prepared to tear him apart limb from limb if my breakfast didn't materialize soon.

He stood back. "You're the sister?"

"The hungry one!"

He eyed me up and down. "I'm Chef Jacques. What can I

bring you?"

"What are my choices?"

He just stared.

"Right. Well, poached eggs and toast…and some kind of meat."

"Coffee or tea?"

"Tea, please."

"Very good. We will serve it to you outside." He gently pushed me backward out of the kitchen.

Nice. I guess he's not the caterer after all. I hope his cooking is better than his manners.

I waded through the piles to the French doors that led out to the pool. They stood open to allow the breeze to aid the cleaning crew in clearing the stagnant foulness from the house.

A separate team of landscapers was making the finishing touches on the pool and backyard. As I stepped through the doorway into the warm sunshine, I was drawn to the end of the pool, where I saw something that had escaped my attention in the dark—the house was perched on a cliff, directly overlooking the ocean. I was in heaven and could only gape at the spectacular scene before me. With the assistance of one of the gardeners, I relocated a table and chair to a flat spot of grass just beyond the pool that offered a perfect view of the water.

My breakfast arrived soon afterward and included a fruit platter and pastries, along with the items I had requested earlier. I eyed an oversized turnover that called to me as soon as the food was deposited on the table. *I guess I can excuse the cook's shortcomings.*

The meal was delicious.

FOR THE LOVE OF MAUDE

I spent so much of my morning appreciating the ocean view and my breakfast that the house had emptied of leftover guests by the time I reentered; in fact, it was almost clean.

Without the people and assorted clothing attached, the house was quite breathtaking. The marble floors were scattered with Persian rugs that had been stowed for safekeeping prior to the party. The paintings, vases, and other decorations had been retrieved from storage as well, and were placed throughout the house. I stepped further inside and watched as several stout men, including Louie, moved couches and other large pieces of furniture from the garages and storage sheds into their normal resting spots. When the transformation was complete, the house looked like a study in understated elegance.

"This can't be the same place as last night," I said out loud.

"Amazing, isn't it?"

I turned to see Shane standing behind me, looking as if a truck had not only struck him but then proceeded to back over him several times, just in case.

"You look fresh as a flower, brother of mine."

He didn't speak; instead, he gestured toward the French doors and walked outside with me, to the far end of the pool.

"You were both quite popular last night." My eyes drifted from his face to the front of his wrinkled trousers and back to his face. "I think I'd have that thing looked at if I were you."

He suddenly found his voice. "Nothing happened, Em."

"Really, Oscar?" I spoke in my best baby-talk voice, "You're such a silly little boy!"

"I suppose I deserve that," he conceded.

"You're right—that and much more!"

"Look, Emily, your haircut pushed me over the edge."

"Cutting my hair isn't exactly the same as what you did, now is it?"

He exhaled. "No. I know I went a little over the top...but I promise you that nothing happened last night."

I didn't care, but he apparently did, because he continued to argue his case.

"Really, Em, I noticed you when you first arrived, when the chef wouldn't let you in the kitchen, so I decided to disrobe. Then I recruited a few of the women around the pool and waited for you to find me. After you went to bed, I regretted every minute of it. It was...I was a fool."

I couldn't argue with him there, but for Dell's sake, I decided to throw him a bone. "My hair grows really fast." I hoped, anyway.

He laughed and looked at the ground briefly before making eye contact again. When he did, we stood facing each other for several seconds without speaking.

I eventually asked, "Why did you knock me out after we arrived?"

He drew a deep breath. "Because I promised Dell I would take care of you."

"By rendering me unconscious?"

"No, Em. I have to ensure that Evergreen doesn't discover you're alive. Your haircut complicated matters and required a quick solution. We only have a warehouse, rather than a safe house established in this era, so we had to rent this property. I didn't have the time or patience to explain the logistics to you when we arrived, and I also didn't know what else you might try once we got here. Knocking you out, as you put it, seemed the best option."

I understand the logistics, smarty pants. I buried the journal in this era. I guess you didn't have the time or patience to do your research on that little detail either. Rather than inform Shane of these facts, I shook my head and scowled, then said, "Lovely, Oscar. I feel so much safer."

He just shook his head.

"By the way, what's *my* name?" I asked.

He hesitated before answering, "Remember that I wasn't too happy with you when I chose it."

Great! I exhaled loudly.

"It's Blanche...Krump."

Nice. "Am I really fifteen?"

"Again—"

"Is that a yes?"

"Yes...and you're my sister."

"Terrific."

He nodded. "Also, many of the staff members are locals from this time period. So we have to make a habit of calling each other by our new names even when we're alone; otherwise, we might forget when we're around outsiders."

"Fine, Oscar, but I'm not going to school."

"It's June."

I then lobbed questions at him in quick succession, resorting to my Tommy Gun Approach. "Good. Where are we?"

He answered just as quickly, "California."

"What city?"

"Near Santa Monica."

"What's the date?"

"Tuesday, June 8, 1926."

"How long are we going to be here?"

"Just for the summer."

"And then?"

"Let's just hope your hair really does grow fast." He gave me a genuine smile that thawed a portion of my frozen heart.

I left him with a smile of my own and returned to my room to shower.

In the daylight and with a full stomach, I was finally able to truly see the room for the first time. It was the size of a luxury hotel suite, furnished with a four-poster bed, night stands, and lamps along one wall and a large dresser and dressing table along the opposite. Before reaching the French doors that led to a balcony, I noticed two large closet doors. But as soon as I opened them, my hopes for a shower disappeared.

"Empty?" I went from one dresser drawer to the next, finding them empty as well.

"Where is my wardrobe?" I had never arrived at a new location without clothes bulging from every available space. I also hadn't been without a lady's maid in years. I looked at my hands and smiled. "At least I'm not sitting on you."

As my search for clothes continued, I surveyed the Maude suitcase the chauffeur had delivered to my room as promised. It was resting on top of the dresser. I expected it to be empty but opened the lid just in case. "Nothing."

I ran my fingers along the false bottom that so often served as a hiding place for the Maude journal, and I gently lifted the cover. It was empty as well. I quickly closed the case, fighting another tear-provoking feeling of nostalgia for the journal that had become my security blanket since my senior year in college.

I shook my head to dislodge the memory and walked into the bathroom, eyeing the empty towel racks and soap dish. "I guess I'm lucky to have toilet paper."

Fortunately, the train case was equipped with a toothbrush and a jar of baking soda paste, so I was able to brush my teeth at least.

After I was finished, I left the room in search of Shane and a change of clothes. I found him nursing a large glass of water on a shaded chaise near the pool. "Sh…er, Oscar?"

He held the glass to his temple without looking up. "Yes?"

"I don't have any other clothes."

He squinted at my wrinkled dress, then at my face. "We left in a rather big hurry."

"I know."

He went back to putting the glass to his temple. "Will a department store do?"

"Yes, that would be fine," I said, trying not to sound too eager. Maude had once told me that buying premade clothing was still a relatively new pastime in the 1920s. Although clothes shopping was never my favorite preoccupation, it reminded me of home. Plus, I was thrilled by the idea of mingling with other humans who weren't employees of the company.

Shane seemed to turn a strange shade of green right before my eyes. "I shouldn't have sat down," he muttered. He slowly lowered the glass and set it on a small table next to him. Then, he swung his legs around and placed his feet on the ground, gripping the sides of his head as he struggled to rise from the chaise. His bloodshot, blue eyes met mine. "You realize I'm counting on you—"

I nodded. "I won't disappoint you."

"Good. We can't afford any more problems." A deep sadness washed over his face. "We really must cooperate,

Em…er, Blanche."

"I'll try harder."

"Me too." He made an effort to smile but failed.

Poor guy!

"That bootlegged stuff doesn't seem to be your friend this morning," I said, offering an olive branch.

"Poison seldom is." His teeth emerged from behind his lips, forming a weak smile.

"You should probably sit back down."

"First, I need to find someone to accompany you to the store."

"Oscar, I think I can handle it."

He just stared at me. "I want to trust you. I really do. I just don't right now."

"Really, Oscar, *you*…don't trust…*me*?"

"Em…Blanche, I can't do this right now." He felt behind him for the back of the chaise and eased himself down onto the cushion, keeping his feet planted on the ground, then sat moaning with his head between his knees.

I stared at his brown locks, just a shade lighter than Dell's. *I sure wish I didn't want to run my fingers through that hair right now!* The thought caught me by surprise and made me take a step back.

"I'm not going to be sick," Shane said to his feet.

"Uh…I know." I fought the urge to run.

"Then why did you move away?" His muffled voice drifted up to me.

"I, just…I wish things were different, that's all."

"Me too."

"Yeah, well, I guess you didn't have a choice."

He suddenly looked up at me, reached for my hand, and

pulled me toward him. "I'm a little slow this morning, but we're not talking about clothes anymore, are we?"

I shook my head.

"Most men would give anything to be loved the way you love Dell. I'm not asking you to forget him. I just need you to stop blaming me for his absence."

"Then you need to trust me," I said. *And it wouldn't hurt if you'd stopped looking like Dell!*

He kissed my hand. "I'll work on it, but in the meantime, Louie will accompany you, and I won't hear any arguments to the contrary."

"Thank you, Oscar."

"You're welcome. Now, can you please find Louie for me?"

I smiled and went in search of my bodyguard. After I returned with him, I listened from just inside the house as Shane proceeded to speak to Louie in fluent Italian. It was such a turn-on. *He's not Dell. He's not Dell*, I chanted to myself.

When they were finished, Shane handed him a stack of bills. Louie smiled at me and gestured to the front door. I couldn't even look at Shane; instead, I smiled at Louie in reply and accompanied him to the front of the house, where I waited until he returned with the chauffeur and the limousine.

Unable to communicate with Louie, I spent the entire ride from Santa Monica to downtown Los Angeles just thinking about Shane and the many ways he differed from Dell. *He's cocky, he has a temper, he's a flirt, and, worst of all, he might have cheated on me last night.* I stared out the window but didn't notice the scenery. *How do you cheat on someone you're not even dating yet?* I thought for a minute. *Still, he's going to marry me in ten years—or at least when he's ten years older.*

Then, I shook my head. *But it's almost identical to an arranged marriage. Shane didn't choose me. His so-called family did.*

God, I'm so confused! Why does he have to resemble Dell so much?

I wanted to slap myself. *Duh, Em. Maybe that's because he is Dell!*

No he's not. Shane's the enemy.

I held that thought as we pulled up under a brown and gold awning that read, "Shaver's Department Store."

Never heard of it! I suddenly wasn't in the mood to shop. My opinion and mood changed dramatically, however, once I stepped out of the car and walked up the stairs and past the doorman. The store was absolutely beautiful. From the marble floors to the chandeliers that dripped crystals from the ceiling like manna from heaven, the entire place gleamed with the opulence that had helped to build it.

"May I help you?" A female voice from behind me jerked me out of my trance.

"Uh…" I turned around and jumped at the sight of a matronly woman dressed in black, standing mere inches from me. *Where's the funeral?*

The woman stood expressionless as I tried to store my comments away.

Great. She's looking at me as if I'm some loser off the street. I think I went to college with one of your descendants—or con-de-scendants. I smiled to myself. Maude always said, "We all came in the same door, Toots. Sometimes people just need to be reminded." So that was exactly what I set out to do.

"Yes," I finally said in the most snobbish tone I could fabricate on the spot. "My things were unavoidably detained in

Europe and shan't be arriving in an acceptable time frame. Thus, my dear brother suggested that I purchase replacements while we await their arrival." I scanned the store and frowned. "I hope I haven't made an error in judgment." With that, I placed my right index finger on my bottom lip and stared into the woman's suddenly bright eyes. *Never judge a girl by her two-day-old dress!*

"Oh, no, miss. I can assure you that you've come to the right place."

I again sized up the store around me. "Yes, well, I'll be the judge of that."

"Of c-course," she stammered. "What can I help you to find?"

I blinked several times at her before I spoke, enunciating periodically for effect. "I'm sorry. I thought I already made myself per-fect-ly clear. I will require ev-er-y-thing!"

The woman blushed and stood staring at the floor.

"Now, my patience is slowly disappearing, so unless you want me and my money to leave through the doors from which we just arrived, I suggest that you direct me to someone who might properly assist me."

Fortunately for her, a stout, gray-haired man of about fifty came to her rescue by offering me his hand. "Welcome to Shaver's. How may I assist you?"

I looked the man directly in his bespectacled, dark brown eyes and shook his hand with little conviction. "Charmed."

"The pleasure is mine, Miss …?"

"I'm Blanche Krump."

"Oh, of course! I understand you are renting the Essex House for the summer."

"Quite right. And you are?"

"My apologies. I'm Stanley Shaver. This is my store, and the Essex family and mine are quite close."

What a coincidence. My husband's younger self and about a hundred others got "quite close" to destroying your best friend's house last night. Weird.

As my snob act began to take on new dimensions, I smiled warmly at the now bright-eyed Mr. Shaver. "How nice! I haven't met them personally, but I've heard such wonderful things about the Essex family."

"Yes, they are quite accomplished pianists. Surely, you've heard that they're touring Europe this summer."

"I believe my brother might have mentioned that." I added a knowing smile for good measure.

"Speaking of Europe, Mr. Shaver, as I told your associate here..." I turned to the woman and frowned. "My things were detained, and I must purchase anew."

"Yes, well I'm sure Mrs. Norman can assist you with that."

"I'm sure she could." I looked at her doubtfully. "However, I would prefer someone who is—shall we say—more knowledgeable in the fashions of my peers."

"Miss Krump, I can assure you that any one of our associates can assist you in that manner." His lips formed a nervous smile.

"Ducky!" I led with one of Maude's favorite sayings, hoping to sound as if I belonged to the time. "Then I shall wait while you bring me your best young associate."

"Uh..." he stammered.

"Is there a problem, Mr. Shaver?"

"Well, Miss Krump, I'm sure you can understand that our associates are quite good at their trade and have developed their skills over time—"

"Mr. Shaver, are you trying to inform me that you only have older associates on your staff?" I continued before I let him find another excuse. "Nice to meet you, Mr. Shaver. If I'm ever in need of a pair of driving gloves for my grandmother, I will consider revisiting your establishment."

I turned to go, but he touched my elbow. "Miss Krump, please forgive me. I take pride in my staff and their professionalism and will make every effort to find an appropriate associate for you."

I looked past his shoulder at a young girl who was carrying a stack of boxes to a nearby service elevator. "How about her?" I pointed toward the girl.

Mr. Shaver and Mrs. Norman both turned to look at the small girl, who I noticed was struggling to press the button for the elevator without losing her load. She didn't succeed. On the third try, the boxes fell from her grasp and toppled to the ground, losing their lids and spilling their folded contents.

I laughed out loud, but Mr. Shaver and Mrs. Norman looked mortified.

We all walked over to the unfortunate girl while she scrambled to reload the boxes in the neatest formation she could assemble. She was so engrossed in her work that she failed to see us approach.

Mr. Shaver cleared his throat as we stood staring down at the poor thing. The girl looked up in surprise and struggled to stand amid the chaos she had created on the floor around her.

"Miss...?" Mr. Shaver boomed down at her.

She stood about six inches shorter than me, a mere five feet tall, and almost trembled like a Chihuahua as her large blue eyes traveled from the store owner to Mrs. Norman and finally rested on me. "Mr. Shaver, I apologize for my clumsiness. I'll clean it up. My name is—"

"Never mind, you're—"

"Perfect!" I interrupted.

The three stood staring at me as I smiled at the young girl.

I broke the silence by announcing, "She'll do just fine, Mr. Shaver."

The store owner remained open mouthed for several seconds before he finally recovered enough to speak. "Oh, Miss Krump, you must be mistaken. She is a mere stock girl."

"That is precisely why I require her assistance. Who better than a stock girl to know what's available in your lovely store?" I smiled at the pretty girl standing wide-eyed before me. "Perhaps Mrs. Norman could clear away this mess, so we can begin," I suggested.

Mr. Shaver remained motionless for several seconds before speaking again. "Mrs. Norman, if you wouldn't mind?"

She simply stared at the floor, red-faced, before reluctantly bending down to clear the jumble of boxes and clothing before her.

"Shall we?" I asked the stock girl.

"Yes, of course, miss." She smiled and walked around the pile and Mrs. Norman, joining me and Mr. Shaver on the other side.

He escorted us to a different, more ornate set of elevators and waited on the marble floor before them, until the art deco brass doors opened and an attendant emerged.

"Miss Krump, if there is anything else I can do for you, please feel free to ask." He offered me a fake smile and a handshake.

"Mr. Shaver, I do appreciate your assistance."

Louie had been waiting silently a short distance behind me during the whole ordeal and now walked toward me and the open elevator, beaming from ear to ear.

He does have teeth, after all.

"Oh, I do apologize." Mr. Shaver extended his hand, clearly surprised by the addition of Louie. "And this is your—"

"Bodyguard," I said, stepping into the elevator.

His eyebrows darted up in surprise, and he seemed to debate whether he should pull his hand back or just hope Louie would accept the shake. Louie just stared at the now embarrassed Mr. Shaver who slowly lowered his hand to his side, then Louie joined me and the sales girl in the elevator.

"One can't be too careful these days." I smiled, giving the store owner a knowing wink.

He just stood facing us, without expression, from his spot on the marble floor.

Before the elevator doors were closed, I caught Mr. Shaver removing a white handkerchief from his pocket and mopping his brow with it. I had to laugh.

"You saved my job, miss. Thank you," the young girl whispered from behind a smile.

"You're welcome. What's your name?"

"Elizabeth, miss."

"Nice to meet you, Elizabeth. I'm Blanche Krump."

"Oh, I've heard…" She clamped her hand over her mouth.

I laughed. "You'll have to tell me all about it later."

"What floor, ma'am?" the attendant asked.

"What do you wish to purchase today, miss?" the girl

asked.

"Everything. My wardrobe was lost."

I thought she would faint, but she held her composure enough to answer the elevator operator's question. "Ladies', please," she said.

The attendant pressed a button, and we stood inside the stuffy elevator as it ascended to the appropriate floor, powered by what sounded like a series of large chains, that, for some reason, had missed any recent form of renovation. It was a bit creepy, and I suddenly wished that I had insisted upon taking the abundant marble staircase. The elevator was so slow that I was sure a normal pace on the stairs would have allowed me to arrive before the noisy beast.

"Second floor, ladies' clothing," the attendant finally announced.

We exited the elevator, and I fought the urge to kiss the floor before Elizabeth led us to an open space in front of the contraption.

"What style do you prefer?" she asked.

"Excuse me?"

"Do you prefer modern dress or a more conservative style?"

"Modern, please, especially things other women won't be wearing."

"I know just the place to begin. Right this way, please."

As she led us toward an area that prominently displayed flapper dresses, dripping with beads and crystals from lifelike mannequins, I noted that her tiny frame was topped with some of the thickest blonde hair I had ever seen. Her bobbed hair almost had a life of its own.

She was quiet, so I tried to make small talk. "Elizabeth is

a pretty name."

"Thank you, miss, but I only go by that at work."

"Oh? What do they call you at home?"

"Well, my name is Maude. Maude Beckwith."

Shocked into silence, I could only stare in disbelief at Nana Rosie's aunt and my buried journal's namesake. In the next instant, a whirring noise inside my head descended upon me and enveloped the world in darkness before I even knew it came. Fortunately, Louie caught me before my limp body could hit the floor.

CHAPTER FIVE

The shade of the palm tree blocked the direct sun as I swayed in the tropical breeze from the comfort of a hammock. A troubadour was singing Italian love songs in the distance, and the overwhelming peace I felt brought a smile to my face. *This must be a dream!*

It was.

Cradled in Louie's arms on the floor of the department store, I smiled up at him, at first not realizing I was awake. He smiled back, gently rocking me and softly singing something in Italian.

Why can't the men in my life be ugly?

Before I could make an even bigger fool of myself, a female voice caught my attention: "Miss Krump, are you all right?"

I turned to Maude and noticed the concern on her face, as well as that of Mr. Shaver, who was now standing behind her.

Great, Em. So much for your snob routine.

"Yes, I'm fine."

But I wasn't. Maude had never mentioned working at a department store, not once, and the shock of having the younger version of my deceased great-great-aunt and best friend standing mere feet from me almost sent me reeling right back to my imaginary hammock.

Louie had to help me sit up, then held my hand as I struggled to stand on trembling legs.

I could have just swallowed my pride, ignored the onlookers, and continued my shopping trip with Maude's assistance, had I not noticed Mrs. Norman standing nearby with her hand over her mouth, stifling a laugh. That was something I couldn't overlook. Thus, when Mr. Shaver asked, "Miss Krump, is there anything I can do for you?" I had to take the opportunity to strike back.

"Yes, Mr. Shaver, there most certainly is. This whole business with trying to find an associate was very unsettling." I turned to look at Mrs. Norman. "Yes, very unsettling indeed."

Mr. Shaver followed my gaze to Mrs. Norman, who was now biting her lips to hide a smirk. He nodded. "I understand. I will personally ensure that the remainder of your time with us meets your complete satisfaction."

"Thank you."

Mr. Shaver waited until Maude was leading me toward the flapper dresses before he walked briskly to the waiting Mrs. Norman. I turned around to see his red-faced head bobbing at her pale one as she made eye contact with the brown and gold carpeted floor and constantly nodded.

Customer Service Lesson Number One: Never prejudge a potential customer—not ever! Also, never underestimate an Emily or Blanche or whatever my name is.

By the time we reached the dresses, I had recovered my pride and disposition and was ready to shop; however, that shopping trip was destined to be unlike anything I'd experienced before.

"Would you prefer the salon?" Maude's request sounded as uncertain as my response.

"The salon?" The last thing I wanted or thought I needed was another haircut.

"It may not compare with the ones in Paris, but you might feel more comfortable," she added.

Paris?! I wasn't trained in the 1920s, but I was familiar enough with earlier periods, as well as my own, to know that Paris trends were always in fashion. "Yes, of course. Thank you." I felt my hair and hoped for the best.

Maude smiled and led me past the mannequins I had seen earlier, to a room that held an abundance of natural light from four large, curtained windows lining one wall. Several tables and chairs sat before the windows, and more mannequins, garbed in various gowns and sporting outfits, lined the center of the room on round podiums.

The salon.

Louie scanned the room briefly and waited just outside.

"Can I offer you a seat, miss?" Maude gestured to the chairs.

"Yes, thank you, Elizabeth." I sat and looked around the room, in which I appeared to be the only customer. The wall opposite the windows was lined with rows of framed mirrors that made the rectangular room seem larger and even emptier. "Is it always so crowded?" I asked.

Apparently my normally outgoing, quick-witted aunt didn't start out that way, because her response came in the wake of a small, almost mouse-like, nervous laugh. "Our salons are very exclusive, miss," she said, wringing her hands.

Poor Maude!

I smiled warmly and scrubbed the snobbiness from my

tone. "Exactly as I prefer them."

"Oh, I'm so glad." Her shoulders, which were almost touching her ears, moved back to their normal position, and her hands relaxed and fell loosely to her sides.

With a smile I hadn't seen since the elevator, Maude looked me directly in the eyes and asked, "May I assume this is your first time at Shaver's?"

"It is."

"May I have your measurements?"

Uh, my…

When I didn't answer right away, she shook her head at my confusion. "I'm so sorry, miss. I should have realized…They must be with your lost wardrobe."

"Yes, they are." I tried for a convincing smile.

Maude didn't seem to notice my ignorance. "If you'll please follow me, then, I will take you to the fitting room so our tailor can measure you."

We walked to a set of large curtains in the corner of the room, behind which stood a tailor's platform surrounded by mirrors that formed a crescent shape around it. The room was enormous, with several couches and chairs arranged around an oval table that held a large vase of flowers and several handheld mirrors.

Almost immediately, a brunette of about thirty, wearing a pin cushion on her wrist and a measuring tape around her neck, entered the room.

"Good morning, Pearl. This is Miss Krump."

Pearl offered a slight curtsey and proceeded to take measurements of everything just shy of my earlobes. When she was finished, she curtseyed again and left the room.

"She doesn't speak English," Maude said.

I offered yet another smile. *I'm fluent, but it's not helping me much here. This store seems like another country. Where are the racks of clothes organized by size and the changing room with an eight item limit? This must be part of my on-the-job training.*

Once I was safely back in my seat in the still empty salon, I watched Maude transform into my personal shopper, assembling dozens of outfits, including shoes, purses, and accessories. She ran from one department to the next, bringing in new items and changing her mind on existing ones. When she was finally finished and slightly out of breath, Maude asked, "Shall I fetch a model?"

I felt certain that I had heard her wrong, but having been mistaken about the salon, I decided to just play along. "Yes, thank you."

She smiled and grabbed the stack of outfits off a nearby table, hefting them into her tiny arms. I watched her disappear behind a set of much smaller curtains next to the fitting room, her petite form bouncing along as she went.

God, I've missed you! The shock of seeing Maude was wearing off, and the reality was setting in. *My life is such a mess. I need a friend. I need you, Maude. I really hope you found the journal.* Although I'd buried the journal beneath the tree she'd dug around as a child, I had to know if she had uncovered it.

However, before I could formulate a useful strategy of discovery in my head, a thin girl about my size emerged from behind the curtains and stood before me, wearing the first outfit Maude had chosen. The sleeveless dress was beige with a gold floral pattern and a drop waist. It reminded me of a set of curtains the older Maude had in her living room.

"Is this—" I began.

"Yes, miss. It is real silk, not the artificial kind."

The proud look on her face kept me from commenting on the curtains. Instead, I replied, "It's beautiful."

"I'm glad you think so." She bent down next to the model and adjusted the hemline that fell just below the knees. "Is this too short, miss?"

I tried not to laugh, picturing the dresses from my time that revealed more than just a little skin. "No, Elizabeth, the length is perfect."

Maude nodded politely to the model and sent her back behind the curtains.

She amazed me. With the exception of the curtain-like dress, Maude selected dresses that, judging by the model, looked as if they would complement both my figure and complexion. Growing up, she always had a highly developed fashion sense that was definitely not genetic. I didn't know anyone else in my family who could coordinate anything; they had enough trouble wearing matching socks beneath their sandals.

"I would like to gather a few more selections for you, miss."

"Of course, Elizabeth."

Only moments before the model reemerged, a breathless Maude arrived, holding several more dresses.

Once she caught her breath, she stood next to the model on the platform, adjusting the dress she was wearing and smoothing out the wrinkles. I noticed that in her effort to collect outfits for me, Maude's bobbed hair stood almost perpendicular to her head in parts. It was a look I would have certainly remembered from family photo albums had any pictures of young Maude existed, but they didn't. *Weird. No wonder I didn't recognize you when we first met.* I stared at her, trying unsuccessfully to guess her age.

"Elizabeth, you're quite good at what you do," I finally said. "How old are you?"

"Thank you. I'm fifteen, miss."

I did some quick mental math. *Wow. You were eighty years older the last time I saw you.* Then I shared Shane's recent revelation. "I'm fifteen too!"

Her jaw dropped. "You are?"

"I'll be sixteen soon." I pretended to admire the model's next outfit. "And as a surprise for my brother, I cut my hair!"

"Thank you, Millie," she said.

The model smiled at Maude and quickly disappeared behind the curtain.

"What did he do?" Maude whispered.

"Oh, the usual, but he took me to someone in Paris to have it fixed."

She studied my hair. "It looks beautiful!" Then she looked at her own image in a nearby floor mirror. "I sure wish I could get mine to look that way."

I watched her unsuccessful attempt to direct her hair downward.

Her eyebrows almost touched while she spoke seriously to her own reflection. "My father sure wasn't happy with me when I cut mine. My younger brother laughs at me every morning. He says I look like a blowfish."

"Brothers!" I shook my head, then stopped abruptly, realizing that *her* brother was *my* great-grandfather. The whole thing was almost too weird to comprehend.

She nodded, then looked at the floor, fortunately missing my reaction. I studied the brown and gold carpet beneath Maude's feet, looking for the object that drew her eyes downward. Her shyness was the only thing I saw, until the top of her crazy hairdo captured my attention.

"Say, do you have any hats in that collection of yours?" I asked.

She looked up and smiled, then walked to the nearby table filled with the scarves, broaches, and hats she had gathered and produced a tan cloche with a fabric flower on the side. "We offer this hat in other colors too, miss."

"This shade is lovely. Could you please try it on?"

Maude looked around. "The model should be out shortly, miss."

"I'm afraid patience has never been a virtue of mine," I said. Then, I stood and placed the hat on Maude's head and turned her toward the mirror.

She beamed, and in that moment, I saw both my mom and Nana Rosie in that smile. *Now, I recognize you!* Seeing the resemblance made me miss the women in my family so much that, without thinking, I pulled her into an enormous embrace. She just stood there at first, until I finally felt her hug me back. *There it is!* Maude was the family hugger, and it had been almost ten years since I'd received one of hers.

"You're an angel!" I said. "Now, I would appreciate doing something for you."

The smile that had consumed her face quickly faded. "Thank you, Miss Krump, but you've been so generous already. I couldn't possibly—"

"But, Maude, I thought we were friends." I used her nickname and threw out my bottom lip for effect.

The smile surfaced again and remained on her face as she met my gaze. "Well, I supposed that's different," she said confidently.

"And how!" I responded, using another of the older Maude's famous phrases. "Now, wait right here."

"But—"

I walked to a mannequin in the salon that was wearing a beaded flapper dress in Maude's favorite shade of pale pink. It was small and looked as if it would fit her, so I stripped the mannequin and handed Maude the dress. "Try it on."

Her hands flew to her mouth.

"Change quickly before someone else comes in!"

Without further hesitation, she took the dress into the fitting room. Moments later, she emerged, wearing the gown and an enormous smile on her face. It looked amazing on her; from the beaded pattern on the bodice to the strands of beads dripping in layers that surrounded it, the dress flattered every inch of her tiny form.

"You look beautiful, Maude!"

She stood in front of the floor mirror. "And it's even pink!"

I'm glad your favorite color didn't change over the years.

She twirled in the mirror, watching the beads crash into each other with every move.

"Do you enjoy dancing, Maude?"

"Oh, I'm not very good." She stopped twirling and looked at her feet again.

I couldn't believe what I was hearing. The Maude I knew didn't live to be an old lady by sitting in a chair. She loved to dance and seldom walked past Tom or Papa Bob without grabbing one of them and engaging him in a foxtrot or tango, saying, "I have ants in my pants...and jitterbugs too!" And she did.

"I'm sorry, Maude, but you didn't answer my question.

Do you *enjoy* dancing?"

She grinned at my reflection. "Yes."

"Better! Do you know the Charleston?"

Her eyes lit up. "No, but I would love to learn!"

"Me too. I'll make the arrangements for lessons, and once we're good enough, we'll dazzle them all in our new dresses."

Her face fell. "Oh. Well, Miss Krump, I—"

"Maude?"

"I'm afraid Papa would never allow that."

"If you think it might help, I can tell him that it will be at our house with my brother chaperoning."

"Oh, no, Miss Krump! Papa would never approve. No offense, but if the rumors about you and your brother are all true, then he won't even let me take the dance lessons with you."

I laughed. "And what do the rumors have to say?"

She hesitated.

"Really, Maude. Tell me. I won't be upset."

"Well, it is said that you have all-night parties, during which men and women lose their morals and their clothes in your swimming pool...and that is only one of the rumors."

Wonderful. I had no idea how I was going to discuss the journal with Maude, and at the rate I was going, I wasn't sure if I would ever get a chance. Still, I wasn't one to go down without a fight. "I understand why your father would be hesitant. It sure would be a shame, though, not to wear that dress somewhere—a real shame." I shook my head.

Suddenly, a familiar smile overtook her face, the same wicked look I remembered seeing whenever her scheming mind wanted to cause trouble. "I think you need a nickname," she said.

"Excuse me?"

"See, Papa might recognize you as Blanche Krump, but not as...let's say, 'Daisy.'"

I knew you were in there somewhere, Maude!

I couldn't stop smiling at how her brain operated. "And what's my last name?"

"Murk."

"Murk?"

"Right. It's Krump backward, without the -p."

Emily Stanton, Mrs. Holtz, Lady Milton, Blanche Krump...Why not Daisy too? What the heck? "Daisy Murk it is then!"

We both burst into laughter.

"Do you work this Saturday?" I finally asked.

"No."

"Then I'll try to find dance lessons by then. Do you have a telephone?"

"No, Papa refuses to buy one. He says that it's the devil's mouthpiece."

Her answer took me by surprise. I couldn't imagine what he would think of the television, cell phones, and the internet. I, on the other hand, was having trouble thinking outside the technology box. "How will I let you know about the lessons?" I finally asked.

"Let's meet at nine in the morning, at the front entrance here. Papa insists upon driving me everywhere in his old car, so if you see one held together with rust and baling wire, you'll know we've arrived."

"Nifty, but what will you tell him?" I asked, still trying to add Maude terms into my speech.

She rubbed her hands together as she spoke. "I'll say that

I have to work for a few hours. He will be in his office on Saturday, too, but all day, so I'll suggest that I take the streetcar home. You'll have to keep the dress for me," she added.

"Your father won't approve of that either?" I asked with a smile.

She shook her head. "He'd never let me out of his sight wearing it."

"I'll keep it safe for you, Maude."

After Maude changed, and I made my remaining dress and accessory selections, she walked with me into the fitting room, where the pre-modeled choices awaited me.

I looked at the group of dresses, hanging from a rod, as well as the additional items Maude was carrying, and said, "That's a lot."

"Goodness, no! Only last week, a customer bought one of each dress at our fashion show. The stockroom could hardly keep up. We have her measurements on file, of course, but it took Pearl until yesterday to tailor everything. She comes in tomorrow for the final fitting and will have them delivered to her house once they're finished."

So that's how it works.

"I suppose replacing an entire wardrobe in a day doesn't happen too often."

Maude laughed. "Not with salon clothes."

One by one, I tried on the dresses, enlisting Pearl's assistance who nipped and tucked her way through each outfit. It took hours, and in that time, a team of seamstresses tailored the ready-made dresses for me.

With the assistance of Louie, the chauffeur, the doorman, and several others, my purchases were loaded into every free space the limousine offered. Even with three of us sitting in the front seat, we couldn't fit all of the boxed or brown paper-wrapped purchases, so the remaining items had to be delivered to the house later in the day.

We arrived home just as Shane was driving out of the gate in a shiny yellow roadster. He looked like a movie star. He pulled up next to us and eyed the boxes and packages vying for space in the back of the limousine and just shook his head. "Looks as if you had a successful trip."

"So did you." I was almost drooling at how good he looked in the car. His blue eyes drew me to his perfect smile, surrounded by full lips my own suddenly yearned to visit. *He's not Dell. He's the enemy.* My thoughts forced me to look away, focusing on the roadster instead. "What kind of car is this?"

"A 1926 Mercedes 24/100/140 PS. If you're a good little girl, I'll let you have a ride later." That crooked grin surfaced and thawed yet another piece of my frozen heart.

I didn't trust myself to respond with words, so I simply smiled.

He just laughed and drove away.

I spent the remainder of the afternoon stowing my new purchases in my closets and drawers, periodically stopping to don an outfit and admire my reflection in the mirror. I hung Maude's dress on the left side of one of the closets for easy retrieval.

By evening, Shane still hadn't returned, and I felt like Lady Milton all over again, lonely and bored. *I wish I could talk to Maude. At least I will see her on Saturday.*

Without Shane's advice or guidance regarding the dance lessons, I began to interview the staff, hoping they could assist me. Fortunately, the chauffeur, who finally introduced himself as Perry, claimed to have an "acquaintance" who taught dance. I didn't ask too many questions. Within an hour, he made arrangements for Maude and me to meet at Madam Perdot's Dance Studio at ten o'clock, Saturday morning.

Shane finally arrived home around eleven that night, followed by a convoy of other convertibles, the loud occupants of which descended upon the house in search of a few games of mahjong. Instead, they lay waste our remaining store of alcohol from the previous evening, then disappeared into the night as soon as the last drop was consumed. Shane spent his time in the company of an overly attentive, unnaturally blonde admirer, who made a show of smoking from a long cigarette holder while also running her free hand along whatever part of Shane's body he allowed, which from my bedroom balcony view, seemed to be without limits. Once again, I was crushed, and I didn't bother answering my door when he knocked hours later.

CHAPTER SIX

I was surprised to see Shane at breakfast the next morning, fully dressed and seated near the pool, which lacked any visible signs of the previous night's party. The morning was clear and warm, and a gentle breeze off the water beckoned for me to ignore Shane and find a different spot overlooking the ocean. For want of another table, however, I decided to join him and try to be civil, if only for Dell's sake. "Morning, Oscar."

He smiled at me as if he had just donned a halo and performed six miracles before sitting down to eat. I hated him. "I hope my friends and I didn't keep you up too late last night," he said.

I wanted to slap him. Instead, I offered him a fake smile as I smoothed my napkin across my lap. "No, I slept as sound as a baby." *Yeah, one with colic.*

He just stared at me from across the table. "Nothing happened."

"Interesting how you seem to feel it necessary to answer a question I didn't ask...Guilty conscience, have we, brother?"

"No, sweetheart. I just didn't want you to have to ask."

"You can't call me that!"

"Call you what?"

"'Sweetheart'—you can't call me that!"

"Em...Blanche..." He reached across the table to grab my hand. I tried to pull away, but his grip held me there. "What's wrong?"

Are you that clueless? I fought the urge to roll my eyes at him. "I'm lonely, I miss my husband, and it breaks my heart that you throw your girlfriends in my face. Then you have the nerve to call me 'Sweetheart.'" I shook my head. "Only Dell has that right!"

Shane opened his mouth but nothing came out.

Coward!

He released his grip as a kitchen maid walked toward us, carrying a breakfast tray. I spent the next few minutes chasing the eggs around my plate with a fork until they were cold.

Once the dishes were cleared, Shane broke the silence. "I'm lonely too."

I looked up and caught intense blue eyes staring back at me; they were Dell's.

"In my time," he said, "most women only behaved as they do now for a fee. That's no longer the case. The temptations afforded to a time traveler are immeasurable." He pounded the table, causing the legs to clang loudly against the concrete deck below. "I despise Dell for putting me in this position!"

"Just take me to him, and you can return to your time, Oscar. I guarantee I won't cause any more problems for you."

"I can't, Em...Blanche."

"Can't or won't?"

He looked at me for a few seconds before continuing, "I

made a promise."

"You made a promise to yourself. Does that really count? Who has to know? I certainly won't say anything." I pretended to zip my lips closed, lock them, and throw the invisible key over my shoulder.

"*I'll* know, Em."

"Blanche," I corrected him.

The lack of enthusiasm in his eyes was palpable.

"You're the one who named me."

"Okay, Blanche." He ran his fingers across the tablecloth in front of him, playing with the bits of his breakfast that had escaped his plate. After a few seconds of that, he finally looked up. "I wish you were ugly."

I met his eyes. "I wish you were ten years older."

We then focused on the crumbs scattered mainly across his side of the table. I accidently caught the corner of one with my fingernail and flicked it at him; it hit him in the nose.

I burst into laughter. "I'm so sorry."

"Not half as sorry as you're going to be!" He returned fire using his middle finger and thumb.

After taking one in the eye, I decided to change my tactics. I rubbed my eye while reaching beneath the table to grab the edge of the tablecloth. Shane sat back with his arms behind his head, looking satisfied. Then I struck. With one side of the tablecloth in my fist, I stood and pulled the fabric into the air, depositing the remaining crumbs into Shane's lap. He sprang from his chair like a cheetah. I dropped the cloth and tried to run, but he grabbed me by the waist and spun me around several times as I struggled to free myself. Then, without warning, he tucked me under his arm like a football and jumped into the pool.

FOR THE LOVE OF MAUDE

Alone in the knowledge that I wasn't much of a swimmer, I flailed about for several seconds before Shane realized I was in trouble and had to dive nearly to the bottom to recover me. He brought me to the surface and guided me to the edge of the pool so I could cough up the water I had swallowed. Then he pushed me up and onto the deck.

I rolled onto my back and closed my eyes. A few seconds later, I felt him pushing my hair to the side, one wet clump at a time, until my face was free.

"I assumed you could swim since you tried to row yourself to freedom," he said. "I guess there are a few things we don't know about each other." I could hear the laughter in his voice.

I opened my eyes to see him lying next to me. "You've no idea…" I said, smiling up at him.

Unfortunately, the commotion drew a crowd from the house, and just as his lips were nearly touching mine, someone cleared his throat. It sounded like Louie. Shane shifted his attention to my forehead where he deposited a kiss.

I closed my eyes again to block out the shame and humiliation of being the chief form of entertainment for a group of people who thought we were siblings.

"She's fine!" Shane shouted.

He helped me to my feet, where I proceeded to cough uncontrollably.

Louie flew to my side and nearly pushed Shane out of the way and back into the pool in the process. Then, he practically carried me to my room, where a maid helped me out of my wet things and into a hot bath. By the time I was out of the tub, Shane was in dry clothes and pacing the hallway outside my room. When I opened the door, he stopped moving and just stared at me. His blue eyes seemed to pierce through me like a dagger. I couldn't look away—his wet hair was the same shade as Dell's.

Why is Shane the enemy again? Seeing him there made me forget.

Suddenly, Louie came from behind, resembling a bull charging a matador. He stood between Shane and me and wouldn't move. Shane spoke to him in Italian, but Louie stood his ground. Shane repeated himself, raising his voice to no avail. My stubborn bodyguard was going to protect me from my incestuous brother regardless of the consequences, and Shane was no match for my giant champion. From that point forward, Louie seldom left my side.

By lunchtime, the entire staff had heard about the pool incident, and by dinnertime, Shane was public enemy number one. His only friend was the chauffeur, Perry.

"I can't believe these people hate me so much," Shane whispered over dinner, then stared through the open dining room door into the living room beyond.

"You've only yourself to blame." I lifted my glass in a mock toast, then brought it to my lips and drank.

He shook his head. "With a few exceptions, such as Perry and your friend Louie, most of the staff is from this time frame. I could just replace them with people from H&S."

"Nice idea, Oscar, but you have one giant problem."

"Which is?"

"Louie. He might be an H&S employee, but he's sure not a fan of yours. In fact, if he wasn't carbo-loading in the kitchen right now, he'd be in here, guarding me from you." I thought for a minute. "And I don't understand why. He traveled with us from the past, where I was Lady Milton, so why does he think I'm your sister?"

"Oh, he doesn't know you as Lady Milton, just as Emily and Blanche; and me as Shane and Oscar. As is the case with all H&S staff, Louie was given only enough information to do his job. I was angry with you when I hired him, so I told him that you were my spoiled sister who needed to be watched at all times."

"Didn't you later tell him otherwise?"

"You bet I did, just this morning after your bath, only he wouldn't listen. Stupid fool!"

"No he's not; he's sweet!"

"Yeah, he's sweet on you!" Shane stared at his silverware and fumed. He bore the same expression Dell had the day I met Shane.

"Are we jealous, big brother?"

The angry eyes that met mine left me instantly mute and expressionless.

He abruptly departed without another word, leaving the front door open to the night. I sat trembling at the table as I heard his squealing tires taking him and his new car away from the house.

Many of the staff came running to stare into the darkness at the source of the noise.

Wow, the gossip trail from this house must be a juicy one. I took a deep breath, determined not to cry. *I'm not going to give them anything else to talk about.*

Chef Jacques emerged from the kitchen and stared in disgust at Shane's untouched plate of food before returning with it to the kitchen. I heard him screaming in French, muffled slightly behind the closed kitchen door.

I just shook my head and tried to eat my dinner. *I could*

sure use a friend right now.

Louie must have read my mind and somehow translated it into Italian because he quietly eased himself into the chair next to me. I tried to ignore him, but he gently reached across, touched my chin, and turned my face toward his. His sad eyes met mine and almost drew the torrent of tears I was trying to suppress.

I'm not going to cry!

Then he said something to me in Italian that sounded like a song and pulled me into burly arms that enveloped me in muscular safety. Had he been flexing, I would have snapped like a twig, but he just held me there. When he finally released me, he cradled my face in his enormous hands and shook his head, spewing angry words in Italian and breaking eye contact only long enough to turn his head toward the seat Shane had just occupied.

He kissed me on the forehead and walked away. It was the sweetest, kindest thing I had experienced in a long time, and I felt horrible for being part of a lie in which I was Shane's sister. *I need to learn Italian!*

I watched him walk away, trying not to stare at his well-formed glutes as he went. *You're a married woman, Em…or whatever your name is; to whom, I don't know, but you're married just the same.*

I went to bed feeling confused and lonely. Shane didn't return home that night, and although I only slightly sympathized, I still worried. The birds were chirping when I finally found a few hours of peace. I awoke with dark circles and heavy bags under my eyes.

"Bags? Heck, these babies resemble steamer trunks!" I stood in front of the bathroom mirror, pulling my cheeks down in an effort to smooth out my face.

I opened my train case and removed the cache of cosmetics, hoping they would miraculously apply themselves to my face, no questions asked. When that didn't happen, I started to mop the makeup onto my skin in an attempt to conceal the obvious. It looked horrible, so I removed the mess and proceeded to rummage through my case again to find something, anything, which would hide my face. I almost experienced a heavenly ray of light and an angelic choir when I moved a large tub of cold cream out of the way and found a sight I hadn't seen for years—an eyeglasses case.

"It can't be!" I picked up the case and held it in front of me as if it were some kind of offering, then I opened the lid and reached in to retrieve the object of my affection.

They were round, and the lenses were kind of blurry—nothing like my favorite pair of aviators at home, but I didn't care. I donned the sunglasses and wore them proudly to breakfast. Fortunately, no one said anything.

After breakfast, I noticed that my luck in the mirror had changed, and I could store the sunglasses for future reference. "Thank you!" I kissed the glasses case, checked my hair, and ran downstairs to meet my chariot.

Louie held the door open for me so I could enter the limousine. We arrived at the entrance of Shaver's just as Maude was stepping out of a black Model T at the epicenter of a dark plume of smoke.

"Circle the block if you please, Perry," I said from the back seat.

Perry slowly drove around the building and returned within a few minutes. By that time, Maude was waiting by the entrance, wearing a smile that nearly consumed her petite face. She almost jumped in place when she saw us approach.

"She's so cute," I said, laughing out loud.

My laughter soon turned to horror, however, when I saw what she was wearing. The shapeless black frock she bore lacked any identifiable style. As we pulled up to the curb, I was able to catch a better look. It was so hideous, I winced. *No time frame, no matter how desperate, would lay claim to that horrible thing.*

When the car stopped, Louie stepped out and opened the door for Maude. Carrying a parcel wrapped in brown paper and tied with string, she jumped inside and slid along the seat next to me.

"Maude, what in the world are you wearing?"

She looked down at her dress and giggled. "This is what I wear when I don't want Papa to know I'm being naughty."

I shook my head and smiled. "Don't you think he might become wise to you?"

She winked at me. "Don't worry about me, Daisy. I have more than just a few tricks up my sleeve."

There's my Maude! I wanted to hug her. "What's in the parcel?"

She gave a bigger wink. "That's my uniform." Then, with the package on her lap, she proceeded to untie the string and unwrap the paper, revealing a delicate yellow flapper dress and matching shoes.

"Wow. They're beautiful!"

She smiled down at the outfit. "Thank you. I saved up for months."

We continued to admire the dress as Perry maneuvered the Ghost through the downtown Los Angeles streets that were home to a chaotic mixture of automobiles, trucks, streetcars, and pedestrians, all vying for street space. During a lull in the conversation, I noticed the traffic had thinned and was no longer blocking my view outside the window. Single-story storefronts, displaying everything from shovels to bread behind large picture windows, competed for my attention. It reminded me of a scene from an old black-and-white movie that had been colorized.

As the overcast morning skies began to clear, I was quickly reminded that air conditioning was not an added feature in the Ghost or any vehicle and wouldn't be for decades. Cranking the window down, I leaned my head out like a dog, enjoying the passing scenery and the salty air that met me.

"Where are we going, Perry?" I asked, poking my head back inside.

"Ocean Park."

Well, that isn't much help. With the exception of the time I buried the Maude journal, I'd only been to California once before, when I was three, and knew as much about the state as I did the 1920s.

Several minutes later, we were driving down Third Street, in a residential area lined with cottages, Craftsman-style houses, and Spanish Revivals, each different from their neighbors. Perry pulled up in front of a white, single-story Spanish Colonial with a grassy lawn and picket fence to greet us, along with a small sign next to the doorbell that read, "Ring Twice to Dance."

We arrived at the dance studio early, giving Maude time to change inside before the lesson began. With her blonde hair lying much flatter than on our last visit and wearing a matching yellow outfit, she was a ray of sunshine. I caught Louie admiring her as well. She seemed as drawn to him as he was to her, and the two just stared from across the room. I excused myself and offered to take her black disguise to the car. She absently handed me the clothes, and I made my escape, wondering if I was doing the right thing by leaving them alone. *What if she marries Louie and it changes history?*

To my knowledge, Maude had never married; if she had, she kept her maiden name, and no one in my family ever spoke of her husband. She loved men and I could never figure out why she remained single all her life. She would always say, "Toots, the love of your life only comes around once, and when he does, you need to hold on to your hat for dear life!" The Maude I knew enjoyed wearing hats.

I was walking back to the studio when it all clicked into place.

When I was young, Maude had stacks of photo albums filled with photographs and postcards from her many adventures. The stories that went along with them were probably more outrageous than my tiny ears should have heard. However, rain or shine, we shared them just the same on the couch in her little house that was tucked behind my grandparents' in St. Helens, Oregon. The photos were of an adult Maude atop camels or horses, in cars, holding strange creatures, etc. None of them contained other people.

One day, I asked, "Maude, who took all of these pictures?"

She paused and stared at the album we were looking at, then set it beside her on the couch. "I'll be right back, Toots." When she returned, she was holding a mother-of-pearl picture frame. She joined me on the couch and gently ran a shaky hand across the surface of the frame, as if she were stroking the hair of the man whose picture it held. "It was my Lou."

FOR THE LOVE OF MAUDE

That was the only time I ever saw her cry.
  Now it all made sense: *Her "Lou" was Louie!*

CHAPTER SEVEN

By our second dance lesson, Maude and I were ready to challenge the untrained masses to a dance-off. Unlike the ballet lessons I took as a child, these were actually fun. Our feet flew and our dresses dangled in all the right places, while Louie smiled at our progress. Maude absolutely glowed in his presence, and she was just the distraction I needed to keep Louie from killing Shane. It didn't hurt that Shane hadn't come home yet either. A week had passed since he left, and I was beside myself with worry.

At the end of dance class, while Maude stood outside the studio, gesturing and giggling to the delight of my bodyguard, I approached the only person I could to ask about Shane, our trusty chauffeur. "Perry?" I asked in a whisper.

He walked to my side. "Yes, miss?"

"Have you given Mr. Krump a ride anywhere lately?" I stared, unblinking, into his eyes, so he would understand the true meaning of my question.

He hesitated before answering; it came in the form of a nod.

"So he asked you not to say?"

He nodded again.

"Did you take him to his time?"

Perry looked away.

I was losing patience. "Yes or no?"

He shook his head.

Great. Nothing like a game of twenty questions with a mute! I drew in and expelled a deep, cleansing breath before continuing, "Okay, then did he join Dell in the future?"

The look on Perry's face was almost painful to watch; I would have felt sorry for him if I hadn't wanted to shake him so much.

"Perry!"

He nodded.

"Do you know when he will return?"

He shook his head and walked away.

I'm in hell. I need a friend. I have to tell Maude about the journal. I wasted no time in almost yelling my request in her direction. "Maude, may I invite you to my house for lunch?"

She clapped her hands eagerly and ran to my side. "Jeepers creepers, would I ever!"

I loved Maude's 1920s slang, and I, once again, had to search my memory for a few expressions I could use as well.

"Is your father picking you up at the store?" I asked.

"No, he's sick, so I rode the streetcar."

"Swell," I said, trying not to laugh at my word choice. "Let's go!"

Louie escorted us to the car. I entered first so that Maude could sit next to him. During the whole ride home, their whispers and near-handholding almost made me nauseous. I tried to be happy for them, but I just wanted to open the door and kick them both out.

Once we finally reached the house, its grandeur proved a

bit much for Maude, who walked openmouthed, while commenting and pointing.

"Maude." I tried to gently summon her back to reality.

She stopped mid-gape to turn glassy eyed in my direction.

"I need to talk to you about something."

She smiled as if she had just had her wisdom teeth pulled and hadn't fully come out of the anesthesia. I took her by the hand and led her to the table and chairs that now sat permanently on the grassy area overlooking the ocean. It was a poor choice of locations, however, because she couldn't take her eyes off the view.

"Maude?"

She didn't even offer a nod.

"Elizabeth Beckwith?"

Batting her eyelashes, she gave me a confused look as though I had just addressed her for the first time.

"I need to talk to you about something."

"Okay…"

I took a deep breath before asking, "Did you enjoy finding buried treasure as a child?"

Her furrowed eyebrows was her only response.

"Please, just humor me, Maude."

"Yes. I loved searching for buried treasure…as most children might."

I nodded. "Did you ever find any?"

She sat back in her seat and folded her arms across her chest. "Why do you ask?"

I drew a deep breath and held it, slowly releasing a little at a time, like a leaky bicycle tire. I stared at the ocean before continuing, "Does the name 'Emily Stanton' sound familiar to you?"

Poor Maude sucked in so much air through her mouth that I thought she would blow away in the wind. The funny little noise that accompanied it drew the attention of a nearby gardener. I waved at him, and he nodded, then quickly returned to his work.

The diversion was just enough for Maude to start breathing normally again. "You're Emily?"

I nodded.

She shook her head in disbelief. "My goodness. I-I certainly didn't expect to meet you before you were born!"

I tried to laugh but made a strange gurgling noise instead. When I was finally able to speak somewhat coherently, my words came out in pieces: "I didn't expect...to meet you again...after you passed away." Tears flowed down my cheeks, setting off a chain reaction and causing Maude to cry along with me.

After a few blubbering minutes, Maude blew her nose on a dainty, embroidered handkerchief she withdrew from a small, beaded purse she was carrying. Then, she scooted her chair closer to mine and held my hand. "Your journal changed my life, Emily."

"Well, you and your little words of wisdom changed mine." I sniffed and continued, "How old were you when you found it?"

"I was ten, and we had just moved into our house. I was digging around the oak tree in the front yard and there it was."

"I'm glad you found it."

"So am I. It really did change my life."

"How?" I asked, hoping it hadn't also changed the future.

"I found it at a time when I needed a friend," she said. Tears formed in her eyes. "Mama died of the influenza, and Papa hasn't been the same since. He loves my brother and me, but he just doesn't know how to show it anymore. He always told her that she was the light of his world. When she died, all the light went out of his life."

I remembered reading about the Spanish Influenza of 1918 in my grandfather's vast library of medical books. Although Papa Bob retired from the medical profession when I was young, he continued to prove his knowledge by embellishing upon the diseases his books had to offer—but he always left that one alone. "It hit too close to home," he would say. Now I understood why.

Deep in thought, Maude played with the handkerchief in her hand, twisting it between her fingers. Finally, she said, "He boarded up his heart and stopped smiling entirely. I think Papa wanted to move from our old house to run away from her memory, but it didn't work. He calls for her in his sleep at our new house too. It doesn't help that I resemble her so strongly either."

Maude turned to the ocean, then to me. "Thank you for the note and the journal. At first, I wasn't sure what to make of it. I don't know many girls who go to college, and your life seemed so swell until your Papa Bob died and your Nana Rosie passed only days later of a broken heart. I gave my papa such a hug after I read that! He felt my forehead a few times before letting me go back to my room. Then, I nearly fell off my bed when I read about Evergreen and your job." Her face grew serious. "They made you take the job before telling you about the time travel bit."

I nodded.

"And they wanted all their scholarship money back if you refused." She just shook her head. "Now isn't that just a load of baloney!"

"I thought so too," I said. "Although I didn't know what I was getting into, I couldn't let Mom sell *her* house to pay for *my* choice."

"No, you did the right thing, Emily."

"It was supposed to be a four-year commitment…until Dell came along and showed me how hard Evergreen works to manipulate the past and how Holtz & Sons stops them," I said.

"And Evergreen still doesn't know about them?" she asked.

"I don't think so."

"So many secrets, Emily…and no one to trust. You didn't just know about Evergreen's operation, you were a part of it. Those names, dates, and details—you couldn't keep all that balled up inside. No." She shook her head. "You had to write it down.

"I was always able to confide in you, Maude. Your journal became a good friend, just like you."

"Well, I hope I can live up to that," she said. "I realize you took a chance in burying the journal and trusting me with it. Your words were too important to be destroyed. They needed to live. I promise you that I will never break the confidence you have in me."

"I know, Maude. That's why I buried it for you."

A serious look washed over her face. "How long are you here?"

"Until the end of summer."

She nearly jumped into my lap. "Why not longer?"

"We shouldn't be here at all; in fact, we're simply waiting for my hair to grow. It should be longer by the end of August."

She smiled. "So you really did cut it to make your 'brother' mad?"

"Yes, and he was."

"By the way, why is Dell your brother instead of your husband?" she asked.

I exhaled loudly. "Oscar is Shane, not Dell."

"Where's Dell?"

"Still recovering from his injuries."

"From your honeymoon?"

I nodded.

"And they still won't allow you to join him?"

I shook my head. "He's in the future."

"How far?"

"He's in the year 2125."

Maude's hands flew to cover her gaping mouth.

I spent the next few hours explaining everything that had occurred since my last entry in the Maude journal, including Shane's disappearance. During that time, we devoured croissant sandwiches and fruit, trying not to spit on each other as we discussed my ever-confusing love life.

"Jeepers, Em, you sure have it bad!" Maude sat back in her chair and shook her head.

"And how! There are a couple more things too," I whispered.

Maude leaned forward in her chair again.

I drew closer as well. "I'm not Emily here, so let's stick with Blanche or Daisy."

"I prefer Daisy, if that's all right with you," she said.

I laughed. "Sure."

She leaned in even more. "What's the other thing?"

I stared into her eyes. "No one knows about you or the journal, and I need to keep it that way."

"I can do that, but what should we say if someone begins to question who I am?"

I thought for a minute. "You're my friend from dance class."

She smiled. "And you're mine."

Throughout the entire lunch and accompanying conversation, Louie remained near the pool. He frequently paced the length of the shaded area or simply stood behind a bush or one of the palm trees. I wasn't sure if he was trying to appear incognito or just wanted to stay out of the sun while he watched us; regardless, his sheer physical size made the scene ridiculous whenever he stood behind the much smaller planters or shrubs. Then he would appear to examine the plant whose shade he was sharing, as if he were studying for a botany exam. Periodically, he would gaze in our direction, then return to his pacing.

After several hours of that, I could no longer contain myself: "He's so obvious."

"Who?"

Maude started to turn around, but I grabbed her hand that was resting on the table. "Don't look!"

She just stared at me.

"It's Louie. He won't sit down. He's been pacing by the pool ever since you came over here."

She smiled shyly. "Do you think he likes me?"

I fought the urge to ask her if she was the original blonde from all of the jokes. It was difficult, but she had the face of an angel. Besides, I needed to remember that she was only fifteen. "Yes."

"Really?"

I nodded.

Then her smile faded. "Could my being with him affect the future?"

I panicked slightly inside. The simple act of telling her *anything* might actually do just that. I hadn't told her much about Louie, and I couldn't risk influencing her actions; especially regarding her future. The journal's impact was already a big unknown. "They don't inform me of much," I finally answered.

Her face fell and her eyes dove to her lap.

How do I tell her that Louie's the love of her life without telling her that he's the love of her life? I was drawing a blank until I remembered one of the older Maude's wise sayings. "Maude?"

She looked up.

"One thing you often told me, and now I'm going to tell you, 'Always follow your heart.'"

The light returned to her eyes. "Gee, I'm smarter than I thought!"

I laughed. "I think he's walked about a hundred miles since we arrived. You might want to save him from a hundred more."

When she turned around to look at Louie, he stopped pacing.

She turned back to me. "I do love him."

"I know you do. Can I ask you something?"

"Yes."

"How do you communicate?"

"Oh, that's easy. I've studied Latin in school for years now." She smiled. "Close enough."

Then, she hugged me and joined Louie by the pool.

Several hours of hand-holding and footsie-playing later, I had to inform the happy couple of the sun's slow disappearance. "Excuse me."

They looked up from their chaise by the pool, gawking at me as if I had emerged from a shiny starship that had just crash landed on their secluded desert island.

"It's late," I offered.

Both pairs of eyes simply stared at me.

"I'll ask Perry to bring the car around." I sulked away in the direction of the garages. *Great. I've created a monster. No, make that two.*

Several minutes later, they unglued themselves from the chair and joined me on the front stairs.

Before we entered the limousine, I pulled Maude aside. "Can you help me with something?" I asked.

She smiled and spoke almost breathlessly, "Anything."

"I can't speak Italian, but I really want Louie to know that Shane, or Oscar, is not my brother. I'd appreciate your help, but how can you, when no one—not even Louie—can know what you and I discuss? We can't tell anyone about Shane's true identity or the journal or anything."

She thought for a moment. "He told me that he hates your brother and wants to kill him when he returns."

Great.

"Say, maybe that's not such a bad thing," she added.

"Excuse me?"

"Your heart's confused about Shane, right?"

I nodded.

"Then, let Louie protect you from your feelings. He won't let the poor guy within ten feet of you. Meanwhile, you can decide how you really feel about him…from a distance."

"But who will keep Louie from killing him?"

A wicked smile consumed her face. "Just leave that up to me. My Lou won't hurt a fly."

Her devious little mind impressed me again. With the face of an angel and the mind of a devil, Maude was a difficult one not to love.

CHAPTER EIGHT

Another week came and went, and there was still no sign of Shane. I was in a foul mood that even my final dance lesson couldn't alleviate. I despised the world and everyone in it. "Let's do this thing!" I barked.

Perry gave me a curious look as he held the door of the limo open for me.

Louie came bounding down the front stairs and entered the back seat, smelling as if he'd spilled a whole bottle of cologne on himself. I surveyed his suit for stains, then turned to stare out the window.

He tapped me on the arm twice before I rolled my eyes and looked in his direction, exhaling loudly in the process.

A grin consumed his face from ear to ear. He was so excited to see Maude that his whole body radiated enough energy to power a small town. It was impossible to be mad at him; he loved my favorite aunt, and she loved him.

I finally smiled. "*Buon giorno*, Louie."

"Gooda morning, Meesa Krumpa!"

He's learning to speak English. I wanted to cry. "Good job, Louie!"

He nodded proudly.

The mood swiftly changed, however, when we arrived at Shaver's and found Maude's father's car waiting at the entrance. They were both standing on the sidewalk, and he was shaking an index finger at her while she just hung her head. As we inched closer, I noticed that, with his free hand, he was holding a peach-colored dress that dragged across a sheet of brown paper and string on the sidewalk.

"Oh, poor Maude!" I cried into my hand.

Louie started to growl like a guard dog on a short leash. His hand was resting on the door handle by the time we approached the curb outside the entrance. I tugged at his arm until I drew his attention away from the sidewalk scene. The look in his eyes was almost feral, accompanied by steeply sloping eyebrows and lips connected so tightly they seemed to merge into one.

I shook my head vigorously. He looked from me to Maude, then back again. I pointed at my chest and simply said, "*I* will go."

Perry pulled to the curb and stopped, and Louie stepped out and opened the door for me. He started to follow, but I placed my hand on his chest and pushed him gently back to the car.

"No," I said and left Louie scowling with his arms folded across his chest. Then, I squared my shoulders and tried to save my aunt by building on the snob routine I'd used days earlier. "Oh, there you are!"

Maude and her father looked at me. Her face was red and tear stained, and her father's mouth was half-open, apparently in midsentence.

"Miss Beckwith, darling, it's so good of you to meet me out front. And who is this, dear?"

"I'm her father."

"Oh, my, yes, you most certainly are!" I eyed his gray suit, then rested my gaze on him. He had light brown hair and stood about five-nine, with a thin build and a young-looking face that might have been considered handsome had he a different disposition.

He backed down slightly.

I looked at Maude, then the dress her father was holding. "Oh, and I see you brought the dress. May I?" I reached for it.

He reluctantly handed me the dress, and I held it in front of me.

"Now I understand your distress, Mr. Beckwith. This certainly is not my color—no, not my color at all."

His jaw dropped.

"Please don't blame Miss Beckwith here. No, the lapse in judgment was entirely mine. See, I have the most exquisite shoes from Paris, and I simply *must* find a dress to pair with them. However, upon closer examination, this particular shade won't do at all." I turned the dress around to examine the back. "My little cousin might enjoy it, though. I think it will suit her just fine. What say you, Miss Beckwith?"

I saw a smile start to emerge at the corner of Maude's lips, and she cleared her throat before responding. "Yes, I think you're quite right, miss."

"I'm so glad you agree." I draped the dress across the crook of my arm and directed my attention to Maude's dad. "Thank you so much for meeting me here on a Saturday. I do appreciate the extra effort, Mr. Beckwith, and I hope my mistake has not caused you any inconvenience."

He shook his head and stared at me, dumbfounded, as if waking from a trance. "Uh, no inconvenience at all, Miss...?"

I held out my hand. "My apologies, Mr. Beckwith. I am Daisy Murk, of the Chicago Murk's. It's a pleasure."

He hesitated but finally accepted my handshake. "Uh, the pleasure is mine, miss," he said.

I offered the sweetest smile I could. "Dear Mr. Beckwith, you must be quite burdened with activities on such a fine day as this. However, I was wondering if I might borrow Miss Beckwith for a few hours to help me choose an appropriate replacement," I said, holding up the dress.

Speechless, he simply stared.

"Oh, dear. I fear I've offended you in some way, Mr. Beckwith."

"No," he said with a cough. "No offense taken."

"Splendid, then can I expect her most gifted assistance with this matter?"

He slowly looked from Maude to me.

I swallowed hard behind the confident smile I was trying to display.

"Yes, of course. That would be fine," he finally said.

I handed the dress to Louie behind me and clapped my hands. "Oh, I'm so grateful, Mr. Beckwith. You don't know how much this means to me."

He reached down to pick up the brown paper and string.

I stepped closer to him as he stood up. "And one more thing, Mr. Beckwith."

"Yes?"

I eyed the store, then looked into his puzzled eyes. "Her employer doesn't compensate her nearly enough for her trouble." I rubbed my nose, then stared intensely into his eyes. "As such, I ask your permission to purchase a few outfits for your daughter to replace this one." I motioned to the ugly black frock that Maude was wearing and returned my gaze to her father. "They would all be school-appropriate dresses, of course." I flashed the biggest smile I could summon and stood staring at him and the confused expression on his face.

He looked down at the brown paper, then at me. "We don't take charity, Miss Murk."

"Mr. Beckwith! Charity and compensation are two entirely different things." I shook my head as if I had been insulted. "Furthermore, I insist that my assistants dress appropriately for the job."

He took a step back. "Assistant?"

"Yes, of course. I thought you knew."

He shook his head.

"Miss Beckwith is indispensable. She has been assisting me with my wardrobe choices on Saturdays, when she's not working here." I gestured to the store. "Mr. Shaver truly has no idea what a gem he has here in dear Miss Beckwith...and such modesty for her not to inform you. She truly is a gem, sir. You must be so proud." I paused, and glanced sideways at Maude's father. "I only wish I had her for Sundays as well."

He was speechless, and I hoped I hadn't overdone it. I glanced at Maude for reassurance. Her hand was covering her mouth, and she was staring at the sidewalk—I took it as a good sign.

We stood in silence for several more agonizing seconds before he said, "Yes, of course...if Maude is agreeable."

She just nodded.

"Nifty!" I shook his hand with enthusiasm. "Pleased to meet you, Mr. Beckwith. I will deposit your daughter at your doorstep later this afternoon and retrieve her again tomorrow morning at nine o'clock sharp!"

Then, before he could change his mind, I looped my arm through Maude's and escorted her to the back seat of the Ghost.

Her father remained motionless on the sidewalk with the exception of his eyes that followed us as we drove away.

I sat trembling in my seat, wondering from what part of my being those words had just escaped and if it was too late to return them. *Wow, Em. Wonderful. You just lied to your great-great-whatever-grandfather and might have changed your own future in the process. You should have majored in theater in school, not sociology.* I filled my cheeks with air and held it. *What am I doing here? First a snob and now this? I'm not a liar, and I'm certainly not an actress. I really need some guidance, some training—something so I don't have to keep making this up as I go. Maude must be mortified!*

Just then, Maude poked my cheek. The pressure from my ballooned face buckled beneath her imposing index finger, causing my lips to expel an extremely loud, unladylike noise that made Louie jump. I quietly blew the remaining air from my mouth and closed my eyes to block out my embarrassment. I could feel my face burning when Maude tapped me on the arm. I opened my eyes to a smile that put all my fears to rest.

"I've never seen anyone stand up to Papa the way you just did," she said.

"You're not upset?"

"Upset? Why on Earth would I be upset? Even *I* almost believed you!" She looked at Louie, then back at me. "You had *him* going too."

Maude hugged my arm as we laughed at Louie's expense; he just grinned, shook his head and looked out the window.

FOR THE LOVE OF MAUDE

His reaction suddenly struck me as odd. *He's almost acting as if he can understand everything we're saying.* I stared at his profile and shook my head in wonder until Maude's giggles regained my attention.

"The Chicago Murks?" She doubled over in her seat, laughing uncontrollably. "You're the bee's knees!"

The remainder of the trip to the dance studio was filled with brief moments of silence that were quickly replaced with Maude's bouts of hysteria. She continued to talk, but her giggles made her words nearly impossible to understand.

It was contagious, and Louie finally joined in by laughing and speaking to her softly in Italian. I could only watch, while a nervous, nagging fear grew inside me that I, somehow, might have just changed my future or Maude's.

When we arrived at the studio, Louie exited the car with Maude and left me sitting in the lurch, so Perry walked around and stood beside the open door, offering me his hand. "Spectacular performance, Miss Murk," he said.

I took Perry's hand and stepped out of the car, my eyes following his outstretched arm to his face. He wasn't smiling; I froze. *I'm in so much trouble!*

Maude and Louie were almost to the door of the studio when she called over her shoulder, "Are you coming, Daisy?"

Perry was still holding my hand and squeezed it to draw my attention back to him. He simply shook his head.

I tried to sound normal when I answered, "Uh...I'll meet you inside." I heard the studio door close as I continued to be held captive by Perry's almost unblinking eyes.

"We're going to take a ride," he said.

I swallowed hard, assuming it would be my last. I watched too many gangster movies as a kid and could only picture Perry loading me in the front seat, while three of his friends climbed in the back, bearing violin cases and piano wire. *I hope he doesn't want to visit any corn fields.*

Fortunately, he gestured to the back seat and quietly closed the door once I was seated, then resumed his position in the front. I exhaled in relief as we pulled away from the curb without adding any other passengers.

Perry drove for several miles, past the residential area, to a street filled with multistory buildings.

"Where are we, Perry?"

He didn't answer but soon parked in front of a large, ostentatious hotel that seemed to have devoured an entire city block. It stood less than ten stories in height but overshadowed the surrounding buildings with its massive stone façade and blue and gold awnings that read "The Strand" and covered every entrance and window surrounding the first floor of the building. The front boasted an enormous glass and brass revolving door that seemed to inhale and exhale an endless stream of well-appointed men and women.

I stared down at my bland outfit, feeling completely underdressed in my flimsy light green taffeta dress. *I could really use a few beads right about now.*

A doorman approached my side of the car, dressed in dark blue slacks with a gold stripe down the outer sides of each leg; a gold-buttoned, blue overcoat with tails trimmed in gold; and a matching blue top hat.

When the man's gloved hand reached for the door handle, Perry turned to speak to me. "Tell the gentleman at the front desk you're here to see Mr. Star in the penthouse. You're Catherine Merit. I'll be waiting for you upon your return." He then turned around and faced the front window, just as the doorman opened the door.

I nervously placed my hand in his and allowed him to assist me out of the car. On wobbly legs, I walked to the uptight, blue-suited man at the front desk and informed him of the nature of my visit.

He just stared down his nose at me. His actions instantly inspired me to find my confident snob routine.

I raised my left eyebrow as he continued to stare. "Is there some form of problem you would prefer to discuss?" I asked. "Because I'm sure Mr. Star would be delighted to hear what you might have to say."

A look of uncertainty clouded his formerly arrogant face.

"Simply delighted!" I cocked my head to the side and smiled for emphasis.

The man broke his stare and snapped his fingers above his head, revealing gold buttons along his lower sleeves. When he put his arm down and began to scribble on a piece of paper, I scrutinized his uniform, which appeared to be a size too large. *You need a tailor…an attitude adjustment wouldn't hurt either.*

Within seconds, a young boy appeared as if out of nowhere and took the note. As he did so, I noticed the desk clerk's gold nametag: "L. Styles." My smile quickly gravitated into a smirk and was fast approaching an outright laugh, when Mr. Styles' gaze again met mine.

He seemed to be studying my expression, then attempted a smile but failed. "It will be one moment, Miss Merit."

"Thank you."

I turned away, pretending to be interested in the surrounding decorations. *I wonder if the L stands for "Lack of," or maybe he put on someone else's tag by mistake, and now he has his.*

I scanned the room for another employee who had a nametag such as "Duh," or "Blah" written on it, but I saw no such person.

It didn't take long for me to forget my nametag search entirely and actually be in awe of the hotel lobby. The floor was covered in an off-white marble, edged with a navy-blue art deco tile that outlined the entire expanse of the first floor. The golden coffered ceilings boasted numerous chandeliers that sprung from ornate medallions. Potted plants lined the lobby and led entrants to the intricately carved wooden front desk that spanned more than twenty feet and was covered with a gigantic slab of white marble. I was so preoccupied by my surroundings that I didn't notice the man at the counter, even when he loudly cleared his throat.

A second attempt, sprinkled with, "Miss?" drew my attention back to his arrogant face.

"Yes?"

"Charles will escort you to Mr. Star now."

I looked down at a sweet-faced boy of about ten, standing next to me and dressed in a miniature version of the dark blue and gold uniform the front desk man wore. His brown hair was greased along the contours of his head in an attempt to control the stubborn curls that still occasionally poked their edges out in various locations. A cherub-like face beamed up at me, revealing a few missing teeth on one side, along with several more baby teeth that seemed to be happy where they were. He was adorable; I just wanted to hug him.

"Any bags today, ma'am?"

"No, Charles, but thank you for asking."

"My pleasure. Right this way, please."

Charles led me to an elevator and rode with me to the top

floor, where we emerged into a short, ornately decorated hallway that ended at a single door. A chubby set of knuckles rapped softly on the door, then disappeared behind Charles's back while he waited patiently for a reply. Within a few seconds, a brown-suited man met us at the door, smiled at me, and handed Charles three silver coins.

The young boy's face lit up. "Oh, thank you, sir! Thank you, very much!"

"You're welcome, my boy."

Then, Charles turned to me and bowed. "I do hope your time with us will be enjoyable, ma'am."

Me too, I thought, but said, "Thank you, Charles." I again fought the urge to kiss and/or pinch his chubby cheeks.

He smiled and returned to the still open elevator and was gone before I could enter the room.

"Are you Mr. Star?" I asked the man at the door.

"No, but he will join you momentarily. Please come in." He stood aside and gestured toward the interior.

I nervously walked in. *What kind of trouble have you found yourself in this time, Em?*

The suite was even more ornate than the lobby. The marble floors resembled an upgraded version of those located elsewhere in the hotel and were polished to such a shine that it seemed walking on them would be met with a cracking sound and a big, cold splash. The artwork covering the walls was museum quality and held small lights above each, and the sculptures that complemented the paintings only lent to the feeling that I should have been charged for admission.

"Beautiful, isn't it?"

I jumped and turned to see a man of about sixty standing just a few feet away.

He stepped forward, offering me his hand and flashing a crooked smile. "I'm Johann Holtz."

I instantly felt lightheaded.

CHAPTER NINE

Although my marriage wasn't exactly conventional, it did offer an advantage that few others could—I was able to see how my husband would appear when he grew older; fortunately, mine aged well.

Johann was the same smiling Dell who I had met at the opera in 1910—aged another twenty-five years. His light brown hair was just starting to turn gray along the sideburns, and his skin held fewer lines than that of most men his age.

I stared foolishly at him for so long I forgot to blink.

"It's nice to finally meet my young bride!"

Really, old man? Try...creepy.

His eyes gleamed at my horror. "Dell was right, you are fun to tease!"

Ha-ha.

"It appears we have a few things to discuss, Emily. Won't you please sit down?"

I looked at the wingback chair to which he was gesturing and gratefully eased myself into it, still unable to say a word.

He sat in a matching chair opposite mine and met my troubled eyes before speaking again. "You're very special to us."

Us? Oh, that's right. There's a Johann behind every tree! I didn't know whether to laugh, cry, or pull my hair and run screaming from the room, and my nonexistent poker face didn't help matters.

He nodded and reached for my hand, addressing me as if he could read not only my reaction but my mind: "I understand your dilemma. Truly. Your future with Dell is quite uncertain, and Shane isn't exactly the man to whom you gave your heart. Then there's the issue of my legacy."

Great. Please don't tell me that I have a third Johann—you, for example—who wants to father a son with me.

I instinctively tried to retrieve my hand, but he held fast.

"No, dear, not that! That's a young man's game, something Dell and Shane must consider. My concern is for *you*."

"It is?" I finally asked.

"Yes, of course. I could manipulate time in such a way that you could meet your Dell in college and never endure the trauma you are now facing."

"You could? Really?"

"Of course."

"I would love that!" I knew it was too good to be true, but for that instant, the hope his words brought was immeasurable.

He looked at my hand in his before continuing, "But at what cost?"

And just like that, the moment was gone.

"Everything comes at a price, my dear. When my peers in the scientific community were courting their wives, I was holed up in a laboratory, trading one kind of future for another. My success was a lonely accomplishment when I realized my life's work would pass to strangers one day."

He rubbed my hand as he spoke. "I knew it was too late for me at my age, so I enlisted my younger but mature self, Dell, to carry out my wishes and find a wife and family. I was content with the idea of playing the doting grandfather instead of fathering my own son. That was a consequence I anticipated and accepted." Johann now looked into my eyes. "But a different element surfaced, one I didn't expect—one that came as a result of my company's mission to let history occur organically without undue interference." He shook his head, and the pained expression on his face almost took my breath away. "If I had foreseen the extent of Dell's injuries, I would have prevented them."

"Is Dell...?" I couldn't even say the word.

"No, my dear, but he might not recover from his injuries, and that is something we both have to accept."

My lip started to tremble as Johann continued.

"Shane was never intended to serve as more than Dell's younger 'brother,' someone who could manage Dell's affairs after your faked honeymoon deaths, then return to his time. It was meant to be a small taste of his future. That was all." He shook his head again. "Dell was not supposed to be in that car, let alone jump from it. The plan was to find an isolated road and push the thing over the cliff, but...Well, he refused to tell me what went wrong. Stubborn me." His attempt at a joke failed to draw a smile from either of us, and several seconds passed before he spoke again, "Shane is in love with you, you know."

I shook my head. "No. I don't."

"Well, he is, but he doesn't know what to do with you. Then there's the issue of Dell recovering. Shane has never been in love before and doesn't want to be hurt. I could summon another one of my past selves, maybe one who resembles Dell more, but what if the original Dell recovers? Then what? And what about *your* feelings, my dear?"

My feelings? Oh, they're dead, but thanks for asking. Can I vomit now?

"How many times can I let you fall in love with the same man?" he asked. "At what point is this sacred thing we call 'love' no longer precious? It would soon become ridiculous."

I nodded but couldn't speak. I drew a shaky breath and continued to look into his eyes for the answers I hoped would soon surface.

"I could allow your college self to meet a different Dell, but again, at what cost?"

I wanted to scream, "Get to the point!" but somehow held my tongue.

He patted the back of my hand. "The Emily whose hand I am holding now would have to sacrifice her happiness for that of her other self."

Great, so the new Emily would have the new Dell, and I would be stuck holding hands with Grandpa here. Lovely.

"Do you see the dilemma we face?" Johann asked.

"I understand, but I'm too selfish for that to be an option."

He chuckled lightly. "Me too, my dear. That is why I won't request the assistance of any more of my past selves in order to further my legacy. It's not worth the risk or the sacrifice."

"What now?" I asked.

"Well, that brings us to the reason you are here today. As you may have already guessed, Perry is not just a chauffeur and member of my staff, he is also a trusted friend. I asked him to deliver you here as soon as you reached the edge of the precipice, so to speak, and needed the assistance that only our meeting could provide. Frankly, I'm impressed. I thought I would have seen you much sooner!" The smile reemerged.

"In other words, I really messed up?"

He grinned at my hand, then met my eyes. "Yes."

Terrific. I stared into his familiar blue eyes. When I finally spoke, my response revealed the anger I had been trying to suppress for months. "You created this monster. Now you need to take responsibility for it."

"You're correct. I did create this, and I *am* taking responsibility for it, but you must understand that it's not easy."

"No, Johann. On the contrary, it *is* easy. In fact, I have the perfect solution for you."

"And what is that?"

"Simple. Go into the future and tell me if Dell is going to recover."

"You know I can't do that. It would defy his wishes, *my* wishes."

"Then we have nothing further to discuss!" I snapped.

I rose to storm out of the room, but Johann was still holding my hand and pulled me back into my seat. "Sit down, young lady!" He took both my hands in his and held them firmly on my lap. I knew better than to try and struggle to become free; I had never won with his younger selves and guessed I probably didn't stand a chance with the original.

"Emily…" His eyes were far nicer than the ones I knew I was offering him.

"Yes?"

"I know who Maude is."

"Excuse me?"

"I know everything about her and the journal."

I stared at Johann in disbelief.

Visions of Evergreen Research and its "one strike, you're out" policy danced in my head. Failing to accomplish an Evergreen assignment often meant being trapped in the past forever, in a bordello or worse, but at least I knew what to expect with them. When it came to Johann and H&S, I had no idea. I shivered at the thought.

"Emily…" Johann's voice jerked me back from the edge of my impending doom.

When I looked at him, I also noticed that he was sitting between me and the exit. I quickly surveyed the room for another escape route and soon discovered that my only remaining option was through one of the many windows that surrounded the room.

"Emily…" Johann again brought my head back to my body.

"Yes?"

"I'm not going to punish you."

Of course you're not. That's why you have employees. I searched the room for the brown-suited man who opened the door.

"And neither is anyone else," he added.

I looked into his eyes and saw them almost laughing at me.

"Emily, if your punishment was my goal, I would have simply fitted you with a wig and sent you to the time and location of my choosing, safe or otherwise." He paused for a moment, while I struggled to maintain eye contact. "We don't operate in a similar fashion to Evergreen. We don't demean or abandon our employees—or worse. H&S is a team, and we all have a part to play. Emily, you are part of our team now."

I looked down at his hand holding mine and felt idiotic. "How am I part of a team when I don't even have a job?"

"Oh, but you do, my dear."

I met his eyes. "You mean…to have a son?"

"No, Emily. Your job is to create a future."

I swallowed hard before continuing, "Did my journal jeopardize that?"

He shook his head and released my hands. "You chose to entrust it to someone who will never divulge the information. Likewise, her…comingling, if you will, with one of our employees will not pose a threat to the company or its future—or your future."

Relief flooded me. I spanned the distance that separated us and offered a hug, then pulled away to see his smiling face.

"I enjoy having you as a 'daughter-in-law,'" he said.

"The only problem is trying to decide which of your 'sons' I just married!"

We finally shared a laugh.

By the time Johann and I were finished with our meeting, the sun was starting to make its descent.

"It's late, my dear. I hope I have eased your mind, as well as given you some food for thought."

We stood, and he walked me to the door.

"Yes, thank you for taking the time to explain things to me." I gave him another hug. "Will I be able to visit with you again?"

He held my chin between his thumb and index finger. "Not likely, Emily. I seldom travel into the past. I only came to see you this one time."

"But, Johann, I still don't know what to do. I need you!"

He looked into my eyes for several seconds, smiling at my

cracking voice. "I'm sorry to say this, but what you need is already within you. I can't answer your questions for you. No one can. You must find those answers for yourself."

Why does he have to sound like a fortune cookie? I shook my head. "Johann, please. I need help with Shane."

He chuckled. "Yes, I remember being Shane." He turned away and continued to laugh, shaking his head at the floor.

I wasn't amused and offered a scowl to prove it.

It took several seconds for him to notice, but once he did, he returned his attention to me and immediately stopped laughing. "How insensitive of me, Emily. Do forgive me. I've been waiting a long time for a family, and I sometimes forget that you and my past selves don't have the advantages I do. However, I can tell you one more thing before I bid you fare-well."

"What's that?"

Johann reached for my hands and held them. "Everything will be all right."

"Thank you. I needed that."

The smile on his face was so genuine that I completely lost all doubts about my future.

"Another thing to remember, Emily. Regardless of who you choose, Dell or Shane, one will win and the other will not; however, both are aware of the consequences."

"Either way, someone will be hurt," I said.

"Yes, my dear. I'm afraid so."

"And Dell thought of this when he suggested Shane and I...become acquainted while he recovers?"

Johann just nodded.

"Is Shane prepared?"

"When you see him again, he will be ready for you."

"Where has he been?"

He kissed me on the cheek and reached behind me to open the door. "That is a question for Shane, my dear."

I nodded and walked into the entryway. "I didn't study this time period. I'm really not prepared to be here."

"Although a certain haircut prompted Shane to bring you here untrained, it is uncharacteristic for H&S to send unequipped people to new posts. Regardless, the future and the training we could provide there is not yours to have, I'm afraid."

"Then who can answer my questions?"

"Dear Who …?" He smiled and closed the door.

Maude! Of course! I laughed at my own stupidity and turned to press the elevator button.

As soon as I reached the lobby, Charles rushed to my side. "Good evening, ma'am! Can I be of any assistance?"

I thought for a moment. Although Johann's words were still absorbing, they already offered a sense of relief I hadn't felt in months. In fact, I was in a good mood and didn't mind sharing it. "Yes, Charles, there is something."

"Anything, ma'am!"

I slowly bent closer to him and did what I had wanted to do earlier; I planted an enormous kiss on each of his chubby cheeks. Then I stood up and looked at the stunned expression on his blushing face and the two dimpled hands that now cradled it. I exhaled and smiled down at him. "Thank you for your assistance, Master Charles!"

He opened his mouth as if to speak, then closed it again and nodded.

I smiled and winked at him as I walked away.

Perry was waiting for me just beyond the revolving door

and assisted while I entered the limo. Once I was seated, I looked out the window and noticed that Charles was now standing on the curb next to the doorman. I waved and blew him a kiss as we drove away. That caught the attention of the doorman, who looked down at the boy and smiled. Charles simply waved in reply.

CHAPTER TEN

My time with Johann had not only consumed most of my day but also my thoughts. By the time we reached the house, I was so deeply immersed in my internal turmoil that I failed to notice the car stopping and Louie reaching to open the door for me from his curbside post. I took his hand and stepped out onto the walkway and smiled absently at him before the smile on his face jolted me back to reality.

I had completely forgotten about Maude. I looked from left to right along the walkway, then up the empty stairs leading to the open front doors, before resting my gaze once again on Louie. "Where is Maude?"

He had a confused look on his face.

I held my palms up in the air and asked, "Maude?"

Louie nodded and made a waving gesture with his hands.

"Tomorrow?" I asked.

He just stared.

I had too much on my mind to deal in hand gestures, but I waited until Perry drove in the direction of the garages before continuing. "Louie?"

He smiled.

"I know you can understand me, so I'm only going to ask once more. Will she be available tomorrow as we discussed?"

Louie looked at the ground, then back at me before responding in perfect English, "Please don't tell her."

I knew it! "I cannot believe this, Louie! Why do you act as if you only speak Italian?"

"Shane requested a bodyguard from Italy to communicate with him in Italian. He just assumed I can't speak English."

"And you didn't correct him?"

Louie shook his head and grinned. "I'm good at what I do. Shane doesn't need me to speak English, so I don't."

"Gooda morning, Meesa Krumpa," I said in a thick accent.

He laughed. "I couldn't resist."

"And what about Maude, Louie? I love her dearly and would never do anything to hurt her. I just hope *your* intentions are pure."

"I assure you they are, miss."

"Do you love her?"

"With my whole heart."

I stepped a little closer. "Then I'm sure you understand it when I say that, although you are much larger than me, if you ever hurt her, I will risk my own well-being to stalk you throughout space and time and make sure you rue the day you were ever born! *Capisce*?"

He maintained eye contact. "Yes...and I would expect nothing less."

"Good. The truth needs to come from you, so I will keep your secret for now, but you had better tell her soon."

"I will, miss."

"And one more thing, Louie."

"Yes?"

"Shane, Oscar, or whatever you want to call him, is not really my brother."

He squinted, peering into my eyes. "Are you telling me the truth?"

"Yes, but I appreciate your protection."

"Who else knows?" he asked.

"Just you, Perry, and Maude, and we need to keep it that way."

"Maude?"

"Of course. She's my best friend."

He nodded, apparently satisfied with my reply, then he laughed at the ground. "I wish both you and Shane luck."

"Thanks. Now can you please tell me if we're going to see Maude in the morning as planned?"

"Yes, at nine o'clock."

"And was she okay with my absence today?" I asked.

"Yes, I told her that you had business to attend. She was very understanding."

"Good." Then I grabbed his hand and held it in mine. "Thank you for taking care of her Louie. It means a lot to me."

He looked into my eyes and nodded without offering a verbal reply.

Leave it alone, Em. If you keep talking, you might accidently tell him who Maude really is to you.

I smiled and walked up the stairs, into the house. I barely crossed the threshold when a hand came from out of nowhere and grabbed me by the wrist and twirled me to the right.

It belonged to Shane. "So are you falling for your body-guard now?"

I looked back out the door and saw where Louie was still standing at the bottom of the stairs. Shane had a perfect view of our conversation—the one in which I occupied space within inches of Louie's face, then held his hand. It couldn't have looked good.

I stared into Shane's humorless eyes. "No," I said.

"Oh, so you just cozy up to anyone you can?"

I tried to find my patience within the depths of my soul, then remembered I was fresh out. "Really, Oscar? You're gone for weeks and come back to scold me because I'm having a discussion with my bodyguard? He can't speak English, remember?" I continued without a reply, "Therefore, it kind of takes a while to make even the simplest request. Maybe if you were around more, you wouldn't jump to such ridiculous conclusions!"

And then it happened.

I felt his full lips touch mine so quickly that I wasn't sure if I'd finished my sentence or just thought I had. He pushed me against the wall and pressed his body to mine. His lips seemed to have a mind of their own in their search to satisfy some deep hunger. I couldn't think; I could only react, so I pulled his head closer to me and buried my hands in his soft hair. I'd never been kissed that way before—not by Dell or by anyone. I was sweating so much it felt as if my internal thermostat had ceased operation. I needed air and tried to turn my lips from his in an effort to find it.

He continued kissing my cheeks and nose until his lips finally settled on my forehead. Then he pressed his head to mine. "I love you," he murmured breathlessly.

I didn't reply.

He pulled slightly away. "I know you love Dell, and you

may never love me in that way. But I promise you that he and I are the same man inside…and I'll do whatever it takes to prove it to you."

I looked into his eyes and saw a sincerity that had been missing before. "What changed your mind?" I asked.

"You."

"How? You've been gone for weeks."

Shane just smiled and ran an index finger along the tip of my nose and down toward my chin, slowly using my bottom lip to open my mouth.

I quickly recovered my lip and its use. "Shane!"

"Oscar," he corrected me and continued to smile. "You write one mean movie review."

"Excuse me?"

"And I sure wouldn't want to own that burger joint you crucified for not serving their meat bunless."

I thought of the articles I had submitted to my college newspaper when I was a freshman and shook my head.

"Need a hint?" Shane appeared to be enjoying every second.

I wanted to slap him.

"You interviewed me once."

I hesitated, still searching my memory. "I interviewed a lot of people."

"Not expert frog whisperers."

"Johnny Wood?" I remembered the hot but nerdy, bearded and spectacled senior I had interviewed for a piece regarding unusual pastimes.

"The one and only!" Shane said proudly.

I shook my head, recalling how Dell also went into my past and posed as my second grade teacher, as well as the gardener at Winston Manor, the house I occupied while working for Evergreen in 1910.

"You Johanns aren't very original."

He smirked. "What's that expression? If it ain't broke…?"

I imagined the things I could break at that moment, but refrained out of self-preservation; I opted to have my question answered instead. "How did that change your mind?"

"Remember our trip into the muddy marshlands that night?" he asked.

"Yeah. Who could forget that? Instead of listening to you whisper to frogs, the only non-cricket-related sound I heard was my hand slapping my skin, where about a dozen mosquitoes decided to feast. Then there was the dreaded, hissing opossum."

"But you didn't complain."

Not to you!

He laughed, still caught up in the memory of that night. "And I bought you dinner."

Right. Rubbery corn dogs and potato wedges from the bait shop down the road. I burped them for days. "I wouldn't call that dinner, Oscar."

He kissed my cheek. "You surprised me."

"How?"

"You didn't give up. The entire time, you continued to ask me questions. Didn't that article win an award?"

I nodded.

"I have found it difficult to admit my feelings for you, but after that night, I couldn't help falling for you even harder. I put you in an uncomfortable situation and not only did you persevere, but you also triumphed…I love you."

Johann had told me that Shane was in love with me, but

hearing it from the source made it all the more real. "Shane…Oscar, I'm so confused right now. I love Dell. I married *him*."

"I—" He tried to speak, but I put my finger to his lips.

"Please listen. I know that you and Dell are the same person, so I'm sure this sounds crazy, but I feel as if I'm cheating on him by being with you."

He kissed my finger and nodded. Then he started to kiss my jaw bone and deposited a trail of kisses across my neck and throat.

"Sh…Oscar?"

"Hmm?"

"Please stop and look at me."

He slowly let his nose travel along my skin, the distance of my neck and face, up to my forehead, where he left another kiss before making eye contact with me.

You're so naughty, I thought, staring at him. "Did you hear what I said?" I finally asked.

"Which part?"

I exhaled into his face.

He grinned. "I'm sorry. Am I making you mad?"

I exhaled again, through my nose that time, and continued to stare.

"Yes, I heard you…but did you hear me?" he asked.

"Yes, but—"

Now it was his turn to keep me from finishing my sentence. He ran his thumb across my lips as he held my face in his hands. "No buts, sweetheart. You might know me as Shane, but I'm also Dell and Johann…and whether you agree with the notion or not, you married us all."

Apparently, he was finished talking, because he replaced

his thumb with his lips and resumed his explorations. Although we remained fully clothed, we spent a sleepless night on display for all to see on the living room couch. By the next morning, Chef Jacques was the only member of the household staff who remained. Several others, including most of the maids, quit simply at the sight of our front door exhibition, and the others just didn't bother showing up for work the next day.

Shane left early in the morning on business that involved letting history occur organically—I didn't inquire about the details. So I was left to eat breakfast alone. Without the assistance of his kitchen staff, Chef Jacques personally deposited my breakfast plate before me and stood next to me until I finally looked up into his waiting eyes.

"Thank you, Chef Jacques."

"Of course."

He didn't move.

I again looked up at him and waited to receive my scolding; instead, he returned my gaze with the hint of a smile surfacing at the corner of his mouth.

"I had a sister like you once," he said, staring off into the distance and smiling. Then he drew the fingertips of his right hand together until they touched and he kissed the tips. *"Magnifique!"*

I smiled at him as he bowed and walked with a slight skip in his step back to the kitchen. *That was weird…and creepy.* I just shook my head. *At least he can cook!*

* * *

By nine o'clock, we arrived at Maude's house, a small, white shingled home with a covered porch that spanned its width and a dormer centered above, like an all-seeing eye. The dog-eared, black-and-white picture Maude often shared with me as a child made the house seem so dull, but seeing it in color brought the house, and her stories about the place, to life. "Papa bought this from a Sears and Roebuck Catalog in 1919 and built the thing himself," Maude once told me. "His job at the newspaper helped him to keep it during the Depression, but many of our neighbors weren't so lucky."

I looked around at the other houses on the working-class block in Los Angeles, which, according to the older Maude, would be razed in the 1970s to make room for a shopping mall. The homes all held a similar look of hope, with manicured lawns and growing hedges, oblivious to their inevitable fate.

I strode up the front walk and past the oak tree under which I had buried the Maude journal in 1920. Its leaves rustled in the slight breeze as if to say, "Why, hello again," and continued to wave at me as I walked past and up the stone stairs that led to the front porch and the doorbell.

Her father answered and eyed my understated navy outfit before resting his eyes on my face. "Nice to see that a girl in your position doesn't feel the need to hide behind layers of powder."

It sounded as if it were a compliment, so I took it as one. "Thank you so kindly, Mr. Beckwith."

He finally smiled. "Please come in. Maude will be with you in just a minute."

I stepped into the front room and realized that, with the exception of the absence of a tacky souvenir or two, the house was decorated similar to the one Maude lived in when I was young. I felt twelve again, as if I had rushed through my homework so I could pay my daily visit to Maude in her little house behind my grandparents', just down the road from ours. *Now I understand your inspiration, Maude.*

A divan was placed under the window, right next to a large bookcase filled with a collection of somewhat tattered hardcovers. A newer looking couch was placed perpendicular to the divan and faced the fireplace, while a wingback chair and ottoman sat on its right. The painting over the fireplace was a beach scene of a young boy and girl playing in the sand. That same painting hung over the older Maude's fireplace. She always said that it was one of her more precious possessions. Now, the familiarity of the room made me homesick.

"What a lovely home, Mr. Beckwith." I felt my friend, the familiar lump, forming in my throat but tried to talk and smile in spite of it.

"Thank you, but I'm sure you're used to much finer," he replied.

I shook my head. "Finery does not make a house a home. It's the people who live within the walls who make it so." I smiled into his now sad eyes and decided to change the subject. "Are those your children?" I pointed to the painting over the fireplace.

He looked at the scene for a few seconds before replying, "Yes, my late wife commissioned an artist to capture them at play. She always said that the sight of playing children set her free. It gave her great comfort when she was ill." He paused before continuing, "I'll see what's keeping Maude." Then, he quickly left the room, heading in the direction of the stairway.

I felt horrible. *Way to go, Em. Why don't you just ask him to relive a few more sad memories? "Remember the time you had to bury your dog in the backyard?"*

"Hi, Daisy!" Maude entered the room, wearing a black dress similar to the one from the previous day.

I shook my head. "You must have a closet full of those."

She just smiled. "Shall we?"

We walked toward the door, but before exiting, I turned to look for her father. He wasn't there, so I called, "Goodbye, Mr. Beckwith!" When I received no reply, I quietly closed the door and walked across the porch and down the stairs in the direction of the waiting limo. "Maude, I'm so sorry. I think I really upset your father."

The smile left her face for a few seconds while she spoke to the ground. "No, Daisy, you didn't. He's just lonely."

Louie stepped out of the car and held the door open for Maude and me to enter.

There was no space between the two as they sat holding hands and whispering to each other in their version of Italian. It was so innocent that it reminded me of Dell and me, so much so that I had to look away.

What we had in 1910 was so sweet and appropriate for that time period. Now, Shane comes along and shows me what I was missing with Dell. I'm so confused! I love Dell, but Shane is…here, and Dell is…not. I closed my eyes and rested my head against the back of the seat, trying to prevent myself from overthinking the whole situation.

"Daisy?" Maude elbowed me.

I turned to her and realized from the impatient look on her face that it wasn't the first time she had said my name. "Sorry, Maude. What were you saying?"

She finally smiled. "We're here!"

I looked outside to see the familiar Shaver's doorman. "Yes, we are. What are we waiting for?"

Louie opened the door and offered each of us a hand.

On the sidewalk, I touched Maude on the sleeve and pointed to the much more expensive department store across the street. "I want to go there!"

Maude's mouth dropped open as she looked from the other entrance, to me and back again. "There?"

I looped my arm through hers. "Yes. Let's go," I said, then half-dragged her across the street to the other store.

The doorman smiled and opened the heavy brass-framed glass door.

Before entering, I turned behind us. Without orders telling them otherwise, Louie and Perry remained standing next to the Ghost. I waved, grateful for the chance to spend a little time alone with Maude.

Inside, we both stopped to admire the décor. Although Shaver spared no expense in decorating his store, he couldn't compete with the interior Maude and I were now experiencing. The entire store was lavished in crystal, gold, and glass and exuded an air of confidence that spilled over into the personalities of those who worked there.

"Welcome to Preswick's. How may I direct you?"

Maude and I turned, in unison, to look at the lady who stood before us. She was an attractive, middle-aged woman who presented herself with such poise that she could have easily been mistaken for a statue. Her brown hair was pulled into a fashionable bun at the nape of her neck, and she wore a fitted black jacket and matching skirt, extending several inches below the knee, that succeeded in flattering her form without divulging any secrets. I struggled not to stare.

I finally smiled warmly and said, "Yes, thank you. We are looking for women's dresses, please."

"Of course! The elevators on your left will take you to the second floor."

"So kind. Thank you." I grabbed Maude by the arm and led her to the elevators.

She leaned close to my ear as we walked. "Mrs. Norman could sure take some advice from her."

"She certainly could," I said.

It was difficult to make it to the elevator without browsing at the various glass cases along the way. The gloves, scarves, perfume, and jewelry kept us from our dress shopping for close to an hour. When we finally reached the second floor, we stepped off the elevator onto marble floors, which bordered black and gold carpeting that flowed into the distance. A mannequin stood before us, wearing an ornately beaded black gown that instantly drew my attention.

Before we could venture forward, however, another well-dressed greeter appeared. "Good morning, ladies. I'm Mrs. Young. How may I assist you?"

I looked behind the attractive lady who was speaking and realized that several others stood in a line behind her. They all looked and dressed alike. *Wow! Talk about customer service. They caught us as soon as we stepped off the elevator.*

Maude was speechless, so I spoke for both of us. "Good morning. I'm Daisy Murk, and this is Maude. We are looking for several school appropriate outfits for my cousin here, as well as some play clothes." I winked at the woman, and she smiled in reply.

"Very good," she said. "Please follow me." She led us to an area that contained mannequins bearing cotton dresses in a variety of patterns and styles that would have easily met the approval of Maude's father. They all had dropped waists with mid-calf hemlines. The attendant glanced at Maude. "Did you bring your measurements, miss?"

Maude reached into her little purse and produced a slip of paper

"Thank you. And how many, miss?"

I answered for her, "At least a dozen…and we'll need them today, I'm afraid."

Mrs. Young reacted by leading us to a nearby salon. Maude, however, looked at me as if I had levitated right before her eyes.

I just smiled. My previous shopping experience taught me that, although ready-made clothes often required alterations, same-day tailoring was both uncommon and expensive. Fortunately, money didn't seem to be a problem in the time travel business, and I'd simply become used to not only having it but spending it as well. I patted the off-white beaded purse Shane had filled from his wallet earlier.

Maude pulled me aside and finally spoke, "Daisy? There are only five school days in a week."

"And 360 other days that require just as much attention!" I locked my arm with hers and hurried to catch up with Mrs. Young.

We entered the salon through a set of red curtains that separated the room from the rest of the store. Chandeliers and mirrors greeted us as we were led to couches along a bank of windows. We sat and drank tea while dresses were modeled by a team of brunettes, all of whom looked related. After approving more than a dozen outfits, we accompanied Mrs. Young to a changing room that held a mirrored platform. It was similar to the one at Shaver's, only with much more comfortable chairs surrounding it. I seated myself on an especially large, light blue one and waited for Maude to don her first outfit. While a gray-haired tailor worked her magic with Maude's measurements, our assistant continued to discover new dresses, as well as shoes and purses that would complement them.

Once the school dresses were sufficiently addressed, we returned to the salon, where the beaded flapper dresses arrived and became more elaborate and equally expensive as the hours passed. I was so impressed by their quality that I, too, had to participate, and I found close to a dozen that I decided I couldn't live without. In the end, similar to my visit to Shaver's, we had to summon the assistance of a delivery van to accommodate the many boxes and parcels that marked our very successful shopping trip.

Maude chose to wear a pale green, cotton dress and matching shoes to Essex House, where a well-deserved lunch was promised. Louie was unable to keep his eyes off her as we drove back to the house, and it was making me crazy.

Maude and I were so close when I was growing up that we could almost finish each other's sentences. We had a mutual respect that was not bound or burdened by age. In fact, whenever I had a problem at school, Maude was always the first in line to defend my honor, regardless of the consequences. Now, looking at the young Maude next to me, still innocent of the world and all it held in store for her, I realized that the tables had turned; now it was *my* turn to defend *her* honor.

Fortunately, as we sat in the back seat of the limo, Maude's small stature made it convenient for me to look over her head and catch Louie's gaze on the other side. He was fixated on Maude as she talked excitedly in a mixture of English and Latin about her new outfits. When I finally caught his attention, he was unable to hide the unmistakable longing for Maude, which he wore like a banner across his face. I recalled a similar expression in Shane's eyes the night before.

I gave him a stern look and shook my head.

Louie turned his gaze skyward for a moment, then back down at the petite hand he was holding in his, before exhaling through a pair of frustrated lips.

Great. All I need is one more thing to worry about!

CHAPTER ELEVEN

W hen we arrived at Essex House, Maude and I ran up the stairs and burst through the front doors to see if our clothes had been delivered. Unfortunately, the entryway held only the sound of muffled voices coming from the dining room.

"Everyone must be admiring our dresses," Maude said. Her excited giggles had us both in a power-walk and out of breath by the time we reached the dining room.

"The table's a good place for that," I said. "Good thing it can seat twenty!"

I swung the door open, but instead of finding our purchases on display, we were met by the startled expressions of Shane and several dozen others, who were either seated or standing around the mahogany dining room table. Although the room was massive, with windows at one end and the door at the other, all the free space in between was lined with people, buffet servers, and artwork.

Shane stood with his hands on his hips, facing us from the head of the table, surrounded by a group of people in matching uniforms—men in black tuxedos with white shirts and women in calf-length black dresses with white aprons. "And this is my darling Blanche," Shane said, flashing that smile of his.

The group burst into laughter.

I took a deep breath and surveyed the smiling faces before me. *Only H&S employees would know to laugh at that one.*

My own face felt like it was on fire as I slowly walked over to join him. Maude remained where she was standing, visibly confused. While shopping, I told her that Shane and I had scared the other staff away, but I could only imagine who she thought their replacements were. "Hello," I said. I tried to act natural, despite my embarrassment.

Shane kissed me on the cheek, instantly adding even more heat to my face.

Well, since I'm already in hell, at least I'm probably the appropriate color. I smiled at the group. *First impressions, Em. Lovely.*

"And this must be Maude." Shane directed his attention to the doorway, then back to me.

How did he know? I looked at Shane, then at my poor aunt, who remained frozen in the entry. *Johann must have told him,* I decided and offered a nod in reply.

He turned to Maude. "Please join us."

I went to escort her over, but Shane held my arm, preventing me from moving. He kissed me on the cheek again, then walked to meet Maude. "Pleased to meet you, Elizabeth."

She extended a trembling hand in his direction, but he drew her into a hug instead. Louie stood with his arms folded across his chest in the doorway, glaring at Shane. The two men's eyes met, locked in a testosterone-fueled staring contest until Shane finally made the first move. His eyes remained glued on Louie as he released Maude and gestured toward the dining room while saying something in Italian.

Louie slowly unfolded his arms and stepped forward to escort Maude to a patch of free wall space. I thought Maude would faint, but she leaned against Louie for support while she composed herself.

"For those of you who have just joined us, I have assembled a new staff to assist us in our stay at Essex House." Shane turned to the group. "So, without further delay, I would ask each of you to introduce yourselves to Miss Blanche and her friends, and tell them what your position is."

They all stood to make their introductions, but I mostly tuned them out, choosing to focus instead on Maude and her recovery. When I was satisfied that she wouldn't fall into a heap on the floor, I turned my attention back to the others just in time to hear "Blanche" and "maid" in the same sentence. I looked to see who was speaking and was met by a beaming face that instantly made me smile.

"Midge!" I almost didn't recognize my former maid in the bobbed haircut she was wearing. I wanted to rush over and give her a hug but thought I'd save us both the embarrassment.

She curtsied to me before reclaiming her seat.

When the introductions were complete, I searched the crowd for our chef but couldn't find him. I turned to Shane and asked, "Is Chef Jacques still with us?"

An audible groan came from the portion of the table that held the kitchen staff.

"Yes. He's simply at the market," Shane replied.

The groaning resumed. Apparently, I wasn't the only one he had rubbed the wrong way at first. *You'll change your minds once you try his croissants!*

Shane ignored the reaction and again addressed the group. "Thank you all for returning with me. I know this was on short notice, and I appreciate your participation. Now, we all have a lot of work to do, so please familiarize yourselves with your posts, and let me know if you have any questions or concerns. Thank you again, and welcome to Essex House!"

After a brief round of applause, the group rose, almost in unison, and began to disperse throughout the house and surrounding estate.

My earlier concern for Maude was quickly dispelled when I heard one of her giggles floating through the crowd. She was standing almost directly across the table from me, leaning against the wall and attempting to stifle a laugh behind both hands while Louie gestured in the air.

I shook my head. *It's just a matter of time before you discover each other's secrets…if you haven't already.* I studied Louie's profile and wondered who he thought Maude really was.

Between the passing handshakes and a "Pleased to meet you" or two, Midge fought the crowd to exchange long-overdue hugs.

"Your hair looks great, Midge!"

She reached up to grab the ends of her brown hair. "Nothing like what you remember from our days at Evergreen, is it ma'am?"

Midge wasn't just my lady's maid; she was also a friend and confidante, an H&S spy who had posed as my maid at Evergreen's Winston Manor. I shook my head and smiled. "I think we're missing a bun and a corset or two."

But before we could catch-up further, the doorbell rang, and several burly men from Preswick's entered the house with our delivery. Midge quickly excused herself and walked toward the open front door, followed by Maude and Louie.

I moved to join them until I heard Shane clear his throat beside me. I turned to see him grinning mere inches from my face.

"You've been busy, my dear." He grabbed me by the waist and enveloped me in his embrace.

"I can say the same about you." I barely finished my sentence before his lips touched mine and made me lose my train of thought.

He gently kissed my upper lip then ran his soft lips along my cheek to my ear, where his warm breath sent goosebumps down my spine. "Not busy enough," he whispered.

My neck muscles failed me, causing my head to fall back and my mouth to open with a sigh. He pulled me closer, and I gripped the back of his shirt for support as his light touch traced my jawline and exposed throat. Every part of me tingled beneath fingers that barely touched my skin.

"Let's go..." His words trailed off when his lips pulled my earlobe into his mouth. For a brief moment, I thought my legs would give way.

When we drew apart, Shane held my hand in his, and we walked past the commotion of deliveries and delegations near the doorway, somehow making our way to his bedroom.

He released my hand and placed his own lightly on the small of my back as we walked through the doorway and to the foot of his bed. "I want you to share this with me," he said.

His words suddenly rang in my ear like an alarm clock on Monday morning. I shook my head. "I'm sorry, Shane, I-I shouldn't be here...with you. I...Shane..."

He stepped back and closed his eyes. "You're my wife, Emily!"

Both Blanche and Oscar seemed so far removed from our conversation that neither of us thought to invite them.

"No, Shane. I married Dell!"

He exhaled loudly and ran the fingers of both hands through his hair. "You married me!" Then, he threw his hands down to his sides and shook his head at the floor.

"Shane?" I reached forward to touch his face.

The eyes that met mine embodied a mixture of sadness and pain that almost broke my heart.

I could hardly look at him as I continued, "I love you...I do." I held his attention with the glimmer of hope my words were imparting. "But—"

He reached forward and pulled me into his arms before I could continue. "Spare me the excuses, Emily. I love you, and you love me. I don't care which me you married in the past— I'm the one who's with you today."

"Please, Shane. I already feel bad enough."

He loosened his hold on me and almost spat fire from his mouth. "For what? For being with me?"

"No!"

"Then what?" He was now standing with his arms folded across his chest.

I exhaled in frustration. "Shane, you don't understand."

"Really, Emily? I hadn't realized...thanks for informing me!"

I closed my eyes to compose myself before continuing, "Shane, I don't see you and Dell as...the same person. I mean, I know you are, but..." I felt as if I were driving in a convertible with my mouth open. I searched for enough saliva to swallow but found none. My voice cracked as I added, "I see you as two different people."

FOR THE LOVE OF MAUDE

His eyes searched mine as though he were looking for the punch line. I couldn't offer him one. Then he slowly nodded. "I can never be Dell in your mind?"

"There's only one Dell."

He just stared at the floor.

"But Shane…"

He refused to look up, so I stepped closer and took his hand in mine, bringing it to my lips and kissing the palm.

"I love you for who you are, not for who you're not."

His eyes left the floor and settled on my lips as if he were still searching for that elusive punch line.

"I love you, Shane, but I'm married to Dell. Until I know whether he will recover or not, I can't be your wife."

His eyes flew to mine. "I won't accept that!"

"You—"

He cradled my face in his hands. "I can accept that you're not ready for my bed, but I will never accept you choosing my older, broken self over the one who is holding you right here and now."

His lips lightly touched mine then traveled to my neck as his hands blazed the trail before them. I was so caught up in the moment that I failed to notice the extent of his travels until a small breeze from the open French doors alerted me to the fact that Shane's actions weren't all that was giving me goosebumps. The floor surrounding our feet was littered with half my outfit and all of his.

I almost screamed; instead, I froze in place, similar to a spoiled two-year-old who couldn't decide between the cotton candy and the caramel apple.

He gently pulled my stiff body into his arms, and I rested my head on his muscular chest as he rubbed my back. His skin smelled amazing; freshly bathed and scented like an out-door stream. Once my body became limber again, I closed my eyes and rubbed my cheek along the contours of his chest that held just the right amount of hair. I turned to face him and ran the tip of my nose and lips along his muscles, unable to resist the urge to kiss him as I went.

"Emily?" he whispered down at me.

I stopped and stared into his eyes.

"I'm so sorry. I realize you're confused, but I…I'm not. I *know* what I want." He paused to kiss my forehead. "Your decision isn't an easy one. I only wish that Johann had chosen me instead of Dell to win your heart."

"Then you'd be in a coma, and Dell would be standing here with me, wishing he were younger."

A grin surfaced on his face as he nodded. "We can't win."

I tried to smile back at him but failed. "I just need time, Shane…and understanding."

"Time is the easy part."

I looked away. "I'm saving myself for my husband, Shane."

"Johann informed me; however, I cannot begin to imagine why my older self didn't enjoy at least one night of his honeymoon with you before the accident. Maybe you're right after all."

"About what?"

"Well, I find it impossible to believe that Dell and I are the same person. I would never have left you alone on our wedding night—never! I can barely contain myself now."

I smiled up at him. "I do love you."

"I know."

The new round of kisses started on my forehead and traveled to my temples and cheeks to finally rest on my lips. I ran my fingers along his muscular back, exploring every inch as his lips continued to make themselves at home on mine. By the time I reached the small of his back, I knew I was entering dangerous waters but chose to throw caution to the wind. The perfectly formed bum that met my eager hands did not disappoint, but it was all proving a bit much for Shane and his almost nonexistent will power.

His lips left mine and went to my forehead, where he planted a lingering kiss. His voice was husky and wavered as he spoke. "We have to stop."

I knew he was right, so I didn't argue; instead, I sadly removed my hands from their new favorite spot, ran them up his back, and brought them together behind his neck.

He shook his head. "I guess I'm going to have to settle for boyfriend instead of husband, at least for now."

"Thank you." I tried to smile.

"Oh, don't thank me, love. It's going to be an uphill battle for you, because I doubt I will be able to be this strong again."

Our eyes met, where I found little humor, so I simply nodded in reply.

"Now, let's gather our things and return to the world of the living," he suggested.

He released his hold so I could separate my clothes from his. I stepped into my blue dress and slowly buttoned it around me. I couldn't take my eyes off him as he started with his pants and worked his way up to his tie. *Boy, he's hot!*

I didn't realize until I was almost finished that I had misaligned my buttons and was left with more buttons than holes to push them through.

Dell who? I shook my head. *This completely stinks!*

Another thing I didn't realize was that Shane was staring at me just as hard as I was staring at him.

"Are you pleased with what you see?" he asked. There was that crooked smile.

I grinned in reply and nodded. "Very!"

"Good." He pulled on his socks and shoes and found a mirror to fix his hair.

I followed him and hugged him from behind, enticing him to lower his comb.

He placed his hands over mine and slowly turned to face me. "I don't want to be without you, Emily. I may have more willpower at times, but I will never just let you go. I can't and won't compete with what you and Dell had, but I will do everything in my power to make you forget." He bent down and kissed me on the cheek, then offered me a brush from his dresser and stepped aside.

I met my reflection with sheer horror as the eyes in the mirror met their mates. My hair was a mess, and the small amount of makeup I had been wearing earlier was now misplaced across various parts of my face. "You'd fight for this?" I asked.

Shane just laughed. "Any day."

I stepped closer to the mirror. "Does insanity run in your family?"

He replied without even looking at my reflection, "It must."

I socked him on the shoulder, but he was already flexing. "Ow!" I shook out my hand and started to kiss the knuckles.

"Allow me." He slowly planted kisses along the knuckles and back of my hand. "Better?"

I pretended to examine my injuries. "For now."

"Well, just let me know if I can be of further assistance."

"Oh, believe me, I will."

He kissed me on the cheek and let me continue making my face and hair once again presentable. It took a little time, but he patiently waited until I was finished, watching me from a nearby chair.

"Join me," he finally said. Then he held out his hand in my direction.

I walked over to him. "How do I look?"

"Beautiful." He reached for my hand and pulled me onto his lap, sniffing my neck in the process. "You smell good too."

"You're not so bad yourself."

He smiled and played with my hair. "Were you surprised to see Midge?"

"Yes! How did you manage that?"

"Well, I was gone for quite a while assembling our new staff."

"How long?"

He tickled my face with a lock of my hair. "Several weeks."

"That long? And here I thought you were only gone a few hours."

"I'm good, but I'm not *that* good."

I shook my head at his arrogance. "And Midge?"

"Well, she quit her job after your honeymoon accident. She just couldn't recover...the grief, you know." He smiled and winked.

"Of course." I paused as he kissed my ear lobe. "Are they all from H&S?"

"Yes."

"How will that work with Chef Jacques?"

His attention was focused on kissing my eyelids, and I had to repeat the question before receiving a response. "Oh...he's from the future."

"Excuse me?" I pulled away, removing any distractions so that he would answer me.

He just smiled. "He owns a very popular 1920s-themed restaurant, The Beaded Lady, and he wanted to gain the full experience by working as a chef in the real era."

"I thought he was from this time."

"I did too. Apparently, they don't tell me everything either. Now, no more questions."

I put my fingertips up to his mouth. "Just one more."

He kissed my fingers. "Fine, but only one."

"Does Chef Jacques really think I'm your sister?"

He shook his head. "I don't know. Why?"

"Well, he said he had a sister like me once."

Shane smiled. "All I can tell you is they showed me his file, and Chef Jacques is an only child."

Then he reached up, grabbed my wrist, and pulled my hand away from his face. It was dark outside before we left the chair.

CHAPTER TWELVE

Apparently, dating one's brother carried an odd stigma I hadn't anticipated. Rather than being social pariahs banished to a lonely Essex House to wait until my hair finally reached my shoulders, we were considered the 'it' couple at all the summer soirees. By the following weekend, the invitations began to accumulate in such a large pile I had to employ Midge as my secretary to sort through them all.

"Here's one from the Blakes!" Seated across from me at the outdoor breakfast table, Midge triumphantly held a gold-trimmed envelope in her hand.

"Who are they?" I asked.

Shane examined the invitation over the top of his morning paper. "Just one of the wealthiest families on the West Coast. When is that one, Midge?" he asked.

She eagerly opened the envelope and pulled out the gold-embossed card inside. "Oh, such short notice. It's next Saturday, I'm afraid."

"They just didn't know about us before." Shane winked at me. "Please let them know we'll be attending." With that, he returned his attention to the paper before him.

I grew to despise the newspaper or any other distraction

at the table. Where Shane was concerned, all form of conversation was generally ignored or at best took a back seat to the morning edition. That included my failed attempt to draw his attention by modeling a dress that Maude had gifted to me. I felt the urge to lunge across the table, snatch the newspaper from his hands, and crumple it into a ball. His insistence on ignoring me and everyone for those black-and-white pages truly infuriated me and made it impossible for me to start my day off in anything but a sour mood.

"Aren't we even going to discuss this, Oscar?" I asked, sounding far nastier than I intended.

"Sleep well last night, darling?" Shane asked from behind his paper.

"I think I might have slept all of five minutes, *darling*."

The previous evening, I had wanted to watch the stars with Shane on a chaise by the pool. Unfortunately, his snoring spoiled the mood. The crickets didn't even stick around. Somehow, I fell asleep and awoke at dawn with a sore throat and a kink in my neck, so I left the buzz saw behind and went to my own bed. It was miserable.

"Hmm. That's odd," he said. "I slept as sound as a baby."

Really, funny boy? That should be my line. Regardless, I wonder how well you're going to sleep in that big lonely bed of yours—you know, the one I'm never going to share with you? I stared at his newspaper and continued to fume. *Great, I guess that means Dell snores as well. Way to go, Johann! Why not just create a few more snoring yous to make my life a living hell?*

The longer I sat, the angrier I became, until I finally blew. "Shane!" The glassware on the table shook in reply, as I loudly forgot to address him by his new name.

Shane quickly lowered the newspaper and stared, wide-eyed in my direction. Meanwhile, Midge gathered the remaining invitations and nearly ran from the table.

He folded the paper and rested it beside his plate and continued to look at me without expression. "Well, you have my attention."

I found it difficult to speak without spitting. "I don't know which is worse, being kept up all night or being ignored in the morning! Sadly, I have to endure both."

"Oh, now, sweetheart, I wasn't ignoring you."

His use of Dell's favorite term of endearment only fueled my anger. I glared at him, unable to speak.

"Well...maybe just a little." He made a show of the space between his thumb and index finger and tried to offer a half-hearted smile.

I wasn't having any of his charm and just glared.

"Darling, please don't be this way," he said. "I have to read the newspaper. It's part of my job."

"Don't you already know what's going to happen before you read about it?"

"It doesn't hurt to refresh my memory."

I just shook my head.

"I guess those rumors about my snoring are true." He grinned.

My stony reply was impervious.

Then he stood and walked behind me, reaching down to place his hands on the arms of my chair. In one quick motion, he lifted both the chair and me off the ground and carried us to the edge of the pool before depositing me, chair and all, kicking and screaming into the shallow end.

He stood poolside, laughing hysterically, but he gained no reaction from me. Instead, I walked to the stairs and emerged dripping. I tried to wring out my dress, but failed to make much progress. It was ruined.

Shane was holding his side as I approached.

"I would have thought you might have learned something from the last time you so graciously deposited me into the pool."

"Yes, of course. This time I put you in the shallow end!"

I looked down at my dress, then at him, shaking my head. "Wrong, dear brother. Throwing me in water never ends well for you. This was the dress I told you about."

The smile left his face, and his mouth fell agape before his eyes met mine. "Please don't tell me this is the one Maude gave you, the dress she bought as a thank-you."

I nodded. "Gee. I guess you were listening after all. I'm a lucky girl." Without another word, I left him standing with his mouth open again and sloshed my way to my room.

Midge met me there and, without speaking, drew me a bath and helped me to remove my soaked dress. After surveying it for several minutes, she finally spoke. "I can fix this, miss."

I wasn't so sure, so I just smiled in reply and slid my body deeper into the warm water. I tried to clear my head of the earlier drama but found that it bordered on the impossible. A recurring thought kept mingling with the angry and sad ones within my exhausted mind: *He'll never be Dell—not tomorrow and not ten years from now.*

Then, I shook my head and closed my eyes to try and block out the visual of my ruined dress.

Unfortunately, I must have fallen asleep, because when I opened my eyes, I was lying naked on the cold tile floor with Midge kneeling next to me.

"Miss? Oh, miss! I thought you'd drowned!"

"What's all the screaming about?" Shane asked from the doorway, breathlessly holding onto the door jamb.

Midge grabbed a towel from a nearby shelf and covered me. "Oh, I'm so sorry. I only left her for a minute."

Shane stepped into the room and pulled the now sobbing Midge to a standing position. "There, there, Midge. It wasn't your fault. She's going to be just fine." He patted her on the back and whispered, "Why don't you let me take over?"

She nodded and left the room.

Shane knelt at my side and took my hand in his.

Great. I'm a captive audience of Lucifer here. I tried to sit up but found my near-drowning experience and rescue had left me with a spinning, aching head, so I resumed my previous position.

"Em?"

I tried to ignore him by closing my eyes.

"Sweetheart, look at me."

I didn't.

He shifted to a sitting position and ran his index finger along my hairline. "I can sit here all day."

My teeth were starting to chatter, reminding me in a hurry that I was wet and naked on a tile floor with only a flimsy towel to protect me from the devil himself. So I opened my eyes.

Shane was gently staring at me.

I sure wish I could hate you! The thought was enough to send warm tears slowly traveling from the edge of my eyes to my ears.

Shane wiped a few with his fingers before speaking again. "I'm so sorry. I've been self-centered and stupid. I'm not used to having someone else in my life, and I...I'm so sorry."

I simply nodded and closed my eyes again; I really didn't want to see or hear him. I just wanted to be left alone.

He wiped away a few more tears before continuing, "I guess I need to learn how to be with you instead of just assuming you want to be dragged along behind me. I should have warned you about my snoring, and I realize reading the paper at the table is quite disrespectful to you." He kissed me on the forehead and said, "Please open your eyes."

That time, I did as he asked and saw a look of concern on his face.

"I'll only ask this question once, then never again. Were you trying to drown yourself?"

I wanted to scream but found I had so little energy I couldn't even whimper. Eventually, I found my voice and muttered, "Don't flatter yourself."

He smiled and continued to dry my tears. "Good. Then let's remove you from this floor."

Shane helped me to a sitting then standing position as my towel inconveniently fell to the floor. Once I was standing, I couldn't help but feel his eyes devouring me, but I was too weak to complain.

"You're so beautiful," he finally said.

I just shook my head. "You never give up, do you?"

"No, and I never will."

I was still dizzy and found walking difficult, so Shane gathered my listless body into his arms and carried me to the bed. Fortunately, Midge was still there, and she immediately covered me with a blanket as soon as Shane deposited me on top of the covers.

"I can take over from here, Midge," he snarled at her.

FOR THE LOVE OF MAUDE

She looked at me, then at Shane, but she wouldn't move.

The next words that came from his mouth were pure venom: "Midge, are you deaf?"

"No, Shane, and neither am I!" I barked back in her defense. Oscar was the last name on my mind, but I could think of a few others as I felt my strength returning. "You will never speak to her that way again. Do you understand? Midge just saved my life! You should be thanking her rather than berating her."

"Fine," he spat, then abruptly left the room.

"I'm so sorry, miss. I don't know what I did," Midge cried.

I reached for her hand and pulled her closer. "You didn't do anything."

"He's not Mr. Dell, is he, miss?"

I shook my head. "No, Midge, he's not."

Several hours of uninterrupted sleep later, I awoke in a totally different frame of mind, my headache now just a dull throbbing.

Midge had salvaged the dress from earlier, and it was hanging on the outside of my closet door. After admiring the garment for several minutes, I realized how much I loved it. It was a sleeveless, off-white silk dress with a floral pattern on the upper portion. The skirt was made of no fewer than twenty panels that shot in all directions when I spun, making it perfect for dancing. It was beautiful.

I easily found my feet and, within a short time, was dressed and descended the stairs to the first floor.

Shane was sitting on one of the couches with his head buried in his hands. As I approached the ground floor, he looked up and suddenly abandoned his pity party to meet me at the bottom of the stairs. "She saved the dress," he said.

"Yes, she's quite the miracle worker."

Shane exhaled, then sheepishly met my eyes. "I've behaved horribly."

I couldn't disagree, but figured I'd cut him some slack. "Then let's continue in that vein by attending a party this evening." I thought of the many invitations we had recently received. "How about the Vincent's?"

He looked at me sideways. "How would that be horrible behavior?"

"Well, darling brother, we didn't respond to their invitation."

"Ah. So we just show up…unannounced?"

"Exactly."

He smiled and nodded but didn't speak; neither of us did. We just stood staring at each other for what seemed hours.

"You're not wearing *that* out, are you?" I finally asked.

He gazed down at the rumpled, water-stained suit he was wearing. "Do I have time to change?"

"Well, we certainly don't want to be on time."

The kiss that followed happened in an instant and was over even quicker.

"I have a lot to learn, don't I?" he asked.

I nodded.

"Then I'd better get started." He smiled and walked in the direction of the stairs.

I watched him take the steps two at a time, until he reached the top and disappeared down the hallway to his room. *I can't believe I'm giving this guy another chance!*

Within fifteen minutes, Shane reemerged wearing a clean and pressed black tux with a white shirt and black bowtie. His hair was greased back, and his teeth seemed to sparkle in the fading light of the day. He only needed a cigar in one hand and a drink in the other to complete the look.

"Is this what you had in mind?" he asked.

I nodded. "It'll do."

As Shane reached for my hand, I noticed that he was even wearing cuff links. The look suited him well, and I found it difficult to look away. He seemed to have the same problem, because he almost tripped down the front steps as we walked toward Perry and the waiting Ghost. With a house filled with H&S employees, Shane and I weren't as disciplined as we should have been in addressing each other by our new names. On the limo ride to the party, however, we resurrected Oscar and Blanche for our night out on the town.

Unfortunately, the party was a bust.

The silence was deafening as we entered the residence. The entire crowd stopped to stare as a unit, then returned to their conversations in hushed tones that filled the air and landed at our feet. Frantic mothers were eager to steer their eligible young sons in a different direction every time one of them even looked my way. Shane was equally shunned by the remaining guests, who seemed to form a protective barrier between him and their impressionable young daughters. Having no idea who the Vincents were, we were able to slip out the front door without even meeting the hosts. We stayed less than ten minutes—the whole ordeal was over before it started.

"Well, that was miserable," I said from the back seat of the limo. "I guess we look good on guest lists but aren't expected to actually make an appearance."

Shane smiled. "That's why I asked Perry to triage the remaining invitations for more suitable company, just in case."

Perry turned around in his seat and produced three invitations. "I recommend the Stellman party. However, you might also enjoy attending either of the other two. Regardless, all three are sound choices."

I looked at Shane.

"My dear?" he asked.

"Stellman has a nice ring to it."

"It should. They own the largest jewelry business in the state."

I smiled. "Despite the pun, I'm sold."

Perry was right. The minute we entered the party, a crazy-haired girl looped her arm through Shane's and led him off toward a group of laughing teenage girls. I, on the other hand, was greeted by a bevy of middle-aged men who couldn't seem to decide how to phrase what all of them were dying to say: *"Your brother and I have a lot in common. We both prefer little girls."* I, once again, cursed my genes for making me look years younger than my age as the men complimented me on my dress and asked if I enjoyed ice cream.

At first, I tried to smile but found it difficult to be the object of such creepy attention. However, with Shane otherwise distracted, my discomfort soon gave way, and I resurrected my acting abilities and began to exaggerate my part in his absence, just to entertain myself. By the fifth sugar daddy, I was ready to play the promiscuous ingénue.

"Oh? Ice cream? Now, Mister…I'm sorry, what was your name?" I asked a bland-faced, tuxedo-clad man.

"Oh, oh, I'm Mr. Daddy," he stuttered. He stepped closer, offering an eager smile and a rancid whiff of his overly greased hair.

"You're so silly, Mr. Daddy." I slapped him on the sleeve, fighting a wave of nausea. "Well, Mr. Daddy…" I winked before continuing, "I don't appreciate how ice cream makes my hips do this." I extended my arms out from my sides about a foot. Then I looked into his dark eyes. "Do you appreciate my hips, Mr. Daddy?"

He blushed a deeper shade than I thought possible. "Oh, very much, Blanche, my dear."

Ick! I tried to hide my growing disgust behind a smile and a small giggle.

He threw a creepy smile back at me, which succeeded in sending me on a desperate hunt for Shane.

Eew! That wasn't as much fun as I thought it would be! Yuck!

Unfortunately, Shane was nowhere to be found. Instead, I soon discovered myself surrounded by a whole herd of other Mr. Daddies, all desperately vying for my attention.

"Do you want candy, sweetheart?" one particularly obese man asked me.

"No, sir, I do not. I find it rather droll."

His booming laugh summoned some of the worst breath I had ever smelled. I, once again, wanted to vomit.

"And what do you prefer instead?" he asked.

I pointed at a waiter carrying a tray of champagne. "That."

"Ah, you have expensive taste, my dear. The Stellmans ship that directly from France—at great risk and expense, I might add."

I was so caught up in my little world that I had completely forgotten about Prohibition. Looking around at the others at the party, I decided they apparently did too. I hadn't seen that much alcohol since my last frat house kegger in college. The

Essex House party didn't even compare.

The man snapped his pudgy fingers in the air, and within seconds, I was sipping an overfilled glass of bubbly. I was fairly inexperienced with champagne, having only tried it once before. But after one sip, I felt certain I was holding a glass of the good stuff. I studied the bubbles for confirmation but found none.

"Is it not to your liking?" the man asked.

"Oh," I said, giggling, "it's just tickling my nose."

"And do you enjoy being tickled, my pet?" he asked mere inches from my face.

Not by the likes of you, creepo!

"Thank you for the champagne, mister, but I'd better find my brother."

He caught my elbow. "Oh, he won't be back for a while."

"What do you mean?" I tried to nonchalantly take another sip from the glass in my free hand.

"I saw him go outside with a group of sweet young things who reminded me of you."

Think fast here, Em, I coached myself, then pursed my lips and stomped my foot, nearly spilling the remaining contents of my glass on the floor. "Well, we'll just see about that!"

The man laughed at my jealous display. "You sure are a live wire, my dear. I would not want to get on your bad side."

You won't be getting on any of my sides, buddy. I scowled at him.

He reluctantly released my arm. "I can see that I don't stand a chance with your brother around."

I downed the remaining champagne and handed the man my empty glass. Then I curtseyed and continued my hunt for Shane. After a few more interruptions that involved stories of liking jewelry more than dolls, I finally found him sitting poolside, holding court with a group of teenage girls. I walked up to him with my hands on my hips. "Hello, brother."

"There you are, my sweet Blanche. Please join us." He patted his knee and smiled up at me.

I smiled in reply and occupied his lap as the girls' jealous eyes drilled holes into me. I felt as if I were a piece of Swiss cheese.

"Ladies, this is my lovely sister, Blanche."

A few of the girls made some form of response but most just glared. Then, one by one, the group slowly dwindled to one. The remaining overly ambitious girl finally stormed off when Shane made a swatting motion and said, "Go chase yourself!"

I couldn't resist laughing at her reaction.

"Having fun, my dear?" he asked.

"As much fun as one can have at a party filled with pedophiles."

Shane laughed and turned my face toward his. "I love you."

"Then rescue me from this horrible place."

We found a path from the backyard to the front, by way of a few shrubs and a very persistent rosebush. Regardless, a few thorns were far better than another trip through the crowded house to the front door.

Once we were safely inside the car, Perry handed us the remaining two invitations. Shane took the envelopes and looked at me. The activity in the house and surrounding area cast just enough light to discern the writing.

"Are you game?" Shane asked.

I met his eyes in the semidarkness of the back seat. "Are you?"

He handed the cards back to Perry. "I don't think so."

I hadn't made out in a car for ages, but the back seat of the limousine proved to be a good location. By the time we arrived home, I had forgotten why we left the house in the first place.

CHAPTER THIRTEEN

We didn't make it to the Blake's party.

I learned from Shane that access tunnels, leading from the beach to hotel basements and utility tunnels beyond, made rum-running a lucrative business along the California coast. Thus, for the next few weeks, we tried to avoid as many house parties as possible and chose to focus instead on the various speakeasies scattered throughout the area.

"I found another one," Shane triumphantly remarked one morning at breakfast.

I held my excitement to a minimum; the last three places were nothing more than glorified shacks filled with spittoons and dirty glasses. As a result, I made it a habit of bringing my own glass from home.

He met my reluctance with a grin on his face and a touch to my hand from across the table; as much as I hated to admit it, his enthusiasm was contagious. "Really, love, this one is supposed to be the best on the West Coast. Let's go tonight!"

I just shook my head at him as he scooted his chair closer to mine.

"Please? You can even invite Maude if you'd prefer," he

added. Maude had been begging everyone to visit a speak-easy ever since our last dance lesson.

"I won't invite her unless I can see it first with Louie." I knew the only other person who could keep Maude safe from her own curiosity was her boyfriend.

"Then we can go tonight?" He started to kiss my hand.

I pulled it away. "Only with Louie."

He grabbed my hand again and brought it up to his lips, making eye contact over my knuckles. "Yes, my love, with Louie."

"Okay." I smiled.

"Good, but for now, I must bid you adieu."

"Not today, Shane. I really want to spend the day with you."

"Sorry, but duty calls."

Since we arrived at Essex House, Shane and I had spent fewer than a dozen complete days together, and that particular day proved to be no exception. He used the quick recovery, associated with traveling within a shorter time frame, to take care of H&S business in the 1920s. And I was left to await his return.

"No!" I cried.

"Sorry, sweetheart, but the stock market is going to crash soon, and many Evergreen clients are hoping to manipulate the economy for their own gain. I need to make sure they fail."

"And how do you do that?" I asked. Shane seldom discussed his business, so I was eager to take advantage of the rare opportunity; if for no other reason than to keep him from leaving so soon.

"Oh, I wouldn't want to bore you."

"Go right ahead and bore me. I insist."

"All right then. First, I make friends with them, then proceed to plant a little seed of doubt. Evergreen doesn't have the research behind them that we do. As they say, the devil is in the details."

A flash of jealously suddenly entered my brain and left my mouth before I could stop it. "Do you have to woo their eligible daughters as well?"

He leaned across the arm of my chair and turned my face toward his. Then he produced a ring from his pocket and placed it on his finger. "I never travel without this."

I looked from the ring to him and felt my face flush with embarrassment. It wasn't the one I gave to Dell, but it seemed to hold the same meaning. "I'm sorry, I—"

He stopped me with a kiss. "At least I know you care. Want to accompany me to the door?"

We stood together and walked, hand in hand, to the front door.

Once we reached it, he pulled me into his arms and held me close. "I miss you every time I have to leave you alone."

"So just bring me with you."

He shook his head. "Sorry, love, but it's far too dangerous."

"And it's not dangerous for you?"

"I've tried it a time or two." He winked at me and proceeded to kiss me so deeply that I thought I would drown.

When he finally let me go, I felt weak.

"We'll visit the speakeasy when I return…with Louie." With that, he smiled and opened the door, revealing Perry and the Ghost at the bottom of the stairs. "Be good." He touched my check and turned to walk down the stairs.

How can I be bad when you just took the only other ride? The roadster was undergoing some kind of maintenance that would take several days. Without the limo, I was left without any form of transportation. Instead, I spent my morning working on my tan by the pool. By lunchtime, I was sufficiently brown and completely stir crazy, so I went in search of the next best thing to Maude—Louie.

He was a shark from the word go and couldn't resist a game of anything involving cards or gambling. When I was young, Maude had taught me how to play most of the fashionable games of her time, including her own version of mahjong that involved two players. So, with a box of tiles in my hand and a few coins in my pouch, as well as a deck of cards in case a different game was requested, I hunted down my opponent.

After an extensive search of the house, I finally found him outside, sitting in a row of roses and staring at an especially dark red one. "Louie, what are you doing?"

He looked up at me with glazed-over eyes and continued to stare as if looking through a window.

"Louie?"

"She's only fifteen," he said.

"Excuse me?"

"Maude. She is only fifteen."

"Okay. And?"

"I'm twenty-seven," he said, his eyes finally clearing.

"Oh." *I thought you were much younger.* I stared at the ground briefly before continuing, "Louie, that's only twelve years."

"Yes, but she's only *fifteen*!"

"You love her, don't you?"

"Of course, but…she's…only…fifteen."

I wanted to argue my point but couldn't get beyond the anguished look on his face. "I guess that's a little too young."

"And a little too illegal in California."

We didn't speak for a few seconds, so I sat on the ground next to him. "I thought you already knew."

He shook his head. "I never bothered to ask. I just assumed she was eighteen."

"How did you find out?"

Louie reached in his pocket and produced a ring. "I was going to ask her to marry me this morning, but I didn't make it past her father. I sought his permission out of courtesy, but he exploded and threatened to have me arrested." He twirled the ring between his thumb and index finger. "I thought he was just being overly protective, until he informed me of her age."

"Oh, no. Was Maude there?"

"Yes. She translated."

I had almost forgotten that she didn't know he spoke English, but I knew it wasn't the time to remind him of that or his promise to tell her. Instead, I covered my mouth with my hand, then slowly lowered it to my lap. "I'm so sorry, Louie."

"Me too. I'm no cradle-robber."

"Are you from the future?" I asked.

He nodded. "I was born in 2035."

"Doesn't that make Maude the cradle-robber?"

He didn't respond to my attempt at humor.

"I guess marrying someone that young in your time isn't as common as it is in Maude's."

"It's not." He continued to stare at the ring.

"It's beautiful. May I?" I asked.

He handed it to me, and I held it up to the sunlight. Its

single caret gleamed within an intricately carved gold setting. "It looks really old. Has it been in your family a long time?"

"It was my mother's and hers before her, going back several generations. Mama gave it to me before she passed away. I always pictured my wife wearing it. Maude's so tiny, I'm not sure if it would even fit her. Can you try it?" he asked.

I slid the ring onto my pinky finger. "Her ring finger is probably close to this size, and it fits perfectly."

We both stared at my finger.

"Don't hold her age against her, Louie. What you two have is ageless and timeless, similar to this." I removed the ring and placed it back into his hand.

He closed his fingers around it and stared at his fist.

Besides, I've always wanted an Uncle Louie. I kissed him on the cheek and left him to his thoughts. *Poor Maude...and today, of all days, I don't have a car.*

The next few hours dragged along slower than all the previous ones combined. Fortunately, Shane arrived as the sun was setting, just in time to save me from another boring game of solitaire in the living room.

"Let's see. What was that line? Oh, yes. 'You're not wearing *that* out, are you?'" he said.

I turned to see Shane standing behind me, holding a large rectangular box.

"What's that?"

"Well, hello dear. Glad to see you too!" he said sarcastically.

"Hi, you." I offered.

He leaned down, and I gave him a quick peck on the cheek.

"Now, fork over the box!" I said, reaching for it.

But he pulled away, stepping back and holding it above his head. "Who says it's for you?"

I stood from my chair and walked closer to him, arriving within inches of his face. "And who says it's not?"

With his free arm, he closed the gap between us and filled the next few minutes with his unrestrained form of affection in which breathing was always optional.

Eventually, he lowered the box into my waiting hands.

Shane held the bottom as I eagerly opened the lid and let it drop to the floor. Beneath layers of tissue paper, I found a work of art. It was a black dress made of silk georgette with silk-thread fringe along the bottom of the diagonally cut skirt panels. The fringe swung in all directions as I pulled the masterpiece from the box and held it against my body.

"Well? What do you think?" he asked.

"I absolutely love it, Shane!" I spun around with the dress held against me, looking down at the fringe that swished with my every movement.

Shane smiled at my reaction.

"Where did this come from?"

"It's French."

"Ooh-la-la!" I continued to spin until I was dizzy.

His smile grew broader. "Try it on."

"Don't mind if I do." I raced upstairs and wasted no time enlisting the assistance of Midge to help me don the dress and find a suitable pair of shoes, stockings, and purse to match. It didn't take long for us to complete the look, after which I stood to admire myself in my mirror.

"Oh, miss," Midge said to my reflection, "you look beautiful!"

"Thank you. This dress is just amazing." I took one more

look, then descended the stairs to an awaiting Shane.

When he saw me, he just shook his head. "You're not going *anywhere* in that."

I looked down at the dress, then back up at him. "Why not?"

"Because I'll have to fight off every man in the place with a big stick."

"Well, you'd better find one to bring with you, because I'm not changing!"

He kissed me on the cheek. "I'll be quick."

As usual, I watched him ascend the stairs from my spot on the marble floor. *Nice!* His backside never seemed to disappoint.

Once he was out of sight, I continued to admire my outfit in the mirror next to the door. The swishing sound of the skirt echoed in the marble-clad entryway as I tried to see how horizontal I could make the fringe.

Just as I turned to view the back of my dress in the mirror, the door opened, and a hysterical Maude entered behind a red-faced Louie. Their entrance drew the attention of several staff members, who discreetly disappeared as soon as they saw the scene unfolding before them.

"What happened?" I asked.

"My father was furious," Maude cried.

"Are you okay?"

She shook her head and ran into my arms, and Louie just stood helplessly behind her, staring at the floor.

When she finally calmed down, I walked her over to the couch and joined her on one of the cushions. "Maude?"

Her tear-filled eyes met mine.

"What happened?" I asked.

"Louie came to visit me."

I stared at Louie, who was now sitting silently on the couch next to her. *I guess fifteen wasn't that young after all. You certainly wasted no time getting Perry to drive you there after Shane came home, did you?* I admired his determination, but Maude's sniffing drew my attention back to her. I shook my head. "And your father was home?"

She nodded. "Yes."

"He was upset?"

"No. He was furious. I've never seen him so red."

Louie handed her a handkerchief.

"I said such awful things to him." She blew her nose before continuing, "I told him that he is stuck in the past and that Mama isn't coming back. Then I held Louie's hand and said that if I can't marry him, I would just as soon join her." She blew her nose again, then added, "He just sort of collapsed into his chair and put his head in his hands. I wanted to go over to him and hug him, but I knew that if I did, my courage would be gone, so I just left him there. Oh, I'm such a horrible daughter! What have I done?" She proceeded to renew her tears and employed the use of Louie's waiting arms instead of mine.

Maude was so loud that I didn't even hear Shane until he was standing next to the couch, dressed for a night on the town. "What's happened?" he asked.

I got up and stepped outside with Shane, so I could give him all the sordid details.

He spent a considerable amount of time staring off toward the sound of the ocean in the darkness before finally asking, "Now what?"

"Right now, Maude needs a friend."

"Great. Can't Louie be her friend so that we can go out?"

"You must be joking."

I waited for him to acknowledge me, but he didn't reply, so I returned to the living room to console Maude, only to find her and Louie kissing on the couch. I felt like some kind of voyeur or third wheel, but when I tried to turn away, I found Shane standing mere inches from me.

"I'm sorry," he said.

I nodded but was growing less understanding by the minute.

Shane turned me toward him and put his arms around my waist. "I think they might have it under control."

I looked at the couch and the two consoling one another and knew he was right. Without further discussion, I walked to the couch and cleared my throat.

Both blushed at being caught.

"I realize it might not be the most appropriate time to bring this up, but we were just on our way out." I looked at Maude before continuing, "We don't have to go, Maude."

She smiled up at me from the couch. "Yes, you do." Then she added, "Where are you going?"

I looked at Shane, then back at her. I had wanted Louie's approval of the place first, but I couldn't lie to Maude, so I tried to downplay my answer by saying it quickly. "I'm not sure. It's some kind of speakeasy."

Maude immediately clapped her hands and bounced on the couch cushion. "Oh! May we come along?"

Dang! "Oh, Maude, I don't know if that's such a good idea. It's really up to Louie, and I don't know if—."

Before I could finish trying to talk her out of it, she turned to him and put her arms around his neck, and they began to communicate in their own special language. When they were finished, Louie looked from me to Maude and reluctantly nodded.

"That's swell!" She clapped her hands again and jumped from the couch. "I need to change."

Within thirty minutes, the four of us were appropriately attired and loaded into the limousine. The pink dress I bought for Maude from Shaver's finally made its debut. It flattered her tiny shape but seemed to reveal more than Louie was comfortable sharing; sweat rolled down the side of his face whenever he looked her direction.

This is going to be an interesting night.

In another half hour, we were quickly exiting the limo and making our way into the entrance of a tiny bookstore.

Shane strolled confidently to the man behind the counter and leaned close to whisper something to him.

The man walked to the front of the store and turned his "Open" sign to the "Closed" side and locked the door. Then he escorted us to the back and removed a book from the shelf. When he did, the entire shelf, books and all, slid out of the way, exposing a large door.

The only thing that made the gray-colored door resemble anything other than a concrete wall was a covered rectangular opening that occupied a portion of the door at eye level. The owner of the bookstore knocked on the opening cover, and it slid to the side, revealing a pair of dark, beady eyes. They looked from the storeowner to each of us before the cover slid back into place. At that point, the door made a loud noise, similar to the movement of a dead bolt, and slowly swung inward.

Shane thanked the store owner and led the way into the

darkness on the other side. Once we were inside, the door closed with a *thump*, making us all jump. Regardless, no one spoke.

I felt for Shane's hand in the dark and hoped that I wasn't holding Louie's as the doorman struck a match and lit a candle. In the semidarkness, I noticed Shane's hand in mine. *Phew!*

"Over there." The doorman pointed the candle toward a second door, which Shane led us to and opened.

Beyond the door was a world, I was certain, none of us could have ever imagined. We stood at the top of a giant staircase that opened into an area the size of an enormous ballroom. A full jazz band played at the opposite end before a crowded dance floor. A bar occupied the right side of the room and housed hundreds of bottles of alcohol, all lined up on glass shelves within reach of one of the many bartenders who scampered to and fro, making and serving drinks. Booths and tables dominated the left portion of the room and were filled with cigarette-smoking people whose laughter hovered in the air as much as their smoke did. In the center of the room, dozens of felt-covered tables occupied the time and pocketbooks of dozens of well-dressed men and women. It reminded me of one of the smaller casinos in Las Vegas.

"How does something such as this exist without anyone knowing about it?" I asked.

Shane just looked at me and laughed. "Sweetheart, it looks as if a few hundred people already do."

I felt pretty blonde at that moment but tried to recover my pride by adding, "No, I mean the authorities."

"Oh. They probably just pay them off. Regardless, let's leave these stairs and explore."

FOR THE LOVE OF MAUDE

We slowly descended into the abyss before us, but unlike the house parties we had been attending, no one seemed to notice our arrival.

Shane led us to the bar and crowded out another couple in order to gain the attention of one of the bartenders. "Champagne and four glasses!"

His request made me realize that I had forgotten to bring a clean glass from home. *Oh well. Worst-case scenario, I'll just drink out of the bottle!*

The bartender leaned his elbows on the bar and looked Shane directly in the eyes. "It'll cost you, sir."

"I can cover it."

The bartender motioned for a large, blocky man behind the bar to bring the bottle, and stepped aside to help another customer. When the man returned, the bartender showed Shane the bottle and handed it back to the other man. "You need to pay first."

"Fine. How much?"

"That one's a $500 bottle."

Without even flinching, Shane reached into his pocket and produced the payment.

In seconds, the man holding the bottle walked around the bar and escorted us to one of the large booths. Although another group was already occupying it, they immediately left, and a second man quickly wiped the table and crescent-shaped seat before offering them to us. Maude and I sat in the middle with Louie and Shane flanking us.

Once the bottle was uncorked and the champagne was poured, I finally leaned over to Shane. "What just happened?"

"A friend told me that if you order an expensive bottle, you receive a booth." He grinned at me. "I'm glad it worked.

I don't prefer standing."

I just shook my head.

Then, he raised his glass toward Maude and me. "I want to propose a toast to the beautiful women in our lives. May their presence always surround us!" Then he smiled at Louie. "*Salute di belle donne!*" He received three cheers and one "*Salute!*" before we tried the bubbling liquid.

It was so horrible that I had to spit it back into my glass, which I soon noticed was covered in various shades of lipstick, none of which I was wearing.

Maude did the same thing and looked at me in disgust. "What is this?" she asked.

I leaned closer to her. "Whatever it is, it's not champagne." I thought of the glasses I'd consumed at the Stellman's party and shook my head.

She looked at her glass and shook her head as well.

Shane and Louie had also returned their drinks to their glasses, and Shane was wiping his mouth with a handkerchief. "Sorry. I'll order us something else," Shane said. "Any requests?"

"What did your friend suggest?" I asked.

"Gin."

"Then I'll try the rum…in a clean glass, if possible."

"Maude? For you?" he asked.

She looked at the table.

"Could you please see if they have a pop…in a bottle?" I suggested.

Then Shane looked at Louie. "*Vino?*"

Louie nodded.

I leaned closer to Maude, "When Shane returns, do you want to dance?"

FOR THE LOVE OF MAUDE

"Oh, very much!"

We spent the next few minutes surveying the boisterous throng before us. Girls in skimpy dresses flashed their skin and beads in front of us, while their dates scrambled to keep them from becoming interested in the other men around them. Louie fidgeted in his seat, his eyes traveling from the crowd to Maude, who was mesmerized by the scene.

The rum and warm, flat pop that Shane delivered to us were only slightly less disgusting than the champagne, so Maude and I decided to skip the drinks and make our way to the dance floor.

I gave Shane a kiss on the cheek. "We'll be back. Maude and I want to try out our dance moves."

"You don't care for the rum either?" he asked, smiling.

I shook my head. "Care to join us?"

Shane stood so that we could exit the booth. "No, thanks, but don't be too long. I fear Louie might have a heart attack."

I looked at Louie and tried to draw his attention, but his eyes were glued on Maude, who was attempting to pull me in the direction of the dance floor. He said something to her in Italian, but either she didn't hear him or just chose to ignore him. Regardless, she succeeded in leading me toward the jazz band.

One song led to the next and before we knew it, the house lights were flickering to warn us of last call. I grabbed Maude's hand and nearly dragged her away from the dance floor. Before we could reach the booth, however, Louie was already bounding across the floor to meet us. He said something to Maude in Italian, and she immediately burst into tears.

Unfortunately for Shane, I spent the remaining hours of

darkness in my room, listening to Maude and the reasons why her current situation was a grave mistake.

As the sun began to rise, Louie knocked on my door, bearing flowers and apologies. Then Maude left me to gain what little sleep I could find. By the time I awoke, Shane had already left the house.

After that experience, the four of us visited every speakeasy we could find along the West Coast. Louie introduced me to the world of fine wines and Maude continued to look for drinkable pop and a way to dance the Charleston without losing her boyfriend in the process. It was an uphill battle that she started to win until one evening, when an unexpected visitor showed up at the Essex House door.

Maude and I were dressing for the night when Midge came to us in a panic. "Miss...uh..." She'd forgotten what to call me, so she just chose to avoid it entirely.

I was running behind and was too preoccupied to notice the urgency in her voice at first. "Midge, do you prefer the pink or the lilac shoes with this dress?" I held up both pair against my dress.

"Miss Maude has a visitor at the front door."

I looked at Maude, then Midge. "Who is it?"

"Her father, miss."

Maude's hands flew to her face, and she turned pale beneath them.

"Please tell him that we'll be down in a minute. And Midge...?

"Yes, miss?"

"Please inform Oscar of his arrival." I offered a wink, guessing she might be having trouble remembering Shane's new name as well.

"Oh, right, miss. Oscar." She nodded and mumbled to herself as she walked to the door.

As soon as she left the room, I turned my attention to Maude, who was now sitting on my bed.

"I can't face him," she said, her shaky voice almost squeaking in fear.

"Yes, you can. I'll be with you, and so will Shane."

"But I...He—"

"Maude, he came here for a reason. Please meet with him. He's your father."

She didn't reply, so I took her by the hand and led her into the hallway. When we reached the top of the stairs, we saw my great-great-grandfather surrounded by Shane, Louie, Perry, and several other staff members. The poor guy's options were limited at best.

"Be strong," I whispered in Maude's ear.

By the time we reached the bottom step, I no longer had to hold onto Maude's hand, figuratively or otherwise; she was already taking my advice. With her shoulders back and her chin held high, she said, "Hello, Father."

"Elizabeth, I've come to take you home."

"No, Father. This is my home."

He looked at Louie. "Have you gone against my wishes and left the state to marry this—"

"Don't say it, Papa!"

He paused for a moment, then continued, "Are you married?"

"No."

"So you're living in sin?"

"No! I'm living with Daisy."

He gave me such a disgusted look I thought he would spit

on the floor at my feet. Instead, he replied, "You mean, Blanche?"

"I mean, Daisy!" She proudly looped her arm through mine.

"And your honor is still intact?"

"I said we weren't married or living in sin, Papa. My honor is just as it's always been."

We watched as he calmed himself, staring at the floor and eventually at Louie. "I appreciate the respect you showed me in asking for my daughter's hand in marriage. I didn't understand the depth of your feelings or my daughter's." He looked at Maude, then back at Louie. "I apologize for my rudeness, and will give my blessing on one condition."

Maude quickly translated her father's words. "What condition, Papa?"

"That you come home with me and live there until your wedding day."

Maude smiled as she relayed her father's words to Louie. He remained unmoved, though, like a statue at the park. I half-expected a bird to fly in through the door and land—or worse—on his head.

"Excuse us, Papa." Maude walked up to Louie and took him by the hand. She led him outside, where they sat on one of the chairs by the pool.

I didn't know what to say to the man in front of me, who was also my great-plus grandfather. I realized that he had lost his wife and didn't want to also lose his daughter, but I had no idea what kind of conversation to make with him. Talking about the weather or the price of wheat didn't seem to be worthwhile, and I certainly couldn't tell him I finally understood from whom my mom inherited her nose. Instead, we stood in silence and awaited Maude's return.

When she finally walked back into the house, Maude was alone. "Goodbye, Daisy, and thank you for everything."

I was stunned but returned the hug that she gave me.

"And Oscar, thank you too." She gave him a hug as well, and Shane followed with a peck on the cheek. Then, just like that, Maude walked out the door with her father and didn't look back.

CHAPTER FOURTEEN

After our fifth night without Maude and any form of social activity, I was going completely stir crazy. The speakeasies lost their appeal without my favorite dance partner, and Louie spent most of his time visiting Maude at her house, so Shane and I resorted to our previous form of entertainment—the house party.

The Monroe's began in a fashion similar to the other uneventful ones we had attended. Although the home, its selection of bootlegged and otherwise illegal alcohol, and staff-served trays of hors d'oeuvres were far superior to others we had recently experienced, the stuffy guest list was nearly identical. Fortunately, Shane didn't leave my side. He offered his arm for me to hang from as we scanned the room for possible excitement. I didn't see any.

"This is boring," I whispered in Shane's ear.

Suddenly, he spun me in a complete circle and drew me into his arms. "Shall we spice things up a bit?" Without waiting for a reply, Shane dipped me backward dramatically and pulled me upright into a long, passionate kiss.

The crowd seemed to share a collective gasp as their conversations ceased. By the time we were finished, the only noticeable sound in the room was coming from the jazz band playing on the opposite side.

Shane smiled. "That wasn't boring, now was it?"

I just shook my head. "No, darling, not boring at all."

He stared at my lips for several seconds and was preparing for a second act, when an older gentleman in a black tuxedo tapped him on the shoulder. Shane turned to find the man standing behind him, wearing a nervous smile.

The man cleared his throat before speaking. "Excuse me, but we haven't been formally introduced. I'm Charles Monroe."

Shane released me and offered the man his hand. "Very pleased to meet you, Mr. Monroe. I'm Oscar Krump, and this is, uh…this is Blanche."

The man stared at Shane's outstretched hand, then at me, finally resting his dark eyes on Shane without shaking his hand. "I'm sorry, Mr. Krump. There are many things of which I do not approve, yet I endure them for the sake of those around me. However, I cannot ignore siblings behaving in this fashion, especially when it involves a child." Mr. Monroe shot a sad look in my direction before continuing, "If I were a younger man, I would challenge you to a dual." His eyes slowly left mine and concentrated an almost venomous hold on Shane. "I see many things in my profession—horrible things—but this, Mr. Krump, is intolerable. Why, I have a good mind to—"

Shane finally spoke. "Now, now, Mr. Monroe, we don't need to resort to that."

Our host ignored Shane and walked over to where I was standing. He reached forward and took my chin in his hand. "You remind me of my little Sara. The influenza took her from us." A small tear rolled down his cheek and onto his lapel.

"No brother has the right to take what doesn't belong to him."

His words played havoc on my conscience. *What are we doing to Dell?*

I felt the urge to distance myself from his words, as if more space between us would make them less true. Unfortunately, I didn't realize we were within inches from three, wide marble steps that led into an open living area. One step would have caused me to stumble and recover quickly, but the other two steps made such a feat impossible. My last memory was of falling toward the marble floor below.

* * *

When I finally opened my eyes, I was lying in an enormous bed beneath a blue velvet canopy. It was daylight, but the room seemed to have missed that subtle detail, opting instead for a cave-like ambiance, complete with dark red wallpaper and gilded French furniture. It was obnoxious. I felt as if I were about to be the victim in an old horror flick. Fortunately, as soon as my panic subsided, I realized that Midge was sitting on the bed next to me.

"Oh, miss, we sure are in a pickle!" she cried.

I felt the aching knot on my head. "I guess it doesn't pay to be clumsy."

"No, it's not that, miss."

"Then what?"

"Oh, dear…"

"Midge!"

"It's Mr. Oscar."

"What about him?"

She looked around before continuing, "Mr. Monroe and several other men...Well...You see, Mr. Oscar didn't stand a chance."

"Is he okay?"

"The doctors say he'll make a full recovery."

"Where is he?"

She looked at her hands. "In the hospital, miss."

"Oh, not another one!" I pictured Dell and Shane in twin hospital beds, separated only by a nightstand. *These Johanns really know how to break themselves!*

I scanned the strange room. "Midge, are we still at the Monroe residence?"

"Yes."

"Why?"

"That's the other part, miss. You see, Mr. Monroe wants to adopt you."

"Excuse me?"

She simply nodded and continued to stare at her hands.

"We have to escape, Midge."

She leaned closer and whispered into my ear, "There is a guard posted outside your door and one in the garden beneath your window."

I flopped back onto the pillow and stared at the enormous canopy above me. *Great, Shane. Why did you have to make me your sister?*

"Midge." I whispered. "Has anyone been contacted?"

She offered a confused look, then started to wring her hands.

"Midge?"

The look on her face was riddled with fear. "We're in so

much trouble, miss."

I exhaled loudly and sat up. "We'll worry about that later. First, we need to leave here."

"Mr. Johann is already downstairs, miss, telling tall tales and trying to convince Mr. Monroe to change his mind."

"Johann's *here*?"

"Yes, miss, and I've never seen him so angry."

"Okay, I guess I'll worry about that later too." I pulled back the covers, swung my legs out of bed and placed my feet on the floor. At that moment, the nightgown I was wearing caught my attention and held it there. *I don't even want to know how this thing found itself on me*! But I quickly changed my mind. "When did they send for you, Midge?"

She followed my gaze to the nightgown. "I was summoned this morning, miss...and you were already in bed."

Great. I couldn't stop picturing Mr. Monroe dressing my floppy, unconscious body as if I were a Sara doll—or a similar tribute to his deceased daughter. *Rainbows and unicorns, Em, rainbows and unicorns!*

I quickly changed the subject. "Midge, do you know where my clothes are?"

"No, but I brought you a fresh change, miss." She handed me a small parcel.

"Thank you." I took the package and my pride into the adjoining restroom so I could bathe and don my clean outfit.

When I was finished, the burly man who guarded the door helped Midge and I traverse the halls and stairways of the monster of a house. I felt like a rat in a maze. Fortunately, the guard was familiar with the labyrinth-like layout and assisted us in reaching the first floor before Christmas. He escorted us into the library and left us to the angry stares of

FOR THE LOVE OF MAUDE

Johann and Mr. Monroe.

Johann was the first to rise and greet me. "Blanche, my dear, sweet granddaughter, I was so very worried." He then pulled me into a hug and whispered into my ear, "You and I have a lot to talk about, my dear."

My knees went weak, so I quickly located a chair and practically fell into it.

Mr. Monroe hurried to my side. "Are you all right, dear?"

I smiled at his concerned face. "Yes, sir. I'm just not used to all of this." I gestured to the two men.

"Of course. We just want what's best for you."

"Well, if that is the case, Mr. Monroe, I would greatly appreciate being able to go home with my grandfather."

His face dropped and his concerned look was replaced by one of sadness. "Is that what you wish, my dear?"

I nodded.

"But I can give you so much more."

"No, sir, you wouldn't be giving anything to *me*...exactly."

He suddenly looked into my eyes.

"You would be giving it to Sara, but I'm not your daughter, and I never will be—I'm Blanche."

He turned away.

"I'm truly sorry about your daughter. You obviously loved her very much, but I have a grandfather who loves me too. You can trust him to take care of me, Mr. Monroe."

He looked at Johann, then at me. "I believe I can."

I tried to smile, but his sad face made me reconsider.

"I promise you one thing, my dear. If I ever see that brother of yours, I personally guarantee he will never walk again."

"No, sir, you won't see him again—I promise."

He nodded. "So do I."

I felt a chill run through me. *Who is this guy?*

Mr. Monroe kissed me on the cheek and walked over to Johann to shake his hand. "I'll leave you two."

"Thank you, Mr. Monroe, for taking care of my dear Blanche."

"Second chances only come around once, if at all. Make sure your grandson knows that."

"I will, sir…and thank you, again."

As soon as Mr. Monroe left the room, Johann hurried to my side and quickly pulled me to standing. "We go now!"

My feet were barely touching the floor as Johann escorted me to the waiting Perry; Midge had to run to keep up.

"Midge, you ride up front!" Johann barked at the poor maid.

Speechless, she occupied the seat next to Perry's and shut the door behind her.

Perry had barely closed our door before Johann unleashed on me. "Do you realize the jeopardy you have put this company in?

"Johann, I—"

"I talk, you listen!" he snapped. "Your little escapade with Shane has cost us dearly. It drew more attention to you than you can possibly imagine. Incest? The times were changing, but that is something society will never accept—never!"

In an instant, the man I met at The Strand was gone, replaced by his finger-shaking, evil twin. I was so belittled that I felt microscopic.

"Mr. Monroe is a very wealthy and powerful man. His bootlegging empire spans the entire coast. You two have been mingling in society without sufficient research or regard for the consequences of your actions. We cannot even afford to be on his radar, yet one of his cars is following us right now."

I turned to look out the back window, but Johann's words stopped me in mid-turn.

"We will return to the house, and you will pack your things. This will take months or years to rectify. I cannot have you interfering any longer!" His face turned a different shade of scary with each word that escaped his clenched teeth. "Louie will escort you to your next destination and will remain vigilant."

At that point, I couldn't hold my tongue any longer. "But what about Maude?"

"She's the least of my worries."

"Well, she's *my* greatest concern."

His eyes burned through me as he responded, "You should have considered that before you and Shane made such a display of yourselves."

"I told you that I needed your help." I reminded him.

"As I said in our last meeting, only you can help yourself. As for Shane, he has no excuse. He has certainly received enough training to know better than to behave in this manner; especially in public. Unfortunately, I didn't anticipate the fire you and Shane would ignite." He shook his head and stared out the window. "I never should have brought him to you. I should have known better."

Silence filled the car as we drew closer to Essex House.

"What will happen to him?" I finally asked.

Johann's eyes met mine. "He'll go back to his time."

"Will I even be able to say goodbye?"

He shook his head.

I closed my eyes and fought the cramp in my throat. "Please?"

Several minutes passed, filled with my pleading looks, until he finally shook his head again and exhaled. "Perry, please take us to the hospital."

Perry nodded his reply and turned the car in the direction he was requested. He zigzagged his way along, finally losing our tail. When we arrived, Johann immediately ushered me into the hospital. After dropping us off, Perry quickly pulled up between two delivery vans in an effort to hide the limousine from anyone else who might be pursuing us.

Then, Johann escorted me to Shane's room and stood outside the door as I slowly entered. Shane was lying in a white iron hospital bed, swollen and covered with cuts and bruises. His left eye was completely closed, and the right was just a slit beneath a mountain of red and purple. Casts covered his arms and right leg, which was in traction. I hardly recognized him.

I occupied the chair beside him and kissed the slightly exposed fingertips of his left hand.

"Morning, sweetheart," he mumbled.

The sound of his voice made me jump, and seeing him so helpless in bed made me regret many things, including the times I snapped at him for calling me that.

"I thought you were asleep," I said.

"What? And miss seeing you?"

When he offered a smile, I noticed a vacancy in the front tooth department. I tried not to stare but failed miserably.

"They sure worked me over, didn't they?"

"Oh, Shane, I'm so sorry!"

He caught my hand with his fingertips and wouldn't let

go. "No, *I'm* sorry. If I hadn't made you my sister, this never would have happened."

"Well, cutting my hair didn't help matters."

"No, I suppose not." He stared at me through the slit in his eye. "You probably already know they're sending me back."

I nodded.

"It's probably for the best," he added.

"Are you joking?"

He attempted another smile. "We don't exactly bring out the best in each other."

I closed my eyes and tried to block out his words. At that moment, I realized that although he wasn't the man I married, he also wasn't someone I wanted to live without. "Shane, I love you so much. I don't care if I have to go back in time and wear a corset for the rest of my life. I want to be with you. Please don't leave me!" I couldn't fight the tears as they poured down my face.

A second later, I felt a hand on my shoulder and turned to see Johann standing there. "It's time," he said.

I turned back to Shane and followed a single tear that was rolling down his cheek.

"I love you too, sweetheart, and if I could leave this bed and take you away with me, I would do so without hesitation." His fingertips squeezed mine. "I've never felt so helpless, but it was my own doing. Now, all I can do is watch you leave and love you for the rest of my life."

"Say goodbye," Johann said from behind me.

I shook my head and bent down to kiss Shane's fingers.

"Sweetheart, there's no other way," Shane said.

I knew he was right, but I ignored him.

He pulled his arm away from me and placed it on his stomach. "Why do I always have to be the strong one?" he asked.

I looked up to see Shane's new attempt at a smile, but his toothless grin made me laugh between sobs. Then he stuck his tongue sideways through the gap.

"Stop!" I cried. "You look ridiculous."

"Yet you look beautiful."

Johann reached down and slowly lifted me from the chair by my arm. "Goodbye, Shane," he said quietly.

"Goodbye, Johann," Shane said. Then he looked at me. "Em…"

I couldn't speak and struggled to see him through the tears.

"My lips aren't too sore," he added.

Johann released my arm, allowing me to reach down and kiss Shane gently on the lips. He tried to kiss back but winced instead.

"This is looking awfully familiar." I thought of the last time I saw Dell and the similar kiss we shared.

"Well, at least we have that much in common."

I shook my head and looked down at his broken body. "I love you, Shane."

"I love you too, Emily."

Without waiting for another round of tearful goodbyes, Johann placed my hand on his forearm and escorted me out of the room and down the hallway.

I thought my heart would break.

The ride to the house was nearly silent, with the exception of my sobs in the back seat. When we arrived at Essex House, the staff was on edge as Midge flew through the house, trying to gather my things into trunks that one of the men had hoisted up the stairs on a dolly.

I was useless and spent the entire time sitting at the table outside, staring out at the ocean in search of an elusive answer or two.

The sound of a paper bag being deposited next to me finally gained my attention. I looked at the bag, then the person standing next to it.

"I packed a few things for you to eat once your appetite returns," Chef Jacques said.

I tried to smile but was met with a new round of tears instead.

He nodded and patted me on the shoulder. "I understand. I will never forget you or the kindness you have shown me." With that, he turned to walk away, but I quickly rose from my chair and touched him on the sleeve.

"Chef Jacques…"

"Yes?"

"Thank you too." I put my arms around his neck and hugged him tightly.

My reaction seemed to surprise him at first, but he soon returned the affection. "You are a remarkable woman, and I wish you nothing but the best."

"Thank you, Chef. Your food surpasses all others in any time, including my own…and you make the best pastries I have ever tasted."

He released me from our hug and stepped back to adjust his white chef coat. "I am a new man! *Au revoir!*"

I noticed the familiar skip in his step as he walked away.

Finally, I said my goodbyes to the ocean and went back into the house, carrying my bag of goodies.

The activity that surrounded me was both noisy and hurried, but I felt detached, still struggling with my own internal drama. I walked toward the stairway, only stopping once to grab the newspaper that was resting on a table by the door.

I ascended the stairs amidst the bustling staff members who weaved around me and each other on their way to their next task. When I entered the bedroom, I found Midge in the middle of packing several trunks with my recent purchases. "Midge?"

She stopped and looked absently at me, as if I weren't there.

"Do we have a trunk to spare?"

Her confusion was almost audible, but I didn't wait for her to find her voice.

"I want to send some of these dresses to Maude. They're hers."

With her open mouth and wide eyes suddenly competing for space on her face, Midge looked as if she might lose something vital and lapse into a coma—all without speaking.

I walked over and touched her on the sleeve. "Midge, *I* will pack them. Please, just tell me if we have an extra trunk."

Her dazed look didn't leave her face; she simply shook her head.

"Okay, well, please just don't pack those dresses." I pointed to the part of the closet that held Maude's things.

She nodded and went back to her other packing.

Dang, she could sure use a few lessons in multitasking. I shook my head. *She's in good company, though.* I thought of my first maid, Rose, and the frantic experience she had endured, preparing me and my things to be transported to the past for the first time.

FOR THE LOVE OF MAUDE

Fortunately, I found one of the men who had delivered the trunks to my room earlier, and he knew of another I could use. When it arrived, the giant trunk brought a smile to my face. It was the same one that was locked and stored in Nana Rosie and Papa Bob's attic—the Maude trunk, minus her name and the travel stickers she would later add.

I ran to it and did what I had wanted to do since I was four—I opened it. Of course the trunk was empty, but it did not disappoint. A removable, divided tray designed to hold toiletries and other necessities slid along the top portion of the trunk. The interior was lined with a floral fabric and looked as if it were large enough to sleep two comfortably. I easily fit the dresses inside with plenty of room to spare. I left the lid open as I located a pen, paper, and envelope, then walked with my writing supplies, as well as the newspaper from earlier, to the table that stood on my balcony. I found the date on the newspaper and began to write:

Sunday, August 22, 1926

Dear Maude,

I'm sure you know by now I am no longer allowed to live in your time. I truly feel horrible about not saying goodbye, but we have to leave in a hurry. Shane and I attended the Monroe party, where we proceeded to act scandalously in front of the other guests. They didn't approve. Worse, I reminded Mr. Monroe of Sara, the daughter he lost to the influenza, so he wanted to "save" me from my "evil" brother. Fortunately, Johann arrived to keep me from being adopted by Mr. Monroe, but he sure wasn't happy about it. The attention Shane and I drew as siblings has hurt the company, and Johann didn't want to take any more chances. I'm not sure where they are going to send me, but I'm certain if they have a safe house in Siberia, I might be calling Russia home.

I'm so sorry about Louie having to come with me. I hope someday you two will be able to be together again and that you can both forgive me. I love you, Maude, and I will miss you.

These dresses are for you. I imagine you may never be allowed to wear them again, but maybe they will remind you of the fun we had.

Goodbye for now, Maude, and please take care of my favorite aunt for me.

Love,

Emily

***P.S.** Louie is going to tell you something that will make communication between you two much easier. Please don't be too upset with him (or me). Also, that will be a good time to let him know who you really are—it's okay if you tell only him. Thanks for keeping it a secret, even from Louie. I realize it wasn't easy.*

I didn't ask anyone's permission for Maude to reveal her identity to Louie, and I didn't care. *Johann and Shane seem to know about her...why shouldn't Louie?*

I fanned the letter in the air to allow the ink to dry before folding it and placing it in the envelope. I addressed the envelope to Maude, then rested it and the newspaper on top of the dresses in the trunk. I closed the lid and went on a hunt for Louie.

When I found him, he was clearly not himself. He had forgotten his Italian entirely and was yelling at everyone around him in English, turning simple tasks into complicated messes.

"Louie?"

The look on his face pierced straight through me, but my question diverted his attention long enough for the staff he had just been scolding to skirt away in opposite directions.

I tried to ignore the angry look on his face and said, "I have something for you."

He approached me and whispered into my ear, "I don't want anything more from you. You've caused enough damage already."

"Please, Louie. I have a trunk of Maude's clothes that need to be delivered to her."

"Why, so she can be reminded of everything she is losing?" he hissed in my ear.

"No, so you can finally tell her in English that you love her and give her something by which she can remember you."

He pulled a chain from beneath his shirt that bore his mother's engagement ring. "How did you know I haven't given it to her yet?"

"When I didn't see it on her finger after she came to live here, I just assumed you lost your nerve."

He nodded. "Even with her father's permission, I just couldn't—"

"It's a big step." I interrupted.

His anger dissolved, and he stood motionless for a minute, then shook his head. "I'm not supposed to leave Essex House."

"If Johann asks, I'll say that I forgot something at her house. He certainly doesn't want any more loose ends. I'll make sure he doesn't stop you." My voice cracked as I continued, "Please tell her goodbye for me…and please have her read the letter inside the trunk before you leave."

He thought for a second then responded, "Where's the trunk?"

I led him to my room, and he quickly took hold of the trunk and lugged it down the stairs. He and Perry somehow fit it in the Ghost, and I watched as they drove away.

CHAPTER FIFTEEN

Louie and Perry returned to Essex House just in time to load me into the limo.

Johann walked me to the car, opened the door to the back seat, and offered his hand as I found my seat. "Your trunks will follow," he said.

"Aren't you joining me?"

He shook his head. "No, I must attend to Shane." Then, he looked down at me in the car and added, "Please don't take this the wrong way, Emily, but I truly hope I never see you again."

Of course, I did the opposite and took it the wrong way.

Johann anticipated my reaction and countered it before I could even open my mouth. "Whenever I visit you, it means that something has gone wrong. You truly don't want to see me again, Emily."

I attempted to respond, but he closed the door, leaving me speechless instead. He was already walking up the front stairs when we pulled away from the house. Fortunately, I had my Maude suitcase with me that contained the bag Chef Jacques had given me—I hugged the case to me as if it were a doll.

Our trip back to the warehouse through which I arrived, or the "Time Travel Warehouse" as I called it, was anything but uneventful. In the days before freeways, main streets and their intersecting side streets served as substitutes. Without an alternate route available, Perry was forced to wedge our conspicuous limousine between a farm truck with wooden rails and a streetcar in order to shield it from any of Monroe's men who might have been following us.

Lovely view. I looked out my right window and through the truck slats at a dripping pig snout on a squealing creature who, by the sound of it, seemed to know its days were numbered. The red electric streetcar out the other window was too close to reveal its passengers and offered little distraction from the thoughts in my head.

Man, I sure hate making bad choices. I looked at the Maude suitcase and wanted to cry. *I finally become friends with Maude as a teenager, and I proceed to ruin her life.* Then, I studied the back of Louie's head in the seat in front of me and shook my own head. *He's such a great guy, and they're so perfect together. Boy, I've sure made a mess of things. How could Shane and I have been so stupid? We're supposed to observe history, not make it. I'd be in the bordello business for sure if I were still with Evergreen Research. I guess I should be grateful, but my guilty conscience is a punishment all its own.*

A whistle-blowing, white-gloved traffic cop, perched precariously on a wooden box in the middle of an intersection, pointed at Perry and waved him into the open. Louie looked past me, out the rear window. I turned as well, just in time to see a black Packard pull out from behind the truck that had been sheltering us.

Perry turned to Louie. "Monroe?"

FOR THE LOVE OF MAUDE

Louie nodded and faced forward, reaching for the dash in front of him.

Nice. Since I can't be Mr. Monroe's new daughter, I guess I get to join his old one.

I was so engrossed in my thoughts that I hardly noticed how fast the car was traveling until I was rolling along the floorboards like a pinball. Seatbelts weren't standard equipment yet, so I chose to remain on the floor until the car came to a complete and sudden stop, leaving me nearly one with the back of the seat in front of me.

I didn't hear any screaming or smell smoke, so I slowly peeked my head up from my cozy position behind the front seat and surveyed the surroundings. We had finally reached our destination. Perry and Louie were facing forward as they waited for two men to close the warehouse doors behind us. Once the doors were secured, Louie turned to find me peering over the back of the seat; he exploded into laughter.

Thanks, Louie. I don't feel foolish, really—no, not at all. Gee, thanks for the vote of confidence.

He wiped the tears of laughter from his eyes and again faced forward.

All things considered, though, I guess laughing at me is a whole lot better than hissing at me. I quickly brushed off my knees and adjusted my dress, then settled back in my seat. I looked around the dark warehouse and recalled my arrival vividly. *Nice, Em. You seem to only come here when you've done something really stupid. At least they didn't knock you out for the ride this time.*

I shook my head and touched the small cloche that was occupying it. My hair had grown to nearly touch my shoulders, so Midge usually styled it into a fashionable wave that led to a small almost unnoticeable bun at the back of my head. That particular day, however, we didn't have time, so I just tucked it beneath a hat. *I guess they can send me almost anywhere now.*

We drove to the far end of the building and descended into the floor, using the same lift we had on our arrival. When we reached the basement level, we didn't bother to converse with any of the lab workers who surrounded us; instead, we drove directly toward the tunnel and accelerated until we arrived before a different group of waiting lab assistants, several of whom I unfortunately recognized—We were at The 1908 House again. I wanted to cry but lacked the energy or hydration necessary to accomplish the task, so I just stared at the group.

As soon as Louie opened my door, one of the female assistants stepped forward with a hooded, floor-length, white chenille robe and helped me into it. It completely covered the time-frame inappropriate dress I wore beneath. Then she removed my hat and drew the hood over my head. When she was finished, Louie resumed his position as my bodyguard, pushed the onlookers out of the way, and escorted me through the vault doors and to the elevator.

As I gripped his arm, I noticed that he was flexing his muscles for me. I didn't want to let go and held tight until we reached my bedroom.

He led me into the room and watched me place the Maude suitcase on the bed. "Is that hers?" he asked.

I nodded. I could tell he was trying to make peace, so I attempted to maintain eye contact.

"She wanted me to give you this." He reached behind him and produced something that had been tucked beneath his shirt.

I was speechless and could only stare at the new journal he was holding in his hand. It took a few seconds for me to finally ask, "Did Maude read the letter I left in the trunk?"

He nodded and looked down at his hand.

"How did it go when you confessed that you speak English?"

Louie simply shook his head.

"She must have forgiven you, Louie."

He still spoke to his hand. "It took a while, but the storm passed." When he finally looked up, a smile had consumed his face. "Then I found out something even more exciting."

"What's that?"

"I'm going to be your uncle!"

"You gave her the ring?" I could feel my cheeks ache with happiness and relief. The moment quickly ended, however, when my thoughts and questions went back to Maude. "Do you think she will ever forgive me for taking you from her?"

He met my eyes with a sincerity in his own. "She's not upset with you, Emily. She's just disappointed that your adventures are going to continue without her."

The tears found me after all.

Louie stepped forward with the journal in one hand and a handkerchief in the other.

I used the handkerchief first, then ran my fingers along the cover of the book and slowly took it from his hand. I sobbed and hugged it as if Maude were inside. "Thank you," I finally said.

"Come here." Louie grabbed me by the shoulders and pulled me into a big bear hug that reminded me of one of Papa Bob's. Once his shirt was sufficiently saturated with my tears, he released me to find a dry spot on the handkerchief.

"Sorry. I cry too much."

He held my shoulders and smiled down at me. "Not as much as your aunt does."

I met his eyes. "I'm so sorry about the problems I've caused for you and Maude. I never meant to hurt either of you."

"Don't worry. It is not the end for us. It's just the beginning—I know it. I don't doubt our lives will be quite…unconventional. However, we are meant to be together, and I won't let time dictate our love."

"Will you let me call you 'Uncle Louie'?"

He shook his head and laughed out loud. "You and your aunt could be sisters."

"I know. She's the sister I never had."

He nodded and kissed me on the cheek. When he released me, he looked at the journal I was holding. "She said she wants all the details."

My eyes left the journal and rested on Louie. "I miss her already."

"Me too." He smiled and left the room.

Within minutes, Goodwin and a crew of familiar housemaids descended on me and my wardrobe and quickly transformed me back to the perfect 1908 lady of the manor. *Wow. Nothing says "I messed up beyond belief" better than a tight-fitting corset.* The maids didn't even comment about my 1920s clothing, which confirmed my suspicion that they all worked for H&S, as usual.

"Milady, do you wish the cook to prepare lunch for you?" Goodwin asked, drawing me from my thoughts.

Lunch? I had time-travel jet lag and couldn't even think of food.

She continued to stand before me, waiting for a reply.

"No, thank you, Goodwin. I think I'll just wait until later."

"Shall I call you for tea, then?"

"Yes, that would be perfect. Thank you, Goodwin."

She smiled, nodded, and left the room.

I tried to flop myself down on the bed but found the corset had other plans and insisted upon goring me in the ribs until I sat upright again. As I did, Maude's journal slid next to me on the bed, reminding me that I had a job to perform. "You are as persistent as your namesake," I said to the book.

Soon, I was seated at the desk with a bottle of ink, a pen, and a blotter, all ready to write my first words. My appetite suddenly returned; fortunately, I remembered Chef Jacque's bag of goodies and munched on two almond-filled croissants, and apple and cheese slices as I wrote:

Probably sometime in 1908…

Dear Maude,

I'm sorry, but I have no idea what the date is, and for the first time, I don't care. (Okay, I do care, but for now, I just want to write.)

I love the journal—thank you! I just wish that you could be here instead. I'm sorry for the separation from your Louie. He is a special man, and I look forward to him becoming my uncle. Congratulations! I'm so happy for you! Hopefully, he can arrange to return to you within a short time, in your time, so that you won't have to wait too long.

DENISE LIEBIG

We arrived at The 1908 House just a few hours ago, and I have been shoved into the usual implement of torture, hidden beneath layers of patterned and pressed fabric and lace. My hair is just long enough to be pulled into a slightly fashionable bun that makes me look at least a little period appropriate. Who cares really? It's not as if we entertain a lot of visitors here.

Oh well. I just see it as part of the punishment. Johann sent me here to be out of the way while H&S cleans up our mess. I think Shane and I enjoyed our freedom a little too much and forgot our true purpose. We weren't supposed to make history; we were only meant to become acquainted in case Dell doesn't recover—what a risky venture that turned out to be. I feel so foolish! I don't know what else H&S has in store for me, but whatever it is, the guilt is worse than any form of outside punishment.

You always told me, "Pull yourself up by the bootstraps and empty the pity pot," so I guess I'm finished complaining.

I miss you, Maude—the one I knew as a child, and the one I've known as an adult.

This stupid corset is killing me. I need to stand up and move around. I'll write more later, when I can breathe again without breaking a rib.

Love,

Emily

FOR THE LOVE OF MAUDE

I returned the lid to the ink bottle, cleaned the pen, and searched the room for a new hiding place for the journal. Although my previous Maude journal was no longer a secret, its memory and the importance associated with its secrecy carried on to the new one. *Private words are just as precious as secrets, and both are worth protecting,* I decided.

I couldn't find an adequate spot, so I stored the new journal in my usual secret compartment within the Maude suitcase. "I'll find something better later, Maude," I whispered to the journal.

Once I stowed the suitcase above the wardrobe, I opened the bedroom door and made my way downstairs and out to the expanse of lawn that led to the sea. The salty air and seagulls overhead made me want to lie on the grass and forget my behavior of the last few months, but it had recently rained, and the damp lawn soon lost its appeal.

I wish I could escape myself!

When I reached the edge of the cliff and looked down at the dock and hut below, I was reminded of my ridiculous failed escape attempt. *Oh, that was a brilliant one, Em. Why didn't you just try your luck at cliff diving and save everyone the misery?* I had always been my own worst enemy and found it impossible to cut myself any slack. *You must be possessed or something!*

Once I was finished scolding myself for my poor choices, I finally turned away from the dock, the shack, and the familiar sound of its snoring occupant and walked along the edge of the cliff in the opposite direction.

A large boulder at the far end of the lawn caught my attention and became my resting spot for several hours until my grumbling stomach reminded me of the tea I had been promised. "I don't suppose Chef Jacques' pastries counted as tea?" I asked my angry stomach.

It simply rumbled in reply.

"Fine, I'll go."

I reluctantly stood and walked across the great lawn to the French doors that led me back into the house. Within my first few steps inside, however, I was met by Stevens, the butler.

"There you are, milady." He stood red-faced with his normally immaculate hair out of place in at least two spots. "You're expected in the library."

Terror filled my being and kept me rooted to the ground. *Hello, bordello!* I took a few breaths and tried to regain some form of composure as Stevens left me to my breakdown. I held my stomach in an effort to breathe deeply despite my corset but failed miserably and found myself panting instead. *Stop, Em! You sound as if you're giving birth.* Finally, I composed myself enough to leave my post and walk toward the library.

When I arrived, the door was slightly ajar, so I pushed it open enough to enter. I started to walk into the room and froze in the doorway, unable to take another step. I expected to see a group of men in vintage suits, assembled in various positions throughout the room, all glaring in my direction and eager to dole out their punishment. Instead, I was met by a single occupant, who was sitting slightly against the massive wooden desk, with an intricately carved wooden cane at his side.

Although my feet were frozen, my mouth wasn't. "Dell?"

It reminded me of our first library meeting, only with a twist—Instead of reading Twain, he was just sitting there with his arms folded across his chest, and the expression on his face was neither angry nor welcoming. "I hear you've been busy," he said.

My mouth suddenly went dry, making my reply sound like a squeaking mouse. "I, uh…" I searched the floor for the answers but it failed to produce anything.

Dell spoke instead, "Please, close the door."

I exhaled loudly through my lips and turned to push the door into the threshold I had barely managed to pass through. Then I slowly faced Dell.

"Come here," he requested.

Since escape wasn't an option, I found my feet slowly moving forward, as if I were no longer controlling them. When I was within a foot of Dell, I stopped and tried to meet his eyes. I only made it to his shoulders.

He unfolded his arms and reached forward, then took my chin and tilted my head and eyes up to meet his. "I shouldn't have left you alone with Shane." He shook his head. "I only have myself to blame."

"No, Dell, I never thought of him as you, and I should have—"

"I put you in an impossible position. You had no choice."

I felt pathetic. "Am I that predictable?"

"No, but I am. I knew that Shane wouldn't be able to settle for just being your friend." He hesitated, then continued, "Regardless of what you want to admit, he and I are the same person."

"Not to me!"

"You don't think so?"

"No."

"Then explain to me why you gave him so many chances."

"Excuse me?"

"He disappointed you countless times, yet you always let him win you back." He shook his head. "Convince me that your love for me didn't play a part."

I searched the usual places in my mind that typically shot words through my mouth in situations such as that one, but my lips weren't moving.

He stroked my chin with his thumb and let it go. "How many chances did you give your previous boyfriends—Hodges, for example?"

I stared at a button on his shirt for what seemed forever, picturing the face of my former flame, until I finally found my voice. "I didn't love him."

"And you love Shane?"

I nodded.

"Why?"

My gaze traveled from his shirt to his mouth and finally met his eyes. I lost my voice again, but Dell didn't.

"Was it his handsome good looks? His wit? His charm?"

I didn't respond.

"No?" he asked.

I was so confused that I wanted to crawl into whatever kind of hole my corset would allow me to enter.

"Was it the way you felt when he touched you?"

I could feel my signature blush turning my face and neck into a burning testament of my guilt.

"Oh? So you enjoyed that?"

I wanted to die and would have gone to my grave without speaking again.

"You and I never made it that far, sweetheart, yet you only went to a certain point with Shane. You never consummated our marriage with him. Did you wonder about that too?"

I felt as if someone had just knocked the wind out of me and somehow resurrected my voice in the process. "No! I...We...I married *you*, Dell. You! I didn't walk down the aisle with anyone but you!" I backed away from him and tried to catch my breath. "I'm so confused right now. I don't know if you are actually you or a slightly older Shane. All I know is that I'm sick of the games. I'm tired of wondering who I am and whether my husband is dead or alive." I started to pace the floor. "I never wanted to fall in love with Shane, but he was there. Where were *you*, Dell? Johann told me you were aware of the consequences of Shane and me becoming ac-quainted—of me choosing him over you. If you were so concerned about Shane and me, why didn't you prevent it by coming to the past as soon as you recovered? Why did you make me suffer in real time?"

He tried to reach for me, but I stepped back.

"No, Dell. I can't do this anymore."

"Sweetheart, I—"

"No!" I screamed at him. "I'm tired of this...all of it!" I felt the bile rise in my throat, competing for space around the fa-miliar lump that was lodged there. "If you truly loved me, you wouldn't have put me through this!" I ran to the door and almost made it out before a crashing noise jolted my attention back to the room.

Dell was lying in a heap on the floor, holding his right leg.

I immediately joined him. "Oh, Dell, I'm so sorry!"

"I guess I should have waited a little longer before com-ing here," he said. His handsome features were twisted in ag-ony.

Fortunately, Stevens heard the noise and assisted Dell into one of the wingback chairs. "Lord Milton, would you prefer I summon a doctor?"

"No, Stevens. I just need to rest for a moment."

"Well, if you change your mind—"

"I will let you know. Thank you, Stevens."

The butler left the room, closing the door behind him.

"I guess you and Shane share a title here, after all," I said, now standing beside his chair.

He just smiled and rubbed his leg.

I let him catch his breath for a few minutes before I spoke again. "Why didn't you wait until you were fully recovered?"

Dell looked up at me from the chair with a sadness so deep I thought I might drown if I stared too long. "I missed you."

"I missed you too, but you still should have waited."

He shook his head. "I couldn't bear being away from you."

Great. Just when I thought I couldn't feel more horrible, I have to taste the icing on the cake.

Unfortunately, he wasn't finished. "I have one more question for you, and then I'll stop. Please, Emily, don't answer until you've thought it through."

"Okay."

He reached for my hand and held it for several seconds before continuing, "Was Shane just my temporary substitute or would you rather be with him?"

There it was, the dreaded question I had feared since the first moment of our reunion. Fortunately, being by his side again put everything back into perspective; something I was missing since I saw him last. I took a deep breath and knelt next to his chair and held his large, strong hands in both of mine. "I love *you*, Dell, and I guess...Well, I probably wasn't being honest with myself or Shane. You're correct about some things, I have to admit. Yes, I gave Shane many more chances than he probably deserved. Ultimately, however, it wasn't because he reminded me of you or because his looks and charm were unavoidable." I shook my head. "That wasn't it exactly."

"What was it, then?" he asked.

I brought his hand to my face and rubbed it along my cheek, then looked into his eyes. "Dell, although I felt you were two different people, I missed *you* and wanted him to be you. I kept waiting for that to happen, but it never did. Still, I thought loving him would be the same as loving you, but...Well, I was wrong. I just hope you can forgive me for having feelings for him."

He took his hand from mine and continued to run it along my cheek to my jawbone. "I cannot lie about being jealous, but that is something I will have to overcome." His other hand joined the first to cradle my face. "I guess in many ways, I don't see him as myself. In others, though, I realize only I am responsible for his actions. They are, after all, my actions as well."

The whole thing was making me crazy. "Please, Dell, can we just be us again?"

"As long as you are willing to be around a jealous, broken man such as me."

I smiled. "How broken?"

"Don't worry, sweetheart, the important things are still in working order."

CHAPTER SIXTEEN

I hoped that having Dell back in my life would mark the beginning of something wonderful, but I was wrong. The man who claimed to be my husband was nothing like the one I had married; in fact, I hardly recognized him.

When I first met Dell in 1910 New York, I thought he was the best looking man I had ever seen. A muscular six feet tall with light brown hair that pushed the limits of length and style, Dell, posing as a Southern gentleman, didn't just stand out in the crowded opera house lobby; he made it disappear. My Evergreen assignment to discover Dell's secrets faded into the background as soon as the pearls along my sleeve caught his watch chain and held me there, staring into his blue eyes, while he introduced himself as Wendell Beringer.

Now, the spark was gone from those same eyes, and he spent his days limping around the estate and barking at the staff. Although Dell was respectful to me, he seemed to constantly walk a fine line, and Louie was always close at hand in case he crossed it.

By the third day, I'd had enough. "Dell?" I caught him at breakfast doing what I despised—hiding behind a newspaper.

He didn't answer.

After a few more failed attempts, I finally stood and walked over to him and tapped him on the shoulder.

He impatiently lowered the corner of the paper I was standing beside and stared at me without expression. "Yes?"

"I want to talk to you."

"Aren't you doing that already?" His cold stare almost gave me the chills.

I exhaled and arrived at the point. "Dell, I think you should return to the future so that you can finish recovering."

"Are you trying to rid yourself of me?"

"No, of course not! You said yourself that you should have waited a little longer before coming here. Besides, I just thought you might be more comfortable there, especially at night." I was referring to the many pillows he had to prop under his injuries in order to sleep. That seldom worked for too long, and he usually spent the night sleeping in a chair.

"Really, or are you just disappointed that I haven't fulfilled my duties as a husband yet?"

I instantly felt red-faced and humiliated. Stevens immediately departed, but Louie remained undeterred.

"Dell, please. I didn't mean that, and you know it."

"Do I, Emily? Really?"

"What do you mean?"

"All I really know is that I can't look at you without picturing you with Shane!"

"Dell—"

"No! I'm tired of pretending to be okay with another man touching my wife. I don't care if he's my younger self. I have no memory of his actions, so he might as well have been another man."

"Dell, please! I didn't—"

"And by the way, Dell's dead. You need to start calling me 'Johann.'"

So much for respect and civility!

I just stood next to him in shock as he raised the corner of his newspaper and once again hid behind its pages. Louie, the consummate gentleman, rose from his chair and offered me his arm. I silently took it and let him escort me from the room.

Wednesday, August 5, 1908

Dear Maude,

I wish I was writing to tell you how happy I am, but I'm not much of a liar. Dell made an appearance three days ago, saying how much he missed me and how he understood why I had feelings for Shane. Then he proceeded to become my worst nightmare. He hasn't completely recovered from his injuries or my time with Shane after all—ironic, considering he could have prevented both. I'm sure he hates me. He is the grumpiest, most ill-tempered man I have ever met. Now he claims that Dell is dead, and he wants me to call him "Johann." Can you believe that, Maude?

I miss the man I married, but I have to wonder if I will ever see him again.

At least I finally know what date it is. I should, since it was plastered across the front page of the newspaper he insisted upon hiding behind this morning at breakfast.

I'm too sad to write any more.

FOR THE LOVE OF MAUDE

Love,

Emily

After I stored the journal, I decided to escape to my boulder on the cliff's edge; however, once I looked out the window, I quickly changed my mind. A little rain might have been acceptable, but the torrential exodus of liquid from the sky that formed lakes across the lawn was a bit much. I looked down at my light yellow dress, finished with a floral-patterned hemline that almost brushed the floor. *Yeah, this would wick up the rainwater like a sponge! Now what?*

A dank basement didn't seem so appealing, especially after my issue with the whiskey and Mr. Hogg.

It's a good day for a book. I imagined myself bonding with a classic in one of the library chairs as the fireplace kept the chill from the room. Mostly first editions, the books still creaked when I opened them, and the smell of fresh ink made turning their crisp pages as much of an experience as reading the words they held. When I reached the library, however, I noticed the door was open and the fire was not lit. I stepped inside and saw Dell at the desk, thumbing through a ledger.

"Don't you know how to knock?" he barked.

"Why? The door was already open."

"Yes, and a simple knock would have been a remarkable display of manners…uncharacteristic on your part, I suppose." He eyed me up and down.

I charged into the room. "Who do you think you are, speaking to me that way?"

He slammed the ledger closed, sending a miniature plume of dust into air. His angry eyes reached me before his words even left his mouth. "Who am I? Really, Emily, you have the nerve to ask me that question? Who am I?" He shook his head. "I know who I am—I'm the man who foolishly married a young girl, thinking she would be faithful to me. I endured months of therapy trying to recover from the injuries I sustained trying to save our future. That's who I am!" Using his cane for support, he walked from behind the desk he was occupying and stood within inches of my face. "And you know how she repaid me?"

I stood seething, wanting to kick the cane from beneath his grasp.

"She cheated on me!"

I laughed in his face. "Really, Dell? How is that even possible? I was with *you* the whole time! Besides, as you said yourself, you're to blame. You created this no-win situation and insisted upon recovering in real time while your younger self kept me company. How can you blame *me* for something *you* orchestrated?"

"Regardless, you didn't have to fall for him. No is a very powerful word, Emily!"

"So is goodbye!" I shouted at a volume to match his own.

"Oh, so now you're leaving me?"

"Who would I be leaving exactly? The Dell I knew never came back. You might think you know who you are, but I'm standing in front of a man I don't recognize!"

He leaned closer. "I'm the man you married, Emily."

I shook my head. "No. The man I married abandoned me."

We both stood there breathing heavily through our inflated nostrils at each other, resembling two bulls ready to charge.

"It certainly didn't take you long to replace me," he hissed.

"I didn't sleep with Shane."

"No, but you weren't far from it. He told me everything. It took every fiber of my being not to break what few bones remained intact in his body." He exhaled into my face before continuing, "I hate him for loving you."

"Then you only hate yourself!"

He stepped back as if he had just sustained a blow.

I stood facing him, with my fists clenched at my sides, waiting for the bell to ring me into the next round.

Instead, after a few seconds, Dell took a deep breath and nodded in defeat. "I suppose I do."

His words caught me off guard, and I remained speechless as he continued.

"I suppose you were also right this morning at breakfast. I shouldn't have come back so soon. My ego impeded any form of sound judgment. Apparently, my injuries aren't merely physical."

That hurt, but I still had no response for him.

"To make matters worse, Johann is furious with all of us right now. His legacy, our future, has been compromised. I would prefer to think that years from now, we all will be able to laugh about this."

I took a deep breath and nodded. "That's a nice thought."

Dell's eyes met mine, and the anger from earlier was replaced with a deep sadness. "I've made a decision I suppose I should have mentioned to you before my temper made a fool of me. For everyone's sake, I've arranged to go away and heal myself. I won't return until that has been accomplished."

"Please don't tell me it's going to be in real time again," I said.

He shook his head. "No. I'll be gone less than a week. I want to give you some time to think as well."

"Will you really come back?"

"Yes."

"Do I actually have to call you 'Johann'?"

He laughed. "No."

"Good." I looked at the floor, unable to make eye contact with him as I asked, "Do you still love me?"

He leaned on his cane and walked to my side. "I've never stopped loving you. I'm not even capable of it, sweetheart." Then he took my hand and led me to the desk, where he sat on the edge and pulled me into his arms. "I'm sorry for my behavior these past few days, Em. My jealousy is overwhelming, something I didn't expect. I need to leave for a while, before I do or say something else we'll both regret."

The emotion was too much for me and left me without words as I examined the face I had missed for so long. Scars presented themselves in places that used to hold smooth skin. They felt swollen under my touch as I traced the curve of his jawline and cheeks with my fingertips. He closed his tired blue eyes, while I gently ran my thumbs across his eyelids, up to his eyebrows and across to his ears. I finally buried my hands in his hair, kissed his forehead, and gently ran my lips down his nose to his waiting lips.

It didn't take long to realize that the passion wasn't gone; in fact, it was even more intense. He finally kissed me as if I wouldn't break, just as Shane had. Unlike with Shane, however, I kissed him back without any sense of guilt—I didn't hold anything back. His lips found all the right spots and I let them.

FOR THE LOVE OF MAUDE

Unfortunately, the library door was still open and an ill-timed knock spoiled our long-awaited reunion.

"Yes?" Dell's irritated voice filled the room.

"Sir?"

Although my back was to the door, I recognized the voice as Perry's.

Dell leaned his forehead against mine and kissed my nose. "My ride is here."

I wanted to cry but refused to waste even a second of the time I had left with him. "I don't want you to leave me again."

"It won't be long." He smiled and kissed me one last time before standing up from his seat on the desk. His wobbly legs brought Perry to his side within seconds. "I'm fine, Perry," Dell said, but he wasn't; the pain was etched across his face.

Perry reached under his arms and held him while he gained his balance.

Dell turned to me. "You'd better go, Em. I don't want you to see me this way."

I knew it would have been selfish to argue, as well as pointless, so I gave him a quick peck on the cheek and walked from the room. I fought the urge to stand in the hall, until Louie rolled a wheelchair into the library. That was the catalyst needed to send me to my room, where the tears found me and soon covered my cheeks like the sheets of rain already cascading down the manor house windows.

* * *

Eventually, my tears dried, but the torrential downpour outside did not. After the second day, I conveniently discovered from one of the staff members that it was an early start to their wet season—it felt more like monsoon season. *Great. Yet another amenity for this stinking place.*

That same day, over a game of cards, Louie presented me with some news of his own. "They're letting me go back."

I gazed at him over my hand while he looked as if he were pretending to rearrange the cards in his. "Excuse me?"

He played with his cards for a few more seconds then finally met my gaze with a nod.

I tried to be mature about it but found it almost impossible. "Good for you, Louie." *Bad for me.* I looked at him and offered the best smile I could muster. "I'm happy for you. Really." Then I resorted to rearranging my own cards. When I made eye contact with Louie again, the smile on his face brought me back from the brink of pouting. His grin was contagious, and I didn't have to dig too deep to offer him a genuine one in return. "I'm sorry, Louie. I really am happy for you. Please give Maude a huge hug for me."

"Maybe, but only after I give her one of my own first." He smiled even wider.

You're adorable.

We didn't bother finishing our game, and within an hour, Louie was gone.

I paced the main floor, staring at the rain and accompanying wind that was pelting the house and the grounds outside. I was bored out of my mind.

The next few days were spent admiring the artwork around the house and trying to find a staircase that would lead me to the attic. I couldn't even find an access door in the ceiling. However, just before I was reduced to implementing my own version of the Dewey Decimal System in the library, my savior arrived.

"Excuse me, milady."

I looked up from a stack of books I had just removed from one of the shelves. "Perry? Is everything all right?"

"Yes, just fine."

"Is Dell with you?" I asked, remaining hopeful.

"No, but I've been instructed to take you to him."

I placed the pile of books on the floor and exhaled down at them, putting my hands on my hips before replying, "I've heard this all before, Perry. I was shuffled around for months with the same promise of seeing Dell. I'm not going to do that again."

Perry stepped into the room with Louie in tow.

"I've been employed to make sure you follow the instructions," Louie said, smiling broadly.

I smiled right back. "Your English has improved considerably since I last saw you."

"He knows." Louie gestured toward Perry.

"Well, that's helpful," I said sarcastically. With the odds clearly not in my favor, I looked at the two men, then at the books scattered across the floor. "I've sure made a mess of the place."

Louie chuckled lightly. "I'm certain the staff can manage. I'll inform them while you prepare for our departure."

I stepped around the piles and gave both men a big hug before making my way to the bedroom, where I grabbed the Maude suitcase and checked for the journal. "It's there," I said to myself, "and it's as good a hiding place as any."

Time travel had become so routine that I hardly noticed the process anymore, and that trip was identical to all the recent others, with one exception.

"Where's the Ghost?" I asked in horror.

Perry fielded the question for me. "It was a little too difficult to conceal, so we had to downgrade." He looked at Louie, and they both laughed.

I glanced from one to the other, then finally asked, "What's so funny?"

"You couldn't touch a car similar to this in your time for less than fifteen million dollars. It's not the trusty limousine to which we're all accustomed, but it's nothing to be embarrassed by either," Perry said with a wink.

My eyes traveled from the elongated black front end to the open driver seat, then to the convertible passenger area that had the top up and was safely enclosed behind a partition window. "What is it?"

"It's another H&S creation, made to resemble a 1931 Bugatti Royale Coup de Ville—not the average chauffeur-driven vehicle of the 1930s," Perry replied.

"So we're going to the thirties?"

Louie nodded. "Yes, and that's all you need to know for now."

Right on cue, two female staff members arrived at my side and escorted me to a nearby room where they helped me to remove my corset and dress and replaced them with a far more comfortable outfit. When one of the women handed me a real bra—or at least something closer to one than what I was wearing—I thought I would pass out. I just stood there, holding it in my hand as if I had just won an unexpected award. I was grateful that a speech wasn't required. *It's only been a few days, but I've really missed your kind.*

I finally put on the bra, underwear, slip, and stockings that the two women were patiently holding for me. Then, a third woman entered the room carrying an amazing dark red, silk chiffon dress that boasted a white pattern resembling sea urchins. The sheer, cape-like sleeves hung loosely over my shoulders and drew my eye to the layers of fabric that flowed like ripples to the tops of my ankles. It had such a delicate look and feel that I thought it might tear when I stepped into it, but it held together nicely as I twirled in the mirror. "I love this!" Next came the red, silk-covered pumps and a matching handbag.

After I was finished admiring myself, I was escorted into a different room, where I was greeted by a chair and another employee who quickly curled my hair and waved it into a loose bun gathered at the base of my head. Then she applied a dab of red lipstick.

I walked back to the car looking and feeling amazing, almost like a new woman.

The men were standing outside the car and turned to admire my outfit. Both smiled as Perry walked over to the back door and opened it so Louie and I could enter.

Once we were settled, Louie smiled and nodded at my dress. "If I wasn't already in love with your aunt…"

I slugged him in the arm and nearly bruised my knuckles on his enormous muscles in the process.

He just laughed and left me staring at the back of his head as he turned away from me.

"So, Louie—"

"Save your breath. I'm still not going to answer any questions," he interrupted, fogging up the window with his own breath.

I exhaled loudly in disgust. I was hoping he'd forgotten his vow to deny me any details of our trip.

"Not working!" He continued to speak to the window

while reaching over to offer a patronizing pat on my leg.

I pushed his hand off and stared out my own window. *These people make me crazy!*

CHAPTER SEVENTEEN

A lthough the journey from the past was similar to other occasions, the arrival at my destination was not. When the car came to a stop, I was still so deep in thought that I found it easy to ignore the employees milling around in their lab coats and the instruments they were using to scan our every movement. Somewhere along the way, I lost all hope of seeing Dell. Even my new outfit didn't help. I was tired of the whole process and didn't bother to root out my "Willy" and make his life miserable. I eventually stopped staring out the window entirely and just focused on my Maude suitcase that was resting at my feet.

We remained in the car and ascended from the basement into the Time Travel Warehouse, where I continued to study the familiar cracks and creases my suitcase held. It was the only constant in my life—the only thing that never changed— and at that moment, my longing for consistency was stronger than a hormonal woman's craving for chocolate.

I hardly noticed the car stopping at our destination, Essex House, until Louie tapped me on the arm.

"Miss Emily?"

I didn't look up. "Is that still my name?"

He opened the passenger door and stepped out, reaching his arm back inside toward me. I slid listlessly across the seat and deposited my hand onto his, while reaching with my free hand to grab the Maude suitcase from the floorboards. Once I was on the curb, I hugged my suitcase close to me and walked up the front stairs, paying no attention to anything but the next step.

As I approached the top, I saw a pair of wingtip shoes pointing in my direction. I followed the shoes up the cuffed, tan pant leg to the belt and then the trail of buttons up the perfectly pressed white shirt, to the clean-shaven chin of its wearer. My eyes froze on the lips, full and inviting, with a smile hovering along the edges. I skipped the rest of the face and was drawn immediately to the laughing blue eyes. "Dell?"

He nodded and held his arms out to me.

I placed my suitcase on the closest step and flew up the remaining stairs into his warm embrace. I heard the car door close behind me while Dell and I remained unmoved. I just closed my eyes and hoped it wasn't some sick joke, but the rippled muscles beneath his shirt felt too familiar. My hand traveled along his back and up to his head, where I buried my fingers in his ungreased hair. It felt as if it was all there, but I had to know for sure, so I slowly opened my eyes and met the light brown locks that I was hoping to find. I pulled back from his hold and ran my fingers across the fading scars on his face. "How long has it been?" I asked, almost in a whisper.

He didn't answer at first; instead, he seemed to be focusing on a loose hair that he tucked behind my ear. "A year."

"I don't see a cane."

He shook his head and continued to explore my face with

236

his hands. "No need for one. I'm good as new."

As I looked into his eyes, a thought crept into my head, one I couldn't seem to suppress. Apparently, it showed on my face as well.

"What's the matter, sweetheart?" he asked.

I closed my eyes and thought for a moment before opening them again and replying, "Please don't take this the wrong way, but I really have to know the answer to this one."

"Okay."

I exhaled, then jumped in before I lost my nerve. "Are you Dell or Shane?"

His laughter echoed throughout the courtyard that surrounded the front of the house.

"I mean, you both have scars, and—"

"Yes, we do, but mine are…deeper."

I immediately broke eye contact. *Here we go again.*

"Oh, no, not that, sweetheart!" He gently brought my face back to his. "I only meant that his injuries were superficial and, once healed, were almost undetectable. Mine left actual scars."

"And you're…?"

He smiled. "Dell, of course."

I still wasn't certain and searched his face for further confirmation.

"Emily, I would never deceive you in that way. I am the man you met in the opera house, the same man you married. Besides," he said, then hesitated a moment, "Shane chose to have his memory of you removed."

I had no idea which flew open wider, my eyes or my mouth, but I felt certain that both worked together to consume my face. Also, my old friend, the lump in my throat, was paying another unwelcome visit, so I could only stand there and gape pathetically.

"He was miserable without you, Emily, and he couldn't bear to endure the next ten years alone. Plus, our first meeting needed to feel natural."

I could almost smell the smoke my poor brain was emitting as it worked overtime to try to grasp the logistics of what he was describing. "Then is Shane the real you of today?" I couldn't formulate a logical sentence for my life, but I wanted another shot. "What I'm trying to ask is whether Shane and you are living parallel lives, or if he is really you?" I shook my smoking head at the ground. "Does that make any sense?"

He smiled. "Yes, it does. Without the memories of you, it was safe for us to reinsert him back into my direct past—not a parallel life but an identical one. He is me and vice versa."

I was suddenly grateful for the big breakfast I'd eaten before leaving The 1908 House and the energy it gave me to deal with all I was hearing. Still, it was a struggle to keep my eyes from rolling back into my head.

Dell recovered the suitcase from the step where I had left it. "I can see this comes as a bit of a shock to you, Em. Let's go inside, where we'll be more comfortable."

"Good idea."

Once inside, I almost forgot everything else. The entire interior of the house had undergone a major transformation, inspired by the Great Depression. Gone were the expensive paintings and decorations that had adorned the house in 1926. In their place, hung modestly framed mirrors and artwork, as well as figurines and other accessories that appeared more mass produced than museum quality. The furniture looked entirely different without its accompanying Jazz Age glitz. It was as if I had just walked into the stripped down version of Essex House, one I preferred over the previous version. It was much more comfortable, and I didn't feel the need to take my shoes off at the door.

Dell walked with me to one of the couches. "Do you want a drink?"

Thinking clearly at that moment was optional, so drinking seemed completely out of the question. "No thanks."

He joined me on the couch and took my hand in his. "Where were we?"

I looked at his hand in mine. "Are you and Johann existing on the same...whatever you called it?"

"No. What you already know still holds true. Johann was married to his science but knew that logically, he needed a bloodline. I was his solution. There was a brief time in his past when he was ready for a family, before his work consumed him. This is the time frame from which Johann selected me, his younger self."

I nodded. "He told me that he traded one kind of future for another—time travel for a family."

"Yes, that's true. However, by the time he came to that conclusion, he was older and too set in his ways to marry, so he enlisted my assistance to find a wife. This allowed him to continue his work without the burden of a legacy or loneliness looming over him."

"I guess he learned how to have it both ways."

"Exactly, but the two of us must live separate lives for this to occur."

I shook my head. "So you're not Johann?"

"No, not in the sense that our lives will ever become one again. However, we share a past that saw us into adulthood;

a past in which we were given the name 'Johann' at birth."

"Are you changing your name again? After all, you asked that I call you 'Johann.'"

"I was just angry then, Em. Besides, I don't want to confuse things any more than they already are. I might have to make an adjustment or two, though."

"Has anyone ever called you 'Hans'?"

Dell looked off into the distance as if he were watching one of his memories on a television screen. "Yes. My grandmother called me that or 'Hänschen.'" He looked down at our entwined hands. "The wedding ring I gave you belonged to her."

I looked at the open space on my finger where the ring should have been; I hadn't worn it since I became Blanche. I tried to change the subject before Dell could comment on its absence. "You've never told me about your grandmother."

"Oma Holtz. She died when I was young, but she loved me with her whole heart. I never felt wanted at home and spent most of my early years in her little cottage. She kept the best vegetable garden around. That was where I developed my passion for the life sciences and where Johann eventually learned his love for quantum physics. My own mother was cold and insisted upon addressing me by my given name, and my scientist father hid behind volumes of texts so he didn't have to feel anything. I guess I eventually followed in his footsteps—or at least Johann did."

I rubbed his hand. "How sad."

He nodded. "Now you can see why I don't mind being called 'Dell'?"

"Yes."

We sat in silence while I tried to absorb Dell's words.

After a few seconds, he leaned toward me and kissed me on the cheek. "Are you okay?"

"I guess."

He scooted closer and put his arm around me, drawing me to him. "I know this is overwhelming."

That's an understatement! I thought but only nodded.

"Emily?"

I turned to see his face next to mine.

"I know a lot has happened since our wedding day, but if you'll still have me, I want to start building a future with you."

"Excuse me?"

He tried to answer, but I immediately interrupted, "Do you think I would constantly travel from one safe house to the next an ungodly number of times if I didn't want to be with you?"

"Em—"

"No, you've been talking for the last half hour. Now it's my turn. Dell, I love you—not Shane, not Johann, and not my lab partner in chemistry, although he was super cute. It's you I love, and the only way we can build anything is to rid ourselves of our past. Therefore, I need to ask one more question."

He nodded, acting as if he were afraid to speak.

I tried to ignore the movement of his head and the smile that was forming on his lips. "Can you ever forgive me for my relationship with Shane? If you can't, then I don't see how we can move forward."

The smile left his face, and he removed his arm from around my shoulders.

Great.

Next, he stood up and turned to look down at me, offering his hand. "Let's go outside."

We walked into the backyard, past the pool, to the area where my breakfast table once sat overlooking the ocean.

"I can't lie to you, Emily. I was insanely jealous of Shane, and in many ways I still am."

I turned toward the ocean.

"But not in the way you think. He's part of me, and although they erased his memories of you, I don't think it's possible for the emotions to be removed." Dell paused for a moment, the span of two or three crashing waves. Then he continued, "Every time I think of you, I feel drawn to the idea of us being together in this house. The passion is overwhelming. Now that you're here, I can't stop thinking about the honeymoon we never had."

I wasn't sure where he was going with the conversation, but I hoped watching the ocean below would keep me calm in the meantime.

"Yes, I'm jealous of Shane—not because of what he had with you but because of what I didn't have." He reached for my hands and turned me back to him. "I intend to spend the rest of my life making up for those months I lost."

"And the anger?" I asked.

"It's gone. I promise."

I shook my head in disbelief. "You were seething, though."

"I was in more pain than I could tolerate. It kept me from sleeping and eating…and thinking. Although I knew your relationship with Shane was of my own creation, that still didn't stop me from despising it or him."

"Or me?" I almost whispered.

He hesitated and exhaled several times before answering, "My anger was…misdirected. I was furious."

I wanted to cry. *Super stupid question, Emily!* I held my lips between my teeth to avoid any similar queries.

"I've loved you since the first day I met you at the opera house, Emily. Whether it was with Shane's emotional help or not, I just know I can't imagine any kind of future without you by my side."

I shook my head. "You still haven't answered my question."

The confused look on his face was followed by his own shaking head. "I thought I just did."

"Not really. I asked if you could forgive me for my relationship with Shane."

"Oh." He pulled me closer and put his arms around my waist. "It's been a year since I last saw you. I needed to recover not only physically but also emotionally, and in that time, I realized that I never really blamed you for anything. I only took it out on those around me because I was angry with myself. When I started to turn my wrath on you, I had sense enough to know I had to remove myself from your presence. I had to learn to forgive myself. As for your question…Where you're concerned, there's really nothing to forgive."

I wrapped my arms around his neck and pulled him toward me. "Then prove it by kissing me."

In an instant, all my misgivings vanished on the ocean breeze that swirled around us. Dell's maturity, mixed with Shane's youthful passion, formed an intensity of emotion that overwhelmed me. I thought I would explode as Dell's tongue sent chills down my spine in its path from my lips to my neck.

Just then a woman's blood curdling scream not only

spoiled the mood but also caused me to lose my balance and nearly tumble backward over the cliff. My heart almost leapt from my chest as Dell held me precariously in his arms and hoisted me back to a standing position.

We looked toward the source of the noise and saw a woman standing on one of the dining room chairs in the house, shrieking at the floor. "A rat!"

I wanted to scream, too, but asked instead, "Who is that?"

"She represents the home owners. I was considering renting the place, to clear the air, so to speak."

I cringed. "You mean create memories of our own that might replace the ones I made with Shane in this same house?"

"It's a thought," he replied with a shrug.

I shook my head. "It's kind of…weird."

The woman's screams, accompanied by the sound of heels clicking on the wooden chair, made their way to our spot on the lawn.

Dell kept talking. "There's always the honeymoon. What do you think?"

"I think if I don't go on my honeymoon soon, I'm going to file for divorce!"

"Sold!"

"Besides," I said, "I thought my so-called brother was on Mr. Monroe's most-despised list. You might resemble him just a bit too much for this time frame."

"Ah, the infamous Mr. Monroe," Dell said. "Well, with the repeal of Prohibition, he needed a new line of work. Unfortunately for him, he chose a profession in which others were already well established. He took a little swim with the fishes, and his bloated body washed ashore a few weeks later."

"Yuck," I said, then added, "but I guess one good thing came of it."

"What's that?"

"He's with his daughter Sara right now."

Dell nodded and walked with me to the woman who was finally coming to meet us.

"Good afternoon, you love birds," she said. "I'm Mrs. Jones." She offered a gloved hand in our direction.

Dell reached for her palm but received only a set of fingertips in return.

The Maude of my youth always said, "Never trust a woman with a wimpy handshake. She's all show and no go." Maude seldom wasted an opportunity to show me the proper, firm way to grasp someone's hand, and as I sized the woman up, I decided that Maude was right yet again. Mrs. Jones's face was caked with far too much makeup, and her scrawny body stood atop a pair of heels that didn't appear stable enough to compensate for her lack of leg muscles. Upon closer examination, I was confused why the rodent on the floor would have frightened her, considering she could have passed for a close relative.

She reminded me of the overindulged designer who wanted to make my wedding dress, Mr. Wert, and I couldn't resist giving her the same treatment I gave him.

Thus, when it came time for me to shake her hand, I didn't hesitate to slam my palm home and give her scrawny arm a run for the money. She jiggled like a bowl of gelatin while I enthusiastically threw a "Nice to meet you," and a "So good of you to let us see the place" into the mix. She tried to recover her hand, but I held it in mine, covering it with my other hand

and warmly smiling into her horror-stricken face.

Dell had to step in by offering, "Sweetheart, have you seen the kitchen?"

I slowly released the woman's hand and looked into Dell's amused eyes. "Not yet, dear, but I can't wait to have a look."

We left the poor woman to recover and walked toward the kitchen and through the swinging door.

"What was that?" Dell whispered.

"I can't stand a wimpy handshake."

"Well, that's one of those things I'm glad I found out early in our marriage," he said, then pulled me into his arms and planted a huge kiss on my lips. "You never cease to throw a surprise or two in my direction."

"You're one to talk!" I said, laughing.

The agent found us in the same position several minutes later as she timidly poked her head into the room. "Uh, excuse me, Mr. & Mrs. Blanchet…"

At her words, I instantly lost control of myself and descended into a series of giggles that left my sides hurting. Dell poked and elbowed me, but my laughter only grew louder until he finally joined in my ridiculous display.

"Well, I never!" Mrs. Jones's parting comments were absorbed by our laughter and the sound of the kitchen door swinging behind her.

"Blanchet?" I tried to whisper, but the snort that came out of my nose sounded like an elephant trumpeting across the Savanna.

Dell wiped his eyes with a handkerchief, then offered it to me. "I had to think fast, and I know how much you loved the name Blanche."

"I love you!" I said and nearly jumped back into his arms.

"And I love you."

We resumed our previous preoccupation until Mrs. Jones impatiently burst through the door and blurted, "Are you going to take the place or not?"

"Or not!" I replied.

"Then I must ask you to leave!"

"Gladly." I walked past the woman, who somehow managed to pale beneath her many coats of paint, then I made my way to the living room and my Maude suitcase that had been deposited on the couch.

I could hear Dell apologizing behind me with a bevy of excuses, including: "She would prefer a larger pool."

The speechless Mrs. Jones simply stood in the middle of the floor and watched our exit from the house.

Thursday, April 28, 1932

Dear Maude,

I saw the date on a newspaper Perry left in the front seat, and while Dell and the guys mill around outside the car, discussing our next move, I thought I would write a quick update for you.

Louie and Perry finally came to spring me from The 1908 House today. Talk about frozen in time! The place was cemetery quiet. Nothing new ever happened there. I went from speakeasies and house parties to torrential rain storms and endless cups of tasteless tea. They failed to mention their wet season in the brochure. I was bored out of my mind there. Sadly, I was actually in the process of cataloging all of the books in the library when my heroes, Perry and Louie, saved me. (Thank you for sharing Louie, by the way!) Speaking of which, I'm glad you two are still together. Apparently, Dell and I are together as well. They promised me Dell, and for the first time, they delivered. He was waiting for me at Essex House with plans to rent the place, but the notion of a honeymoon helped to change his mind. Good thing, because spending time with Dell in the house where I lived with Shane wasn't the most comfortable of choices. Besides, the real estate agent annoyed me.

I'll write more later. Better yet, I hope to see you later!

Love,

Emily

CHAPTER EIGHTEEN

The morning after our first time was anything but romantic. I awoke completely stuck to the sheets, next to my sweet-faced husband, whose snoring would have directly competed with an oncoming freight train had we been sleeping next to the tracks. By morning, I actually missed Shane's snoring, which apparently grew worse with age. Since we opted not to rent Essex House again, our official consummation took place in the honeymoon suite of The Waveshore Hotel near Santa Monica, which Dell had booked just in case.

When we entered the hotel on the previous afternoon, my expectations were extremely high. The light filtering through the glass skylights that housed the atrium-like lobby only seemed to add to my already enamored mood. I was in love, and all heads turned in our direction as Dell and I walked, self-confidence in tow, to the front desk.

The desk clerk announced our arrival to the surrounding onlookers. "Mr. Blanchet, so good to see you again...and good afternoon, Mrs. Blanchet."

I looked at the man's nametag. "Thank you, Lionel."

He smiled and returned to the paperwork on the desk in

front of him. "Your room is ready for you." He looked around us and stared at the empty ground in our shadows before continuing, "Will your luggage be arriving later?"

Dell held up my Maude suitcase. "We have this for now. The rest were delayed."

"I see." Lionel then dangled a room key in the air and looked at a young bellhop who was standing nearby.

The boy quickly walked to the waiting clerk.

"Mr. and Mrs. Blanchet, Harvey will assist you to your room."

The towheaded Harvey smiled and took the key. "Good afternoon. May I take your case?"

"Certainly, Harvey." Dell handed the boy the Maude suitcase, then threw his arm around my shoulders.

Harvey escorted us to a waiting elevator. "Congratulations," he offered as soon as the elevator doors had closed.

I smiled. "Thank you, Harvey," I said, but I wasn't so thankful. With that one word, the bellhop brought me to the realization that I was finally on my honeymoon. The expectations and disappointments I was certain Dell would feel swirled in my head, making me almost nauseous.

Dell and Harvey chatted idly as the sudden onset of nerves overcame me and my tongue.

I started to sweat and reached up to wipe a bead from my forehead.

"Are you okay?" Dell whispered in my ear.

I just smiled until he returned to his conversation with Harvey. *No, I'm absolutely not okay! I'm about to consummate my marriage with you, and I have no idea what I'm doing.* My virginity wasn't a moral choice but a practical one. Both my mom and Nana Rosie had become pregnant in college, and I was determined to break the chain and be the first to graduate. Of course, my personal victory seemed more and more meaning-less with every floor we ascended. By the time we finally reached our destination, the sweat was seeping from every pore; I was drenched when Harvey unlocked the door to our room.

Fortunately, the honeymoon suite was just the distraction I needed to keep a full-fledged panic attack at bay. Large, or-nately carved French doors led into a marble entryway and flowed to an enormous living area that showed few signs of the Depression. The couches and chairs that filled the space were leftovers from previous eras, but blended nicely to-gether bound by one common thread—gold. The gilded wood and patterned fabrics would have been obnoxious in any other setting, but there, they seemed to glow in the midst of the muted, white marble floors and off-white plaster walls.

Harvey turned on the lights and opened the curtains to show us the remaining features that the multi-room suite had to offer, including a black-and-white tiled bathroom that was home to an enormous clawfoot tub.

While Dell offered Harvey a generous tip, I walked around the main room, running my fingers along the surfaces and trying to avoid the obvious, the bedroom. When the door closed behind me, I was afraid to turn around, and secretly hoped Dell had left with Harvey.

But Dell's arms surrounding me from behind and pulling me into his embrace told me otherwise. He kissed me on the neck and whispered in my ear, "Don't be nervous, sweet-heart."

At that point, telling me not to breathe would have been easier to accomplish and far more satisfying—I could have just fainted and put myself out of my misery. It didn't seem to be the right time to point out that fact, so I chose not to speak at all. My panic had turned to terror.

Dell stopped kissing my neck and turned me toward him. "Emily?"

I had to grit my teeth to keep them from chattering, but that only made my head bob instead. I couldn't make eye contact with him.

He kissed me on the cheek, then forced my eyes to meet his by using the tip of his nose to guide my face upward. "Emily, I love you, and I know you've waited a long time to be with someone. I also realize that deep down, you might not consider ours a real marriage. If that's the case, we can wait until you feel otherwise."

I knew I needed to summon my voice to set him straight. "I didn't consider this a real marriage when you first proposed. Then, when you were in the future recovering from your injuries, I also had my doubts." I reached up and locked my fingers behind Dell's neck. "Being with you today, though, I feel as if we are finally moving in the direction we should have after our wedding reception. When I married you, Dell, I didn't just fake my vows to you. I meant every word. Everything that has happened since has been both a distraction and a test of my true feelings for you." I pulled him closer to me. "I love you, and I want to be your wife."

He leaned forward and whispered in my ear, "Then let go."

So I did, and in return, he didn't judge. Instead, his gentle touch released me from years of self-imposed inadequacy and fear. My heart pounded as he slowly ran his fingers from my forehead to my toes, where he received goosebumps in reply beneath his fingertips.

Although Shane and I had never consummated our own relationship, we sure made a good show of it. In fact, it was the furthest I'd gone with anyone prior, so it was my closest point of reference. I soon discovered, oddly enough, that Shane and Dell were like night and day. Where Shane groped, Dell caressed; where Shane devoured, Dell anticipated and enjoyed; and where Shane demanded, Dell gently summoned. Hours passed as the bed, floor, couch, and finally the enormous tub became bonding sites of our passion.

We hadn't spoken much all evening and remained in our own thoughts while I leaned back against Dell's chest, enjoying his warm, wet kisses on the back of my neck as the water filled the tub. I tried to lean forward to turn off the faucet, but Dell held me back, reaching his foot toward the knobs and turning them with his toes instead.

"Ooh!" I clapped. "You're multitalented!"

"You've no idea where all of my talents lie, Mrs. Blanchet." He nibbled on my earlobes, sending chills down my spine, despite the warmth of the bath.

The water was cold and covered a substantial amount of floor outside the tub before Dell finally slid the chain attached to the stopper between two toes, curled them, and dislodged the plug from its post.

I turned my head along his chest to meet his eyes. "I have a feeling you've tried this before."

"Many times!" He smiled at the glare I shot him. "But always alone, of course."

I tried to splash him, but he caught me by the wrist and held me there.

"I love you," he said.

"I suppose I love you too." I tried to sound upset, but failed miserably. I was far too happy to pretend otherwise.

We slipped and shivered our way out of the bathroom and to the bed, where we recovered the blankets from the floor and tried to find warmth wherever and however we could.

I thought I understood my feelings for Dell, but I didn't know the depth of his for me until we were entwined under the covers, trying to catch our breath.

Dell kissed the top of my head. "This is a first for me as well."

My brain returned to my body in such a hurry that I almost jumped. "What do you mean?"

"I've never truly been with anyone before."

I shook my head. "I don't believe you."

He let out a laugh through his nose that made his chest rise beneath my head that was resting on it. Then, he spoke with the slight Southern drawl I hadn't heard since our wedding day.

"I'm no angel, darlin', but I've never made love before."

I sat up on one elbow to look into his face. We hadn't bothered to close the curtains, and the street lamps offered just enough light that I could see his serious features perfectly. I swallowed what little saliva I had left, then opened my mouth to speak but didn't know what to say; instead, I simply stared into his face and ran my fingers along his early morning stubble.

He caught my hand and held it in place once I reached the scars on his cheeks. "I'd do anything for you," he said. His sincerity filled the semidarkness.

I suddenly felt so guilty about my relationship with Shane

that I wanted to cry.

Dell brought my hand to his lips so he could kiss it. "Please don't keep rehashing the past, sweetheart."

My face seemed the only place that expressed what I wanted to say, because my mouth still couldn't find the right words.

Dell spoke instead. "We each have a past of our own, but it's the present with which I'm concerned. You're my wife— with whatever name we take and in whatever time we find ourselves living." He then gently released my hand and brought his up to my face. "My life is nothing without you. You're my always."

My tear rolled into his hand and disappeared along his fingers. He wiped it away and pulled me toward his waiting lips. He kissed me softly, then returned my head to his chest. Within seconds, he was quietly snoring. I sniffed and played with his chest hairs, and somehow let his snores lull me to sleep.

The same sound that helped me find sleep made for an alarm clock only a few hours later, when I awoke face down on the sheets.

I felt my cheek and realized I must have slept with my mouth open, because a nice, crusty trail of yuck greeted me along with my nasty breath. The bathroom floor was still wet, and I spent a considerable amount of time, effort, and towels to safely reach the sink and my hotel-supplied toothbrush. After a good brushing and a much-needed solo bath, I left the bathroom feeling alive again.

"Nice look!" Dell was propped up on his elbows and referred to the hand towel, my only dry option, which I had tried to tie around my waist. It kept falling off, and I kept trying to replace it.

I looked over at him and the grin that consumed his face. "I should have known you were awake," I said. "The snoring finally stopped."

He laughed and continued to watch me struggle with the towel. "I have a solution for that," he finally said.

"I bet you do."

"Come here, and I'll show you what it is."

"I'm good," I said and remained standing at the foot of the bed.

He sat up. "Oh, so you need a little incentive this morning?"

"Breakfast would be a good start."

He put his head back and spoke to the ceiling. "It's happening already."

I grinned at his disappointment. "I can't fulfill my wifely duties without food."

Dell threw the sheets back and nearly flew off the bed in search of the hotel phone and a promise of room service.

"You might want to ask for more towels too," I called after him.

Within an hour, a grinning Harvey was wheeling a cart of covered plates, as well as coffee and tea pots, into our room. I peeked out from behind our slightly ajar bedroom door, not wanting to miss a second of Harvey's reaction to Dell and his appearance—my husband was a mess. His partially tucked shirt was buttoned in only four places, and his hair was sticking out in crazy clumps all over his head. One of his pant legs was tucked into a sock, and the other was so rumpled that it resembled a worn paper bag.

The boy was almost entirely speechless until Dell handed

him what must have been a large sum of money.

"Your discretion," Dell said to the openmouthed, wide-eyed bellhop.

"Of course, Mr. B-Blanchet," Harvey said. Then, still staring at the tip in his hand, he turned to leave the room but was met by the unavoidable pile of wet towels that had formed just outside the bathroom door. "Oh, that reminds me, Mr. Blanchet. Clean towels are under the cart. I will take these to the maid's bin for you. You can just leave the cart in the hall when you're finished."

"Thank you, Harvey."

The boy reached down and exited the room with the dripping heap of towels.

Must have been some kind of tip, I thought with a smile. As soon as the door was closed, I emerged from our room, wearing the slip I had retrieved from our pile of clothes on the bedroom floor. It was fairly sheer and caught the daylight just right as I walked toward my disheveled husband and the breakfast that waited on the cart next to him.

He couldn't seem to take his eyes off my slip.

I knew where his thoughts were heading, however I was starving. As I drew closer, he reached toward me, but I swatted his hand gently away. "No, no, Dell." I spoke to him as if he were a child.

He played along, sticking his bottom lip out and sighing while continuing to stare at my slip in an almost trance-like state.

"You're adorable, but I'm not nice when I'm hungry," I informed him. "And sometimes, I even pass out." I smiled and winked, referring to our first date, when a lack of breakfast caused me to faint after a morning spent riding horses.

The spell was broken, and he immediately pushed the cart to the table next to the window and slid a chair out for me to occupy. He then pulled lids off plates and poured my tea like a pro.

I smiled and clapped. "You're hired!"

"Thank you, Mrs. Blanchet, but I don't come cheap."

"Oh, I don't want cheap. I only want good. Are you good?"

"The best!"

I ate breakfast, but I have no idea what I had. I spent the entire time being fed bites from Dell's fork that sometimes missed my mouth entirely and required Dell's expert assistance with the mess. "Oh, Mrs. Blanchet, I'm so sorry. Let me take care of that for you," he said.

Dell had a unique way of taking care of things without the use of a napkin. For the sake of convenience, I eventually sat on his lap, and he offered me one bite for his every two. In the end, we were both full and lying in a sticky pile of syrup and jam on the floor beside the cart.

"I'll never look at breakfast the same way again." I smiled up at him as he sucked something from my hair.

Our meals during the next two days were spent in a similar fashion; we weren't able to finish one without wearing at least some of it. Although we made a mess, Harvey and our maid, Edith, didn't seem to mind it or the silence Dell's generous compensation brought them.

Before we could order our third breakfast, however, Harvey arrived at our door with Louie and a half-dozen leather-trimmed, hard-sided suitcases of various sizes.

I wasn't ready for our time to end and almost despised the sight of the luggage when I finally exited our bedroom, wearing a robe Dell delivered to me from one of the suitcases once Harvey left. Regardless, it was good to see Louie again. I hugged him so tightly that I was glad I had double knotted the tie that held my robe closed.

Louie looked from Dell to me and burst into laughter.

Dell finally brought him out of his hysteria. "Just you wait for your honeymoon. Emily and I will be sure to visit you as well."

With that, Louie suddenly went silent.

It took a moment or two for it to register in my brain that Dell was speaking to Louie in English.

Louie looked at my confused face and smiled. "Dell has always known."

"By the way, when *are* you two celebrating your nuptials?" Dell asked with a grin.

Louie again went quiet.

I finally had to ask, "Have you set a date?"

He reached in his pocket and produced an envelope, which he handed to me. Then he spoke without taking his eyes from the invitation. "She's been waiting for you."

When he finally made eye contact with me, I realized he was also waiting for me.

"Maude wanted you to be here for the wedding."

And then, recalling the date from the newspaper several days prior, I suddenly understood something that took my breath away. "Louie? Before you and Perry brought me to this time, how long had it been since you'd seen me?"

"Six years."

I shook my head in disbelief. "What?! You just left a few days ago."

"I couldn't bear to let her be alone."

"When did you arrive here?"

"The day after I delivered the trunk to her."

"And you waited with Maude for six years to be married?"

He nodded.

I tried to be positive but *six whole years* kept rattling around in my brain. *Shane and I made such a mess of things that it took years to resolve, and Maude wouldn't get married until I could travel here again.* I knew it would have been embarrassingly inadequate for me to offer an apology. The only thing I could think to say in my guilt-riddled position was, "It's a big decision."

Dell grew serious. "It's their choice, but the rules are clear."

"I'm confused. What rules?" I asked. *First, a six-year-wait, and now this? When did we cover "the rules"?* I felt as if a whole conversation had taken place while I was sleeping, only I was wide awake, and no one had been talking.

I looked from one to the other, but neither Dell nor Louie would acknowledge me. Instead, the two men stared at each other for what seemed forever before Dell continued, ignoring my question. "Theirs will not be a conventional marriage with a mister and missus and children, Emily."

"Excuse me?"

Neither spoke.

With a sigh, I continued, "What kind of stupid rules are those? I can't believe they're even rules! Who would ever agree to them?"

The daggers their eyes shot at me would have easily pinned me to a wall before I had time to finish my last sentence.

"They're aware of the conditions, Emily," Dell said sternly. "I need you to understand as well."

"Well, I don't!"

Louie left without another word.

"Emily—" Dell tried to speak, but my tornado-mouth consumed the room and held him midsentence.

"There's no way you can expect them not to have children! Maude was the aunt everyone wished they had. All the kids flocked around her—she was the best. And Louie talks about his family constantly. How can you deny them one of their own?"

"*I'm* not denying anyone anything, Emily!"

"Dell, why can't they have children together? I don't understand."

"Emily, did your childhood aunt ever have a husband or children?"

I shook my head, then handed Dell the envelope from Louie.

"No, she didn't. And what was her last name when you were young?" he asked.

"Beckwith."

"Right, the same one she received at birth," Dell added.

I wanted to scream. "Dell, this isn't right. It's…a death sentence. I feel horrible for them and for being a party to this. Plus, I don't understand. Johann said that their relationship wouldn't be a problem."

He shook his head. "It isn't, but their marriage is different. We're not in the business of changing history, not even Maude's. Our research determined that they can wed, but Maude will have to keep her maiden name, and they cannot have a family."

I couldn't breathe and had to find a chair I could slump into. I buried my head in my hands and covered my face in shame. "I'm such a horrible person. Maude was an amazing aunt, who showed me so much love as a kid, and I repay her by introducing her to the love of her life and denying her motherhood."

"It's their choice, Emily, and they have already made it. They're both happy with their decision. You should try to be happy for them."

I looked up at his face, hovering inches from mine and realized that it was not a battle I could win. "Have they set a date?" I finally asked, defeated.

Dell opened the envelope and pulled out the invitation. After skimming the page for a few seconds, he answered, "Apparently, it's this afternoon."

CHAPTER NINETEEN

The Los Angeles County Courthouse stood before us, a Romanesque-style, red sandstone building covered with an abundance of ivy that didn't quite reach the dormers several stories above. Wide stone stairs led to an arched front entrance beneath a tower that once held an enormous clock. In its shadow stood my aunt, scanning the horizon for our arrival.

The last time I saw Maude, she was a somewhat mousy fifteen-year-old, trying to shock her father into paying attention to her. In my mind, that was the girl who was marrying Louie. After all, it had only been a few weeks since I saw her last. However, the woman who met me at the courthouse was anything but a child. In fact, if I had a sister, her name would have been Maude; aside from her being at least six inches shorter than me, her hair, physique, and even her style was a mirror image of mine.

"I've been cloned in miniature," I said, squeezing Dell's arm as we walked up the courthouse stairs toward the wedding party at the top.

"That's all we need," he whispered in reply.

Maude's squeal of delight at our approach saved Dell

from a well-deserved slug. "Oh, Daisy!" she cried.

Louie grabbed her by the arm, preventing her from running down the stairs toward me in the ankle-turning pumps she was wearing.

I quickened my pace. "Maude!" I reached the top of the stairs and my impatient aunt, who finally broke away from Louie to give me a hug.

"I've missed you so much," she cried into my ear.

"I missed you too. Let me look at you."

She stood back and modeled her dress for me. It was a simple white taffeta with a beaded bodice and a short-sleeved lace cape. A beaded comb held a single veil in place above her shoulder-length hair that was curled under on the edges and framed her sweet face like a golden halo. Although her outfit was beautiful, she could have worn a flour sack and been just as lovely. She was simply glowing.

"You look gorgeous," I said, hovering near tears.

She kissed me on the cheek. "Don't you start, now."

I smiled and nodded, trying to take her advice.

"And look at *your* dress!" She felt the fabric of my sleeveless, seafoam dress covered in a large shell pattern. "Silk?" she asked. Her unblinking blue eyes were a perfect match to the sky.

"Yes."

"It's beautiful."

"Thank you," I said, my voice cracking.

"You were right, Daisy!" She held her engagement ring out for me to admire. "It fits!" Louie's mother's ring sparkled on Maude's petite finger.

"I knew it would," I said.

Louie kept smiling at us. His black suit was clearly specially tailored to fit him and his enormous muscles, and it did him justice. After a few minutes of appearing to listen to the others who were surrounding him, he finally walked over to join Maude and me. He couldn't keep his eyes off his future wife, and I couldn't help but notice. My staring gave his approach away. Maude turned to meet his eyes, and I felt the electricity between them—it was overwhelming. He bent to kiss her on the cheek, then stood next to me.

"Louie, you look so handsome. I couldn't be happier for you two!"

He smiled and pulled me into such a bear hug I thought the buttons would fly from my dress and injure someone. "Thank you…for everything," he whispered before giving me a kiss on the cheek.

I nodded. "You better take care of her."

"My life and heart are hers forever." The sincere look on his face made doubting his words impossible.

"Quit whispering, you two." Maude reached her tiny arms around Louie and me and gave us both a hug. It was a simple act, but it reminded me just how much I loved my aunt.

Fortunately, before I could dwell on it too much, a woman exited the courthouse through the large archway and broke-up our reunion. "They're ready for you now," she announced.

Louie let me go and offered his arm to Maude, who eagerly accepted it. I just stood and watched them walk through the front entrance. They were so in love.

Dell approached and offered me his arm as well.

"You were right. They're happy. Were we like that?" I asked, smiling up at him.

"Happier," he replied.

We waited for Maude's father and brother, as well as Perry to enter the building before following. My great-great-grandfather hardly glanced my direction.

He hates me!

When her brother Phil, my great-grandfather, filtered through the entryway, I tried to picture him as an older man with Nana Rosie on his knee, the pose he held in the old photo that used to hang on Nana's living room wall. It would have been a stretch if it hadn't been for the nose. *They all have it, don't they?* I fought the sudden urge to check my reflection in the glass doors for similarities but ultimately chose to examine his nose more closely instead.

He caught me staring at him and smiled, and there it was; the resemblance to the man in the picture was unmistakable.

I smiled back. *Not everyone can say they met their great-grandfather when he was sixteen!*

Aside from the nose and the smile, Great-Grandfather was much taller than his own father and far more muscular, standing almost six feet tall, with a boyish face and blonde hair that was greased back. He wore a suit that was at least a size or possibly two sizes too small. Likewise, his brown shoes didn't seem to fit either his feet or the black suit he was wearing. It looked as if he had borrowed the whole outfit from his much smaller father's closet. Regardless, he had made the effort, and the sweet look on his face would have made anyone who saw him immediately forget and forgive him for his wardrobe. His appearance, coupled with the fact that he was carefully holding Maude's flowers, made me wish I could have snapped a quick photo of him with my cell phone that was collecting dust on my dresser more than eighty years in the future.

FOR THE LOVE OF MAUDE

Shortly before entering the judge's chambers, Maude took a nosegay of wildflowers from her brother, then turned to me and smiled. "I almost forgot. I would be thrilled if you could please be my matron of honor."

I was flattered beyond belief. "The honor would be mine."

She handed me the flowers, then kissed me on the cheek before entering the room. The space was large and sparsely decorated with floor-to-ceiling mahogany paneling, broken only by a set of large windows and several rows of books. We waited for the judge's arrival, standing in front of a rectangular wooden desk that consumed more than a third of the room. When the graying, black-robed judge entered, he wasted no time in performing the ceremony.

Hold it together, sister! I lectured myself. I somehow made it through the vows without shedding a single tear.

The reception afterward was held at my great-great-grandfather's house, where all the eligible ladies from his office and neighborhood seemed to be in a culinary competition for his widower heart. From stews and bologna casseroles to fresh-baked breads and pot pies, the dining room tablecloth was lost beneath the Depression-era dishes and desserts that covered it.

Maude's father didn't seem to mind, and neither did the other men at the reception. In fact, at some point shortly after a simple but tasty banana cake was served, most of the chairs inside the house and out were occupied by the male guests, engaging in some form of food-induced stupor. After a brief search, I wasn't surprised to find my snoring husband rocking gently in a hammock in the backyard. The only two men not napping were the groom and his father-in-law.

My great-great-grandfather wasn't a big man, but he had a set of blue eyes that could cut through steel in a fashion similar to a well-engineered laser. Saying he intimidated me would have been an understatement—he scared the daylights out of me. Therefore, when I saw him walking my direction in the front room, I wanted to run and hide. Unfortunately, I considered finding refuge behind the ample form of his neighbor, Mrs. Carter, a little too late.

"Daisy…" he said.

"Hello, Mr. Beckwith." I tried to sound nonchalant.

"May I have a word with you?"

Okay, but just one. I smiled and nodded to avoid giving him my real answer.

"Shall we?" He led me to the front porch, where, surprisingly, two free chairs awaited us.

I attempted to act as if I weren't afraid that he could possibly dismember me with his eyes, but my lightly chattering teeth were waiting to give me away; so I chose to avoid making eye contact instead.

Fortunately, he didn't make me suffer too long. "Daisy, I can't say I approved of you or your lifestyle. Regardless, you have somehow brought my daughter more happiness than I could have ever imagined." He reached out to take my hand in his. "My new son-in-law is a true gentleman, and I am honored to welcome him into my family. And as for you, Daisy…Well, I apologize for misjudging you. Maude told me about your humble beginnings in the garment factory and how Oscar rescued you from that life. I guess posing as his sister made travel easier for both of you."

I had to press my free hand firmly against my lips to keep them from parting and revealing the smile that was lying just below the surface. *You always were quite the storyteller, Maude.* I just nodded as he continued to hold my other hand.

"I also understand that "congratulations' are in order for you and Oscar."

Great. How does this work when Oscar is really Dell instead of Shane? Now it was my turn to spin a yarn. "Yes, thank you so much, Mr. Beckwith. Only, I don't know if Maude told you that Oscar goes by 'Dell' now. It makes forgetting the past that much easier."

I watched him nod while my words seemed to hang in the air as they took on new meaning. *I haven't thought of Shane since I came back here, and I don't feel guilty. In fact, it took Great-Great-Grandpa mentioning Oscar twice for me to even consider Shane. Dell is my now, and Oscar and Shane are my past. I guess I buried them without even realizing it, and I have Dell to thank for that.*

"Dear?"

A gentle pat on the hand brought me back from my thoughts. I smiled at my great-great-grandfather's concerned face.

"I'm afraid I have brought up a difficult subject for you. I apologize."

"No, that's quite all right, Mr. Beckwith."

"You're both welcome in our home any time." He squeezed my hand. "I always wanted more children."

His words were so sweet that I fought the urge to come clean about the stories Maude and I told but knew the real truth would cause more problems than it would solve. Instead, I settled for a version that would satisfy both our needs. "Thank you, Mr. Beckwith. I'm sorry for not telling you the truth sooner, but we had to protect ourselves."

"No, dear, I understand."

Then he rose and drew me into a hug. He and Papa Bob shared the same bay rum aftershave, and it was just enough of a nostalgic nudge to close the remaining gap that stood between us. With a kiss on the cheek, he left me alone on the porch with my thoughts; in that instant, I wished that I had never come.

I can't stand lies. Maybe there's a nice rock for me to crawl under. I scanned the front lawn for an appropriate specimen but came across Maude's oak tree instead. It had aged significantly in the twelve years since I'd buried the original Maude journal. The trunk had at least doubled in size, and the shade its sturdy branches imparted spanned the entire front lawn and a good portion of the street in front of the house. I couldn't resist the urge to touch it, so I left the safety of the porch and walked toward its trunk. "Remember me?" I asked, then caressed its bark as if it were an old dog. I reached down to pick up one of the few leaves that were strewn at my feet. "I think I need a souvenir. Can you part with this one?"

"I think he can manage." Maude was standing next to me with a smile spread across her face. "This is what started it all," she said.

I nodded and looked up through the sea of branches to the sky. "Did you ever imagine…?"

"Not in my wildest dreams."

I looked at her again and saw another side of her, the mature Maude I knew as a child. The guilt I felt over her limited future was overwhelming. "I'm so sorry, Maude. I'm so very sorry!"

She shook her head. "Don't be. I'm not."

"But the rules say—"

"All rules are made to be broken, Daisy. You, of anyone, should know that about me." She flashed the devious smile I remembered from my childhood.

"Maude, you don't understand. I know how your future goes, and—"

"Shh! Don't tell me! You'll spoil the surprise."

"Seriously, Maude."

"I *am* being serious, Daisy. Louie and I have it all worked out. After all, we've had six years to think about it."

I just shook my head and focused on the leaf I was twirling in my hand. "I want to protect you."

"Oh, Daisy, that's so sweet, but I'll be fine."

"I want to believe that."

"Then do! Besides, you have your own life to live now."

I smiled at the thought of Dell.

"You and I now have our men to try to tame us," she said.

"Good luck to them," I said, smiling.

She put her arm around my waist. "Yes, they're certainly going to need it. By the way, did you receive my journal?"

"Yes, and I loved it, but I have to admit I haven't been a very faithful author. It's only been a few weeks since Louie gave it to me."

She laughed out loud. "Then I guess I'll need to be more patient."

"Well, I never knew you to be good at that, Maude."

She rolled her eyes at my grinning face and gave me the biggest hug her small arms could offer. "I love you like a sister, Daisy."

I hugged her back. "You're the one I never had."

We continued to embrace beneath the tree until male voices behind us captured our attention. Louie and Dell were standing there, side by side, within a few feet of our display.

Louie extended his arm toward Maude. "We need to say goodbye to our guests, my love."

I looked at Dell, and he nodded.

Maude hugged me tighter and shook her head. "No!"

I wanted to grab her and run down the street but knew our heeled shoes wouldn't let us make it too far. Then I looked at the tree and thought of one of Papa Bob and Nana Rosie's infamous 1960s-era tree house sit-ins they used to proudly talk about. "We didn't end any wars, but we did save a few old trees from becoming firewood," Papa said. "Sometimes winning enough battles can change perceptions."

You could support two blonde chicks, couldn't you, old tree? Maude was also looking at the tree and smiling, but I could only wonder what she was thinking.

Louie and Dell knew us well enough to step forward and try to take control before our imaginations beat them to it.

"Congratulations," I finally said to my now-sobbing aunt.

She just nodded and fought to keep her bottom lip from quivering.

I tried to see Louie through my own tears but only saw him in parts. I offered a soggy smile in his direction regardless.

My great-great-grandfather was now standing next to Louie, obviously confused by our emotion. "It's only a honeymoon, girls. You'll see each other soon enough."

The trouble was, we knew better. With time travel, there were no guarantees. Our lives might cross paths again, but we didn't know when or how. We just had to be prepared for the reunions as well as the separations.

Somehow, Maude found words through her tears. "Bye,

Toots. I'll be seeing ya."

I never knew where the expression came from, but she always said that to me when I left her little house as a child. They were also the last words I whispered in her ear when I was fifteen, as she rested peacefully in her casket. The memory of her funeral only made it more difficult for me to speak, but I pulled the strength from somewhere to offer my usual reply, "Not if I see ya first."

Our poor husbands had to shuffle their waterlogged wives in opposite directions in order to ensure that the new-lyweds wouldn't miss the train and eventual steamer to Italy.

"Isn't Perry taking them?" I finally asked Dell on our trip back to the hotel.

"Yes. That's why we drove separately. Maude's father, however, insisted upon seeing them off at the train station. Therefore, we had to coordinate a believable travel schedule."

"Oh," I said, the only syllable I could offer.

He reached over and took my hand. "Maude will be just fine, Em. She's not a child anymore."

"I realize that, but—"

"You need to focus less on their honeymoon and more on ours."

"What do you mean? I thought we just had our honey-moon?"

He laughed. "No, sweetheart. That was just a precursor, an extended and grossly overdue wedding night." Focusing on the road, Dell shook his head. "No, we haven't gone on our honeymoon yet."

"Where are we going then?" I asked.

"I was hoping to discuss that once we arrive back at the room."

I laughed. "Dell, I don't think we've strung more than a couple dozen words together in the last few days inside that room."

"You're correct, Mrs. Blanchet. What a sage observation!"

Within ten minutes, we had pulled off the main road and were parked on the sand within walking distance of the ocean.

"A few decades from now, driving on the beach will reward you with a ticket," I said.

"A few decades from now, houses will cover this whole stretch of beach and make access impossible," he added.

A smile finally found me. "Then let's access it."

I reached down and removed my pumps as Dell left his seat and opened the trunk, which resembled a big piece of matching luggage that had been attached to the back. I heard him rummaging around inside for several seconds before he closed it and returned with a blanket.

He opened my door and offered me his arm. "Milady…"

I slid across the red leather seat and stepped outside, then turned to admire the car's shiny gray and black exterior. "I really like this one. What is it?"

"She's made to resemble a 1932 Chrysler CL Imperial, one of only forty-nine ever made."

"I guess this makes fifty," I said.

Dell smiled and nodded. "Shall we?"

The sand was cool beneath my bare feet as we walked to the ocean's edge, where I proceeded to wade in the water and collect seashells.

He spread the blanket on the sand, removed his wingtips, and joined my treasure hunt. "Here's a good one." He held a perfect hermit crab shell for my inspection.

"Very good!"

"And what do I receive for my trouble?" he asked.

I took the shell from his hand and smiled into his eyes. "That depends."

"On what?"

"On how many more whole shells you can find."

Dell quickly became a shell-finding fool, and within minutes, he had accumulated so many that he had to start carrying them in his pockets.

"How is this possible?" I finally asked.

"What do you mean?"

"Well, in Oregon, I would have spent hours only to find two whole shells of any kind and massive cramps in my frozen feet! Who are you?"

Dell smelled and looked like a creature from the deep as he walked his sand-covered hands and feet closer to me. "I'm Seashell Man!" He pulled a clam shell from one pocket and a sand dollar from the other, holding one triumphantly in each hand.

"You are so strange," I said, giggling.

"But you like strange."

"Correction. I *love* strange."

He dropped the shells and lunged at me. I zigged when I should have zagged and was quickly gathered up into Dell's unyielding arms.

"Look! I found the catch of the day!" he cried.

I tried to kick my feet in the air, but succeeded in throwing sand on us instead. Once we reached the blanket, he laid me down and held me there with a good measure of his body weight.

"Hey! I-I c-can't breathe," I moaned.

He rolled to one side to give me air and proceeded to crack the shells in his pocket. Then he rolled to the other side and cracked the remaining ones. He stood and briefly emptied the shell shrapnel, distributing the pieces evenly on the sand around the blanket.

"Why did you do that?" I asked, mortified.

"I thought broken shells on the beach would remind you of home."

Needless to say, we didn't make much progress with our honeymoon discussions.

Sunday, May 1, 1932

Dear Maude,

Today is your wedding day, and I have to say you were the most beautiful bride I have ever seen. You glowed. Louie is a lucky man, and believe me, I have lectured him on more than one occasion about treating you well. I know I don't have to worry about that with him, but I needed to make the threats for my own piece of mind. He's a great guy, and I'm happy for both of you! I hope your honeymoon is all you expect it to be and more. Dell and I are still trying to plan ours, but…Well, we haven't exactly made it too far. I'd ask you to wish us luck, but I'm kind of enjoying the process the way it is.

Love,

Emily

P.S. My days are so bungled that I didn't realize until after your wedding that it was on a Sunday. Sunday? The courthouse should have been closed. I guess a judge has no say when his extremely demanding wife wants her favorite salesgirl to have her wedding "whenever she pleases," and "he's the man to make it so." I met his wife at your reception, and she sure talked my ear off! Wow! I can only imagine what kind of amazing wardrobe you put together for her. I've always been in awe of your abilities, Maude. You're my hero.

P.P.S. *I'm so sorry for making you wait six years to be married. Shane and I were selfish beyond words. Still, after all that, you asked me to be the matron of honor in your wedding. You really are my hero, Maude.*

CHAPTER TWENTY

After four days of supposed honeymoon planning, Dell and I were no closer to determining our destination than we were when we started. By the fifth day of our impromptu extended stay, the hotel management started offering nervous smiles and hints regarding another couple meant to occupy our suite that evening.

Neither of us wanted to be the responsible one, but when the bill for our stay was discreetly slipped under our door, we knew a timely decision had to be made. Dell reached down to retrieve the folded tally of our weeklong precursor.

"Think they're trying to tell us something?" I asked sarcastically.

He nodded but didn't look away from the paper for several seconds. When he did, the expression that met me was far more serious than I expected.

"Dell? Is something wrong?"

He exhaled, then nodded. "I've been putting this off long enough. There is something I need to tell you, Emily."

"Okay…"

"Your mom and her boyfriend have been in an accident."

"Excuse me?" I loved my mom beyond words, and Tom,

the man who stuck around despite my teenage years, had grown to be a father to me. The thought of them being hurt or worse was almost unbearable. I stared at the floor before asking the obvious question. "Are they…?"

He shook his head. "No. They're recovering."

"What happened?"

"Their brakes failed as they were driving to Mt. Hood. Fortunately, they were going uphill."

I shook my head in disbelief. "But that's not possible. Tom's a gearhead. He knows how to fix everything and maintains cars better than most mechanics. The man performs tune-ups for fun!" I searched Dell's face for more answers, but he didn't speak. "What else aren't you telling me?" I reluctantly asked.

"We think Evergreen knows we're still alive."

"How?" I asked, then instantly whispered, "Was it Shane and I?"

He shook his head. "I doubt it. As you know, H&S spent years tidying things up. We were very thorough." Dell spoke matter-of-factly, as if he were addressing a business associate.

I was mortified. *What does "thorough" mean? Forget it. I don't want to know. It's bad enough discussing the mess I made with my boyfriend while my husband was fighting for his life. Wow, I feel awesome.*

I stared, unblinking, at the floor as Dell continued, "We aren't certain. We're still investigating, but one theory seems to stand out."

I was almost afraid to know, so I just raised my eyes to meet Dell's until he spoke again.

"Some of our researchers believe one of the Evergreen staff who was close to you grew suspicious and decided to micromanage your life there, including going back and posing as someone else just to spy on you."

"Who?" I asked. But I knew the answer. "Hodges?"

"We think so."

I shook my head, thinking about the man Evergreen had wanted me to marry before Dell became their love interest for me. "Love can turn to hate in a hurry, I guess."

Dell pulled me to him and held me there, my head resting on his chest.

I closed my eyes. "I almost wish you hadn't told me."

He kissed the top of my head. "That was why I waited. I didn't know how to tell you or even if I should."

"How long have you known?"

"I found out shortly before I returned to you."

I hesitated for several seconds, then slowly lifted my head from his chest. "I know what your answer is going to be, but I have to see them."

"Em, you can't—"

"No, Dell. Please don't tell me Mom and Tom are hurt, then say I can't go to them."

He took several deep breaths before replying, "Emily, that's exactly what they want you to do. They're watching your family, waiting to flush you out, so to speak. I realize you won't be able to think of anything else until you have proof of their safety. I understand that, but you also have to understand that going to them will put them in jeopardy as well."

Then my tongue took over and left a mess behind in its unfortunate wake. "Are you worried about them or your company?"

He instantly released me and took two steps backward.

"Emily, how can you ask me that? Do you really think that H&S is all I'm considering here?"

I shot back with a venomous hiss, "I know what *my* priorities are!"

"So do I, and I'm not as shallow as you take me to be! I have been tortured by this knowledge for days now. I wanted to protect you but knew I needed to tell you the truth as well." He ran his fingers through his hair and filled his cheeks with air, then forcefully blew it out through his lips. "Can't you see how difficult this decision was? Yes, I am concerned with my company, but how could you possibly think I'd put that above the people you love? What kind of monster do you think I am?" Then he threw out the zinger: "Do you question my love for you?"

I preferred to win arguments and would have added a few more comments had I been with anyone else, but something new overcame me in that moment, a depth of emotion I had never felt before. I saw the anger mixed with sadness in Dell's eyes and knew I had already crossed a line with my words. "No," I said, shaking my head. "I don't question that."

He exhaled through his nose at me. "Then why do you doubt my motives?"

I couldn't offer an answer, so I found a nice spot on the carpet, where I focused my eyes and attention and remained silent. After a few seconds, I watched Dell's feet walk closer to me, until his bare chest was almost touching my down-turned head.

"Emily?"

I was too ashamed to look up, so I closed my eyes and leaned my forehead against him.

He didn't seem to mind and continued to talk regardless.

"I love you more than I have ever loved or will ever love. I would never do anything to hurt you or your family. After all, they're *my* family now."

I lifted my head and looked into his face, reaching up to touch the scars on his cheeks. "You already hurt someone I love." He shook his head and tried to speak, but I stood on my tiptoes and kissed his lips. "You never should have been in that car on our fake honeymoon. You could have died, Dell."

"That doesn't count," he replied.

"You're wrong!"

"Emily, I—"

"No, I could have lost you forever, Dell. You need to promise me right now that you will never do anything even remotely similar to that again. I don't care who you think you're protecting or why. Promise!"

"I can't make that promise, Em."

The lump in my throat was enormous and felt as if it were bulging through my skin, yet somehow I spoke around it. "In that case, I don't think—"

"Don't even say that!" he cried, his voice stern and un-yielding. "You're correct. I wasn't supposed to be in the car, but I had to ensure that the accident occurred as planned. Long ago, I promised I would never hurt you, Emily. I can't honor that promise if I also agree to keep myself from harm. It doesn't work that way."

"I can't lose you, Dell. I won't." I wrapped my arms around his neck.

His voice softened. "Then don't."

I didn't want to do anything more than hug him, and he held me there until we heard a knock at the door.

Neither of us were dressed, so Dell spoke through the closed door, "Yes?"

"I've come to collect your things, sir," the young voice of Harvey said.

Dell turned to me and whispered, "They're kicking us out."

I looked around the suite at the prior day's wardrobe, strewn about the room, and shook my head.

"Harvey, my boy, could you please give us a few minutes?" Dell asked.

"Of course, sir. I'll just wait here."

Dell returned to my side. "I have a plan, sweetheart. We can talk about it once we're on our way."

I nodded at the mess on the floor.

He kissed me on the forehead. "Everything will be okay."

I wasn't convinced but decided to focus my energy on packing and making myself and the room somewhat presentable.

After thirty minutes, filled with baths and rushing about the suite, Dell opened the doors to find a sheepish Harvey standing next to a luggage cart.

"Good morning, Mr. Blanchet."

"Good morning, Harvey."

The boy wasted no time in pulling the cart into the room and loading our suitcases, then pushing it back into the hallway. My train case had appeared when Louie brought our other things, so I retrieved it from the bathroom and placed it on the cart as well. The bellhop patiently stood in the hall and waited until Dell and I took the hint and joined him.

Dell smiled at the boy's persistence. "You'll be a fine businessman someday, Harvey." He reached into his pocket and handed him his final tip. "I hope you have big plans for your future."

Harvey's eyes lit up at the sight of the 100-dollar bill. "Oh, yes, Mr. Blanchet. I am going to be the first in my family to attend college."

"Keep dreaming big, Harvey."

The boy pocketed the cash and pushed the cart toward a waiting elevator. We barely fit, but Harvey refused to let us out of his sight, so we squeezed inside with just enough room for the door to close.

At the front desk, a clearly nervous Lionel counted our payment and offered change in return.

"Keep it for your troubles, Lionel." Dell offered him a smile in addition to the tip.

Lionel just looked at the large sum, dumbfounded. We exited the lobby without another word.

As we approached the sidewalk, however, I noticed that the curb was empty. "Where is Perry?"

"He's still working on Maude and Louie's travel arrangements. Apparently, her father decided to accompany them to New York," he said with a smirk.

"Poor Maude."

Dell squeezed my hand. "The women in your family are hard to live without."

I leaned my head on his shoulder and reached my other arm around to hug his muscular biceps while he kissed the top of my head.

Within seconds, a valet drove the Chrysler to the front of the hotel. With the assistance of two other men, the valet divided the luggage between the armchair-looking back seats, piling them well above the height of the car sides.

Dell playfully elbowed me. "Good thing it's a convertible."

I simply smiled.

We loaded into the car and drove to the same beach we had visited several days prior. On the way, I looked at the passing scenery, trying to make sense of everything. Stone-faced buildings surrounded by the bustle of cars, streetcars, and pedestrians were soon replaced by palm trees and sun-kissed tourists, covered in smiles and more yards of spring fabric than the generations that would replace them.

Once we arrived at the beach, Dell turned off the engine and reached both arms toward me, pulling me sideways across the front seat. "Speak, my love."

My body was still facing forward, but I turned my head to meet his smiling face. "Are you sure you really want that, because I have about a million questions for you?"

"I'd be worried if you didn't!" He knew me too well.

"Are you comfortable?" I asked.

He pulled me closer. "Very."

Good, because we're going to be here a while.

Dell patiently waited while I gathered my thoughts.

"First, I want to apologize for what I said earlier. It was thoughtless."

He kissed me on the cheek. "Forgiven."

"Thank you." I looked at the ocean and hoped for inspiration, but found none, so I took a deep breath and moved forward on my own. "Is Maude going to be all right?"

He nodded. "That is why Louie is taking her to Italy."

"Okay. And what are you doing about Hodges?"

He didn't seem to expect that question, because he tried tapping the ocean for assistance as well. "I don't know how to say this, but he, uh…approached Midge and tried to woo her with his charm."

"Charm?" Hodges was tall, dark, and strikingly handsome and could match wits with any opponent, worthy or otherwise; however, he could have lived his entire lifetime and several others without adding "charming" to his resume. "Boring" was a more fitting term and much more likely to make the top five in his repertoire.

"I know," Dell continued, "but Midge enjoyed the attention regardless. They're engaged, Em."

"Excuse me? When did that happen? Was it before or after we faked our deaths?"

"Just after."

"Dell, I'm confused. Didn't Midge quit her job after we died in 1910, then travel to the 1920s to be with me at Essex House?"

"Things have changed. It's all so sudden."

I shook my head. "You're losing me. How can something that happened in the past ever be sudden?"

"Well, when someone is trying to manipulate past events, we have to slow things down and examine every miniscule detail. That's what Evergreen is doing, and it has forced us to do the same."

I put my own past under a microscope and thought back to the day when Midge appeared at Essex House, when I was Blanche, and Shane and I were creating such a controversy. "When Midge finally travels to Essex House, will she know you survived?"

He shook his head.

"What a relief! That would have been a big secret to keep, and poor Midge isn't the best with stress, you know."

"Yes, I know," Dell agreed.

"And her relationship with Hodges?"

"She understands that her love affair will be short-lived. She is also developing tuberculosis."

My mouth flew open to speak, but Dell beat me to it.

"It's not the real disease, Em—just believable symptoms."

"Is she going to die?" I used finger quotes around the last word.

"Yes. Then she will join you at Essex House."

"Well, she does have a flair for the dramatic."

Dell held his grinning lips tight for several seconds but broke out into laughter anyway, scaring nearby seagulls from their sandy search for food.

"What's so funny?"

"Well, sweetheart, Midge isn't the only one with that talent!"

"Jerk!" I said. But I smiled inside, secretly thinking of Maude, my inspiration.

He moved his arm toward me. "Want to slug me?"

I offered a view of my tongue instead.

"Tease!" Dell smiled.

I rolled my eyes and tried to look angry, but it didn't work. "So what will Midge and her alleged death accomplish?"

"The distraction we need to investigate Hodges and his motives."

"Okay. And are you investigating other theories as well?"

"Yes, there are several others. Do you remember Sybil?"

I thought back to the housemaid who made my life hell at Winston Manor. "How could I forget her?"

"Well, she didn't forget you either. She even followed me

and other H&S employees on our pretend honeymoon, posing as a nanny for a wealthy family in Nice."

"You're kidding!"

"I wish I were. She followed us up until the day before our accident."

"Was she acting alone?"

"That is what we are investigating."

A horrible thought crept into my mind. "And how are you protecting Mom and Tom?"

"Your mom's new best friend, Jane, was the nurse who cared for her after her accident. And Tom befriended two local mechanics who helped to investigate the accident and clear Tom's name in the process. They're all H&S employees."

"Poor Tom. I bet he blamed himself."

"He did, but his new friends have eased his mind."

"He's a good guy."

"I know."

I looked at Dell. "How?"

He hesitated, then finally said, "I met him."

I sat up in my seat and turned my entire body toward him, without breaking eye contact.

Dell shook his head. "Now, Em…"

"Why are you allowed to go and I'm not? They're *my* family!"

"Sweetheart, I was in greasy coveralls and had my hair in a ponytail. My tattered ball cap and goatee didn't hurt either."

"Dell, I can wear a disguise just as easily as you can."

"No, Em."

"Why not?"

"Because Evergreen wants you, not me. They came out of the woodwork to watch Jane and her every movement. She's one of our best, yet she almost quit as a result. They've infiltrated the hospital and parking garage, as well as her apartment complex. They even pump her gas, bag her groceries, and offer her help to the car. They've swarmed her and won't back off. They easily overlooked a greasy male friend of Tom's, but they'd never give you a pass."

I was beyond frustrated and wanted to scream, so I did. Not only did all the newly gathered seagulls fly away, but the ocean almost seemed to stop crashing to shore from the time I opened my mouth until I closed it again.

Dell tried to reach for me, but I exited the car, stepped out of my pumps, and stormed off in the opposite direction, toward the water. At first, he just called after me from the front seat, but then I started to run. I considered entering the water, but knew that my swimming inabilities would not allow me to make it too far. I also really loved my red and yellow silk dress, so I chose to run toward the water, then fake a right and continue on my way down the beach. Dell, however, seemed to have a strategy of his own. He caught up to me within seconds, grabbed me around the waist, and pulled me down onto the sand.

My instincts kicked in, and I tried to push him off but failed under his weight. I felt as if I were a feather trying to escape from beneath a rock.

Dell slid the hair from my angry face. "Your mom read the letter from Maude."

I'd forgotten all about it and the note I'd buried with my journal, asking young Maude to one day write a letter that would explain everything to my mom. As I pondered his words, I stopped struggling. "I miss her so much, Dell."

He kissed my forehead and rolled off, then helped me to

sit next to him on the sand. "I know, and she misses you as well."

I leaned my head against his chest, where the sound of his heart beating in my ear gave me the courage to finally ask, "So she knows about Evergreen's involvement in her accident?"

"I told her."

"Is she okay?" I asked, then lifted my head to see his face.

"She's strong, similar to someone else I know."

"I don't feel so strong. In fact, I feel pretty pathetic."

"Well, considering what you've been through, I'd say you're doing better than most."

I offered a weak smile. "Thank you for checking on them for me."

"You're welcome. Can we go back to the car now?"

I laughed. "Yes."

Dell stood and reached for my hand and helped me to my feet. I brushed myself off and held his hand as we walked to the car.

"You know I was quite the athlete in school, Em."

"Apparently," I replied, shaking my head.

He opened the door for me and helped me into the seat, but before he joined me, he opened one of the suitcases and rooted around for several seconds before closing the lid. "Here. This is for you."

I looked at the envelope in his hand, the fiber-covered, recycled variety that Mom usually purchased. I took it from him and turned it over, noticing the signature tape that Mom insisted upon using on all of her correspondence. "Never lick an envelope. It's coated with carcinogens!" she always warned. I held it to my chest and closed my eyes before open-

FOR THE LOVE OF MAUDE

ing it to read:

Sunday, February 24, 2013

My Sweet Little Girl,

I am so proud of you! You have become the woman I always knew you would be—strong, independent, and loving beyond my hopes and dreams. Speaking of dreams, this Dell of yours is sure a hunk. He and Tom just disappeared down to the garage and are talking parts and lubricants. You know guys and their toys.

I am sorry we missed your wedding, but I understand a corset was involved and…well, I'd be hard pressed to wear a bra, let alone one of those things. Still, for you, baby, I'd even wear an underwire. (Please destroy this letter. I don't want you using it against me in the future!) When you come home, we'll have a wedding of our own.

This business with the accident has left us all frazzled, but please don't worry about us. We can take care of ourselves. I know you, Treasure. Please don't blame yourself for any of this. It's certainly not your fault. Tom and I were becoming bored anyway.

Glass-A-Fras is keeping us busy. Apparently, hand-blown glass has become really popular, and business has never been so good. I took a few more classes and am now making some pretty wild jewelry. I've saved a few of my extra special pieces for you. In case I forget, they're waiting for you on your dresser next to your cell phone. (Yes, I received the note asking me to put the phone on your dresser. You know me too well. I might have misplaced it otherwise.)

Dell also said you have become good friends with our crazy Maude. You two always had a special connection that transcended the age barrier. Now I understand why. Next time you see her, please give her a big squeeze for me, and if you could put a good word in for me in advance for wrecking her car when I was in high school, I would appreciate it.

I'm so proud of you! I can't wait to finally see you and hear about all of your adventures—at least the ones you can talk about. I love you, darling, and want you to know that we support you in everything you do.

Take care of yourself and your eggs. I might want grandchildren someday.

Love,

Your Favorite Mom

P.S. *Thank you for asking Maude to write that letter. It blew my mind and eased it at the same time. I'm sure you know what I mean. I am grateful that I finally have the opportunity to reply to it and you. I'm also happy to finally open the trunk—as I'm sure you remember, I promised Maude before she died that I wouldn't open it until a certain date, one I couldn't reveal. Well, the day came on the fifteenth of last month, which was also the date I was able to open your letter. It wasn't easy to keep such secrets for all these years, especially from you, but it was sure worth it. Wow! I bet when you first saw Maude's old trunk as a* *child, you never imagined your secrets were the reason it was chained and locked in the attic. I grew up with the same trunk, and I'm having trouble with the concept as well. I also can't imagine the life you are living, but I hope you and I can discuss it soon over a cup of cocoa—with extra marshmallows, just the way you like it. We have a lot of catching up to do, so please hurry home!*

I folded the letter, replaced it in the envelope, and ran my fingers along the tape to reseal it. Dell silently handed me a handkerchief and started the engine.

CHAPTER TWENTY-ONE

Without a clear honeymoon destination in mind, Dell drove us to the Time Travel Warehouse, where we descended into the laboratory to explore our options. It couldn't have been less romantic. We were seated in a windowless room, stark white from floor to ceiling and filled with lab-coated employees who insisted on offering their personal suggestions on the best and safest honeymoon locations. I wanted to vomit.

"There's always the house where you're known as Lady Milton." Dell said, an obvious ploy to coax a smile from me.

"My favorite," I said, though it clearly wasn't.

Finally, Dell looked at the people milling around. "Will all of you please give us a moment?"

The drove of clipboards left without another word.

"Thank you," I said once the door was firmly closed.

"You're welcome, sweetheart. This wasn't what I had in mind."

I stared at the table filled with safe house pictures spread out neatly before us. "Me neither. This isn't exactly the epitome of romance."

"Emily..." He pulled his chair closer to mine and reached

for my hand.

I met his eyes.

"I'll take you anywhere you want to go regardless of the safety. We'll figure it out somehow." He read my mind before I could respond. "With the exception of your family."

I nodded. "I understand, but it's difficult to think of anything else right now."

"I know." Dell's voice was calm, almost resigned.

I closed my eyes for a few seconds and tried to picture my ideal spot. I couldn't. I'd never dreamed of a honeymoon as a child. In fact, I'd never dreamed I would be married; after all, Mom hadn't walked down the aisle, and my father was a taboo family topic that left my very curious, little mind to fend for itself. Thus, when my friends insisted upon playing wedding when I was younger, I always avoided being the bride and chose to be the DJ or singer at the reception instead. I couldn't carry a tune, but it beat having to kiss Jimmy Delgado at the end of the imaginary ceremony; he had chronic halitosis and never cleaned under his nails. I shuddered at the memory.

"Are you cold, Em?"

I opened my eyes to see Dell staring at me, within inches of my face. "No. I, uh...No. Thank you. I'm fine." I chose to keep the memory of Jimmy to myself.

"Any ideas?" he asked.

I thought for a moment, then offered a suggestion that I quickly grew to regret. "Well, this might sound kind of strange..." I said.

"That's okay. What is it?"

"You were able to meet my family, to see where I grew up, to talk to them. I want to do the same with your family."

Dell grew pale before my eyes, suddenly matching the color of the room around us. "No!"

"Why not?"

He was on his feet, his booming voice filling the room. "Because they're not who you think they are, Em. Your family loves you. They're kind and caring. Mine is the opposite. They're loathsome and hateful. I would never take anyone as precious as you into that world."

No, but you'd make me feel horrible for asking! I hadn't seen him so distraught since our stay at The 1908 House, and I had no interest in a repeat performance, so I swallowed my pride and comments. "Dell, I didn't mean to upset you. I just thought it would be nice to—"

"Can we just drop it?"

I nodded up at him.

He looked at me for several seconds, then pulled me into his arms. "I'm so sorry, sweetheart. I didn't mean to erupt."

"Dell, you've just told me so little about yourself. I want to know everything about you, and meeting your family seemed to be such a perfect solution."

He shook his head. "The only solution you'd find there is a divorce. If you met them, you'd definitely file for one. In fact, you'd leave in the night without ever turning back."

"I doubt that."

"I don't, and I'm not willing to take the risk."

"How about your grandma, Oma Holtz?" I asked.

I could feel Dell's arms finally relaxing. "I have to admit she was the exception, but I don't know how she'd take the arrival of her adult grandson and his bride from the future. She passed when I was quite young, and I'm not sure if it would be a safe risk for her or us."

"I understand," I said. I didn't, but I took a deep breath and exhaled slowly in relief, grateful his anger had passed.

Dell's past was a mystery to me. I knew he was born a century or more before me, but I didn't know exactly when, and the Dickens-themed nightmare I was picturing in my head wasn't worth pursuing. Therefore, I turned to look at the safe house pictures on the table next to us. "Some of them look really nice," I said.

"They are," he said.

"Are they fully staffed?"

"Yes."

"Are we limited to the house itself, or would we be able to mingle with society a little?"

A smile started to surface on his face. "We could mingle."

"Well, then I guess I've made up my mind."

"Okay." He looked at the pictures, then back at me. "Which one have you chosen?"

"All of them!"

"Excuse me?"

"I want to tour them all, like a Fifty Best Time Travel Safe Houses of the World tour. It would make a great television series, wouldn't it?"

He smiled and shook his head. "I'm ignoring your brilliant idea regarding the series, but it will still take months."

"Exactly."

"But—"

"Okay," I said before he could protest too much. "Just to make it easier, I'll eliminate one right off the top. Pardon me." Dell released his hold so I could reach across the table toward the pictures. I retrieved the photo of The 1908 House and showed it to him. "This one." Then I flung it over my shoulder and onto the floor.

"Oh, and this one too." I picked up the photo of Dunston House and held it in my hand. Its massive stone façade and perfectly manicured hedges appeared uninviting, almost arrogant. I truly despised that house. It stood just across the road from Winston Manor and was where Dell lived when we first met. Dunston House was also where I discovered Dell had faked our deaths without me, then left me so he could recover from his injuries. My memory of our original wedding night spent alone in the basement laboratory of that house made me cringe. I felt my cheek where the putrid green couch I'd occupied unaccompanied that night had left a woven pattern on my face. "There!" Flinging the photo on the floor was liberating, as if I were throwing the nightmare away.

Dell's voice drew me back to the moment. "Em, really, you want to visit all of them?"

I nodded triumphantly. "All except those."

"Well, I have to warn you that the ideal time frame for at least half of them would involve your wearing your favorite undergarment."

My smile fell. I hadn't considered the dreaded corset. "Which ones?"

Dell shuffled through the pile. "This one, this...and oh, this one. This too."

When he was finished, there were six remaining, and most were located in cold climates.

I shook my head at the pictures. I grew up in the Oregon rain, with occasional black ice and snow, then went to college and worked for Evergreen, where I suffered through the bitter winters of Upstate New York. The idea of freezing to death on my honeymoon just wasn't an option.

Dell separated two photos from the group and brought one closer to me. "This is one of my favorite locations. It is on a tropical island in the Pacific, and we wouldn't have to worry about our wardrobes."

"I bet," I said, picturing myself in nothing but coconut shell bras and grass skirts. *If I'm lucky.*

He smiled at the house in the picture, confirming my thoughts.

I quickly brought him back to reality. "And the other one?"

"Well, this is one of my other favorites. It overlooks the Mediterranean and isn't far from a local fishing village."

"Is this where Maude and Louie are on their honeymoon?"

He shook his head. "No. This location is farther south."

I studied the two photos he was holding.

"No corset?"

He laughed and shook his head.

"If my choice isn't as great as it appears in the photo, can I pick the other one?" I asked.

"Yes, or you can choose both if you prefer."

They both looked appealing: one a secluded white plantation house, surrounded by a porch and palm trees; the other, a Mediterranean villa with a perfect view of the sea.

Some of my earliest memories involved my family telling stories of their travels. Maude shared her many photo albums, and Mom brought the sights and sounds of Italy to my bedside every night as she relived her college years, one cathedral and museum at a time. The thought of their adventures brought some normalcy into my life and left me with one clear choice. "I've always wanted to go to Europe," I said.

"Okay, I'll make the arrangements." He gathered the remaining photos, as well as the ones on the floor, and returned to my side. "Are you happy, Em?" he asked.

I nodded. "I'm finally going on my honeymoon...every girl's dream. How could I not be happy?" But I wasn't.

Dell had posed that same question the day before our wedding, when having my family in attendance wasn't an option. Now, the thought of honeymooning when I knew Mom and Tom were being stalked by Evergreen didn't create much joy either. *Happiness is a relative term. I'm not exactly lying about being happy now if it finds me eventually*, I decided. *Close enough.*

He leaned forward and kissed me on the cheek before leaving the room, then returned within minutes, accompanied by two women bearing tape measures. They spent a considerable amount of time circling me with their tapes and making notes on clipboards.

"Is this really necessary?" I asked Dell offhandedly.

Both of the women stopped and stared, looking offended.

"Yes. Louise and Talia are specialists in clothing of this region and time frame."

I had to think fast, fearing the possible loose stitch that would lead to a serious wardrobe malfunction at some point in the near future or past, as the case might be. "Oh, Dell, you spoil me!"

The ladies smiled at each other and returned to their work.

Dell just shook his head and grinned.

While the ladies were busy taking measurements, I started to feel lightheaded. By the time they left, my ears were ringing, and I was seeing stars. I must have looked pale, because Dell ran to my side and eased me into a chair.

"Are you okay?" my husband asked, his eyes wide as saucers.

I was confused by the question and could only look into his eyes for the answer I wasn't able to produce on my own. Then my stomach growled and gave us both the clue we were seeking.

Dell knelt next to my chair. "Oh, Em, I'm so sorry! We lost our room before we could order breakfast." He suddenly checked his watch. "Now it's past five."

"I don't feel so good, Dell," I muttered just before the tunnel that seemed to be closing in around me finally swallowed the remaining light in the room.

CHAPTER TWENTY-TWO

A lone, I awoke in yet another new and unfamiliar location, a room filled with natural light, in which I was buried beneath the largest, warmest blanket I'd ever been fortunate enough to experience. "This is growing old," I said to the ceiling.

Its large wooden beams loomed down at me as if to say, *"So are you!"*

Regardless, I rose on my elbows and began to study the room. My eyes were immediately drawn just beyond the footboard of the large wooden bed I was occupying, to a set of double-windows that opened outward like shutters. White lace curtains rustled as the fragrant scent of flowers drifted into the room on a light breeze. A small, narrow dresser sat beneath the window and was covered with a lace runner. The room was sparse but adequate, with a nightstand and candle next to the bed and a small table and single wooden chair on the opposite side. A wardrobe consumed the remaining portion of wall beside the dresser and window.

The fresh air called to me, so I pulled my covers back to inhale more deeply, only to discover I was wearing an unfamiliar long, white nightgown. I was tempted to once again wonder how I had managed to be wearing such a garment, but I quickly convinced myself not to overthink it. Instead, I sat on the edge of the bed and forced myself to focus on the headboard with flowers carved into its thick wooden face, until my attention was stolen by the frigid, planked floor that met my bare feet.

I quickly recovered them. *Great, I think I have frostbite!*

I rubbed my feet vigorously while formulating a plan to use the woven rugs scattered across the room as stepping stones to lead me to the window. Once there, I rested my hands on the dresser and leaned toward the open air. The yard beyond was bordered by neatly trimmed hedges and flowerbeds filled with more varieties than I could count. "Where am I?" I asked out the window, as if Mother Nature might answer me.

A flock of little birds descended on the shrubs outside the window. My presence didn't seem to keep them from their search for insects. Once they had their fill, they quickly flew around the outside walls and out of sight.

"Bye, little guys!" I called after them.

I felt as if I had just entered a fairy tale. At any moment, I expected to see a half-dozen small men carrying picks and whistling as they marched through the doorway. I searched the room for a robe, just in case, and I was happy to find one lying along the foot of the bed.

I was working on the last button, when I heard a knock at the door. I turned toward the door just in time to see it open slightly and produce a small, shoeless foot, then another, until a boy of about three was standing beside it, grasping the door latch as if he were holding a shield. I couldn't help but smile down at his cherub-like face surrounded by golden curls.

"*Guten Morgen,*" he said shyly to the ground in front of his feet.

I guess that answers the "Where am I?" question. Mom's subtitled movies to the rescue again. "*Guten Morgen,*" I replied.

"*Möchten Sie etwas zum Frühstück?*" he asked.

Uh…yeah. So much for Mom's movies. I just smiled at the little guy and the earnest look on his face. Then my stomach growled.

He giggled. "*Sie haben einen grossen Hunger!*"

Hunger? Yeah, I guess skipping breakfast and lunch is what landed me here.

When he held out his hand, I let him lead me from the bedroom into the living area beyond. It was filled with more large wooden furniture that matched the bedroom pieces in their simplicity and functionality. We walked a few more feet, into a large kitchen that housed a wood-burning cook stove and a corner booth. The table was covered in an amazing, aromatic array of baked goods, including rolls and sliced dark bread, as well as bowls of fresh fruit and slabs of cooked ham and cheese.

I was starving and couldn't keep my eyes or nose from the table. I was so focused on the feast that I didn't notice the woman standing nearby until I was almost upon her, and I jumped backward at the sound of her voice in a thick German accent.

"Emily?"

I caught my breath and turned to see the kindly, gray-haired woman smiling at me. She wore a dark red dirndl with a white apron tied around her waist and knotted in the back. Her sturdy arms reached for me and pulled me into a hug before I could register another thought.

FOR THE LOVE OF MAUDE

She squeezed tightly, then released, holding me at arm's length and examining me from head to toe. After gripping my shoulders for a few seconds, she suddenly grasped me by the waist with both hands and held them on my hips. She shook her head. *"Nein, das geht nicht!"* Still holding my waist, she guided me backward to the booth and gently pushed until I sat down.

I looked from the table to her face that was smiling down at me, and then I froze; those were Dell's eyes looking back at me. "Oma Holtz?"

She nodded. *"Ja."* Without wasting any time on further introductions, she reached for a plate that was resting on the table and proceeded to fill it with an ample amount of food from the selection before me.

I must have been in shock, because I could only stare at her smiling face and the eyes that seemed to run in the family.

The plate was mounded when she finally deposited it in front of me. *"Guten Appetit!"* she said.

It was more food than I had consumed in the previous week, but I smiled just the same. *"Danke!"*

"Bitte schön!"

Everything on my plate looked so good that I didn't know where to start. *If her plan is to fatten me up, I guess I'll let her have her way just this once,* I decided. I reached for a heavily buttered piece of rye bread and took a bite; it was heaven.

She nodded in satisfaction and left the room, returning with a pitcher of milk from which she filled a giant mug and deposited it next to my plate.

My mouth was full, so I just nodded at her.

She smiled in reply and left me to my meal. The little boy, however, decided to stick around and stare at me as I ate. At first, he simply hovered near the edge of the table and shyly looked at my plate. Then his eyes wandered to the other items that surrounded it. I could almost see the drool forming around his mouth.

I offered him a Kaiser roll and felt as if I had made a friend for life. The little guy devoured the bread within seconds and looked back at me, pleading for more. I removed a berry from my plate and held it out for him.

He followed the progress of the fruit from my plate to within inches of his mouth. "*Danke schön!*" He snapped the berry up like a lion being fed a juicy steak.

"*Bitte schön!*" I replied, hoping my feeble attempt at his language wasn't butchering it.

The boy didn't seem to notice. As he chewed, his eyes finally left the table and met mine. There they were again, Dell's eyes. Only on that occasion, they weren't just hereditary, they were actually his.

"Johann?" I finally asked.

"*Nein, ich heisse 'Hans,'*" he said proudly. His sweet little voice sounded similar to one of the birds that had greeted me earlier.

"Hans?"

"*Ja.*" He nodded.

Little Dell! I was instantly in love.

I beckoned him to me with my index finger, and he slowly walked closer until he was sharing the booth next to me. I offered him another item from my plate and slid the mug of milk in his direction. That continued for a few more minutes, until I eventually just pushed my plate in front of him and let him help himself. As he ate, I noticed that his face and hands were filthy and his dirty clothes were worn on the edges. It brought tears to my eyes, and I didn't have the heart or the German vocabulary to ask him to wash his hands before taking another bite.

"Johann!" Oma scolded from the kitchen.

Neither of us had noticed her return, but she caught Hans mid-chew, where he remained.

She pointed to a kid-sized table and stool near the cook stove; the table held a small plate and mug. Hans didn't leave my side, but Oma wasn't upset for long when my sad eyes caught hers.

She just nodded and brought me another plate and poured a different mug of milk. I helped myself to the breakfast and also resupplied Hans's plate as I went.

When he was finished, he scooted closer to me and put his tiny arms around my waist. I pulled him into a hug, and he squeezed me tightly. I looked at Oma, who dabbed the corner of her eyes with her apron before clearing the table.

What kind of monsters are your parents? I couldn't imagine the amount of neglect poor Dell suffered throughout his childhood.

It didn't take long before his full belly overcame him, and he drifted off to sleep. Oma heard his light snores and gathered him into her arms. I followed her as she gently laid him on a pillow-covered chair in the other room and draped a soft blanket over him. Then she drew me into a hug and held me there for several seconds before kissing me on the cheek. Even if I could have communicated with her at that moment, it wouldn't have mattered; her sweetness was beyond words.

We spent the next few minutes clearing the table, storing the leftovers on shelves in the larder, and washing the dishes in her enormous, trough-like basin that didn't have the advantage of indoor plumbing. As we worked, Oma told me the names of all of the food items and continued to repeat herself as I dried the dishes and put them away.

My attempt at learning her language was met by suppressed giggles that turned to peals of laughter. *I just thought I'd earn my breakfast by lending a little comic relief.* Similar to little Hans, Oma was sweet, and I couldn't be upset with her sense of humor; it was contagious, and in the end, she had me laughing at myself as well.

When we were finished, I helped her carry large pots of steaming water from the cook stove into a small room, where we poured their contents into a giant tub that was situated under an open window. After several similar trips, the pots were empty and were followed with several more of cold water that we filled from a well in the backyard. It was quite the process, but we eventually brought the bath water to a manageable temperature. She closed the window, offered me a bar of soap and towels, then started to leave the room.

"Oma?"

She turned and smiled at me.

"Hans?" I motioned to the bath.

She shook her head and made a sleeping gesture with her hands and cheek.

I felt guilty for her efforts and knew that even if I hadn't bathed in weeks, I was far cleaner than the precious little boy sleeping in the other room. I also knew that bathing in a house without indoor plumbing was a luxury and was usually accommodated in a trough in front of the stove or fireplace. I appreciated the privacy.

Oma stepped closer and placed her hand on my cheek and smiled. Then she left the room.

FOR THE LOVE OF MAUDE

I stared at the tub and imagined the many ways in which I could use it to inflict pain and suffering upon Hans's parents. I spent the entire bath fantasizing about other more inhumane methods, involving such things as dirty clothes and starvation. By the time I was finished, I was more than just a little motivated to put my plans into action.

Fortunately for Oma's son and his evil wife, I didn't know where to find them or how to circumvent the communication barrier enough to make a successful attempt. *A minor technicality*, I decided.

My vengeful thoughts consumed me as I exited the room with the tub and entered the bedroom to find a rose-colored dirndl of my own resting on the freshly made bed. The top was covered with embroidered flowers connected by vines. A similar pattern ran the length of the detached skirt's hem. A cropped, white, short-sleeved blouse rested just under the other clothing on the bed.

"Yes! No corset." I was happy there wasn't one until my struggle to fit into the tight bodice made everything clear. "This thing is its own corset!"

I cursed the big breakfast I'd just eaten as I gingerly pulled on the skirt. Despite the hold the bodice had on my ribs, I successfully avoided pushing my stomach and its contents up and into my esophagus in the process of donning the skirt. *This thing needs to come with instructions—in English. I'll definitely put the skirt on first next time.*

When the outfit was complete, I stood in front of a strange mirror that covered the inside portion of one of the wardrobe doors. *What makes you reflective?* I thought of the old mirrors I'd learned about in chemistry class, and stepped closer to take a better look. *Mercury or silver?* My curiosity was soon replaced by the image that stared back at me. With the exception of my face and the wet hair that surrounded it, I didn't recognize the woman in the glass. I looked as if my head had been superimposed on a picture of a well-endowed girl wearing a dirndl, possibly from a beer ad. "Dang girl. You're hot!" I turned to admire my newly enhanced figure further, adjusting the top of the little blouse and smoothing the fabric along my ribcage.

"Who are your friends?"

I almost screamed. Dell was poking his head into the room from the garden, ogling my cleavage. I fought the urge to pull the window closed but greeted him with my hands on my hips instead. "You scared me to death. Where did you come from?"

"Here, actually, but the real question is, where did *they* come from?" His eyes couldn't seem to find mine.

"Don't you wish you knew?"

"Why don't you come here and —"

Before he could finish, Oma knocked on the bedroom door and opened it, bearing a brush and hair pins. She looked from me to Dell and laughed, then swatted at him with the brush. "*Auf Wiedersehen!*"

I giggled at him too as he walked away in a mock sulk. *Poor guy!*

Once he was gone, she handed me the brush and hairpins and deposited me into the wooden chair she had placed in front of the wardrobe mirror. I spent the next few minutes watching in wonder as her hands nimbly brushed and braided my wet hair into a halo-like formation around my head. The pins were inserted in strategic locations until she seemed satisfied with the finished look. I sat in amazement at how quickly she transformed me into Frau Holtz.

"*Danke!*" I smiled.

"*Bitte schön.*"

I exited the room a new woman, both in body and spirit, and I was eager to see Dell's reaction. I expected him to be waiting in the other room, panting and pacing the floor, but he wasn't. Instead, I was greeted by the sound of voices coming from the kitchen. As I drew closer, I also heard the sound of water. Dell didn't notice my approach as I entered the kitchen to find him bathing young Hans in the basin. Oma looped her arm in mine and we stood in the doorway, watching the two laugh as the younger Johann splashed in the water.

I wanted my camera—and a handkerchief. However, the smile on my face suddenly fell when I spotted Hans's dirty clothes on the floor. They were so filthy they practically stood up on their own. Oma must have noticed as well, because she pulled her arm free from mine and left the room. When she returned, she was holding a pair of lederhosen, a clean shirt, and socks. They smelled as if they had just come from a cedar chest.

She carried the outfit, along with a clean towel, to a dry table next to Dell and deposited the stack. He smiled at her and kissed her on the cheek. She looked at me, removed the dirty clothes from the floor, and left the room.

Dell followed her gaze to where I was still standing in the doorway. He tried to smile, but I could tell it was difficult for him to hide the pain of his childhood. As I walked closer, I could see the tears forming in his eyes. We both turned back to little Hans, who was making a mess splashing water all over Dell and the area around the basin. He acted as if he'd never taken a bath before, and from the looks of the dark brown water he was sitting in, I doubted he had.

"I'm sorry," I whispered in Dell's ear.

He couldn't speak and only nodded his reply.

I remembered one of my favorite tub pastimes as a child and began to search the kitchen for a cup and spoon. I found them on a shelf and gave them to Hans, so I could introduce him to the world of Fill Me Up and Pour Me Out. He loved it so much that he didn't want to stop, even when his little teeth were chattering. The promise of a warm towel and comfortable chair finally convinced him to leave the tepid, filthy water.

Dell held him tightly in the fluffy towel, singing softly to him. Hans just looked up at him and smiled, eventually singing along in his sweet little voice.

It was a heartbreaker I couldn't bear to watch; nor did I feel I had the right to participate, so I left them and joined Oma in the backyard, where she was washing Hans's threadbare clothes in a trough. I wrung them out for her and looked around for somewhere to hang them, but no line existed. Oma noticed my confusion and took the clothes from me and gently hung them over a nearby tree branch. I was too engrossed with the state of the items to bother pondering the lack of a proper clothesline; in fact, I couldn't stop staring at them. *How on Earth have these held together this long? They're barely stitched!* I walked in circles around the little outfit and shook my head in amazement and disgust.

My blood boiled as I closed my eyes and pictured myself delivering an arsenic-laced torte to his parents' front door, knocking, then hiding behind a bush while they happily carried it inside to devour it and meet their doom. The plan quickly fell apart, however, when I considered the possibility of Johann having a few siblings who might be fed the dessert as well. *Okay, Plan B, then.*

Smoke must have been pouring from my ears, because Oma suddenly tapped me on the arm, causing me to open my eyes and turn toward her. She shook her head. *"Nein, Emily!"*

I exhaled forcefully through my lips in an effort to calm myself. I knew she was right, but I couldn't help wishing for some form of accident to befall them. I paced the garden for several minutes before I was nearly knocked down by the force of young Hans as he hurled himself at me, wearing the outfit Oma laid out for him. I caught him while he was hugging my legs and quickly wrestled him to the ground and rooted out all of his most ticklish spots. He was wracked with giggles before I finally joined him on the grass. I was out of breath, but he wasn't, and he quickly jumped up and began to chase a butterfly.

Dell came to my side and helped me to my feet.

"Can he be our son?" I asked.

"No." He stared sadly at the little boy who jumped toward the butterfly with his hands in the air, squealing in delight.

"It's not as if it hasn't been attempted before. What's another Johann?" I asked, a failed attempt to lighten his mood.

"If it were possible to spare him from the upcoming years spent under our parents' roof..." He looked at the now giggling boy rolling in the grass. "If I could do so, I would, without hesitation."

We continued to watch Hans running rampant throughout the yard before I finally spoke. "Thank you for not introducing me to your parents."

Dell turned to reveal such a deep sadness in his eyes that

I almost couldn't breathe.

I hesitated for a moment, then continued, "I may have been forced to commit a double-homicide, and I doubt the jails of this time had internet."

He reached for me and pulled me into his arms and kissed the top of my head. "They don't have libraries either."

"Well, there goes my dream of working on my master's."

He held me tight for several minutes with his chin resting on my head. "If I didn't know that he'd be okay, I'd gladly share a cell next to you."

I nodded with my head against his chest and squeezed him as hard as I could. "Thank you for letting me meet Oma, though. I love her, and she sure loves you."

"You're welcome. Although, at first, I didn't care for the idea of revisiting my past, I'm glad we're here. I've missed her. She taught me how to love. Shortly before she died, she also convinced my father to send me to boarding school. I always assumed she must have known she was sick and wouldn't be there to protect me, but now…"

"Have you spoken to her about your schooling?" I asked.

"Yes, I wanted to plant the seed just in case. She wasn't too receptive at first, but when my scrawny, neglected little self appeared on her doorstep this morning, she couldn't refuse."

I shook my head along his chest. "What happened to him…you?"

Dell took a deep, shaky breath before replying, "My father is away on business, and my mother locked herself in her room."

"How long will he be gone?"

"Months," he said, sounding defeated.

I tried to speak calmly. "Are there other children? Why don't they take care of Hans?"

"My oldest brother is only eight."

I wanted to cry again but knew I needed to be strong for his sake. "I hate her."

He drew in another deep breath and exhaled loudly before replying, "There's a long line forming before you." I could hear his heart pounding in his chest.

I knew it was difficult for Dell to relive his childhood, but I wanted to keep him talking. I feared it might be my only opportunity to learn of his past. "Was your father a good man?" I asked.

"Once, before he married. Then he started to travel to be away from her; unfortunately, he left us behind in the process. I believe he loved us but not enough to shield us from her. I despise him for that."

Hans ran around us and tried to tickle the backs of our legs with a leaf before running toward a neighbor's cat that had just wandered into the yard.

"Can he live here until your father returns?" I asked softly.

"Yes."

I pulled away and gestured toward Hans. "Who does he think we are?"

"Cousins from another part of the country, where people speak in a strange dialect."

"What part of Germany is this?"

"I'm not German, sweetheart. I'm Austrian. We're just outside Salzburg."

"I never would have guessed that the Southern gentleman I met and later married was actually an Austrian one!

Where's your accent?"

"I spent a considerable amount of time and energy trying to shed it…and my past."

"I guess the wife is always the last to know."

He gave a slight chuckle before returning his attention to Hans.

"How did you convince Oma to let you in?" I asked.

He simply replied, "She recognized the eyes."

CHAPTER TWENTY-THREE

S everal days after our arrival, Oma surprised Dell with a pictorial tour down Memory Lane. Apparently, he resembled his father more than he realized, and a portrait tucked away in a cupboard left little doubt.

Oma wiped the dust from the framed painting and showed it to us. The man was dressed in a suit and stood next to a woman, who was wearing a white, flowing dress covered in lace. It was obviously a wedding portrait, and its lack of fading told me it had spent a considerable amount of time in the dark. Without being told, I knew we were looking at Dell's parents. His mother's dark hair was gathered onto her head and was decorated periodically with small flowers. The style of clothing was as foreign to me as the country I found myself visiting. Her dress and hair were beautiful, but the smile on her face told a different story. Even the addition of a large bouquet of flowers couldn't lighten her expression; she looked as if she wanted to rip the portrait's artist limb from limb. Dell's father, on the other hand, held a twinkle in his eye that almost compensated for his new bride's sour disposition—almost. His brown hair was combed back neatly and the hint of a crooked smile was dancing beneath his lips. The likeness to his son was almost eerie.

Dell glared at the painting and abruptly left the room. Oma simply shook her head and replaced the portrait deep within the cupboard from which she'd retrieved it and slowly closed the door.

I followed Dell's escape route and found him sitting on a bench in the garden with his head buried in his hands. "Dell?"

He didn't respond, so I sat next to him. After several minutes, he finally spoke. "I really don't know who I am anymore, Em. All these different facets of me—these glimpses of my life—leave me feeling empty. It seems as if parts of me are under a microscope, exposed for all to see and dissect. I'm tired of the scrutiny. That painting! I've never had a clear image of my father in my mind. I guess I blocked it out of my memories. Now, seeing the resemblance, I feel as if I've just viewed the dark side of my own soul. We might not be the same person, but he's inside me just the same."

I tried to console him. "You're not him, Dell."

He turned to reveal the torment on his face. "Emily, I'm not even Dell. I'm Johann Holtz, son of Friedrich Holtz, a man I'm too ashamed to claim as my father. I might not be him, but his blood is running through my veins whether I like it or not." He returned his head to his hands and tugged at his hair as his fingers ran through it.

I reached my arm around his back, but he pulled away.

"I don't deserve your love."

My jaw dropped, and I was speechless. I'd never seen him so defeated, not even when his anger and jealousy caused him to leave me for a second recovery period from our faked deaths. Dell was one of the strongest people I had ever met, ranking right up there with Nana Rosie, who always knew what to do in any situation.

Nana was not someone I sought when I was down in the dumps, because she didn't put up with anything, especially self-pity. If she even sensed a hint of it, Nana would fly into a lecture, filled with stories of the physical and mental difficulties others had not only encountered but conquered. In the end, my so-called problems always seemed ridiculous. Then she topped it with a kiss and sent me on my way. I called it "Nana Rosie Stew"—a jumble of ingredients mixed with love. And at that moment, Dell needed a big bowl of it, possibly seconds.

I didn't have the stories that Nana had, but I had a few ideas of my own that I was eager to throw Dell's direction. "Well, too bad for you!" I finally said.

Dell slowly turned to me, revealing his red, puffy face.

I quickly stared at the grass so I wouldn't lose my nerve. "I just feel sorry for someone who has overcome so much by creating an amazing life for himself—one that includes a superhot wife, mind you—then he simply wants to throw it all away."

Now it was his turn for his jaw to drop.

"I realize we returned to the past physically, Dell, but it's too bad you feel the need to return emotionally as well." I stretched my legs straight out in front of me and crossed them at the ankle. Then I extended my arms down behind me and placed my palms on the bench, leaning my weight on them.

He didn't respond, so I let out a heavy sigh and tilted my face to the overcast sky above us. I was freezing but pretended to bask in the nonexistent sunshine.

It took him several minutes to finally find his tongue. "You are superhot, especially in that dirndl."

I kept my eyes closed. "I know." Then I opened my eyes slightly and squinted in his direction. "It's nice to see that you think so too."

His smile finally surfaced momentarily but faded as he spoke. "You have to understand that this isn't easy for me."

"And you have to understand that none of this is your fault. You're your own man, and you chose not to live your life the way your father did."

He turned away and nodded at the ground. "I feel responsible, though."

I returned to a normal sitting position and placed my hand on his leg. "Well, don't. Just because he's your father, that doesn't mean you're responsible for his actions."

He took my hand in his and brought it to his mouth, kissing each finger individually until he reached the pinky. "I'm lucky to have you."

"Yes, you are…and don't you forget it!"

That drew a laugh out of him, but he quickly grew serious again and looked into my eyes. "Em, I don't want you to think I'm weak."

"Why would I think that?"

"The anger we had toward our father and the lack of love we received from both our parents inspired Johann to build an empire. I've built nothing; in fact, look at me now. One visit to my past, and I fall apart in front of the two women who mean the most to me."

Nice, Em. The whole speech about returning to the past physically instead of emotionally was a real winner. Way to go.

I tried to think a little longer before I spoke again. "Dell, you're the strongest man I know. What you see as Johann's strength is actually his weakness."

Dell's puzzled eyes met mine, forcing me to take a deep breath before continuing.

"Those things might have contributed to Johann creating his company, but they didn't make him strong or complete or satisfied. They produced a weakness in his life, a void that only you can help fill. You have a heart, Dell, and Johann needs that to build his future."

Dell nodded into the hands he was now wringing. "Oma taught me how to love."

"Yes, and deep down, Johann must have remembered that and wanted to experience it with his own grandchild," I added. We sat in silence for a few seconds before I continued, "Didn't you have any other relatives who could care for you?"

"Oma was the only true family I had as a child. After she passed away, I didn't return."

"Not even for holidays?"

He quickly replied, "No one sent for me."

"What about your siblings?"

He shook his head. "They scattered as well. I never knew what became of them, nor did I make it my business to learn."

"Were they treated as badly as you?"

"I was the only one who resembled my father's side of the family. Mother grew to love them eventually, but she never cared for me."

"Why did she have children?" I asked, baffled.

"She thought my father would become as wealthy as hers, but when her dowry began to dwindle, she realized she'd made a poor choice. By then it was too late. There were already five of us. Father worked endlessly to keep her lifestyle afloat, and Mother put an equal amount of effort into making my life miserable. I was the scapegoat for her misery."

"She really must have hated him."

He nodded. "It was mutual."

"She looked so angry in that wedding portrait, but your father looked genuinely happy."

"He was in love with her, but she was spoiled. Her dress, the flowers, the wedding—nothing was good enough for her. Father relished the challenge, but he could never win." He exhaled forcefully at the ground beneath his feet. "Once her ugliness began to overcome her physical beauty, Father simply gave up the effort. The love was gone, and so was his tolerance for her. When he was home, they fought constantly."

"I'm sorry, Dell. I can understand why you preferred boarding school." *I guess it also explains where your temper comes from.*

He didn't respond.

I paused for a few seconds. "How did they die?"

"Father was killed in a carriage accident, and mother moved with my siblings to another village. I heard she remarried. Beyond that, I'm not sure what became of her. She didn't exactly keep in touch...and neither did I."

I struggled to make sense of her actions. "She almost acted as if you were not her child."

He gave me a curious look. "Oma thinks the same thing."

"Are you the youngest?"

"Not quite. I have a younger brother."

"Maybe your father had an affair and your real mother died, possibly in childbirth. That wasn't uncommon back then. And to explain the addition of a baby in their household, your parents could have fabricated something about a well-concealed pregnancy."

"You have a good imagination, Em."

"Your parents both had brown hair. Did you have a blonde nanny?"

For the second time in less than an hour, his jaw dropped.

"I guess that's my answer. What became of her?"

"I never knew."

"Have you ever asked Oma?"

He shook his head.

"Don't you want to know?"

"No."

"But, Dell, that might explain so much."

"Or it might only create more questions and confusion. Please, Em, just drop it."

"But—"

"Emily!" His face was scarlet, and he was almost frothing as he spoke. "Just leave it alone."

So much for the Nana Rosie Stew!

The tears stung in my eyes, but I refused to react. Instead, I rose from the bench and walked back to the house. On the way, I passed Oma, who patted me on the back and walked past me into the garden, joining Dell on the bench. Within seconds, his shoulders were heaving in unison with the muffled sobs he was depositing on her shoulders.

That made me appreciate and miss my family even more. As I turned from the backyard scene, little Hans ran up to me and stopped short, holding a book in his hands. The tears and Dell's words were soon forgotten. I simply smiled down at the boy's sweet face as he handed the book up to me. I looked at the cover that held a profile of a horse and began to thumb through the pages, hoping to find only pictures. Unfortunately, the book contained mostly words—German words— with an occasional black-and-white woodcut picture. A nervous laugh overtook my smile, but Hans was undeterred. He grabbed my hand and led me to a chair and pointed. I was barely seated before he climbed into my lap, took the book from me, and turned to the first page.

Great.

He looked from the book and back up to me in eager anticipation, but I could only shake my head. He nodded and stared at the page for several seconds before closing the cover and pointing to the words in the title. Then he proceeded to read—most likely not the real words, but the ones he decided were there. As we progressed through the book, I felt as if I were viewing one of Mom's old movies where the people say dozens of words, while only five make it to the subtitles. The only difference was that I couldn't understand the language or the subtitles. Nevertheless, Hans augmented his flowery speech with gestures and emotion that made the book come to life in a larger way than the author might have even imagined. Soon, I began to understand the story—at least the one *he* was telling. By the time he finished, he was so proud of himself that he snapped the book closed and clapped for several seconds before jumping off my lap and running back into the yard.

I loved him already and remained in the chair, unable to convince the smile to leave my face. *That imagination's going to come in handy when he gets older.*

"Now I remember you."

I jumped and turned to see Dell standing behind me in the doorway.

"I also remember this visit to Oma's."

"How is that possible? You were so young."

He shrugged. "It stood out." He drew closer and knelt by

my side, then took my hand in his. "I'm sorry, Emily. I lose all control when I think of my past."

I stared into his sad blue eyes. "Why did you bring me here?"

"Because one of the last requests you made before you lost consciousness in the basement laboratory was to visit my family in the past. I felt guilty for refusing, so I made a bargain with your unconscious self that when you awoke, I would introduce you to my Oma."

"Well, now I know how to have my way. I'll just pass out."

Dell's silence sucked the humor from the air. "I need to ask you a favor, Em."

"Okay."

"Oma needs supplies from town, mostly for Hans. I resemble my father too much to join her—people will talk. Would you mind accompanying her?"

"Of course not," I said. Then I asked, "How will I manage without being able to speak the language?"

He continued to hold my hand in his and gently caressed it with his thumb. "I guess that's the favor portion of my request."

"Okay…"

"It would be best, for your sake and Oma's, if you were a little…mute."

I chuckled and shook my head. "And how should I behave if someone happens to ask me a question?"

He grinned. "Well, you're a little hard of hearing as well."

"You mean I'm deaf?"

"Mostly."

"Great, so I need to pretend to be a deaf mute?"

He nodded. "Exactly."

"Awesome." I stared at the wood floor. "Who am I in relation to Oma?"

"You're a neighbor. There are enough farms around here that no one will question it."

"Is it safe?" I had to wonder.

"Serial killers won't be popular for quite some time," he said sarcastically.

Now it was my turn to lack amusement.

He drew my hand to his lips and kissed it gently before returning it to my lap. "I wouldn't put you in harm's way. You know that."

* * *

Unfortunately, he was wrong. The five-mile trek to town early the next morning was more than my feet could bear in my borrowed leather shoes. I winced at the notion of the blisters that would greet me once they were finally free. The dirt road leading to town was lined with trees, bordering open, grassy meadows that stretched to an alpine mountain, Oma called "Der Untersberg," on one side and Hohensalzburg Castle, a stone fortress high upon a hill, on the other. The occasional horse-drawn wooden wagon held drivers who yelled, "*Grüss Gott*" as they passed. Pedestrians were few but offered similar greetings.

Then came the cobblestone streets that meandered through the town, crowded with all forms of wagon, horse, and foot traffic. Dell hadn't shared the time frame with me, and the almost timeless dirndl- and lederhosen-clad passersby didn't offer any clues. Regardless, the overcrowded streets were a hazard beyond description, with people scampering to and fro in a dangerous game of chicken with the other forms of traffic.

When the crowd became almost impassable, Oma looped her arm through mine, and we forced our way to our first destination, a tiny storefront sandwiched among a row of other businesses. I couldn't understand the words in German script on a sign protruding from the building and another just above the door, but the boots and slippers on display behind the store window informed me that it belonged to a shoemaker. Inside, the pungent smell of tannins and leather greeted us before the door could even close. There were surprisingly few customers, but the place was filled instead with rows of leather and cloth shoes, men's on one side and women's on the other.

"*Grüss Gott*," Oma said, smiling at a gray-haired man in a leather apron. His thick glasses and gnarled, arthritic hands were unkind testaments of his profession. After she handed him a paper with a traced outline of Hans's tiny feet, the man walked with Oma to a wooden podium at the back of his shop.

While the two discussed the order, I examined the many pairs of shoes on the shoemaker's shelves. Some were nothing more than flat, style-less strips of leather meant to simply cover one's foot. Others were elaborate patterned silk slippers, each with a chunky heel on the bottom and a giant buckle on the top. None were anything like the shoes I had learned about in my training with Evergreen or my travels with H&S. Whatever their design, they all lacked any form of support, a lesson my throbbing feet were learning firsthand.

Oma signaled the end of her conversations with a *"Wiedersehen,"* and we exited the store to join the crowd outside.

Our next stop was the tailor, where she offered another paper with measurements on it. Similar to the shoemaker, the balding tailor walked to a portion of the shop where they could discuss the order, leaving me to feel and stretch the bolts of cotton, silk, and leather material that lined the walls.

Next to the tailor was a sweets shop with a window filled with chocolates and hard candies I felt compelled to admire. Oma just shook her head and pointed to her teeth, which were white, straight, and still in her head.

Poor Hans! I could feel the saliva accumulating in my mouth and had to swallow to avoid drooling. *Poor Hans? No, poor me!* I felt as if I were five, except I maturely decided to avoid the temper tantrum and listen to reason. We walked on, but I continued to glance over my shoulder, admiring the window and its delicious-looking contents until they were out of sight.

The next shop that caught my eye was the toy store, where, from behind the front window, a group of intricately carved wooden animals held me in their hypnotic stare. Oma tapped me on the shoulder and shook her head. I made a praying gesture with my hands, but she wouldn't budge.

I'll give you the candy, Oma, but you're not going to win with the toys! With that thought on my mind, I walked past her and into the crowded shop, where I examined several horses until I located the one with the cutest face, proudly staring from its perch on the top shelf. It reminded me of the one from the book Hans tried to read me, and I was willing to do just about anything to take it home to him. When I was young, I had a room filled with toys, yet I hadn't noticed Hans playing with any of his own.

Oma reached my side and shook her head.

"Hans," I finally whispered.

Oma looked at my face and arms folded across my chest, then shrugged her shoulders. The owner of the shop retrieved the horse from the shelf at Oma's request and wrapped it in paper, then tied it with string.

Once we were outside, Oma pulled me into a giant hug, nearly spilling the newly deposited horse from her basket. We both laughed as we walked to a nearby butcher, where she added several parcels of bacon, cured meats, and bones to the basket. Most of the remaining space was filled with baking staples, such as salt from another nearby shop. The basket was now mounded and required both of us to walk on either side to share the handle and heavy load. Our final stop was a stationery store, where we added pens, paper, and books to the other items.

As we exited the shop, I noticed something I hadn't seen in a long time—a newspaper, proudly displayed in the front window next to the stationery store. Oma tried to steer me away but failed. Instead, I held fast to the basket handle and nearly dragged it and her to the glass, where I could only stare in amazement. The date on the newspaper stood out like a beacon among the German words that surrounded it: "17. September 1790."

CHAPTER TWENTY-FOUR

F or the first time since my arrival in Austria, I was happy for the language barrier. Oma sang softly or whistled while we carried the overloaded basket between us, sharing the burden on our return trip to her cottage. The basket, however, wasn't the only thing that weighed heavily upon me. I welcomed the lack of conversation so that the date on the newspaper could run around inside my brain. *I thought Dell was born in the 1800s — the late 1800s and not the late 1700s. How did I not know this? Why didn't I ask? The wife really is the last to know. No wonder Shane went crazy in the 1920s!*

With so much on my mind, the return trip seemed to take far less time than I anticipated, causing me to almost pass the road to the house.

Oma stopped at the entrance and tugged on the basket to gain my attention. I was holding onto the handle so tightly that I almost lost my balance and had to quickly recover my footing before spilling the contents of the basket. She just stood smiling at my ridiculous display.

Boy, do I feel stupid! I offered an embarrassed smile in reply and turned in the proper direction, wishing I were somewhere else. Fortunately, Oma simply returned to her whistling as we walked to her cottage. Once inside, we deposited the heavy basket on the kitchen table and shook out our tired arms in unison.

"*Ganz schwer*," she said with a laugh.

I just smiled. "I sure wish I could understand you."

"She said that it was very heavy."

We both jumped at Dell's comment from the doorway.

"Hans!" Oma scolded him.

He pulled her into a big hug and kissed the top of her head.

"*Geh weg*!" She pushed him away in mock disgust.

How cute!

She straightened her apron and walked with blushing cheeks to the overfilled basket.

Dell watched her walk away then met my grin from across the room. Seeing his smiling eyes, I realized how much I had missed him. Although we were staying in the same house, even sharing the same bed, it had been a while since we had been close. Aside from our honeymoon being put on hold, our relationship in general was feeling the strain. He had been struggling with his past during our entire visit with Oma and hadn't been himself since our arrival.

In just three quick strides, he closed the gap between us and pulled me into his arms. I hugged him tightly in return.

"I'm sorry," he whispered down to me.

"It's okay."

"No, it's not."

"Either way, I miss you and want you back," I said. When he didn't reply, I added, "How long do we have here?"

"We should have already left."

I drew back just enough to meet his eyes. "You're attached to Hans, aren't you?"

"I am. Strange as this might sound, he has restored my faith in myself. Oma has played an enormous role as well."

I smiled. "She's wonderful."

"Yes she is." He paused. "I'm going to miss her."

"Thank you for bringing me here and sharing her with me."

"What do you mean?"

"Before we arrived, Oma was just a memory from your childhood, a distant memory. With the aid of time travel, she became someone you could appreciate as an adult and also introduce to me. Now, she's a memory we can both share, and Hans is a part of you, a special part, you shared as well. I love him, and I love you even deeper for trusting me enough with your feelings to bring me here."

Dell took a deep breath and exhaled before saying, "I don't want to leave him here. I want to spare him all the pain I know he will be forced to endure."

"You realize you can't do that—your words, not mine."

"I understand," he said, his voice was rough.

"What you suffered has made you who you are, Dell, which ultimately led you to me. If you change the past, you change...us."

"Yes, but I've become extremely attached to Hans and want to protect him from the grim future he knows nothing about."

I nodded. "He's sweet."

Dell drew another deep breath and slowly let it out. "Please hear me out before you react."

"Okay."

"Being around him makes me want to start a family."

I didn't respond. Instead, I waited for a punchline that I hoped would soon follow. It didn't, and Dell seized the opportunity my silence offered to continue on the same theme.

"I realize you might not be ready, but I am…and I've been waiting a long time."

Centuries. I no longer felt comforted by his embrace. In fact, I suddenly felt the urge to run. I tried to pull away, but Dell tightened his grip around my waist, holding me within a few inches of his chest.

"Emily?"

I looked into his eyes. "Can I react yet?"

He laughed. "Yes."

"I'm not ready to have this conversation right now. The last thing I want is to be living in the 1700s and worrying about becoming pregnant." My voice was panicked, and Oma stopped momentarily from unloading the basket to look at us.

Meanwhile, Dell's eyebrows told the tale of his confusion. "How do you know what time frame we're visiting?"

"You seem to have this thing called a newspaper, or a *Zeitung*. Regardless, I couldn't read the words, but the date was clear."

Dell nodded and exhaled through his nose.

I continued, "I thought you were born in the late 1800s."

"I wasn't forthcoming on purpose, Em."

"Didn't you think I could handle it?"

No, that's not the reason. I just…it's complicated."

"And time travel isn't?"

"Of course it is, but you were mistaken earlier. It's more than just the physical act. There's also an emotional transition. I didn't want to burden you with the details all at once."

Great. Strike Two on that bowl of Nana Rosie Stew and all of its physical and emotional ingredients. I guess it must be cold by now. I cringed as I dared to ask, "Is there more?"

"Much, I'm afraid."

"Such as?"

He shook his head. "The best way to impart such a vast store of information is in increments as we traverse this crazy path."

"Excuse me?" My brain was clearly still on "start a family," and it was beginning to fog.

"I'll tell you as we go," he said.

I offered no reply.

"I apologize in advance if I miss anything. I know you love your details." He tried to draw a smile from me, but I just stared. "Emily?"

An almost comatose reaction was all I could offer.

"I don't expect you to give me a child before you're ready. I simply wanted to make you aware of my feelings."

Then let me make you aware of mine! I finally snapped out of it. "We've been careful to this point, and I want to continue to wait. I'm not finished with our honeymoon."

"Neither am I, Em." His voice had an edge to it.

"I love children, but I don't want one unless I can be with my mom. I know it's been difficult and dangerous to even arrange a visit, but I really want to be home with her."

"You're my wife, and your home is with me, Emily!"

"And where is that Dell?" Since he didn't reply, I continued, "Besides, how does a baby fit into time travel? He or she needs a physical home, someplace stable."

Again, he didn't speak; instead, he bit his lip and stared into my eyes. The flash of anger was gone but rested just below the surface.

"I know my home is with you, and as long as we're together, I don't mind traveling. But, Dell, we can't do that with a baby."

He shook his head as if to dislodge the remaining ill temper he had just tried to suppress. "I'm sorry. I just want to be a father."

"You will, but in this time travel business you created, it all takes patience. I've had to learn that the hard way."

He simply nodded, then said, "Johann's desire to create a legacy was a bit difficult to digest at first, but now it's all I can think about. I've endured this long. I guess I can wait a little longer."

I wrapped my arms around his neck and pulled him in for a kiss before he could change his mind.

With our tempers in check, Oma quietly shuffled toward us and handed me the package containing the wooden horse.

I took the parcel and smiled at her. "*Danke.*"

"*Bitte.*"

"What's this?" Dell asked.

"We bought something for Hans."

I looked around. "Where is he, by the way?"

"He's taking a nap on our bed."

I thought of my sore feet and equally overused mind. "After that hike into town and back, I feel as if I should join him."

"You should."

"I'd rather join you," I said.

Dell shook his head and grinned. "Tease—I thought you didn't want to start a family."

"I don't."

He pulled me closer. "Well, then a nap might cause a problem with some unexpected results."

"If you're not prepared, then I guess you're the one with the problem with results you can definitely expect."

"Hmm, Mrs. Holtz. And to what problem might you be referring?"

"Well, Mr. Holtz, of course the little problem that involves you taking cold showers and sleeping alone."

"Ah." He smiled. "That sounds strangely familiar to our courting days."

"Then I guess you'll have a lot of experience to draw from."

He just shook his head. "Fortunately, for both of us, I came prepared after all."

Sadly, the promise of a little alone time was shattered when a groggy but smiling Hans greeted us from below.

"*Guten Morgen!*" Dell teased the boy and further ruffled his messy hair.

"*Guten Nachmittag,*" Hans corrected.

I wanted to ask Dell to clarify their exchange, but he was in his own world, playing the father figure he never had. Then I remembered the parcel and handed it to Hans.

At first, he just stared at it, then looked at my smiling face, before returning his gaze to the wrapped gift.

I knelt on the ground before him, still holding the package, and again extended it in his direction. "*Bitte,*" also meaning "please," was one of the only words I could offer from my limited vocabulary, but it worked.

Hans slowly took the package and placed it on the floor, using his tiny fingers to untie the string around the parcel and unwrap the paper. When the wooden horse was finally exposed, I thought his precious blue eyes would bulge from his head. He squealed in delight and gently reached for the animal. Then he brought it up to his face and proceeded to kiss and hug it to him. I couldn't make eye contact with Dell or Oma, who were now kneeling on the floor around Hans, but Dell's sniffs and Oma bringing her apron to her face let me know their reactions were similar to mine.

Hans's instant appreciation for the toy filled me with guilt for all of the handmade Christmas and birthday gifts I'd received as a child that quickly found their way to the bottom of my closet or toy box, in lieu of their more expensive, less love-laden electronic competition. *Boy was I spoiled!*

Still deep in thought, I was suddenly caught off guard when Hans and his new toy lunged into my arms, nearly knocking me to the ground and almost impaling me with the wooden legs, all in one swift movement.

I held fast to his giggling body, kissing him on the cheek and squeezing him so tightly I thought I would crush him. His soft, blonde hair tickled my nose, and the clean scent of soap, mixed with the warmth from his nap, seemed to unlock an instinct I didn't know I had, something undeniably maternal. I loved kids and had babysat my way through high school, but the new feeling was different, deeper—scary. And that wasn't the time for its revelation.

I loosened my grip on Hans, and as quickly as he flew into my arms, he was gone, darting out into the yard with his wooden horse in his hands.

It took us adults a little longer to recover. I gathered up the paper and string and stood, fearing that any eye contact with Dell would give my thoughts away. Meanwhile, Dell helped Oma to her feet. Then she reached for the paper in my hand and left the room. I heard her in the kitchen, inserting the bundle into the cook stove.

Walking to the open back door, Dell finally spoke, his voice cracking as he did so. "I remember that horse."

"You do?"

I studied his profile, his eyes following the actions of his younger self, galloping around the yard with his wooden horse leading the way.

"Yes. I also remember the beautiful woman who gave it to me, but I didn't realize it was the same woman to whom I read the storybook. In fact, I never knew if I dreamed of her or if she actually existed. I used to call her my *Engel* or angel."

Little Hans whinnied loudly as he ran past the open door, bringing a smile to Dell's face.

"I imagined I could communicate with her by talking to my horse every night before I went to sleep in boarding school. It comforted me to believe she was looking out for me." Then he turned to hold my eyes in his. "Now, I've married her."

After a few seconds, I finally said, "I'm no angel, Dell. I think we both know that."

He laughed, pulled me toward him, and cradled my face in his hands. "In that case, I'm a happy man."

We kissed for the first time in days. It had been so long that it almost felt like a first kiss—a short one.

A pounding at the door jolted us back to reality.

Dell rushed forward, reaching the door before Oma and shielding her from a red-faced Johann standing on the other side. Johann stormed into the house and glared at Dell with the venom of a den of snakes. Oma ran in the backyard and gathered Hans and his new toy into her arms, then fled to her room and locked the door. I just stood in the middle of the floor, wishing I had visited the outhouse earlier.

FOR THE LOVE OF MAUDE

When Johann finally spoke, his words came out with such force that I felt certain the windows would break. "What in the world are you thinking?"

Dell stepped defiantly toward Johann. "We're leaving."

"You absolutely are...immediately!"

The two men glared at each other again.

"If you remain any longer, you risk everything," Johann added. He shoved a wrapped package at Dell's chest. Then he looked at me and tossed me an even larger parcel. "Change!"

I caught the package and walked to the bedroom, feeling as if the principal had just scolded me for my wardrobe not adhering to the dress code. I laid the bundle on the bed. As I unwrapped the paper, a dress started to unfold like a snake in a can. Caught somewhere between Marie Antoinette and Jane Austin, the final product was enormous, nearly consuming the bed in blue striped silk. Not only did it include a corset but also layers of petticoats that almost helped the thing stand up on its own.

Since it seemed to have a life of its own, I decided it required a name to match. "Oh? You say your name is 'Griselda'? Well, pleased to meet you. I'm Emily." I extended my hand in its direction and curtseyed.

All jokes and laughter quickly disappeared, however, as I concentrated my efforts on the unfamiliar garments. I pulled the shift over my head, rolled the sleeves past my elbows, and smoothed the hem just below the knee. The piece I dreaded the most, the corset, sat like a beacon in the middle of the bed. The minute I withdrew it from the stack of clothes, I realized it was much different than those I had grown to know and despise. Although it had multiple whale bone stays in the front and rear, as well as springs sewn into the sides, the beige corset was in two pieces, already laced in the back. Somewhat relieved, I slipped it on like a vest and laced the front like a pair of tennis shoes. The next object on the pile was a long, wide pad with pieces of ribbon sewn to either side. *What are you?* I held the thing in front of me and soon realized it was about the width of my hips, so I tied it around my waist, adjusted the pad along my back side, and hoped for the best. Then, I pulled the petticoats up over the pad, tied them snugly, and swished from side to side to release the wrinkles before covering them with another blue striped petticoat. The long-sleeved jacket top matched the top petticoat and buttoned in the front.

Just when I thought I was finished, I noticed a sheer white piece of fabric curled, almost catlike, on the bed. "There's always a part left over," Papa Bob often said after completing a project. To prove his point, he kept a jar on his garage shelf filled with stray screws and bolts from things he'd assembled.

I smiled at the memory and lifted the fabric from the bed. My smile quickly faded, though, as a pair of white silk stockings and blue fabric shoes appeared beneath. "Wonderful, Em, can you even find your feet?"

Fortunately my assistance arrived with a small knock at the door, which produced a pale Oma and a scared little boy, who immediately ran under the bed, hugging his horse close to him.

I sat on the bed while Oma rolled the stockings onto my feet, and cuffed them around a garter she'd tied just below the knee. Then, she held my arm so I could step into the shoes. As I admired myself in the mirror, she placed the white scarf around my neck and tucked the ends into the top of the bodice.

FOR THE LOVE OF MAUDE

I stifled a laugh. *You look like one of those crazy tissue box dolls old ladies like to put on their toilet tanks!*

But Oma was all business, scooting the tiny chair next to me and standing upon its seat. Looming above me, she removed the braid from my hair and quickly transformed my closely worn locks into a loose pile upon my head. Then she inserted several fake ringlets on either side and covered it all with a blue, wide-brimmed hat. It was obnoxious but fit the style of the time for society women. Apparently satisfied with my hairstyle, she climbed down off the chair and neatly hung the dirndl I had been wearing on a hook in the wardrobe and handed me my Maude suitcase that had been stored inside.

I wanted to hug her, but she was too preoccupied. Hans, on the other hand, had emerged from under the bed and was standing next to me, clearly expecting to receive attention from his *Engel*. I couldn't resist his little face looking up at me and hugged him as tightly as I could against my full dress. *You're the angel, little guy.*

Oma had to almost pry him from me, as neither of us wanted to let go. We emerged from the bedroom with Oma holding Hans and me holding my suitcase. Fortunately, the environment we entered was far less hostile than earlier. Johann was still clearly upset but was no longer demonstrating it. Dell, on the other hand, seemed beside himself with delight at the sight of the formfitting top I was sporting. He was wearing a white ruffled shirt beneath a waistcoat covered by a coat with tails. The black knee-breeches, white silk stockings, and pointy black shoes all worked together to make his look almost comical. I could only smile and shake my head.

Johann looked at my dress and nodded, then abruptly left the house through the front door. I couldn't believe how rude he was being to his grandmother, especially knowing that he might not see her again. I just stared, dumbfounded, at his exiting form; in fact, we all looked after him. Then, reluctantly, we turned to face the reality within the cottage and the painful goodbye.

Dell's smile was gone, and sadness now consumed his entire body. I couldn't bear to look at him any longer, so I focused my attention on Oma instead.

Her wet eyes met mine. It was most likely the one and only time I would ever meet her, and the weight of the situation was almost excruciating. There were so many things I wanted to say, but all of them would have sounded trite or ridiculous somehow. Then there was the language barrier that further limited my speech. In the end, I tried the only word I thought fit the situation under the circumstances: *"Danke."*

It seemed to be enough, for Oma walked toward me and wrapped her sturdy arms around me in an enormous hug. She held nothing back, and I could feel all of the other words that neither of us could express as tears escaped us both. When we finally pulled away, she handed me a delicately embroidered handkerchief and gathered up her white apron to mop up her own tears.

Oma had barely stepped back when Hans ran to stand between us. Without another word, he grabbed my hand and pulled me to the nearest chair, which he easily climbed. Then, standing on the seat and still holding his horse, he stretched his arms out from his sides in a hugging gesture. I surrounded his little body with my arms and squeezed him until he giggled. Then I kissed him on the cheek and whispered in his ear, *"Ich liebe dich!"* — "I love you" was one of the first phrases Dell taught me after we arrived.

He whispered the same in reply and kissed me on my damp cheek. Then he jumped off the chair and proceeded to latch onto Dell's right leg and would not let go. Dell and Oma were deep in conversation, so he reached down and patted Hans on the head.

I decided to give him his privacy and exited the cottage to join Johann and face the inevitable scolding I imagined I would receive.

Outside stood a large horse-drawn coach. The driver, dressed all in black, sat on a bench seat outside, above the cab, and stared over the top of the horses. Coach lights were mounted high on the carriage on either side of the bench, and a miniature version of the driver shared the seat just to his left. Aside from a few windows and a side door, the black coach was completely enclosed.

An almost chipper Johann beamed from one of the windows. "You look confused, Emily."

His change in demeanor caught me off guard, and I was afraid to speak.

"I'm not going to bite," he said.

"But—"

"Dell knows better. You don't—not this time at least," he said, winking at me. Johann stepped out and assisted me and my layers of dress into the seat across from him in the carriage.

Within a few minutes, Dell joined us, and we watched Oma and Hans wave from the front door of the cottage as we departed. My heart broke for Dell, who was staring out the window, biting his lower lip.

We bumped along the road for several yards before Johann broke the silence. "How could such a tiny hovel have ever earned my love?"

Dell nearly lunged at Johann from the seat he was sharing with me and my dress. "You pitiful old man! How dare you forget the patience and love Oma showed you as a child?!"

Johann simply smirked as Dell continued.

"How can you not see that it wasn't her house you loved but the wonderful woman who occupied it? Then you treat her as if she is some form of criminal by bursting into her home and scaring her."

"I did knock first," Johann retorted.

"You disgust me!"

"Regardless, you're lucky I arrived when I did." He tipped his hat at the occupant of a passing carriage.

The blood drained from Dell's face as he, too, noticed the man in the other carriage as it went by. "Father?"

Johann nodded.

"But—"

"Young Hans was supposed to be taking a nap when he arrived, but your interference changed that. Fortunately, I informed Oma, and she has sent our small self to gather berries with the neighbor children. He'll return in just enough time to miss Father entirely."

"Why did he come?" Dell asked.

"To offer Oma the means with which to support our education. You can't possibly think some silent benefactor cared for you all those years?"

Confusion consumed Dell's features. "But I just gave her money yesterday to care for him."

"And she returned it to me today." Johann handed Dell a pouch filled with coins.

"Keep it!" Dell said with a snort, waving a dismissive hand in the air.

Instead, Johann deposited the pouch into my lap.

The weight of the coins left a dent in my over-fluffed dress. I was too afraid to speak to even say, "Thank you."

"When did you talk to Oma?" Dell finally asked.

"While you and Emily were changing. It took a little coaxing, but I finally convinced her to unlock her bedroom door and speak with me."

"How did you do that?" I couldn't help asking.

Johann cleared his throat. "I become so focused on my work that I don't always remember people's feelings. I might be cold, and my comments might lack tact, but I'm not heartless. Oma was one of the only kind people in my young life, and we shared many great memories. I just reminded her of a few." He cleared his throat again and shifted in his seat before continuing, "Then she scolded me for my behavior and introduced me to my younger self."

"So why didn't you say goodbye?" I asked.

Johann let out a small chuckle. "If you didn't appreciate my hello, you certainly wouldn't have appreciated my goodbye either. I believe I did us all a favor."

Wow! Talk about lacking social skills! I was afraid my comments would cause more problems, so I left the remaining questions to Dell.

He took his cue and continued where he had left off. "Why did she return the money? She could have used it for something else."

"No, Dell. Oma would never spend money on herself if it was meant for Hans. Besides, Father will give her enough to live comfortably and keep us well educated."

Dell stared out the carriage window for a few moments to collect his thoughts, then turned his attention back to Johann. "I recall her dying when I was quite young."

"Yes, however, Oma had the forethought to put the money in the hands of a solicitor who cared for it and us."

"Did we ever meet the solicitor?" Dell asked.

"Not directly, but the remaining funds assisted nicely with our later research into time travel."

Dell leaned forward. "How did father earn his money?"

"He was quite the inventor, our father. He was going to share the profits of his newest invention with our mother, but when he came home to her nasty attitude and his missing son, he changed his mind." He paused, then added, "He loved us, you know."

Dell looked dumbfounded. "But he abandoned us."

"No, he told mother that he needed to finish his business and would return for good in a few weeks. Of course, she only heard what she wanted to hear and decided to tell us her version."

Dell looked at me, then back at Johann. "Is it possible that she isn't our mother?"

"It's a certainty that she isn't."

I thought Dell's eyes would fall out of his head when he asked, "Was father having an affair?"

"No."

"Then how…?"

Johann looked at Dell, then rested his eyes on me. "I wasn't the first Holtz to experiment with time travel."

"Then Hans is really…?" I asked, unable to remain silent.

"He's a younger version of the man we thought was our father. We are all essentially the same person."

FOR THE LOVE OF MAUDE

My thoughts made my head spin. *So I guess we can just add Friedrich to the ever-growing list of Johann's…or should I say I need to add Johann, Dell, Shane, and Hans to the ever-growing list of Friedrich's? But the burning question is, am I still Emily?*

Fortunately, Dell stepped in and rescued me from my internal turmoil—or so I hoped. "Who did Mother think Hans was?"

"An orphan whom Father said he couldn't abandon, but she always thought he was the product of an affair. The resemblance was too strong, and photographs of our childhood weren't exactly available to assist her in her search for the truth, not to mention the absence of DNA testing."

Dell was beside himself. "I always hated Father! Now I find out that we are not only his legacy, but are one in the same man, all from various stages of his life?"

"Yes. As I also discovered, time travel must never fall into the wrong hands. Often, it is only you who can be trusted."

Dell shot a loud, frustrated sigh across the inside of the coach. "So we continue to entrust the company in the hands of our younger selves?"

Johann nodded. "It has worked for hundreds of years now."

Dell just stared out the carriage window at the passing landscape, and I just focused on my lap, wishing I had skipped college entirely and joined Mom and Tom in their glassblowing business straight out of high school.

A few moments of silence were followed by Dell's question that succeeded in pushing me over the edge" "Then Oma is—"

Johann cut in to finish, "Our real mother."

Apparently, the conversation was a bit much for everyone involved, because it brought about an extended measure of silence, which, coupled with the rocking carriage, finally helped give my overworked brain and body the rest it needed.

CHAPTER TWENTY-FIVE

The sound of horse hooves on cobblestone roused me from my sleep. It was dark, and we were traveling through a mass of other carriages and horses.

"Where are we?" I asked into the darkness. I couldn't see any streetlights; in fact, the only light in the carriage came from the ones mounted on the outside of it, as well as those on passing coaches. It was like being in the country or camping.

Dell reached for my hand and held it tight. "We're just approaching Vienna."

"How did we get here so fast?"

"It's been hours, with two stops and a change of horses, sweetheart," he said, handing me a loaf of bread in the darkness. "It's almost dawn."

"Thank you. I guess that walk into Salzburg really tired me out." I took a bite of bread before continuing, "Are you still Friedrich, Johann, Dell, Shane, and Hans, or was that just a nightmare?"

Johann laughed out loud, scaring a passing horse and its rider.

"Yes" was the simple answer I received from Dell.

"I was hoping you'd say it was all just a bad dream."

"I wish I could," Dell again replied.

I tried to picture happy thoughts and imagined little Hans and his curls. "By the way, who is the blonde in your family?"

Johann quickly answered, "Opa Holtz, Oma's husband and our real father."

"Is he a Friedrich too?"

Now both Johann and Dell were laughing at my confusion.

"No, sweetheart. He was a Karl, and there was only one," Dell said gently.

I exhaled loudly. "That's good to know." It was then that I recalled something else that begged an explanation. "Why was Friedrich's hair so dark in his wedding portrait?"

Johann answered, "He greases his hair in the style of the time. Although it makes his hair appear darker, it's actually the same color as Dell's."

"But Shane's hair is lighter than Dell's," I added.

"Yes," Johann replied. "As with many people, our hair has grown darker with age."

I accepted his answer and nibbled on my bread while trying to focus on the passing scenery; people bundled in long, dark cloaks, rushing in the cool, predawn temperatures to rectangular, stone houses, many with window boxes filled with flowers. The occasional lamp-lit carriage clip-clopped past us, briefly hiding the pedestrians from my view.

Within minutes, we came to a stop outside a large stone residence that was set back from the street behind a heavy iron fence. Potted plants and flowers surrounded the entrance and softened the look of the giant wooden door that faced the road. While the driver remained seated, the young man wearing knickers and a long black coat climbed down from the front of the coach and opened the door, allowing Johann to step from the carriage and offer me his hand. I reached for him and attempted to exit but was caught by the many layers that comprised my dress. I felt as if I were the cork in a wine bottle as I nearly flung myself and my skirt through the opening and onto the street below. Fortunately, I landed on my feet, but the coin pouch was still in my lap and fell with a loud *thump* on the ground. Dell exited behind me, recovered the bag, and slipped it into the Maude suitcase for the attendant to carry while I adjusted the oversized monstrosity that surrounded my lower half.

Several passersby tipped their hats and snickered at my performance.

I'm here every Tuesday and Thursday! I kept my thoughts to myself as I felt myself blushing uncontrollably.

"We'll have to work on that," Dell whispered in my ear.

"Ha-ha." I said, failing to see the humor.

We filed into the house, followed by the young man, who deposited the Maude suitcase near the entrance, then he quietly closed the front door. He could have juggled pianos while dancing a jig for all I knew; nothing could have diverted my attention from the room I had just entered.

There's less marble in most quarries, I decided. My feet seemed as if they were glued to the floor, while my head followed my eyes from the floors to the intricately carved furnishings to the paintings on the walls and, finally, to the ceiling and its massive chandeliers. *I could stand in this spot all night and still not see it all!* I had never experienced a house quite its equal.

While I was gaping, Dell grabbed my suitcase and came

to my side. "We aren't staying here, Em."

I couldn't believe my ears. "What do you mean?"

"We're leaving."

"Why?"

"This house belongs to Friedrich—it is a second home that Mother…er, his wife knows nothing about."

"Are we not supposed to be here?"

"Not exactly. It will become the first safe house a few years from now, but he hasn't figured it out yet."

"Why did we come, then? I still don't understand."

"I'll explain everything to you as we walk."

Dell held one arm, and Johann secured the other as they led me through a door to a closed staircase and helped me descend the slippery stone steps that led into an even more unpleasant basement.

As we mostly slid toward the bottom step, an obnoxious squeaking noise and foul stench greeted us long before the source could be determined in the darkness. Nevertheless, I didn't need confirmation. I guessed the identity before we reached the basement floor. "Rats!" I screamed.

Standing at the base of the stairs, I felt the movement of one of them as it scurried over my thin slippers, so I kicked at it, flipping the rodent, along with my shoe, into the darkness before me. I panicked and started to hyperventilate, climbing Dell's back as if he were a tree.

"Emily! I can't breathe!" His strained voice came from beneath my arms that were wrapped like a noose around his neck.

I loosened my grip and tried to wrap my legs around Dell's waist but couldn't maneuver them beneath my layers of skirts, so I just hung along Dell's back like a dead-weighted bell.

"Get off, or I'm dropping your suitcase!" Dell threatened.

Johann finally stepped in and grabbed me by the waist with one arm and used the other to pry me from my poor husband. Then he held me there until Dell could catch his breath.

"Emily, what was that all about?" Dell asked, his voice raspy and irritated.

"Rats!"

"And?"

"I hate them! They're everywhere! Besides, I lost a shoe kicking at one."

"Well, you shouldn't have kicked at it, then!" Johann said.

You think? "Regardless, I'm not taking another step!"

"You most certainly are." Johann firmly plopped me on the ground, sending several of my rodent friends running to safety.

I turned to walk back up the stairs, but Johann grabbed me by the wrist and held me in place.

"If we don't leave now, we'll be stuck in this time frame, and rats will be the least of your worries."

"Excuse me?"

"Here. Take this!" I heard Dell handing the Maude suitcase to Johann in the darkness. In the next instant, he reached for me and gathered me and all of my skirts into his arms. "We don't have time to explain," he snapped.

Both men shuffled as quickly as they could through a sea of squeaking, stinking rats to a beacon of torchlight at the end of the hallway. Once there, a skeleton key resting above the door jamb served as a first-generation H&S security measure that gained us and several of our rodent guests entry into another hallway. It resembled a scaled-down version of the corridors that extended beneath all H&S safe houses. Johann replaced the key and fought to close the door against the rat invasion. Several similar doors later, we were finally free of the pests.

"I need to put you down now, Em."

I kissed Dell on the cheek. "Thank you."

He placed me on the floor and held my hand as we ran in the direction of yet another door.

Once through that door, we were finally met by a familiar sight—Perry and my friend, the Silver Ghost limousine. Our cars from the 1930s were nice, but I'd missed the Ghost.

It would have been easy to reminisce about all the good times I'd spent in that car, but Perry was quick to bring me back to reality. "Hurry!" he called.

We ran to the open rear door through which all three men folded and stuffed my skirts. I felt ridiculous.

"Good thing dresses of this period don't have hoops or you might have had to tie me to the roof," I said, but no one laughed. Instead, tension dominated the free space my dress and hat weren't occupying within the car, so I kept my mouth shut and just looked at the dark walls outside the window.

Within seconds, Perry was guiding the limo into the darkness.

"You might want to close your eyes," Dell suggested.

I followed his advice, and when I heard the car groan and grind as the engine accelerated, I squeezed my eyes even tighter. "It's never sounded this way before. What's happening?"

"It's okay, Em. This is a different process. We're fine," Dell assured me.

I held his hand in a death grip with both of mine, hoping

that the strange sounds weren't building to an explosion. When the car finally started to decelerate, so did my fear of a fiery death. I slowly opened my eyes and noticed that we were in a tunnel surrounded by the bright blue glow of artificial light.

I loosened my grip on Dell's hand. "I'm sorry for being such a baby."

"I guess this is another occasion when we learn something new about each other?" He tried to joke.

"That's an understatement, Fritzie."

He just smiled. "That's right, rat-girl."

I laughed. "Nice one, but why were we in such a hurry?"

Dell pulled my hand onto his lap. "Without access to a well-established safe house and tunnel for time travel, we must create a portal in which to travel. Unfortunately, these portals have time limits on them."

"Expiration dates?" I asked.

He laughed. "In a matter of speaking, yes."

"Did we almost miss our chance?"

"Yes."

Johann must have overheard our conversation from his spot next to Perry in the front and twisted in his seat to scowl at us before turning again to face forward.

I fought the urge to stick my tongue out at Johann and instead asked, "Would we have been stuck there long?"

Dell hesitated before answering, "Yes."

"Wouldn't someone from the future have been able to create another portal for us?"

He shook his head. "No."

"Why not?"

"Because no one other than the inhabitants of this vehicle

knew we were gone. And Johann used our portal to inform me of my father's...er, I mean, Friedrich's visit to Oma's cottage."

"Why didn't Johann just create another portal, closer to Salzburg, and use that one?"

Johann shook his head and spoke without turning around. "No time."

Dell continued, "Johann just learned of our location a few hours before his visit. Friedrich's basement was available, and Johann didn't have time to research a better location. He had to act quickly. Had we been at Oma's when Friedrich arrived, it would have drastically changed the future."

"How?" I asked, again struggling to keep up.

"There would have been four of us at Oma's at the same time. Hans and I were from his past, however, Johann was from his future. It would take Friedrich years of research and dedication to discover that time travel to the future was even possible. Seeing that it was possible in the form of Johann, as well as you, would have altered his dedication, and the outcome may never have occurred." Dell shook his head. "We couldn't risk that."

"Not organic," Johann added from the front seat.

I ignored Johann and looked at Dell. "I thought Johann's research led to all of these discoveries?"

Dell glared at the back of the seat Johann was occupying. "So did I, but I recently discovered that Friedrich left a journal among his effects that his solicitor delivered to Johann on his thirtieth birthday. It contained Friedrich's research which Johann built upon."

"Wasn't it *your* thirtieth birthday too, Dell?"

"No, I was removed from that life two days before my

birthday. I had no knowledge of the journal, its author, or my true identity until just yesterday," he said, still scowling at the back of Johann's head.

"Okay," I conceded, "but I'm still confused. Didn't you once tell me that Johann befriended scientists, such as Tesla, who were also interested in time travel, scientists who would have been born in the mid- to late-1800s?"

Dell nodded.

"Weren't you from the late 1700s?"

Johann answered instead, "Time travel eliminates all barriers, my dear."

"That makes no sense! So is this one of those who-came-first questions, only instead of the chicken and the egg, we're dealing with time travel and the scientists who invented it?"

Johann made a loud barking noise from the front seat and seemed to descend into an obnoxious laugh-fest with himself.

With no hope of an answer from the elder Johann, I turned to Dell, who simply shrugged his shoulders. "Apparently, there's a lot I don't know."

"Great," I said, "and I know even less."

Dell squeezed my hand that was still in his lap. "I'll tell you everything I can."

I clung to the opportunity to ask my usual series of questions. "Why was Hans sent away to pick berries?"

"Hans needed to hate his father," Dell replied. "Had he been there when Friedrich arrived, he would have witnessed his benevolence firsthand and loved him for it."

"Excuse me?"

"This hatred, unfortunately, was his motivation in later years to become the inventor he was meant to be. The future of the company rested on that meeting not taking place."

My eyes glazed over. "I want to request a hammock between two palm trees and something liquid—the stronger the
better—that fits nicely into a coconut, please."

Dell leaned to whisper in my ear, "Make that two."

The limo came to a stop, but before Perry could assist us,
Johann jumped out and opened our door. "This is where we
part."

I sat up straight and slid across the seat toward the door.

The lab-coated assistants, already gathered around the
car, witnessed my less than ladylike ejection from the vehicle
and subsequent loss of balance. Fortunately, Johann steadied
me, while Dell pushed my remaining skirts free of the doorway.

A grinning Willy looked as if he wanted to comment until
I stood within inches of his face and offered a comment of my
own. "Why don't you try it sometime and see how *you* do?"

Similar to all Willys, he sought the comfort of his clipboard rather than show me his flushed face.

Dell reached for my hand from behind and started to pull
me away from the man but lost his grip when Johann took an
even firmer hold of my other hand and spun me around to
face him. "You have a lot of fight in you. You're going to need
that for what lies ahead."

I was tired of the whole ordeal and had lost all patience
in the process. "What are you talking about?"

"I'll let Dell explain that to you." He kissed me on the
cheek and reached into the car to retrieve my suitcase, then
handed it to me. "Good luck," he said. End of conversation.

I looked from the case to him and tried to absorb whatever I could from the previous few hours. I failed; my mind
was having trouble keeping pace with my ever-changing

reality. Instead, I watched as he shook Dell's hand and occupied the seat next to Perry.

"Let's stand over here." Dell gestured to an area several yards from the car.

Once we relocated, the floor beneath the car began to rotate clockwise 180 degrees, until the limo was facing the direction from which we'd come. The engine was still running, and within seconds the limousine and its occupants were fading away, heading down the tunnel in the opposite direction.

I turned to look at my husband, who was still staring at their departure. "What's going on, Dell?"

He slowly faced me. "You're not going to want to hear this."

"I didn't think I would, but tell me anyway."

"I need to take care of some business…in the future."

I exhaled in disgust. "And let me guess. I can't go with you."

He tried to reach for my hand, but I pulled it away and continued to vent.

"And the rest of our honeymoon, or even the hammock I requested earlier?" I asked.

"We're going to have to postpone it for a while."

"Define 'a while,' Dell."

He shook his head.

"Great. So you're leaving me again to take care of something you can't discuss for who knows how long? Am I getting warm?"

"Em, I have to—"

"No, Dell. I don't want to hear it. You know how I hate this part!"

"I do."

"When are you leaving?"

He answered quickly, as if he were pulling off a bandage. "As soon as Perry returns."

"Are we talking about five seconds from now?"

"Sweetheart, we—"

"I'm not okay with this!" I cried.

"Neither am I. Do you think I *want* to leave you again?"

I didn't answer, because the words inside my head weren't pretty.

"Em, please come here."

When he reached for me that time, I didn't pull back. Instead, I yanked the pins from my hat and let it fall to the ground, then walked into his waiting arms and buried my head in his chest. "Will this kind of thing keep happening?" My muffled question rose from the front of his shirt.

"Yes."

"This isn't what I pictured for my life, Dell. I got straight A's in college. That should have earned me a window office by now, as well as clothing and housing stipends, even a new car—and especially a husband who comes home every night."

He laughed. "How could anyone anticipate this kind of life?"

"Where am I?" I finally asked.

"Italy."

"Please don't tell me I'm on Maude and Louie's honeymoon."

Dell didn't speak.

"Great, I guess your silence says it all." I exhaled and pounded my forehead into his chest.

He finally spoke. "This is their safe house."

"Do they know I'm here?"

"Yes."

I cringed, already feeling as if I were invading their privacy. "I feel stupid."

"Don't. Maude is looking forward to seeing you."

"How long have they been here?" I despised the question but needed the answer.

"A year."

"Okay. Well at least it's been more than a day."

"Or an hour," he said, then laughed.

"Right." I tried to feel optimistic about being welcome on their honeymoon but couldn't. "Regardless, won't she think it's strange that you're not joining me?"

"No. She thinks you miss her and wanted a short visit while I'm away on business."

"I do miss her, and I hope more than anything that it truly is just a short visit."

Dell kissed me on the top of my head.

Unfortunately, the sound of an engine echoing in the tunnel and the accompanying headlights sent a chill down my spine.

My head briefly left his chest. "You're really leaving, aren't you?"

He nodded.

"I'm not letting you go!" I squeezed him as tightly as I could, considering the disadvantage my dress was posing.

"You'll be safe here, sweetheart."

"And I wouldn't be safe with you?"

"No."

"Then you won't be safe either."

"That's not what it means. I just can't guarantee your

safety where I'm going, but I can here."

"Now I'm really not letting you go!" My grip tightened, and I held it there as I heard the limousine coming to a stop behind him, followed by the sound of the car being rotated in the opposite direction.

"Emily…"

I wouldn't answer.

"I need to go."

"Good luck," I said, but I still wouldn't budge.

He gently reached beside him and held my arms in his hands.

"Emily, the sooner I leave—"

"Then you should have been back five minutes ago!"

"It doesn't work that way."

"Great. Are we talking real time again?" I asked, moaning in frustration.

"Yes."

"Super. Can't we just have one night together before you have to go?"

"Sir?" Perry interrupted

"Yes?" Dell replied.

"May I speak with you, please?"

I reluctantly released Dell and watched him walk with Perry to stand beside the limo. The engine was still running, so I couldn't hear their conversation, but the pale look on Dell's face when he returned made my stomach fall.

"I can't delay my departure any longer, Em."

"What's wrong?"

"I can't tell you." He pulled me into his arms and began to kiss my surprised mouth with the passion he had first showed me on our real wedding night.

"Sir?" Perry was standing within inches of us, tapping Dell's shoulder.

"I have to go, Em."

Dell gave me another quick kiss, then entered the vehicle through the door Perry was holding open for him. The sound of the door closing echoed throughout the tunnel and left me feeling empty.

I leaned my head through the open car window. "I had better see you again."

Dell's smile failed to reassure me. "I love you."

"I love you too."

Perry put the car in gear, and I quickly backed away to avoid losing something vital, such as my head. In what seemed an instant, I watched the limo being swallowed up by the darkness of the tunnel. Soon, even the sound of the engine disappeared.

I stood there in the silence of the tunnel until a kind-faced lab worker touched me on the sleeve. "I don't suppose you would enjoy a wardrobe change," she said.

I grabbed my Maude suitcase and hat. "Is there a bonfire involved?"

She laughed and led me out of the tunnel, toward a group of window-filled rooms. Inside one of them hung a white blouse with gold buttons and the largest set of shoulder pads I had witnessed since Mom finally decided to clean out her closet. A pair of black walking shorts hung on a separate hanger that hovered just feet over a pair of black sandals. The familiarity of the outfit, as well as the lack of miles of overused or constricting fabric, almost lessened the blow of Dell's departure—almost.

Although she was friendlier than most, the lab worker behaved in a similar fashion to her counterparts, limiting her conversation and not offering me her name.

Who needs names when so few get to use them…or talk for that matter?

True to her training, she retrieved the clothing and led me to the restroom in silence. Inside, stood a shower and toilet area similar to ones I had encountered in other safe house basements. Under a different set of circumstances, I would have been in heaven; after all, I had just spent the previous few days using an outhouse. The lady hung my outfit on a hook and rested the sandals on the floor below. Then she directed my attention to a modern bra and matching panties sitting on a nearby bench. Again, my enthusiasm eluded me.

While I was still trying to decide how to react to my new wardrobe, I found myself being unlaced and unencumbered by the dress I was wearing and the hairstyle and fake ringlets that had somehow remained piled atop my head. The outfit had been so tight that I was halfway through my shower before I felt any relief.

When I was sufficiently cleaned and pruned, I wrapped myself in an oversized white towel and used a second smaller one for my hair. Then I wiped the fog from the mirror and just stood there, looking at my sad face. "Happy honeymoon, alone again."

I brushed and dried my hair before putting on my new outfit, which felt about ten pounds lighter than ones I'd recently worn. I left the bathroom in search of someone who, I was certain, would feel compelled to make my hair big.

That person came in the form of a large woman and her two ultra-skinny stylists-in-training. Although I refused the gaudy, pastel makeup, to their great disappointment, I couldn't escape their successful attempt at transforming my hair into a curled, backcombed, and oversprayed rendition of its formerly flat self.

"Ah, the eighties," I said into the mirror as they emptied what seemed like the tenth can of hairspray into my bangs.

The two girls giggled and clapped in delight; I half-expected them to kiss the ring on the older woman's chubby hand.

Similar to so many other occasions, I looked and felt ridiculous. *Well, at least I'm wearing normal underwear and can sit comfortably in a chair...and they left out the legwarmers. Not bad for a third wheel on someone else's honeymoon. Better than being a third wheel on my own honeymoon, I guess. See? There's always a bright side!*

I could only pretend to be convinced as I entered the elevator that would take me to the safe house level and my waiting family.

CHAPTER TWENTY-SIX

A scending the elevator from every basement laboratory I was fortunate enough to escape was always a nerve-racking experience. It wasn't the elevator ride as much as where those elevators led that put a ball of fear in the pit of my stomach. Regardless of the fact that all the labs and elevators looked fairly similar—sterile stainless with a hint of white—I always felt as if I were traveling into the unknown, and I was often alone in the process. That particular ascent was no exception.

When the elevator bell alerted me that I had arrived at the main level of the safe house, I felt the ball in my gut expand. Once the stainless elevator doors opened, I could almost taste the fear. I took a deep breath and made a wish to the elevator gods before exiting into the center of a long hallway. "Please bring Dell to me soon!"

The doors closed behind me as I hugged my Maude suitcase close and tried to decide which direction to walk. I didn't have to debate the issue for too long, however, before a familiar squeal echoed toward me from the left.

"Daisy!

My fear vanished instantly as I turned in her direction.

FOR THE LOVE OF MAUDE

"Maude!"

She was standing near one end of the hallway, which was filled with the light of the Mediterranean sun. The plastered walls were an off white and appeared to be balancing many sets of dark wooden beams on their ample shoulders. The floor was covered in large, rustic brick-colored tile, with a long tapestry runner that led straight to my smiling aunt. She seemed to glow like a sunbeam just outside a doorway to my right and simply remained in place and clapped her hands excitedly as I approached. Her enthusiasm was so contagious that by the time I was within a few feet of her, my face muscles hurt from smiling. It was obvious that she was genuinely happy to see me, but I found it strange that she didn't run toward the elevator to meet me. It all made sense when I came closer, and she stopped moving for a few seconds.

The sight before me made me lose my grip on the Maude suitcase, sending it crashing to the floor. My hands covered my mouth, and I was unable to take another step. I was trapped in a frozen stare at Maude's slight form and the new tenant residing beneath her oversized blouse. "You're pregnant?" I asked from beneath my hands.

She beamed her reply and proudly put her hands on either side of her belly.

I opened my mouth to speak but decided to keep my thoughts to myself. I couldn't crush her with my knowledge of her future that didn't involve a child.

She spoke instead. "I know what you're going to say, Daisy."

No, you don't. I remained silent as I bridged the gap between us and hugged her around her swollen belly.

She rattled on excitedly, "But the company overcame the

shock and is making arrangements for us."

I didn't care for the sound of that one. "What kind of arrangements?"

"They haven't said."

I bit my tongue.

The sound of the dropped suitcase soon attracted several members of the household staff, as well as Louie; I could hear him running from the opposite end of the hallway.

"They're all so overly protective of me," Maude said with a smile.

Louie reached us out of breath and filled with concern for his wife.

"It's okay, Lou. Our Daisy just dropped her suitcase at the sight of our little friend."

Louie took a deep breath and kissed Maude, then turned in my direction. But the smile he tried to offer me soon melted beneath the fiery glare I was shooting at him. Fortunately, Maude was oblivious.

"Emily," Louie said uneasily, "I'll show you to your room."

Maude continued to rub her belly as Louie escorted her to an oversized couch near a set of open French doors while I waited in the hall.

When Louie joined me again, he reached down for the suitcase and led me toward a row of doors along an adjacent hallway. I couldn't even look at him let alone speak, so we walked in silence as I boiled.

Louie stopped at the last door and opened it. Inside, I momentarily forgot about him. The room was beautiful. White plaster walls and dark wooden rafters gave a sense of openness that was further enhanced by white drapes, billowing in the breeze from the open French doors beyond. The day was clear and warm, with blue skies, and a perfect view of the sea below from a private patio that held two lounge chairs and a table. The waves crashing in the distance brought the fresh scent of the ocean, which had a brief calming effect on my nerves. The furniture inside the room included a simple wooden bed, dresser, and wardrobe, but I would have settled for a cot and a shoebox rather than lose the view from my doors.

The spell was broken, however, when Louie placed my suitcase on the bed, instantly reminding me of his presence.

"What were you thinking?" I spewed at him.

He just stared.

"Did you even wait two days before making her pregnant?"

The floor seemed to be where his eyes and attention felt the need to remain after that.

"Do you have any idea what this means?"

He finally met my angry eyes. "Yes, I understand."

"Does she?"

His gaze found the floor again.

"Great, Louie. That's just great!"

He took a deep breath, then said, "Emily, you're here for a reason."

"Excuse me?"

"I need to join Dell."

"You what?!" I thought my head would explode and didn't bother waiting for his reply. "Does Maude know?"

"No."

"Super." I exhaled in disgust. "When is she due?"

"In about a month."

"Lovely. And I don't suppose you know when you're going to return."

He shook his head. "No."

"I also don't suppose you know how badly I want to rip your head off."

"I can guess."

"You could try, but you'd only scratch the surface!"

Louie met my angry eyes. "This isn't easy for me, Emily. I don't want to leave Maude."

"You'll break her heart!"

He nodded and quietly replied, "I know."

"I won't let you leave without telling me what's going on, Louie. You owe me at least that."

"I can't say, Emily."

"Yes, you can."

"No. I promised Dell."

"Really? You promised? Well, you also promised not to have children with Maude or hurt her, for that matter. You also promised her father you would take care of her. From what I'm seeing, it doesn't look as if promises are high on your list of priorities!"

"Emily—"

"Tell me!" I screamed.

He turned to stare at the sea. "Let's take a walk."

We exited the room through the open French doors and walked onto the stone patio beyond.

Louie's attention was still focused on the water as he spoke. "Evergreen Research found one of our safe houses."

I felt ill. "Which one?"

"Dunston House, across from Winston Manor."

"How?"

He shook his head. "I don't know the details yet."

"Did they find the lab?"

"From what I understand, they only infiltrated the house and not the basements. That's all I know."

I had my suspicions but still needed to ask, "Who was it?"

"Hodges," Louie replied.

Figures. "Won't Dell be in danger?"

"No. He's in disguise, as we all will be."

"Has Evergreen discovered anything?"

"I'm not certain, but H&S isn't taking any chances. All available staff has been called in to assist."

"You're not exactly *available*, Louie."

"I am in their eyes."

I shook my head and planted my hands firmly on my hips. "Thank you for telling me. I won't mention it to anyone, including Maude."

He exhaled and continued to stare at the sea.

"What about the baby?" I finally asked.

He shook his head. "They were naturally furious, but she's your aunt, so they are working on a solution."

"If this so-called solution breaks her heart, I'm going to send you on a one-way trip to some abandoned safe house in the middle of a warzone!"

"If it harms her in any way, you won't have to send me. I will gladly go."

Fair enough. I calmed down slightly, but my heart was still pounding in my chest. "When do you go?"

"I was supposed to leave as soon as you arrived."

"Regardless of what was promised, Dell probably expects you to tell me."

He nodded. "I think you're right."

I looked at the sea as well and tried to make sense of what Louie was telling me. "Why are we in the 1980s?"

"It's safe."

"How?"

"Evergreen prefers events prior to 1940. They seem to be easier for them to manipulate with their less sophisticated science. Likewise, since they haven't perfected the art of disguise, they were caught easily in Dunston House."

"You mean Hodges, right?"

"Yes." He nodded.

I stared at the side of Louie's face.

"He was never convinced that your death was an accident or if it even occurred. He still loves you, Emily."

Great.

A seagull flew overhead and kept my attention for several seconds before I said, "We were supposed to be married before Dell came into the picture."

"I know," he said.

"Does Shane need to be involved?" I quickly asked.

"Yes, but he doesn't remember you."

"Then I guess I don't need to ask you to say hi for me."

He dug the toe of his shoes nervously into the ground. "I guess not."

"Sorry I went mama bear on you, Louie. I don't really want to rip your head off."

He finally turned to look at me. "You'd just hurt yourself."

We both let out a chuckle that finally cleared the air.

"Please take care of my Maude for me," he added.

"You know I will...and you take care of my Dell."

"It's a deal." He reached over to shake my hand, but I

pushed it aside and took a hug instead.

"What are you going to tell her?" I asked, releasing him.

"I can't lie to her, Emily, but I won't be able to give her any details. I will tell her I need to work with Dell on our future and that it must be now."

"There's no easy way, is there?" I asked.

He buried his hands deep in his pockets. "No."

"Will she be going to the hospital to have the baby?"

"No, they've established a delivery room in the lab. A doctor and nurses will arrive this afternoon, just in case."

I panicked. "In case of what?"

"They say the shock of my leaving might cause her to go into early labor."

"Okay…that doesn't add any stress, does it?"

"I'm truly sorry, Emily."

Now it was my turn to stare at the ground. "It's more my fault than anyone else's."

"What do you mean?"

"I introduced you to Maude, and I also used to work for Evergreen, which brought Hodges into the equation as well."

Louie shook his head. "Emily, you can't blame yourself for other people's choices, even if you made a few introductions or had a past relationship. Maude is the best thing that's ever happened to me. We'll be fine…all three of us. Besides, H&S is a much more sophisticated and powerful organization than Evergreen can ever hope to be. We'll tackle this Hodges fellow without any problems."

The reality of the situation was starting to sink in, and I didn't like the consequences that might result from it. "I just don't want anyone to be hurt," I said.

"No one will."

"How do you know?"

"Because I have been with H&S for many years. They're the good guys, and they will prevail. They always do."

"I thought good guys finish last."

"Well, last in time travel is really first," he said with a chuckle.

"You're full of it, Louie!"

"Full of what?" Maude asked, standing in the open doorway leading to the patio.

We both turned to see her smiling face. She was so sweet, and within a few minutes, her world was going to come crashing down around her. I wanted to cry, but I pulled myself together enough to give her a few more minutes of joy.

"Beans!" I answered.

"He's full of beans, all right!" She walked across the patio and stood between us, extending her petite arms behind our backs. "My two favorite people in the world. I couldn't be happier."

I almost lost it, but her sudden giggles kept me from giving myself away.

"I can't forget this one," she said, looking down at her belly. "I guess I have three favorites now."

I had to bite my lip and tried to concentrate on another seagull that was squawking overhead. Louie must have been doing the same thing because he wasn't speaking either.

"Is anyone as hungry as I am?" Maude suddenly asked.

"I doubt it," Louie finally said.

She giggled again. "I seem to be eating even more than you these past few days."

I wanted to fling myself from the cliff and take my chances on the rocks below but remembered my promise to take care of Maude.

"Well, we'd better get you inside." He smiled down at her.

Lunch was served on a large veranda beneath a grape arbor just outside the room where Maude originally greeted me. A rustic rectangular table, surrounded by six blue-cushioned chairs, held platters of antipasto, prosciutto and provolone paninis, fruit, and breads, as well as ice-filled pitchers of water and lemonade.

Louie and I both picked at our lunches as Maude cleaned her plate and part of another before finally sitting back enough to notice the remaining food on the table.

"Are you going to finish that?" Maude asked, eyeing my sliced apples.

"No."

Without delay, she pulled my fruit plate closer to her and unceremoniously scraped the apple slices onto her own.

"You can have those too." I motioned to the oranges and grapes.

She cleared them and slid the empty plate back to me. After finishing my fruit and Louie's, as well as the remaining food on the platters, Maude finally wiped her mouth and sat back in her chair. "I'm kind of full. How about you two?"

"I think I'm finished too," I announced.

Her full belly finally allowed her to notice the small bite out of my sandwich and Louie's untouched version. "What's going on?" she asked.

I looked at Louie, who was still staring at his plate.

"Lou?"

He didn't speak.

"Daisy?"

I couldn't make eye contact.

"You're scaring me! Is the baby okay?"

Louie finally spoke. "Yes, sweetheart. The baby is just fine."

"Then why didn't you eat anything?"

"I need to tell you something." His voice came out as almost a whisper.

"What is it?"

"I'm afraid I need to assist Dell with a company matter."

"You?"

"I'm so sorry, Maude. It just came up, and I must do this."

"When?"

"Well, uh…today," he stammered.

"Today?"

He reached for her hand that was covering her belly. "Yes."

"And when will you be back?"

"I'm not sure."

"Surely before our baby is born, right?"

"I don't know for certain."

"No!" she cried, then instantly grew pale.

Both Louie and I jumped from our seats and went to her side, but Louie was closer and knelt next to her, wrapping his arms around her as she sobbed and trembled.

"I-I can't…do…this… al-lone…" she stuttered.

"You won't have to. Emily will be here," he said, trying to remain calm.

"I know, but I want you here too!"

"I'm sorry, but I have to go."

"This can't be happening!" she screamed.

"Maude, darling, you must calm down. You'll upset the baby," he said gently. But his soothing voice was no match for her hormones.

"The baby's already upset with Daddy leaving!"

Louie looked at me over Maude's wilted head, pleading with his eyes for some sort of assistance.

I felt useless, but I had to try. "Maude, we'll take good care of you while Louie's away."

"You don't understand!" she barked.

I had never seen Maude so upset, not in any time frame, and that really worried me. I knelt by her other side and rubbed her back. "No, I don't, but this can't be helped. Louie and Dell have to work together on your future. Unfortunately, it has to be now."

She sniffed and reached for a napkin to blow her nose. "*My* future?"

I looked at Louie for support, but that was the end of his participation in the lie I was going to have to fabricate. "Yes, and he has to go now."

"Is it dangerous?" She looked at Louie, but I answered for him.

"All time travel is dangerous, Maude. That's why they work so hard to create safe houses similar to this one, for everyone's benefit."

She was still focusing on Louie. "Will you be going to a safe house?"

"Yes," Louie answered for himself.

She nodded and blew her nose again.

"*Thank you*," Louie mouthed over her head, and I smiled.

"I'll leave you two," I said, then kissed Maude on the cheek and left the veranda.

I walked back to my room and unleashed a fair share of my own tears. Still sniffing, I stood at the open patio door, seeking both fresh air and perspective in the cool breeze that was now coming off the water. I felt as if Maude and I were reluctant war brides for whom I needed to find a couple of yellow ribbons to wear or tie on something. "I have no interest in living this way," I said to the sea.

I received a reply from a tiny voice behind me: "Neither do I." I turned to find Maude shaking, just inside the bedroom.

"Is he gone?"

She nodded, and her teeth began to chatter.

I took a blanket from the foot of my bed and wrapped it around her. We walked onto the patio, sat together on a lounge chair, and sobbed in unison for ourselves and the husbands neither of us expected to be apart from, nor could be certain we'd ever see again.

EPILOGUE

The weeks slowly passed as Maude and I awaited the arrival of her baby. To occupy our time, we walked, talked, baked, and even learned to knit from Gina, one of the maids. I shared the pages of the newest Maude journal, and she shared some of the less private details of her honeymoon, including the pictures she had taken along the way.

"I thought you spent the entire honeymoon here," I commented at the variety of photos she had in a well-organized honeymoon album.

"No, this was just home base. There are many safe houses around the world where we traveled, until I started to show." She rubbed her belly before continuing, "And we always took our photos in black and white, just in case."

Her safe house-trotting honeymoon reminded me of the one I had originally wanted to take. *Well, at least one of us was able to do it.* I flipped to the next page and recognized one of the pictures from the album; it was one the older Maude had shared with me as a child. "Where was this one taken?"

"Which?" She scanned the page.

"The one of you on the camel."

"Oh, that one." She laughed. "That was in Egypt. The silly

beast kept spitting at poor Louie."

The next picture in the album nearly stopped my heart; it was the close-up of Louie smiling for the camera, the same photo she kept in the mother-of-pearl frame on her nightstand when I was young. She ran her fingers across the picture, just as she did when she showed it to me for the first time.

This isn't right. We're supposed to share this picture when I'm much younger and you're an old lady.

I tried to ignore the fear that seemed to be creeping in, threatening to consume my thoughts. I searched for distractions but didn't have honeymoon details to share, so I just stuck with the journal, as well as the letter Mom wrote me, including her request for forgiveness for wrecking Maude's car.

Regardless, after swapping suitable stories and memories of our time spent with our husbands, either or both of us would descend into an emotional puddle of tears. Maude usually surpassed my mild sniff or two with a torrent of enormous sobs that required countless hours of consoling and piles of tissue. For her sake, I eventually chose to treat Louie as a nonentity, and the pregnancy was akin to the Immaculate Conception. It worked for about a minute.

Unfortunately, the baby, similar to our husbands, was late. The doctor planned to induce, but Maude was set on having her child "without any help." She was also determined to wait for Louie to return. Luckily the baby had a mind of its own and two days before the scheduled delivery date, Maude's water finally broke.

Without Louie to hold her hand, Maude squeezed the daylights out of mine instead. By the time the baby was born, I wasn't sure if the tears I was shedding were for the cute little girl the doctor was presenting to us or the painful tingling my hand was experiencing as the blood slowly flowed back into it. Either way, once the baby was born, it didn't matter; in fact, nothing did until Maude started to scream in agony.

I looked at her pale body writhing in the bed and knew something had gone terribly wrong. The doctor quickly handed the baby to the nurse and returned his attention to Maude. There was blood everywhere.

"Doctor?" I asked.

He ignored me entirely and yelled, "Nurse, find assistance!"

The nurse placed the infant in an incubator and rushed from the room. She returned with several additional staff members, all scrubbed and ready.

"She's hemorrhaging," the doctor informed the group.

They all seemed to know what that meant and surrounded the bed, then wheeled it to an operating room behind a windowed security door. I was speechless, staring after them in shock. Another nurse entered the room and removed the baby.

I stood alone in tears, shaking out my hand that still hadn't regained all its feeling. Hours passed without word of Maude's well-being or the child's. Every attempt at passing through the security door was met in defeat; neither tears and cries, nor harsh words and threats would grant me entrance. I couldn't sit; all I could do was pace the hall outside the operating room.

After I spent six hours walking the halls, the doctor finally emerged. His expression was drawn and pale. "The surgery went well, but she lost a considerable amount of blood. She's hanging on but is in a coma."

"Will she be okay?"

"We can't say for certain. If she's strong, she stands a chance."

Burying the Maude journal had been a difficult experience for me, but it couldn't compare with the possibility of burying Maude instead. My favorite aunt—the one who had never married or had children, the same one who almost lived to be 100—now stood a good chance of dying at twenty-two after giving birth to her husband's child.

"And the baby? Can I see her?"

"She's just fine, sleeping right now. Maybe you'd like to rest as well. I'll have one of the staff find you once the baby is awake." The doctor smiled and offered me a pat on the shoulder.

The gesture that was meant to console me failed to emit any form of response. I just stood and watched him walk back through the door from which he came.

My thoughts consumed me like an aggressive disease without a cure.

It's all my fault! Johann assured me in The Strand penthouse that Maude and Louie's relationship would not affect the company's future or mine, but I was too selfish to notice that he didn't mention whether it would affect her future. I just assumed it wouldn't, and I didn't bother asking. I could have prevented this! The rules of their marriage were clear, and I am even more responsible for their being broken than Maude and Louie are, because I introduced them—and now we all have to live with the consequences, only Maude might not live at all.

If forgiveness were possible, I would never allow myself to experience it.

I walked down the hall and to the elevator and pressed

the up button. When it arrived, I stepped inside and somehow found the main floor button through my tear-clogged eyes.

On the first floor, the entire staff was waiting for the news, but when they saw my face, they silently stepped back to let me pass. I walked to my room and opened the Maude suitcase to retrieve the bag of gold coins Johann had given me in Vienna. Then, I put it in a purse and returned to the hall. The Maude suitcase, journal, and clothing remained where I left them in the wardrobe. I didn't bother packing. No one spoke as I walked past them and out the front door.

Thank you for reading *For the Love of Maude*! If you enjoyed it, please take a moment to leave a review at your favorite retailer.

Want to know what happens next?
Continue Emily's journey now in *Forever Maude*

A SNEAK PEEK OF FOREVER MAUDE

PROLOGUE

A lthough time travel left me with a bag of several dozen antique coins, capable of supporting a lavish European lifestyle, I had a conscience that would never allow me to enjoy such a life.

A round of drinks at the right club bought more than just alcohol; it often gained a new friendship with a kindred spirit, typically the daughter of a wealthy tycoon whose love was measured within the contents of her daddy's wallet. I acted as either her sidekick or instigator; regardless, I was simply the sponge she needed to foster her rebellion, and I felt no remorse for my actions. In fact, I was oddly comforted by the company of those who used me for either my companionship, my money, or both. After all, I had ruined too many lives to deserve anything more.

Each club was different, but the results were the same. I was in Genoa, Italy, in one of the many bars near the waterfront on a Friday night in April 1989, but it could have been any time. The Riviera teemed with young people looking for fun, and I was willing to fund it.

"Another round!" I called from my perch atop the bar.

I was surrounded by a mass of young smiling faces, raising their glasses and voices toward me. No one seemed to mind that I didn't know Italian. My money bought me fluency in any language. Besides, my hair was long now and bleached by the Mediterranean sun. I didn't exactly blend into the crowd, nor was that my desire—for once in my life, the attention didn't bother me.

So, I smiled in reply and stepped down onto the closest available stool to revel in the gratitude of those paying homage to their new best friend—me. Settled on the seat and with my elbows resting on the marble bar behind me, I surveyed all of the smiling faces that surrounded it. Amid the rustic, plaster-covered stone walls and plank floors, the crowd was filled with mostly twentysomethings—girls with big hair and formfitting spandex dresses, much like the black minidress I was wearing; men in slacks and shirts with turned-up collars, unbuttoned at the top to reveal chains that blended into their abundant chest hair. I acknowledged each *"grazie"* with a smile, wishing their gratitude would fill the void inside me.

It didn't.

In the end, everyone seemed to want my company—everyone, that is, except me. Instead, I pretended to pay attention to the affections of a nearby cuff-linked man whose rings and watch filled the space that separated us. His wedding band glistened despite the darkness of the club, apparently serving as nothing more than another meaningless piece of jewelry. My thoughts drifted to my own wedding ring, stowed safely in the train case I left behind—in another life.

I continued to offer a fake smile at the man I mostly was ignoring, consumed instead by my thoughts, until a gorgeous

Italian man in his late twenties drew my attention back to the club. A perfect smile and twelve layers of confidence preceded him as his intense almond-shaped eyes met mine and held them captive from across the room. His shirt fit like a glove with buttons, flattering his every move as he navigated the crowd, similar to a fish swimming upstream through a sea of my admirers.

I smiled back, knowing how his night would end. In addition to the wealthy young heiresses who frequently adopted me, the men were even more abundant. They soon lost interest, however, when their jewelry and furs rewarded them only with a hug and a kiss on the cheek. Neither their money nor their model-good-looks could compete with the memory of my husband.

I shook my head. *You're not Dell!* Aside from a similar muscular build, my Austrian husband was at least ten years older and six inches taller than the man approaching me, and most likely outweighed him by forty pounds or more. *Fifty*, I decided, finally leaving the man's gaze to size him up. *Dell could snap you like a twig; especially if he saw the way you were looking at me.* I met the man's unwavering eyes again, seeing the brown and wishing they were blue. *I remember when Dell looked at me that way.* I followed the smile forming at the corners of his eyes, then traveled to his temples and to his dark hair that was slicked back, glistening amid the bar lights. It was a stark contrast to Dell's light brown hair, soft and grazing his shoulders, always beckoning me to run my fingers through it.

I missed my husband, but I knew that I also missed my opportunity to deserve him when I walked away from my life—our life—and never looked back.

My newest victim wasn't privy to that. However, before the man could reach my spot at the bar, a loud *"Salute!"* erupted, and its aftermath cut off his approach and the future disappointment that was in store for him.

Although the crowd around me cheered and showered me with their affection, I felt alone; worse, I felt lonely, overwhelmed by the memory of my husband and aunt, whose lives I no longer could share. But I'd made my choice and had to live with it. So I took a deep breath and tried to channel the theater class I'd taken at school or at least the confidence it often gave me, by once again climbing on the bar. "Who wants to party at my place?" I jumped down and headed for the exit.

I didn't have a "place," but no one appeared to notice as they cheered in their ignorance and followed me as if I were the Pied Piper, out the door and to the marina. The owner of the yacht I decided to invade didn't seem to mind the popularity my actions brought either. His false hairpiece and unnaturally whitened teeth had midlife crisis written all over them as he welcomed us aboard. He later offered me unlimited use of an oversized stateroom in exchange for my "discretion."

I didn't mind, nor did my conscience, when, a little before dawn, I heard the remnants of my host's lifestyle choice tiptoeing along the dock just outside my window. Instead, I let the gentle rocking of the ship lull me back to sleep until the sound of a vacuum charging my closed door awakened me with a start. Slightly disoriented and with my heart racing in my ears, I left the stateroom and walked the narrow corridors in search of fresh air. Drawn to a set of glass doors that revealed a seating area at the stern of the ship, I finally saw what

I'd missed the previous evening in the dark. Although the yacht was a monster, able to give at least four school buses a run for the money, it was dwarfed by many of the ships moored on either side. I settled myself into a blue-cushioned chaise to better appreciate the view.

"Location, location, location," I whispered to the mammoth, yacht-shaped silhouettes rocking before the rising sun.

The words barely were spoken when my host's manservant brought me a small, white, steaming cup of coffee, surrounded by sugar cubes on a little saucer. Then he left without a word. I preferred tea but didn't complain. Instead, I scanned the multicolored horizon, stirring my cup and admiring my handiwork.

Aside from my overwhelming desire to walk clumsily along the precipice of self-destruction and make every effort to lose my footing and fall into the void, I had to admit that surviving the 1980s in Italy wasn't such a bad gig.

* * *

Continue reading *Forever Maude*
GET YOUR COPY!

ABOUT THE AUTHOR

DENISE LIEBIG is the author of *Dear Maude, For the Love of Maude*, and *Forever Maude*, the books of the Dear Maude Trilogy. A true fan of historical fiction, she spends her free time researching historical events and writing about the possibilities. Denise also enjoys spending time with her husband and three kids at home in Nevada.

VISIT HER WEBSITE
www.deniseliebig.com

CONNECT WITH DENISE

Twitter - @DeniseWithWords
Facebook - @AuthorDeniseLiebig
Linked In - @AuthorDeniseLiebig

ACKNOWLEDGMENTS

A SPECIAL THANK YOU to Meghan Pinson, My Two Cents Editing, for helping me dig deeper; Autumn Conley, for giving my words the polish they needed; and The Book Khaleesi, for making them look good.

Thanks to my family, friends, and fans of my work, whose support keeps me writing. Thanks, too, to all the people who answered my crazy questions that eventually helped lend authenticity to the eras mentioned in *For the Love of Maude*.

And, of course, thank you to my husband, Doug, who has supported me along the way. I couldn't have done it without him.